Partition Stories

To

My Guru

PROF. PANKAJ K. SINGH

and

My Parents

SMT. KESRI DEVI AND LATE SH. YOG RAJ

Partition Stories

Mapping Community, Communalism and Gender

Vinod K. Chopra

ANAMIKA PUBLISHERS & DISTRIBUTORS (P) LTD.
4697/3, 21A, Ansari Road, Daryaganj, New Delhi 110002
Phone: 2328 1655, 23270239; Fax . : 011-27868035
E-mail : anamikapublishers@yahoo.co.in

First Published 2009

ISBN 978-81-7975-233-3

PRINTED IN INDIA

Published by Anamika Publishers & Distributors (P) Ltd., 4697/3, 21A, Ansari Road, Daryaganj, New Delhi 110002. Typeset by Shivani Computers, Shahdara, Delhi and Printed at Nagri Printers, Delhi.

Contents

Preface

The literature on the Partition poignantly captures the ravages of history on human hearts and lives. It represents not only the unprecedented tragedy and violence of the Partition—arson, murder, rape, uprooting of millions and the emotional scars and unresolved dilemmas of identity and homelessness experienced by the survivors—but also how in individual acts of charity and compassion humanity still survived across communal divide. The brutal impact of the Partition has been haunting the creative imagination even after sixty years, as is evident from the recent novels on the subject.

While the novels on the Partition such as *Tamas, Azadi, Train to Pakistan*, have won great critical acclaim, the short stories by writers from India, Pakistan and Bangladesh, written in such diverse languages as Hindi, Urdu, Punjabi, Bangla, Sindhi, English, Malayalam, etc., have not received the critical attention they deserve. Hence I turned to short stories, which provide more numerous and diverse frames on the Partition, to explore the question that bothered me: how the multiple identities of communities along cultural, ethnic and linguistic lines were obliterated and communities got defined only along communal lines of religious identity, how women suffered not only at the hands of communal 'other' but even at the hands of their own communities, and how a political decision, not of their own making irrevocably changed the lives of the millions.

The present study brings into focus how the short stories

cutting across cultural, religious and linguistic differences sensitively represent the traumatic impact of history on human lives and how those stories engage with the shifting paradigms of community, communalism and gender. In the last chapter these issues are explored in a close textual analysis of the three recent novels—Shauna Singh Baldwin's *What the Body Remembers* (1999), Kamleshwar's *Kitne Pakistan* (2000) translated into English as *Partition* (2006) by Ameena Kazi Ansari and M.J. Akbar's *Blood Brothers* (2006).

The present book would have remained an unrealised dream but for the valuable guidance and constant encouragement of Professor Pankaj K. Singh. I express deep sense of gratitude to her for her painstaking and scholarly help, constant support and motherly affection. I would also like to acknowledge the contribution of all my teachers especially Prof. Girija Sharma and Mr. Deepak Kapoor. I extend my thanks to all my friends and scholars who encouraged me all the time.

I am also thankful to the staff of the libraries of Indian Institute of Advanced Study, Shimla; Himachal Pradesh University, Shimla; Punjab University, Chandigarh; District Library, Una; District Library, Hamirpur and to Mr. V.D. Vashisht, Asstt. Librarian, Govt. Sr. Sec. School, Tauni Devi, for providing valuable resources. Mrs. Madhu Thakur helped with the typing of the manuscript.

I am deeply indebted to my wife Neeta who infused courage in me and never claimed much time. She completely relieved me of household responsibilities to enable me to concentrate on my work. I am indebted, in particular to my little daughter Sona, who is too small to express her claim on my time and attention. She kept watching me working all the time, with a sense of surprise in her eyes and coped with my long absences with some distress. Finally a word of grateful thanks to my mother, and brother, Mr. Subhash Chopra but for whose blessings nothing would have been possible.

Hamirpur (HP) **Vinod K. Chopra**
March, 2008

Introduction

The Partition of India was one of the greatest catastrophes suffered by its people. The political leaders took decisions regarding the Partition within the closed doors of their conference rooms and considered it unnecessary to ask the masses what they thought about it. Even the people of the present Pakistan were not in favour of the Partition of the country.[1] The joy of freedom was overshadowed by the Partition and its aftermath, that is, migrations, uprooting and massacre on communal lines. It was "the most complex divorce action in history, the break up of a family of 400 million human beings along with the assets and household property they'd acquired in centuries of living together on the same piece of earth."[2] The Partition was not peaceful. The violence it unleashed was unprecedented, unexpected and, of course, barbaric. Provoked by the hooligan actions of a few, the vengeance that the ordinary Hindus, Muslims and Sikhs wreaked on each other devastated our moral fabric, distorted our political judgement and deranged our understanding of moral rightness. The worst sufferers of the Partition were women since people of different communities punished one another by targeting their women by raping, dishonouring and abducting them.

Never before or since have so many people lost their homes or country so quickly as during the Partition. Amidst an unparalleled tide of human misery about twelve million people moved between the new, truncated India and the two wings, East and West of the newly created Pakistan. People were crawling like columns of ants[3] across the country. They were migrating in large numbers, in large caravans and one of them alone represented 800,000 people, a caravan almost mind-numbing in dimension, the largest single column of refugees man's turbulent history had ever produced.[4] In north India the Muslims travelled West to Pakistan, the Hindus and the Sikhs towards East to India. Thousands were butchered[5] on the way and many others died of malnutrition and contagious diseases while they were living in refugee camps. Thousands of families were divided, homes were destroyed, crops were left to rot and villages were abandoned. In this ghastly catastrophe women became victims of sexual savagery[6] and physical violence. More then 75,000 women are believed to have been abducted and raped by men of religion different from their own.[7] Sometimes these women fell prey to even men of their own community.

One of the worst consequences of the Partition was that it created mutual mistrust and hatred between the two communities – the Hindus and the Muslims. So the Partition was not just a political divide, or a division of properties, of assets and liabilities; it was a "division of hearts."[8] It brought to an abrupt end a long and communally shared heritage. It was really harrowing that the children of the same motherland became thirsty for one-another's blood.

If we go back to the history, one reality comes to the surface that the Muslims of India are not pure Arabs. It is during the centuries immediately succeeding the capture of Delhi in 1192 that the Muslim community was created[9] within Delhi Sultanate. "The other avenue by which the Muslims found their way to India was trade."[10] But these were only a fraction of the later community. The expansion of Islam further took place with the conversion of the local people during the Mughal rule in India.[11] Thus while a trickle came from the Hindus upper classes the largest element within the Muslim community came from 'voluntary' conversion.[12] It was in this way that one fourth of the Indian population became Muslim. Even Gandhiji believed, "Both Muslims and Christians are converts from Hinduism or are descendents of converts".[13]

Historically, it is a fact that over centuries the Hindus and the Muslims lived amicably a life of peaceful co-existence.[14] Though the foreign Islamic rulers invaded India from time to time, their motive behind invasions was not mainly related to religion. They wanted to plunder the wealth of India. In this process of collecting booty they looted both the Hindu and the Muslim rulers and the masses of India as well. Even these plunderers were sometimes helped by the Hindu or the Muslim rulers with whom they had developed friendly relations. During the medieval period the rulers were generally Muslims and they oppressed both the Hindu and the Muslim masses. The condition of the Hindu and the Muslim peasants and workers was the same.[15] So, it is evident that both the communities lived amicably and in comparative peace and amity over long stretches of time.[16] Though their relations might sometimes have been marred by suspicion, distrust or the angry rejection by one group of the habits and practices of the others leading to minor acts of malevolence, quarrels and squabble, such moments were rare and transient. Such minor clashes that took place occasionally cannot be termed as 'communal riots'. It is clear, then, that communal antagonism was not a problem inherited from the past[17] rather it emerged as a consequence of the emergence of modern politics which marked a sharp break with the politics of the medieval or ancient or pre-1857 period.

Had there been a history of irreconcilable hatred or non-negotiable aversion between the Hindus and the Muslims, it would have been reflected in the cultural and social practices of the two communities. Numerous examples of mutual love and amity between the two communities can be cited. Prem Chand wrote movingly about the need of love between the Hindu and the Muslim friends in his *Karambhumi* (1932). On the other hand Iqbal opened his *Bal-I-Jibril* (1935) with a couplet from Bhartrihari.[18] Even in the love legends of medieval Punjab we find evidence of harmonious co-existence of Muslim and Hindu components of Punjabi life. The seventeenth century poet Pilu's composition of "Mirza Sahiban" and the eighteenth century poet Waris Shah's celebrated composition of the legend of "Hir Ranjha" are among those love legends that move around Muslim protagonists but Hindu characters and customs do frequently figure in these narratives. Ranjha goes to a Hindu *Jogi* to seek *Jog* and is often compared to Kanha (i.e. Krishna) and so on.[19]

There are so many other examples to prove that the Hindus and the Muslims lived together in peace and harmony. For example from Iltumish to Sher Shah Suri, such Hindu symbols as 'lotus' and 'Swastika' could be seen on the coins of Turkish-Afghan rulers in India. Jainul Abadin of Kashmir, Hussain Shah of Bengal, and Yusuf Adilshah, the founder of Bijapur kingdom, worked hard to strengthen communal harmony. Yusuf Adilshah went a step further by declaring Marathi language as the court language. At the end of the fifteenth century a common worshipping sect 'Satya Peer' came into being in Bengal, which still exists. People of both the communities have faith in the 'Satya Peer' sect. Kabir, brought up by a Muslim weaver, tried his best to emphasise the reality in his teachings that God is one whether He is worshipped in the form of Allah or Ram. At the end of the fifteenth century Guru Nanak Dev, the founder of Sikhism, spread his teachings in temples and mosques equally.[20]

During the Mughal Rule in India Akbar is known for promoting Hindu-Muslim unity. He did strengthen his relations with the Hindus by entering into marital relationships with Rajput princesses. He himself listened to the teachings of the Hindu saints and philosophers in his *Ibadat Khana* (house of prayer). A large number of temples were built all over the country by him.[21] It is said that Akbar only drank water from the Ganga and his food was cooked in waters of the Jamuna and the Chenab.[22] The Hindu customs and festivals were celebrated in the court. Common people took part in the procession on 'Moharram'. The Muslim painters, musicians and authors, too, played a vital role in cementing the Hindu-Muslim relationship. During the time of Akbar the *Gita* was *translated* into Persian. Even during Shahjahan's regime there were many Hindu musicians in the court. Hence we cannot ignore the contribution of the Muslim rulers. No doubt, cruel rulers like Aurengzeb were also there who imposed special taxes on the Hindus but such rulers were very few.

With this historical background of largely peaceful co-existence between the two communities one wonders how at the time of the Partition such a wide gulf between the two communities got created and who was responsible for making them each other's enemies? Were these the political leaders of the Hindus and the Muslims who failed to see the consequences of the Partition, or were the British solely responsible for creating the catastrophic communal divide?

The British government had seen the Hindu-Muslim unity during the revolt of 1857, and it grew apprehensive of the National Movement in which both the communities fought shoulder to shoulder for India's freedom. Now the British felt that they could continue their uninterrupted regime in India only if they were able to divide the Hindus and the Muslims. Hence they followed the policy of 'divide and rule.' "The British rulers were neither the true friends of the Muslims nor the foes of the Hindus; they were the true friends of British Imperialism and acted on the tested and tried maxim of *Divide et Impera.*"[23] To weaken the National Movement they created a rift between the Hindu Nationalists and the Muslim Nationalists. After 1872, they brought a shift in their policy towards Muslims through appeasement of Muslims. They fanned religious sentiments of the Muslims and tried their best to sow the seeds of hatred and separation.

The leaders of the Muslim League fell an easy prey to the evil designs of the British rulers who were responsible for giving birth to the Muslim League in 1906 to "counter poise" the rising nationalism.[24] The implementation of the policy resulted in the Partition of Bengal in 1905, which was a move to create a permanent gulf between the two communities. On the other hand the Muslim League leadership, concerned only with their own "narrow and selfish interests, raised the slogan of a separate Muslim State where they could have a free field for exploitation."[25] So a separate State was a demand of hungry-for-power politicians, but generally Indians— Hindus and Muslims— took no interest in the proposed scheme and described it as impracticable.[26] But the Leaguers were stubborn on getting a separate Muslim State, and for this they roused communal feelings to their highest pitch.

Mainly the religious fanatical forces led by the Muslim League demanded the Partition of India on the basis of the theory that the Muslims constituted a different nation from the Hindus. Even the Congress cannot be absolved of its role or responsibility in the Partition of India. "The revivalist tendencies in the Congress accentuated separatist tendencies. As a result the Congress failed to draw the Muslim masses in its fold."[27] It seems as if the Congress leadership was tired of continuing its national movement and the Congress leaders preferred a "safer route"[28] to power. Years later, a British author, Leonard Mosley, recounted a conversation with Nehru that rings true. The Prime Minister told him in 1960:

> The truth is that we were tired men, and we were getting on in years too. Few of us could stand the prospect of going to prison again and if we had stood out for a united India as we wished it, prison obviously awaited us. We saw fires burning in the Punjab and heard everyday of killings. The plan for Partition offered a way out and we took it...."[29]

Besides, in 1937 the Congress refused to share power with the Muslim League, which became the cause of further divide between both the communities since, as one historian puts it, "Nehru made the Muslims realize that they did not care for the Muslims. They could not get honourable place in this country."[30] Due to this Jinnah grew angry and declared 'direct action', which followed in the form of looting, riots, killing and arson on a large scale. Now there was a fear of civil war. Most of the national leaders from the Congress Working Committee came to the conclusion that rather then allowing civil war to continue, it was advisable to accept Mountbatten's plan based on India's Partition. The Working Committee of the Congress was aware that Gandhiji was totally opposed to the Partition. It was the height of impropriety that the decision to endorse India's Partition was taken without Gandhiji's knowledge.[31] Gandhi, for all his rapport with the people, could not counter the lust for quick and easy access to power that his protégés developed.[32] So the fact remains that Muslim leadership demanded Partition and the Hindu leadership accepted it. But it is a matter of sorrow that the peoples of the Punjab and Bengal, the Hindus and the Muslims, consequently had to pay a heavy price for the acts of omission and commission of their leaders and of the mechanizations of the imperialist powers,[33] and were victims of and witness to the most barbaric crimes against humanity.

II

A momentous national experience generally serves as a great source of literary creativity. The French Revolution, the American Civil War, the Russian Revolution and the two World Wars in the previous century provided the basis of great fiction. Likewise, in India, too, sensitive literature has been written on the tragedy of the Partition. The event of the Partition has been captured in its varied aspects by creative writers of India, Pakistan and Bangladesh in the form of novels and short stories. The human tragedy caused by the Partition has found poignant expression in such novels as *Train to Pakistan, Azadi, Tamas, The River Churning, Ice-candy Man* and also in numerous short stories included in three volumes entitled, *Stories About the Partition of India* edited by Alok Bhalla. Even after more than fifty years the partition still haunts the creative minds as is evident from recent novels like Shauna Singh Baldwin's *What the Body Remembers,* Kamleshwar's *Kitne Pakistan*, translated into English as *Partitions* and M.J. Akbar's *Blood Brothers*. Almost all the novelists and short story writers succeed in communicating the grossness and ghastliness and total insanity of the two-nation theory. They poignantly recreate the agony, which victims of the Partition find it difficult to forget.

The present book aims at studying the nature and dynamics of the shifting paradigms of community, communalism and gender in such catastrophic moments of history as the Partition of India as reflected in literature. While the novels on the Partition have drawn great critical acclaim, the short stories on the Partition have not received the critical attention they deserve. A selection of short stories written in different languages including English, Hindi, Urdu, Punjabi, Marathi, Malayalam, Dogri, Sindhi and Bengali by the authors belonging to India, Pakistan and Bangladesh is made for a detailed analysis. Though written by the authors hailing from different religions, culture, location and gender, the stories revolve around the same catastrophic and traumatic incidents during the Partition that left a brutal impact on the human life. The stories give a vivid account of the human agony and suffering that a large section of people suffered in the wake of the Partition. The most notable thing about the stories selected for study is the objectivity with which the Partition is represented by the respective authors. They do not hold one or the other community responsible for the Partition accompanied by mayhem and bloodshed. Due to the diversity of language, writers' location and a more varied representation of the event the stories, in fact, become so many diverse voices against the Partition violence. The stories have a variety of themes. They reveal not only bloodshed and killings but also the love and friendship shared by both the communities. There is a hope that mutual love and trust can still be rebuilt.

The first chapter of the book conceptualizes the terms,

'community', 'communalism', 'gender' and their varying meaning and dimensions in changing social situations. The second chapter examines religious distortions and communal hatred during the Partition, which led to large-scale devastation and mutual hatred between communities. The third chapter presents a study of the ambiguities manifested within the communities—how people of the same community are treated as the 'other' and that, in turn, creates problematic identities for the uprooted, A quest for belonging begins, with no easy solution in sight. Inter-community and Intra-community violence against women, who are always the worst sufferers in communal riots, is discussed in the fourth chapter. Yet amid bloodshed and hatred one could find traces of human goodness, of human values surviving the communal divide, and a full chapter is devoted to the note of optimism sounded in the stories.

Even more than fifty years after the Partition one is pained to see that communal violence and mistrust are still not a thing of the past and that catastrophic events, similar to those witnessed during the Partition, keep on recurring even now. Equally the creative minds even now keep on turning back to the tragic and violent events of the Partition. The final chapter examines three recent novels on the Partition to see how community, communalism and gender are represented in the novels and how they respond to the Partition in general.

NOTES

1. As Mani Shankar Aiyar observes in "Who Wanted Pakistan: The Muslims or Muslim Leaguers?" *Sunday*, March 14-20, 1993. p. 18. Also see Census of India, 1941, Vol.1, Part I, Table XIII, pp. 98-99.
2. Larry Collins and Dominique Lapierre, *Freedom at Midnight*, (1976, rpt. New Delhi: Vikas Publishing House, 1977), p. 168.
3. Ibid., p. 319.
4. Ibid.

5. Ajit Bhattacharjea, *Countdown to Partition: The Final Days,* (New Delhi: Harper Collins, 1997), p. 61.
6. Urvashi Butalia, *The Other Side of Silence,* (New Delhi: Viking, 1998), p. 3.
7. Ibid.
8. Ibid., p. 7.
9. Percival Spear, *A History of India*, Vol. II, (New Delhi: Penguin, Books, 1990), pp. 221-22.
10. Shibani Roy, *Status of Muslim Women in India,* (Delhi: B.R. Publishing Corp., 1979), p. 12.
11. Sabiha Hussain, *The Changing Half: A Study of Indian Muslim Women,* (New Delhi: Classical Publishing Company, 1998), p. 2.
12. Spear, *A History of India*, Vol. II, p. 222.
13. "Gandhi on the Partition of India". Excerpted from *"The Way To Communal Harmony"* by M.K. Gandhi, ed. U.R. Rao. *The Tribune* (Sunday Reading) June 22, 1997, p. 1.
14. M.G. Chitkara, *Indo-Pak Amity: A New Concept,* (New Delhi: Ashish Publishing House, 1994), p. 10.
15. Bipan Chandra, *Communalism in Modern India*, (1984, rpt. New Delhi: Vikas Publishing House, 1996), p.13.
16. K.R. Malkani, "A Treaty to Heal Hindu-Muslim Rift", *The Times of India,* February 9, 1993, p. 8.
17. Bipan Chandra, *Communalism in Modern India*, p. 9.
18. Alok Bhalla, Introduction to *Stories About the Partition of India*, Vol. I, (New Delhi: Harper Collins, 1990), p.1X.
19. Pankaj K. Singh, *Representing Woman: Tradition, Legend and Punjabi Drama,* (Shimla: IIAS, 2000), p. 47.
20. *Bharat Ka Sankshipt Itihas* (Hindi) translated by Dheera Verma from H.R. Ghosal's *An Outline History of the Indian People* (New Delhi: Publication Division, 1962), p. 60. My translation. For details see pp. 56-64.
21. V.D. Mahajan, *India Since 1526,* (New Delhi: S. Chand and Co. Ltd., 1986), p. 90.
22. Khushwant Singh, "What Makes a Man Great?" *The Tribune,* June 9, 2001. p. 3.
23. B.L. Grover and S. Grover, *A New Look at Modern Indian History: From 1707 to the Present day,* (New Delhi: S. Chand and Co., 2000), p. 604.
24. Satya M. Rai, *Partition of the Punjab,* (New Delhi: Asia Publishing House, 1965), p. 5.
25. Ibid., p. 11.

26. Ibid., p. 13.
27. Ibid., Preface, p. VIII
28. Ajit Bhattacharjea, *Countdown to Partition: The Final Days*, (New Delhi: Harper Collins, 1997), p. XXV.
29. Ibid., pp. XXV-XXVI.
30. Milap Kothari, *Ab Bharat Ko Jagna Hoga* (Hindi), (Jaipur: Rajasthan Patrika ISBN, 2000), p. 59.
31. M.G. Chitkara, *Indo-Pak Amity: A New Concept*, (New Delhi: Ashish Publishing House, 1994), p. 8.
32. Bhattacharjea, *Countdown to Partition: The Final Days*, p. XXVI.
33. Rai, *Partition of the Punjab*, p.19.

1
Community, Communalism and Gender: The Shifting Dynamics

COMMUNITY

Innumerable types of groups are found in a society. There may be a family group, economic group, political group or a friendship group. These groups may be primary or secondary, voluntary or involuntary, permanent or transitory, hierarchical or of equal status, territorial or extra-territorial. However, all types of groups are not important from sociological point of view. According to Sorokin the important groups are those which exert a powerful causal meaningful influence upon individual, upon other groups and upon the course of socio-cultural phenomena generally.[1] These groups may be unibonded or multibonded. Among the important unibonded groups he includes groups based on race, sex, age, kinship, territorial proximity, or on occupational, religious and educational affinity, etc. Among the multibonded groups he includes family, clan, tribe, nation, social class, etc.

A person rarely exists alone. He is linked in many ways to his fellows who form a group. It is inevitable that people who over a length of time live in a particular locality should develop social likeness, should have common social ideas, common traditions and the sense of belonging together.[2] This fact of social living and common specific area gives birth to community and the individual starts identifying his interests with larger interest of the group or community who is the "bone of his bone and flesh of his flesh."[3] Community feeling does play a vital role in all human settlements.

Maciver defines community as "an area of social living marked by some degree of social coherence." He further says, "Whenever the members of any group, small or large, live together in such a way that they share not this or that particular interest, but the basic conditions of a common life, we call that group a community."[4] On the other hand, Oxford Advanced Learner's Dictionary defines the word 'community' as the "people living in one place, district or country, considered as a whole" or "a group of people of the same religion, race, occupation, or with shared interests." The encyclopedia of sociology defines community as "a set of social relationship which takes place wholly, or mostly, within a bounded local territory."

According to Robert Redfield a community has the following characteristics:

- Definite territory
- Close social relationship
- Psychological rapport and the 'we feeling'
- Culture similarity
- Organized interaction.[5]

There are different types of communities in a society. In a way a village or neighbourhood forms a community where people share common interest and live collectively. A village can be said to be the smallest unit as a community. The primitive bands were migratory communities. With the passage of time man acquired skill and knowledge in agriculture. With the development of agriculture and with the consequent stabilization of the source of food, people began to lead a settled life and human communities became more stationary. The village, then, emerged which signified that man has passed from nomadic mode of collective life to the settled one. Thus, village is the oldest permanent community of man. Kropotkin writes, "We do not know single human race or one single nation which has not has its period of village communities."[6] And according to Bogardus, "Human society has been cradled in the rural group."[7] A village has almost all the characteristics of a community.

We do find communities within communities such as neighbourhood and school in a village. Colleges and universities are called communities because in these also one finds the feeling of belongingness. On the other hand settlements, cities and metropolises are also communities. People of cities meet and speak without knowing each other. Since they hail from different regions and their languages may be different from that of one another that becomes a cause of impersonality or lack of emotional bonding among them. Hence community feeling is not so strong in urban as in rural context. As community sentiment is lacking in cities, they cannot be termed communities in the strict sense. But we cannot fix rigid definitions of communities today. Definition of communities keeps on changing in different contexts, and times. We know that in modern circumstances of globalization, the people with the same business and professional interests are linked to one another by trade and newspapers and hence they constitute separate business communities despite anonymity and impersonality. Thus we see that nature, structure, and goals of community are undergoing change though it still retains its fundamental characteristics.

At a larger level nation itself forms a community. It contains within it a number of small communities and groups with more close bonds of unity and numerous common qualities. Nation at present is the largest group which is permeated by a common consciousness.[8] There is a general consensus that the nation is a territorial community as distinct from racial, tribal or religious group of people.[9] In this context it is to be noted that many Indians are settled in America, England, Canada, Fiji and so many other countries. These people belong to the 'Indian community' there, irrespective of any specific religion, caste or region. Though religion has been a great cementing force and has played a significant role in the past in consolidating nations yet it cannot be regarded as an indispensable objective factor today. The modern nation is a territorial community. It includes and embraces all persons, of whatever ethnic stock and religious faith. Hence, religion is not a major characteristic of a community.

A community is also defined or identified due to the likeness in language, customs and modes. Every community has some particular ethnicity or name. Each community is something of an individuality or a personality as well, often indicated by the name given to it. In this sense an individual may belong to multiple communities. An individual may simultaneously belong to different communities; such as a person from North India may be an Indian, a Punjabi, and a Hindu at the same time. He is thus part of a national community, a Punjabi cultural community and a religious community. And even beyond these categories he may be part of other communities—as a student, or a businessman and so on. Hence we find that a community is not a fixed or a rigid notion. For example, within the Hindu community one may be a Punjabi, a Kashmiri, or a Brahmin or a 'Baniya'; one may be a worker or an owner. There are multiple streams of identity even within the larger community.

There is no denying the fact that the notion of community keeps on changing with the changing context, and in different socio-political contexts the defining factor of the community may change. In times of social upheavals such meanings undergo a change rather rapidly. The Partition was such a social upheaval that caused change in the definitions of community. It was during the Partition that all the definitions of community based on locality, caste, tribe or region proved fragile. Communities were now no longer defined in terms of area or language or ethnicity but essentially and only on the lines of religion. Communities got defined only in terms of communal rivalry or 'otherness.'

It was due to the emphasis on religion as the determining factor during the Partition that other identities became weak. Now the concept of nation, too, got redefined essentially in terms of religious identity, as a separate country was demanded on religious basis only. The British government divided Indian nation into different religious communities because of its policy of 'divide and rule'.[10] It created communalism, which later on resulted in two-nation theory purely on religious lines.

One of the biggest ironies of the Partition is that it made religion as the sole determining factor in defining an individual and all other identities of language, culture, profession, etc., got blurred. As a result the communities started looking at each other as the 'other'. No doubt, some political motivations, selectively and superficially used some traditions to divide the Hindus and the Muslims.

Once this 'divide' was achieved, the Hindus were made to flee from Pakistan, while the Muslims were forced to evacuate the 'Indian' land. Now these homeless looked for shelter and food within their 'own' communities, in their 'new' homeland. As soon as the Partition was granted and the masses were exchanged, the whole situation took a new turn, a turn for worse, once more for those who had left their homes and shifted to another land. The tragedy of uprooting became more painful when their own communities i.e. religious communities did not accept easily those who came to new countries on both sides. They were rejected and sometimes they became victims of violence by the people of their own community. So another irony that emerged in the perception of identities of communities was that now within the religious communities the divide started emerging. Their Muslim brethren treated the Muslims who fled to Pakistan from India as 'outsiders'. They became 'muhajirs' there. On the other hand, the emigrant Hindus faced the same fate and dilemma and they were labeled as 'refugees'. Ironically these so called 'muhajirs' and 'refugees' had to face negation and indifference from their 'own' people who followed the same religion and worshipped the same God. Even today these 'muhajirs' and 'refugees' are lookedupon as 'others' in their respective countries. So once again the already defined communities, based on religion came under redefinition. The 'refugees' and 'muhajirs' emerged as distinct communities. The refugees of Punjab found themselves bound together by common destinies; and survived, after long ordeal as a distinct community, though there were no such physical factors as territorial demarcation for evolution of a community feeling in those people.[11] And yet this sense of belonging to a single community proved to be of great help in the rehabilitation of those people. Hence we notice that during social and political upheaval or turmoil the notion of 'community' keeps on changing depending upon the new circumstances and new areas or factors of bonding amongst groups of people.

COMMUNALISM

Since during the Partition communities got defined along religious lines and people of one community started looking at those of the other community as enemies, feeling of bitterness and hatred grew rapidly. This was in sharp contrast to the situation in medieval India when the Hindus and the Muslims lived peacefully along with each other, except for the political rivalry between the Muslim Kings and the Hindu rulers here and there. In fact, there was no sharp division among the people of the two communities. Later on the common fight of both the communities, under the leadership of Bahadurshah Zafar, against the British East India Company in 1857 was a unique example of Hindu-Muslim unity. But the British sowed the seeds of communalism whose harvest was very bitter. They did their best to sharpen the communal consciousness among different religious communities. The communal hatred and divide gained so much momentum that it resulted in the Partition of India. This divide became so deep-rooted that it is posing a serious threat even today. After more than fifty years of India's independence, the sinister forces of fundamentalism and rabid communalism have threatened and posed a dangerous challenge to national integrity. Recently, the Gujarat carnage has been a monstrous manifestation of the communal hatred and has certainly pricked the conscience of millions who want peace and amity in the country. And what is most disturbing is the sharpening of beastly instincts on both sides of the communal divide. Communalism, even today, is causing slow destruction of the social fabric, a process that had already divided India in 1947. Nehru's observation about communalism was so correct and significant: "I consider communalism the biggest enemy of India. All of us should work with full might to eradicate communalism because it is the biggest challenge to Indianism and nationalism."[12]

The word communalism has been derived from the word 'Commune' which means consciousness or feeling of oneness or friendliness or community feeling. According to S.L. Malhotra, "Communalism is a type of consciousness, true or false, that makes the members of a community feel that they constitute a distinct group. It is based on the assumption that all members have common interests that distinguish them from other communities.... In other words, the community constitutes an organic whole. It is homogenous or cohesive. This kind of consciousness, if sufficiently strong and real, develops into nationalism."[13] But unfortunately such a nice word has been used in the Indian context in a derogatory sense. In India the word has acquired a notorious meaning.[14] In the Indian context, the word "communal" means antagonism between people belonging to different religions and races. In other word, it gives a negative concept with regard to "religious communities" and "communities of religious interests." Hence a particular community claims that even the secular interests of all its members are identical only because they follow a particular religion. In this way a feeling of separation is developed in these groups. Communal groups prefer religious and linguistic interests to the national interest.[15] According to Smith, "A communal person or group is one who considers every religious and linguistic group as a separate political and social unit and that its interests are different and even antagonistic. The views of such groups will be called communal or communalism."[16] Thus communalism is generally associated with narrow, selfish, divisive and aggressive attitude on part of a religious group. As a matter of fact, communalism is an ideology that advocates that the followers of a religion have common interests and followers of another religions have different interests. It is an ideology that preaches hatred against the followers of other religions or religious communities.[17]

The ideology of communalism consists of three stages. The first stage of communalism appears when it is stated that people who follow the same religion have common secular interests. It means they have common political, economic, social and cultural interests. This is the stage which gives birth to socio-political communities based on religion.[18] The second stage of communalism is reached when it is believed that in a multi-religious society like India, the secular interests of all the followers of one religion are dissimilar and divergent from the interests of the followers of another religion.[19] The believers in this ideology are moderates and this type of communalism can be described as 'moderate communalism.' Though moderates believe in the politics of communalism, they still have faith in liberal, democratic, humanist and nationalist values. These communalists believe that differences, if any, can be gradually accommodated and brought into harmony. In the third stage of communalism the interests of the followers of different religions or of different 'communities' are seen to be mutually incompatible, antagonistic and hostile. The antagonism goes to the extent of falsely accusing and harming deliberately a particular community and extends to looting, burning down their homes and shops, dishonoring their women, and killing persons.[20] This communalism is based on fear and hatred and has a tendency to use violence of language, deed or behaviour, the language of war and enmity against political opponents. It was this kind of extreme communalism that played an important role in the Partition of India. And it was also at this stage that the Hindu communalists and the

Muslim communalists put forward the theories of separate nations based on religion.

Communal divide can be of various kinds—ethnic, social, or religious. The issues of or the strife in different countries are varied. In the United States and United Kingdom it is ethnic. In Ireland and in much of the Islamic world it is religious strife. In South Africa it is social divide based on colour. But in India it is purely based on religion. And the slightest spark can ignite a nationwide communal tension. It was in 1947 that a separate country was carved out on religious ground, as religious communalists demanded it. Even today religion is being used as an instrument to divide people of India to such an extent that the unity of the people and the composite culture and togetherness are on the brink of disaster.

Communalism in India has its roots in modern colonialism. Before the 1870s there was hardly any communal ideology or communal politics. As Jawaharlal Nehru remarks, "One must never forget that communalism in India is a latter day phenomenon which has grown up before our eyes."[21] When the British began to rule India, communalism was almost unknown. There is no doubt that the colonial rulers found that the religion could be profitably exploited to keep the larger community divided against itself and to ensure the permanence of their colonial domination. For creating a divide between the Hindus and the Muslims such views that the Hindus and the Muslims are two different nations were created.

In fact, economic and political interests of both the communities were the same and there was no logic in making a division between these two communities on these issues. The problems that the communalists were projecting were not the real problems at all, and under the pretension of serving their communities' interests the communalists served some of their own political interests. It is rightly said that 'communal persons' are those religious leaders who run their religious communities like business enterprises and raise the sceptre of "Hinduism, Islam, Sikhism or Christianity being in danger" to save their personal interests. For them God and religion are merely instruments to be used to live luxuriously as the 'king parasites'[22] of society and to attain the political goals.

The strongest arm of the communal triangle in pre-independent India was the British rulers.[23] First it suited the imperial interests to support the Hindus, so they supported them. The early British economic and education policies benefited the Hindus more than the Muslims. The British looked upon the Muslims as chief conspirators in the revolt of 1857. They deliberately adopted the policy of suppressing the Muslims. As a punishment 27,000 Muslims were hanged to death in Delhi alone after the suppression of the revolt. But the British also knew that both the Hindus and the Muslims fought the first war of independence against the British. It was a remarkable example of unity between the two communities that created a fear in the British government. To check the tide of unity and National Movement the British slowly extended their friendly hand towards the Muslims. The crafty rulers sought to divide the people along religious lines. On 14th January 1857, Lord Cross, State Secretary, wrote to Viceroy, Lord Duffrin, "The religious divide between the Hindus and the Muslims is very useful to us".[24] They now sought to masquerade as the "champions" of the Muslims, winning over the upper strata among them.[25] It was this policy by which the government of India kept on favouring the Muslims even at the cost of other communities.[26] The Partition of Bengal along religious lines in 1905 was a move to create a permanent gulf between the two communities.[27] In 1906, the Muslim League was formed as a "counterpoise"[28] against the rising nationalism in which people of both the communities were involved.

The British government made one more attempt to woo the loyal Muslims by conferring upon them constitutional safeguard in the form of "separate electorates" made by Lord Minto in 1906. The Morley-Minto Reform Act, 1909, conferred upon the Muslims constitutional safeguards and weightage as a protection against the majority and "reward for the services rendered to the British Empire." The Government of India Act, 1935, provided separate electorates for Muslims and other communities. This was well known as 'communal award'. Under this award the Muslims, the Europeans, the Sikhs, the Indian Christians, the Anglo Indians and among the Hindus the depressed classes were to get separate eloctorates.[29] It was the outcome of the elections fought under Government of India Act, 1935, in the years 1937 and 1946 that led eventually to the communalism, which became the cause of the birth of Pakistan. In this way the seeds of country's Partition were sown by the communal award.[30]

The socio-economic conditions also helped in spreading the communal divide. Majority of the Muslims were economically backward, suffering from poverty, illiteracy and unemployment. Since big businessmen, moneylenders and landlords were largely Hindus who exploited both the Hindus as well as the Muslim masses; the Muslim bourgeoisies gave it a communal colouring by fanning religious sentiments.

The educational backwardness of the Muslims had another harmful consequence. Since the Muslims were lacking modern education, most of the government jobs went to the Hindus who were ahead of the Muslims educationally. The communalists also often distorted or misinterpreted economic struggle against landlords, social tension, class conflict between the exploiters and the exploited belonging to different religions as communal conflict. C.G. Shah has rightly asserted: "Under the pressure of communal propaganda, the masses are unable to locate the real causes for their exploitation, oppression and suffering and imagine a fictitious communal source of their origin."[31]

The manner in which Indian History was taught in schools and colleges also contributed to the growth of communal feelings between both the communities. The British writers on Indian history also served the imperial cause by initiating, developing and emphasising the Hindu-Muslim approach, in their study of Indian history and development of Indian culture.

It was the British historian, James Mill, who described the ancient period of Indian history as the Hindu Period and the medieval period as the Muslim Period. It implied that the religion was the guiding force behind politics during the whole of the medieval period.[32] That is why Gandhiji wrote:

> Communal harmony could not be permanently established in our country so long as highly distorted versions of history were being taught in her schools and colleges, through the history text books.[33]

The government refused to take action against propagation of virulent communal ideas and communal hatred through the press, pamphlets, leaflets, literature, public platform and rumours. On the other hand, the nationalist press's literature, the civil servants' efforts, and propaganda that aimed at spreading unity and brotherhood between different communities were frequently suppressed. On the contrary the British government freely rewarded communal leaders, intellectuals and government servants with titles, positions of profit, high salaries and so on. The British administrators also followed a policy of relative inactivity and irresponsibility in dealing with communal riots.[34]

The British, however, were not alone in executing the plan to divide the Indian Nation along religious lines. They were helped by some selfish and shortsighted native politicians in this nefarious game.[35] These politicians exploited the religious sentiments of innocent masses for personal gains. And communalism became a dominant note in politics during 1945-47 when the Muslim communalists gave the cry of "Islam in danger" and the Hindu communalists cried hoarse about 'Hindu Raj.' The communalists of both the sides were also responsible for the riots and the communalists killed innocent people belonging to both the religions mercilessly. In the frenzy of riots people forgot that no religion teaches violence or hatred towards other sections of humanity, that religion, in fact, is a matter of faith, bonding and spiritual upliftment. Communalism is more a product of political maneuvering than of religious hostilities.[36] In this context Marx was right who considered religion as an illusion[37] which eases the pain produced by exploitation and oppression. Besides, innocent masses are unable to realize that the so-called leaders, who are often their exploiters, use religion to keep away their mind from real issues of economic deprivation by creating the demon of communalism. V.M. Tarkude rightly describes communalism as "unprincipled politics at the top, identified with a collectivity at the bottom."[38] The communalists create differences among people on the basis of religion that are then used to mask or disguise the social needs, aspirations, conflicts, arising in non-religious field. K.M. Ashraf sums up this aspect in an appropriate phrase when he describes communalism as 'Mazhab ki siyasi dukandari' (political trade in religion).[39]

Some individuals were particularly responsible for creating an impassable gulf between the two main religious communities. In fact, the British government played a major role by using some Muslim leaders who had a base among the masses. Among the Muslims the three persons who easily fell prey to the separatist tendencies forcibly created in their minds by the imperialistic power were Sir Sayyid Ahmad Khan, Sir Mohammad Iqbal, and last but not least Mohammad Ali Jinnah. Their minds were so vitiated by the British that they started asking for the separate and sovereign Muslim State. The British created Hindu phobia in the minds of the Muslim leaders so much so that the foundation of Pakistan was laid on the basis of religion, evidently an upshot of communalism. First, it was Sir Sayyid Ahmad Khan who preached the gospel of Muslim isolationalism with unprecedented vigour and thereby laid down the foundation of Muslim nationalism.[40] Ironically, he was the same person who had earlier advocated a united Indian nation and had preached Hindu-Muslim unity, and had described, the Hindus and the Muslims as the "two eyes of a beautiful bride," i.e., India.[41] Soon he fell in line with the British imperialists[42] and became a staunch opponent of the Indian National Congress. He labeled the British rulers as *Khalifatullah,* i.e., God's representatives on earth who would reward the Muslims for their loyalty.[43] He also maintained that the Hindus and the Muslims were not two nations, but two warring nations who could never lead a common political life.[44] He created among the Muslim masses a fear of Hindu rule which, he said, would come in the form of majority rule where the Muslims would be pushed into background. He said about democracy in India, "It would be like a game of dice, in which one man had four dice and the other only one."[45] The second most important Muslim who, miserably, failed to make out the evil designs of the British was Iqbal. Ironically, the writer of "*mazahab nahin sikhata aapas mein bair rakhna*" (religion does not teach animosity) became an ardent advocate of the idea of separate Muslim State for the Indian Muslims. He gave the necessary emotional content to the movement. The surprising development about him was that an arch-nationalist was talking like an arch-communalist. He was the man who discovered an effective instrument of promoting communalism in Mohammad Ali Jinnah. He asked Jinnah to come back from London and assume the leadership of the faction-ridden Muslim League.

It was none other than Mohammd Ali Jinnah whom the British government used against the Hindus. He became an easy instrument in the hands of the British who created the fear of majority rule in India after they would leave. The fear further resulted in communal frenzy among the Muslim masses that led to the Partition of India. Dr. Rafiq Zakaria in his book, *The Man Who Divided India*[46] holds a single individual, i.e. Jinnah, responsible for the mutilation of Mother India. He quotes Dr. Ram Manohar Lohia from his *Guilty Men of India's Partition* to confirm this. Though Jinnah himself was a convert, never prayed or read *The Koran,* yet he fanned religious sentiments of the Muslim masses. In less than a decade he became the sole leader of the Muslims. He was in a hurry to become the supreme leader of the Muslims, and for that he was prepared for any compromise or adjustment.[47] It was Jinnah who converted Pakistan into a reality from a slogan. He, along with other communalists, gave religious tinge to every trivial issue. He did not realize that to paint all cultures with the brush of religion is both erroneous and dangerous.[48] The Muslim League failed to muster majority even in the Muslim-majority province in the elections held in 1937. Even the Congress refused to form a coalition government with the Muslim League. It was a major set back to the Muslim League and particularly to Jinnah. After failing to form government in 1946, in frustration he gave a call to the Muslims 'to do or die' promoting the idea of 'Islam in danger'. On July 29, 1946 when he indulged in rhetoric of violence, he gave a call for 'direct action.' The result was that riots broke out in Calcutta on August 16, 1946, the day appointed for the 'direct action.' The riots were so widespread and horrible that they strengthened the roots of communalism.

Likewise, the Hindu communalism did not lag behind. The Hindu Mahasabha made a sharp turn in the fascist direction under V. D. Savarkar's leadership. Year after year he warned the Hindus of the dangers of being dominated by the Muslims. Among the Hindus some Hindu communalists like M.S. Govalkar, the leader of R.S.S., the leaders of the Hindu Mahasabha and the Arya Samaj were also responsible for accelerating communal feelings among the Hindus. They wanted to bring 'Hindu raj.' They even had their personal armies, which were too often involved in riots. Among the Sikhs it was master Tara Singh the sole leader of the Sikhs who fanned religious sentiments of the Sikhs. At one place he stated that "our motherland is calling for blood and we shall satiate the thirst of our mother with blood."[49]

Some Hindu nationalists also gave a religious tinge to their political movement by worshipping Hindu Gods or by taking a dip in the Ganga when they began political activities. They introduced strong Hindu religious elements in nationalist thought and propaganda. They emphasized ancient Indian purist culture to the exclusion of medieval Indian composite culture. Bal Gangadhar Tilak used the Ganesh Puja and the Shivaji Festival to propagate nationalism. Not only this, the anti-partition movement of Bengal was initiated with dips in the Ganges. What was much worse, Bankim Chandra Chatterjea and many other writers in Bengali, Hindi, Urdu, and other languages often referred to Muslims as foreigners in their novels, poems, and stories and tended to identify nationalism with Hindus. Even leaders like, Lajpat Rai, Aurobindo, Tilak and later Gandhiji who were strong believers in Hindu-Muslim unity often employed in their writings and speeches language, imagery and symbolism derived exclusively from Hindu sources. All this tended to produce resentment among literate Muslims and alienate them from the emerging national movement. The Muslims and the Muslim communalists looked at the Hindu practices with suspicion and that increased the gap between the Muslims and the Hindus.

As a result the year 1947 saw one of the bloodiest upheavals in the history of mankind. Communalism figures as an important component in literature of that time and about that time. The short stories taken for detailed study particularly foreground the irrationality of the whole theory and practice of communalism. The stories tell us how, during the Partition, religion was used as a mobilising factor by the communalists and it led to ghastly crimes and violence against humanity. The communal madness gave rise to the beast in man, thirsty for human blood on the other side of the religious lines, and shattering the centurie's old tradition of brotherhood and harmony. The stories also do not blame only one community for the communal carnage. Whatever the Muslims did to the Hindus in Pakistan the Hindus were doing it to the Muslims in India, while the stories are also replete with the details how the two communities lived with perfect harmony before the Partition. The literature on the Partition and its aftermath is an important social and historical document. The madness of communalism not only led to looting and murder but also caused life-long suffering in terms of uprooting and homelessness.

While both men and women suffered these losses women were much greater sufferers because women became major targets of communal vengeance. Besides women could be tortured and degraded the way men could not be. Abduction, rape and forced captivity led to trauma that could never end in their life time, not to talk of murders of their husbands and children right before their eyes. The short stories vividly depict the trauma experienced by women of both the communities. Men wreaked vengeance on women of other religions to punish their rivals.

GENDER

The perception of gender role and values also gets drastically changed in the communally charged atmosphere. The concept of gender, too, got redefined like community and communalism during the Partition. On the one hand men became worried about their women and suddenly women appeared 'dear' and fragile because they symbolised 'community honour' for men, and on the other hand the Partition brought with it more suffering in the lives of women. They were subjected to the worst kind of violence. Either community attacked women of the other community as a target of vengeance upon their enemies. The lives of men do not get affected even during communal violence the way women's are.

Gender is the social conditioning of the two sexes. It refers to the social roles, responsibilities, or definitions assigned to male and females sexes. 'Gender' is a term that has psychological or cultural rather than biological connotations. If the proper terms for sex are 'male' and 'female', the corresponding terms for gender are 'masculine' and 'feminine'.[50] George Peter Murdock sees biological difference between men and women as the basis of the sexual division of labour in society.[51] He says that man with his superior physical strength can better undertake the more strenuous tasks, such as lumbering, mining, quarrying, land clearance and house building while woman is handicapped by the physiological burdens of pregnancy and nursing. But many sociologists do not agree with Murdock. They begin with the assumption that human behaviour is largely directed and determined by culture. Thus norms, values and roles for individuals are culturally determined and socially transmitted. From this perspective gender roles are a product of culture rather than biology. Much of the childhood period shapes conscious gender identity, and the primary source of influence is parental. It is rather true that conditioning begins right from childhood as upbringing of boys and girls is different and is related to their respective roles in adult life. The girl is trained for the role within home, but boys by being given more independence are prepared for the role outside home. Ann Oakley, a British sociologist and supporter of Women's Liberation Movement, comes down strongly on the side of culture as the determinant of gender roles.[52] She says, "Not only is the division of labour by sex not universal, but there is no reason why should not be human culture diverse and endlessly variable. They are the creation of human inventiveness rather than invincible biological forces". [53] And yet we find that there is sharp discrimination against women merely on the basis of biological difference, in terms of actual equal rights, dignity and justice. Society and culture force women to adopt qualities of submissiveness, self-sacrifice, devotion, love tolerance, generosity, compromise towards their husbands and the family. And there is no denying the fact that woman is not born but made by society.[54]

For man she is the "incidental", the inessential as opposed to the essential.[55] In patriarchy everything associated with male sex gets elevated over everything associated with female sex. Woman is never seen equal to man. She has no 'identity' of her own as an individual. In a patriarchal society where male values are worshipped woman is seen either passive or she does not exist. On the other hand man is seen as active and 'victor'.

Feminine side is always seen as the negative and powerless.

In the Vedic civilization, it is believed women enjoyed equal status with men. They studied Vedas and, even, composed Vedic hymns. The age could boast of the women *rishis* like Gargi and Maitreyi. Widows could remarry and women could own property. The evils like *Sati* were unknown. No ceremony was considered effective without her participation. And yet no desire is expressed for daughters in the *Rig Veda*.[56]

In the post Vedic civilization a daughter was considered the cause of all problems.[57] Woman, wine and gambling were placed in one category and woman was considered one of the three evils.[58] The son was regarded as the saviour of the family.[59] Even Buddhism held women responsible for the downfall of Buddhism. The Buddha is reported to have said to his favourite disciple Ananda: "If women were not admitted into the monasteries Buddhism would have continued for thousands of years".[60] The following ages saw the deterioration in the status of women and the period from 800 to 1200 A.D. witnessed steep downfall in the status of women. Women were considered mentally 'inferior'. Their duty was to obey their husbands blindly. A wife's duty of personal service towards her husband was described saying that she shall shampoo his feet and render him such other services as befits a servant.[61] Beating of wife is justified. The period between 1206 and 1761 recorded evils like female infanticide, child-marriage, *purdah*, *jouhar*, *sati* and slavery. These evils were still in vogue during the British regime. Though they made some laws to check the tide of these evils related to women, they failed to eradicate them completely. Among princely families 'Sati' was seen as a noble act.

The condition of the Muslim women was worse when Islam appeared in Arabia. They were not only regarded as socially 'inferior' but also were treated like slaves and chattels. It was a mark of dishonour for any man to have a daughter. They, too, had the custom of female infanticide. Introducing *Purdah* also imposed a system of seclusion on them. While Islam has given equal status in law to men and women, the position of women has remained miserable. In fact women of both the communities are suffering due to similar social evils in the society.

Girl-foeticide has created an alarming situation these days. The 2001 census figures of the sex ratio are really appalling in the under-six age group all over the country. The lowest female-male ratio in the country is in Haryana—864 women for 1000 men. Nationwide the number has come down to 927 from 945. It is also because the male patriarchal values of the society are deeply internalised by the women as well who feel inferior if they do not produce a male heir. Hence today the female child is being decimated.[62] We can say that condition of woman is the worst at present since she is being denied even the right to be born. Dowry deaths are common these days. Millet claims that if government is patriarchal and serves the interests of men, how do feminist issues such as domestic violence get on to the political agenda?[63]

Religion is often used as a tool to subjugate women. Zamfare, one of the Nigeria's 30 states, has introduced certain laws in the name of Sharia. One of its provisions prohibits women and men from travelling together on public transport.[64] During the Taliban regime in Afghanistan women had no access to education, health care services, jobs and other means of livelihood. It was done in the name of Islam and segregation of sexes. It seems as if we are still living in feudalistic society. On the other hand in Arunachal Pradesh most of the tribes, bring more wives in exchange for an animal called 'mithun'. The people of this state think that it is easier to maintain wives than so many animals.[65] In some African societies female circumcision is still practised.

Different religions of the world also give sanction to the female's subjugation to the male members of the society. *The Bible* clearly tells the women:

> Wives submit yourselves to your husbands, as unto the Lord.... as the church is subject unto Christ, so let the wives be to their husbands in everything.[66]

Woman is regarded subordinate to man because it is believed that she was made out of man.[67] In the Biblical myth man has been made master of all and he rules over and controls every object on this earth including woman. St Paul gives a secondary position to woman:

> Women should be silent during the church meetings. They are not to take part in the discussions, for they are subordinate to men as the scriptures also declare... (I Corinthians 14: 34-35).

The Koran also repeatedly stresses the superiority of men over women. A woman's function in life is to provide the male with sexual gratification and progeny. *The Koran* says, "Men are superior to women on account of the qualities with which God had gifted the one above the other..."[68] In India the Muslim women live in insecurity since their husbands are allowed to divorce them anytime. They just utter the word "talaak" thrice and can get rid of their wives.

Judaism, too, did not award equal status to woman in ancient times. She was not allowed to share man's work in any walk of life [69] A Jew made his morning prayer in the following manner:

Blessed be God... that he did not make me a woman.[70]

The ancient Hindu lawgiver, Manu, whose philosophy occupies a significant place in the mainstream of Indian ideology and culture, constantly stresses the inferiority of women to men. Manu says that woman must remain "dependent"(V.148) on man. He also says that a wife must ever remain devoted to her husband and always please him while he is alive. "Even though the husband be of bad character and seeks pleasure elsewhere he must be constantly worshipped as a god by a faithful wife"(V.154). Manu divides Indian society into four Varnas and position of women has been equated with the lowest class, 'shudras'. Not only this, various smritis have also assigned a subordinate role to women. For instance, Vishnu Smriti says, " A woman should not be free. She must be ruled over by one or another male member throughout her life."[71]

A major practice to perpetuate subjugation of women has been to intimidate them by inflicting violence, violence of all kinds physical, mental, emotional and spiritual. Rape is certainly the worst kind of violence, which is not merely physical but shatters the whole being of a woman. It violates her mind and soul as well since it is related to the concept of "purity" and "virtue" of women. Men have kept themselves above moral indictments of any kind by making the concept of "purity" "honour" and "izzat" rest entirely in women.

Women in peace times remain secondary to men and are subjugated by the men of their own communities. However, during communal riots, as those of the Partition, the equations of gender change within the community. During the Partition riots women became embodiments of "honour" of the whole community. While the men of their own communities considered them "precious", who needed to be carefully guarded from the men of other community, they became the preferred targets. The worst kind of violence was inflicted on women of the 'other' community by raping, abducting and humiliating their women. Defilement of community's honour through the violation of female sexuality is a thesis that resonates through the entire process of our nation building.[72] Since the communities' control over female sexuality lies at the centre of patriarchy the female body has been in our time reduced to a pawn whenever there is a crisis in the social order.[73] It was during the Partition that both the main communities of India— the Hindus and the Muslims—started ill-treating and raping the women of the other community. Susan Brownmiller is right who says that rape is "a political act", for it "imposes humiliation and oppression on the victim".[74] At that time, for men violation of a woman's body was an expression of triumph and intimidation of one community over other.[75] During the Partition the life of women became more tragic since within the community the oppression of women is of one kind but by the other community it is a threat of a more serious nature.

What is more agonising and surprising is that the survivors of rape suffer from an unprecedented sense of guilt and shame. The women first suffered at the hands of men of the 'other' community through rape and abduction and later when they were 'restored' to their families they were looked down upon with contempt as if they had themselves been responsible for their present condition. Both men and women in the families had so internalised the concept of purity that instead of sympathising with the victims they added to their suffering by rejecting them. Since the concept of purity, chastity or 'izzat' is central to men's definition of women, responses to its violence under any circumstances are problematic. When men of both the communities were fighting during the Partition, they were worried that the men of the other communities should not violate their woman's virtue. It would bring 'dishonour' to the whole community. Now men wanted to save the lives and honour of their women at the cost of their own lives. It is ironical since women never seen, as a value in themselves by the community suddenly became a value for the whole community because men thought that if their women were violated it would bring humiliation to the men. It also exposes hypocrisy of the male-world, their medieval and feudal mindset.

The internalisation of this concept by women leads to a sense of 'shame' sometimes in the mind of the victimized women as well, and almost always in the mind of the victim's family. Hence the response to such a woman becomes confusing as she is seen "polluted" by the society while the victimizers do not carry any burden on the minds, nor fear any ostracization by the society. Hence when some of the abducted women were restored to their families many refused to accept them back as part of the family.

Hence during the Partition women faced double violence—

intra-community as well as inter-community. Many women were killed by their own men so that they should not land in the hands of their 'enemies'. Many women jumped into wells to commit suicide. Women of both the communities to avoid greater violence and humiliation at the hands of their enemies took the step towards self-inflicted violence. Even though women themselves opted for self-inflicting violence as they internalised the concept of purity, some men of the same communities took advantage of the upheaval and exploited women of their own community. They raped them, sold them to brothels to make money out of them.

The women were subjected to another agony during the Partition as they were forced to keep silent about their woes. They were not listened to nor were they allowed to express their emotions. Even when some women were restored to their families no one shared their pain and trauma. The injuries to their bodies and psyche remained unhealed as no one consoled them. No one tried to discover or explore what Urvashi Butalia call 'the other side of silence'.[76] Some of the short stories very poignantly portray the agony of such women who become 'exiles' in their own body and mind.

NOTES

1. Quoted in G.R. Madan, *Theoretical Sociology* (Delhi: Atma Ram and Sons, 1983), p. 129.
2. Vidya Bhusan and D.R. Sachdeva, *An Introduction to Sociology* (Allahabad: Kitab Mehal, 1994), pp. 73-74.
3. Ibid., p. 520.
4. Quoted in Ibid., p.73.
5. S.M. Dubey, Dinesh Sharma, *Sociology*: *An Introduction* (New Delhi: NCERT, 1990), p.76. The book is translated into English by Susheela Dobhal.
6. Bhusan and Sachdeva, op.cit., p. 523.
7. Ibid.
8. Ibid., pp.539-40.
9. Ibid., p.554.
10. Akhileshwar Pandey, *Savtantra Bharat Me Hindu-Muslim*

Samasya Ke Aayam (Hindi) (New Delhi: Raj Publishing House, 1998), p. 16. My translation.
11. K. Singh, *Principles of Sociology* (Lucknow: Prakashan Kendra, 1980), p. 120.
12. Quoted in G.N. Rastogi, "Communalism", in *Political Science* (New Delhi: V.K. India Enterprises, 2000), p. 497.
13. Quoted in Ramji Lal, "Communal Scenario in India and Its Way Out," in *Communal Problem in India: A Symposium*, ed. Ramji Lal (Karnal: Dyal Singh College, 1988), p. 3.
14. M.G. Chitkara, *Indo-Pak Amity: A New Concept* (New Delhi: Ashish Publishing House, 1994), p. 33.
15. Pukhraj Jain and B.L. Faria, *Bhartiya Shasan Evam Rajniti* (Hindi) (Agra: Sahitya Bhawan Publication, 1999), pp. 632-33, my translation.
16. Quoted in ibid.
17. Ramji Lal, "Communal Scenario in India and Its Way Out," in *Communal Problem in India: A Symposium*, p. 4.
18. Bipan Chandra and others, *India's Struggle for Independence* (1857-1947) (New Delhi: Penguin Books, 1989), p. 398.
19. Ibid., pp. 398-99.
20. Ram Ahuja, *Social Problems in India* (1994, rpt. New Delhi: Rawat Publications, 2001), p. 120.
21. Quoted in Bipan Chandra and others, op. cit., p. 401.
22. Ahuja, *Social Problems in India*, p.120.
23. B.L. Grover and S. Grover, *A New Look at Modern Indian History* (1707 to the Present day) (New Delhi: S. Chand and Company, 2000) p. 604.
24. R.C. Majumdar, ed., *The British Paramountcy and Indian Renaissance* (Mumbai: Bhartiya Vidya Bhawan, Part X, 1982), p. 322.
25. K.K. Bhardwaj, "Indian National Movement: Communal Politics", *Competition Success Review*, New Delhi, November 1998, Vol xxv. No 5, p. 51.
26. V.D. Mahajan, *India Since 1526* (New Delhi: S. Chand and Co., 1986), p. 356.
27. Satya M. Rai, *Partition of the Punjab* (New Delhi: Asia Publishing House, 1965), p. 5.
28. Ibid.
29. S.N. Sadasivam, *Party and Democracy in India* (New Delhi: Tata McGrow Hill Publishing Co. 1977), p. 61.
30. Chitkara, *Indo-Pak Amity: A New Concept*, pp. 35-36.

31. Bipan Chandra and others, *India's Struggle for Independence*, p. 405.
32. Grover and Grover, *A New Look at Modern Indian History*, p. 606.
33. Quoted in Pandey, *Savtantra Bharat Me Hindu-Muslim Samasya Ke Aayam*, p. 15.
34. Bipan Chandra and others, *India's Struggle for Independence*, p. 409.
35. P.P. Mehta, "Foreword" in *Communal Problem in India: A Symposium*, ed. Ramji Lal (Karnal: Dyal Singh College, 1988), p. iii
36. Chitkara, *Indo-Pak Amity: A New Concept*, p. 33.
37. M. Haralambos and R.M. Heald, *Sociology, Themes and Perspective* (New Delhi: Oxford University Press, 1980), p. 460.
38. "Psychology of Communalism", *The Hindu*, March 24, 1993, p.3.
39. Bipan Chandra and others, *India's Struggle for Independence (1857–1947)* (New Delhi: Penguin Books, 1989), p. 413.
40. J.C. Johar, "Editor's Introduction" in Lal Bahadur, *Struggle for Pakistan: Tragedy of the Triumph of Muslim Communalism in India (1906-47)* (New Delhi: Sterling Publishers, 1988), p.vii.
41. Grover and Grover, *A New Look at Modern Indian History*, p. 605.
42. Ibid.
43. Bipan Chandra, *Communalism in Modern India* (1984, rpt., Delhi: Vikas Publishing House, 1996), pp. 104-5.
44. Grover and Grover, *A New Look at Modern Indian History*, p. 605.
45. Quoted in Pandey, *Savtantra Bharat Me Hindu-Muslim Samasya Ke Aayam*, p. 33.
46. Rafiq Zakaria, *The Man Who Divided India* (Bombay: Popular Prakashan, n.d.).
47. P.K. Ravindranath, "Jinnah's Role in Partition of India: A Reappraisal, *The Tribune*, December 16, 2001, p. 8.
48. Mohammad Hasan, "Communalism in English Literature" in Asghar Ali Engineer and Moin Shakir, ed. *Communalism in India* (New Delhi: Ajanta Publications, 1985), p.196.
49. Quoted in Anders Bjorn Hansen, *Partition and Genocide: Manifestation of Violence in Punjab, 1937-1947* (New Delhi: India Research Press, 2002), p. 111.

50. Robert J.S. Toller, *Sex and Gender* (New York: Science House, 1968) p. 7.
51. Haralembos and Heald, *Sociology, Themes and Perspective*, p. 371.
52. Ibid., p. 373.
53. Quoted in ibid.
54. The epigraph of *Women in Sexist Society: Studies in Power and Powerlessness*, ed. Vivian Gornink and Barbara K. Moran (New York: New American Library, Mentor Books, 1972) says: "The fault lies not in our stars, our hormones, our menstrual cycles or our empty internal spaces, but in our institutions. Woman is made not born."
55. Simone de Beauoir, *The Second Sex,* trans. and ed. M.M. Parshley (1953, rpt. Harmondsworth: Penguin, 1983), p. 16.
56. Ram Sharan Sharma, *Ancient India* (1977, rpt. New Delhi: NCERT, 1986), p. 48.
57. D.N. Jha, *Prachin Bharat* (Hindi) (1980, rpt. New Delhi: Manohar Publishers, 1997), p. 29.
58. Ibid.
59. V.D. Mahajan, *Ancient India* (1960, rpt. New Delhi: S.Chand and Company, 2000), p.141.
60. Ram Sharan Sharma, *Ancient India*, p.66.
61. Satish Chandra, *Medieval India* (1978, rpt. New Delhi: NCERT, 1988), p. 26.
62. Nirupama Dutt, "Where has a girl child gone?" *The Tribune*, June 24, 2001, p. 21.
63. Bela Rani Sharma, *Women: Marriage, Family and Divorce* (Jaipur: Mangal Deep Publications, 1997), p. 84.
64. R.M. Pal, "Where government makes anti-women laws", *The Tribune*, October 26, 2000, p. 10.
65. "Women Lose out to Mithuns" a report under the column "Trends and Pointers", *The Tribune*, December 7, 2000, p. 9.
66. Ephesians 5 : 22-24.
67. In *The Holy Bible*, there is another reference to this effect: "This is now bone of my bone and flesh of my flesh: She shall be called woman, because she is taken out of man". (Genesis 2 : 13).
68. *The Koran*, trans. J.M. Rodwell (Herts: Everyman's Library, 1909), p. 415.
69. Shaikh M.H. Kidwai, *Woman* (Delhi: Seema Publications, 1976), p. 14.

70. Quoted in De Beauvoir, *The Second Sex*, p. 22.
71. Ramnika Jalali, *Indian Women in Smritis* (Jammu: Vinod Publishers and Distributers, 1994), p.5.
72. Jasodhara Bagchi, "Introduction" to Jyotirmoyee Devi's *The River Churning*, trans. Enakshi Chatterjee (1995, rpt. New Delhi: Kali for Women, 1998), pp. XXVIII-IX.
73. Reicha Tanwar, "Combating a mindset that is a fortress", *The Tribune*, July 15, 2001, p. 21.
74. Wayne Fraser, *The Dominion of Women: The Personal and the Political in Canadian Women's Literature* (London: Greenwood Press, 1991), p. 168.
75. Jasodhara Bagchi in Jyotirmoyee Devi, *The River Churning*, p. XXIX.
76. Urvashi Butalia, *The Other Side of Silence* (New Delhi: Viking Penguin India, 1998).

2
Communal Frenzy and the Human Waste: The Price of 'Freedom'

The freedom of India from the British regime in 1947, which was achieved after a long struggle waged against the colonial rule by the Indian irrespective of caste, religion or any other regional affiliations, was however, marred by the colossal tragedy of the Partition of the country. A new nation state of Pakistan for the Muslims was carved out of India. This political decision led to unimaginable human suffering and large-scale migration on both sides of the border. The religious distortions propagated by individuals and political organisations for vested political interests led to monstrous atrocities and large-scale violence and bloodshed virtually unprecedented in human history. People of both the communities turned against each other and riots broke out. Killings, looting, arson, abduction, rape, and bloodshed became a routine affair. The historians have dealt with the political causes of the Partition in detail, particularly the factors that caused the Partition, but they did not record its impact on large sections of humanity. The tragedies of the uprooted masses have remained largely untouched by the historians.

The creative writers of different communities, however, poignantly record the loss and suffering, trauma and agony experienced by humanity during the single historical-political event. The after-effects of the riots were so painful and intense and the violence was so widespread that they stirred the creative imagination of the story writers and novelists. Hundreds of short stories on both sides of the border have been written about traumatic incidents at the time of the Partition. Much of this creative outpouring has been cathartic as many of the writers themselves have been victims of these events and have been witness to the ghastly crimes against humanity. The writers of the short stories have captured the human dimensions of the violent catastrophes very effectively. A study of the fictional writings of that time or about that time can help us understand the pain and trauma of the Partition victims. Gyanendra Pandey emphasizes the need for the histories to 'recover the voices of the marginal', so that history does not end up as the celebration 'of certain victorious concepts'.[1] The historians should also move away from traditional sources and look more towards fictional writings and memories, since it would present a medium for otherwise indescribable horrors and sufferings.[2]

In fact, the literature written on the Partition is historically also very important to get an adequate idea of the impact of the Partition on the people of India. Urvashi Butalia has, in her recent book, *The Other side of Silence*,[3] used selective interviews to obtain insight into how the marginalized groups, especially women, perceived the Partition. She emphasises the need for shifting the focus to groups otherwise neglected, like women and children. And this is in fact what writer of short stories and novels do. They have tried to break the silence of the victims by recording some personal pain as well as the pain of other sufferers like them by talking to them and recording from their memories the true picture of the time. Hence to know the scale of loss and sufferings literature from both sides of the border, probably is the best source.

The consequences of this calamity were damaging in several ways. This chapter focuses on some of these consequences, for example, the large scale gruesome massacres turning land into cities of sorrows with thousands of corpses, fear psychosis and loss of faith, betrayals and utter loss not only of one's dear ones but also of one's home and hearth.

And where children were among the worst sufferers. The stories taken for detailed study are those which poignantly recount these various facets of human suffering: "The Owner of Rubble", "Death", "The Refuge", "A Holy War", "The City of Sorrow", "Avtar: A Hindu Myth", "The Peshawar Express", "Pali", "A Mouthful of Water, A Mouthful of Blood", "Post box", "The Abandoned Child" and " Where is My Mother?"

I

BETRAYAL AND LOSS OF FAITH

The Partition caused great upheaval in the lives of those who used to live amicably sharing one another's joys and sorrows irrespective of religious or ethnic differences. The most serious consequence of the Partition was the gruesome violence that resulted in communal hatred for each other. The communal hatred gave birth to suspicion. People started looking at each other with distrust. Those who were friends turned foes and started to live amid the feelings of insecurity. The twine of faith was snapped giving place to fear and suspicion.

Mohan Rakesh has very poignantly recorded the feeling of 'loss' in "The Owner of Rubble."[4] Gani Miyan is the main character who returns to India after seven and half years after the Partition. He goes to the lane in Amritsar where he had once built a house and where his family had been killed in 1947. He goes back not to claim his house but to see the place where his life had once its roots. It is the love for the land which once belonged to him and nostalgia that attract him to the land of past memories. Ironically, people fail to recognize him at first and regard him with suspicion as a kidnapper. The old sense of fellow feeling has vanished. The Partition has broken all the bonds of love and faith that had once been the main feature of community living.

Here Gani Miyan meets Rakkha who had been a friend of

Chiragdin, Gani's son. Chiragdin had stayed back in India, along with his wife and daughters, because he had faith in Rakkha. When Gani Miyan had asked his son also to move to Pakistan Chiragdin had told his father, "As long as Rekkha was around, no body would dare to hurt him"(p 75). Gani Miyan is ignorant of what had exactly happened and who had killed his son. When he sees Rakkha he asks him with tears in his eyes, "Tell me, Rakkha how did it happen?... You were friends. You loved each other like brothers. Couldn't he have hidden in your house? He was bright enough to have thought of that"(p. 74). And the greatest irony or tragedy is that it was Rakkha who killed Chiragdin and along with other goons raped his wife and daughters before killing them, thus betraying the faith Chiragdin had reposed in Rakkha. Chiragdin perhaps forgot to realize that time had changed then. How could he lean over the shoulder of Rakkha when everyone, generally, had been turned wolfish by the communal hatred and passion? This shows how appropriate this observation is: "Riots are transformatory as well as historical events. They share and alter perceptions and aspirations. People are changed: Their attitude to each other and their ways of thinking about themselves are transformed."[5]

Chiragdin "depended" on Rakkha who betrayed him. Rakkha wanted to "grab" his house, so he attacked him. Chiragdin had refused to migrate to Pakistan as he didn't want to leave his newly built house and he also had faith in Rakkha. Ironically, it was the desire to grab his house which made Rakkha betray his faith and like Chiragdin, he sent his wife and daughters also "to Pakistan" that very night by "a different and longer route." (p. 72). Their bodies were found in the "canal nearby" (p. 72). The manner in which Rakkha killed his 'friend' was awesome. Chiragdin was eating his dinner when Rakkha asked him to come down. Chiragdin got up without finishing his food, and went downstairs to meet him. The moment Chiragdin stepped out of the door Rakkha "grabbed him by his shirt-collar, threw him down in the street and sat on his chest." (p. 72). Chiragdin was terrified. He helplessly screamed,

"Rakkha Pahalwaan, don't kill me! O God help... save me! (p. 72). His wailing had no effect on ruthless Rakkha. Chiragdin's wife and daughters were screaming helplessly. The scene turned heart rending when Rakkha pressed his knee down on his thighs and shouted, "Don't scream, you sister-fucker... you want Pakistan, don't you? I only want to send you there! Now go!" (p. 72.) And Chiragdin was stabbed to death. The house was ransacked after killing Chiragdin. All emotions, all values died, and a mad pursuit of communal hatred combined with selfish interests turned friends into foes.

The trauma of the old man, Gani Miyan, is not less. He has visited India to see the land that belonged to him. He has come to see the house where his family lived once. But the tragedy is that even the house is no more there. It has turned into a heap of rubble. The history of his family's fate is buried in "the pile of rubbish" (p. 72) His agony can be estimated as he sits in the middle of the rubble, scratches ash with his nails and scatters it over his head. The frame of the door is standing isolated like Gani Miyan among the rubbles. It is the only thing left there to remind him of his family which had been annihilated like the house. Gani Miyan puts his arms around the doorframe and wails, "Speak to me, Chirag! Say something! Tell me where you are? O, Kishwar! O Sultana! My Children! O God, why is Gani still alive! "(pp. 72-73). Poor Gani's trauma cannot be explained in words. He is even deprived of the mere joy of seeing his house. There are no signs to relate to his past. There is only a heap of rubble left.

But Gani Miyan accepted all this as 'fated'. He is an epitome of goodness. He is devoid of any feeling of hatred and animosity against anyone. He is a good, humble and god-fearing Muslim. He has no malice against anyone. The greatness of his character is revealed as he says to Rakkha, "What happened was fated Rakkhiya. There is no use moaning about the past! May god bless the virtuous, and may he forgive those who have sinned! Now that I have met all of you, I feel as if I have seen Chirag again. May Allah keep you in good health" (p. 75). It is really a positive sign that even amid bad times people like Gani Miyan are still there.

The author not only depicts the seriousness of the Partition which resulted in large scale destruction and massacre, but also depicts how greed can make individuals inhuman, to grab the property of others one can even kill one's fellow human being. But the author also hints at the truth that evil does not prosper always. Rakkha had killed Chiragdin and his family so that he might grab his house but before he could do this someone else burned down the house. Even the murderer could not own the house. But greed to own and control makes Rakkha claim the ownership of the rubble of the house and he doesn't let anyone touch even the remains of the burnt house. This is how during times of upheavals anti-social elements overpower the common man and even communities.

Exploiting communal frenzy for personal gains people like Rakkha are responsible for widening the gulf between the communities by shattering the faith of the innocent and well-meaning persons.

The author also introduces a crow and a dog in the story. Symbolically, their presence conveys a message that Rakkha is not the only owner of the rubble. When a wandering crow perches on the frame of the door, the dog barks at him to scare it. Both of them also, it seems, claim to be the owners of the rubble.

The title of the story refers to the meaninglessness and futility of motivated acts of looting and murder like those of Rakkha. And the story very sensitively brings out how not only people lost their dear ones and their homes but also the faith in human goodness, and the trust in friends was shattered.

The ghastly shadow of the communal riots also falls on Madan and Saleem and it brings estrangement between friends. The loss of mutual trust is central in Ved Rahi's story "Death,"[6] in which both these characters appear. Both of them have been good friends since childhood. During school days it is Madan who saves Saleem from mischievous classmates. They play together and when Madan visits Saleem's house his mother showers love upon Madan. The bonds of their friendship are so strong that Saleem who does not know how to swim and is afraid of water jumps into the river when he thinks Madan is drowning. He tells Madan innocently, "When you didn't surface for sometime, I thought that you had drowned. I jumped into water to save you" (p. 231). What else could be the measure of love between the two friends? At another time when both of them encounter a snake they are scared but finding themselves "so close to each other", they are "no longer mortally afraid" (p. 231).

However, the mad irrationality of communal hatred creates fear and doubt in the minds of even the best of friends and their relationships are marred. An unprecedented cataclysm[7] takes place. Everywhere the many and the strong have started assaulting the few and the weak. The Partition riots break out and Saleem's parents are forced to flee to Pakistan leaving Saleem behind in Military school's boarding house where he is studying at that time. During these days Madan is worried about Saleem and his parents because he knows that "some Muslims have been lured away, with the promise of helping them reach Pakistan, to a place where they could be easily slaughtered" (p. 234).

Madan invites Saleem to his house from the boarding house when peace returns. He tells Saleem that his own parents have bought a house at a very cheap rate. The house was once owned by a Muslim family but the family was killed during riots and the only surviving son sold it to them. This creates fear in Saleem. Though he drinks tea at Madan's house, he leaves the house hurriedly. A shadow of suspicion is cast over him. Saleem is in a fix whether he should believe Madan or not. He asks Madan with terror in his eyes, "Madan, can you murder me?" (p. 236). Though he does know that Madan cannot harm him, he is apprehensive about his behaviour. It is the riots and religious distortions created by the elders that have created a gulf between such fast friends. The gruesome manifestations of virulent violence stupefied the very sensibility of both the Hindus and the Muslims.

S.H. Vatsayan's "The Refuge"[8] particularly focuses on the mad irrationality of communal riots, which leaves the sane and sensitive human beings utterly helpless. This story is set in Lahore and revolves around Devenderlal who continued to live in his house even after all the Hindus in that *mohalla* had fled their houses, because his Muslim friend Rafiquddin had insisted that he should stay on and that he himself would take responsibility of Devenderlal's safety. In fact Rafiquddin sincerely felt it was his duty as much as that of the other Muslims to protect their Hindu friends and neighbours because what was happening was shameful. When Devenderlal, whose family had already gone to Jullundhar, decides to leave, Rafiquddin persuades him to stay, "No, we'll lose face! How can you leave your own home and become a refugee in your own city? We will not let you go—we will force you to stay. It is the duty of the majority to protect the minority, and to make sure that they don't abandon their homes and run away" (p. 73).

It is not that Devenderlal did not trust his friend and neighbour but as he explains, "Once fear grips people and they begin to run away, then the entire scenario changes completely. Each one suspects the other; begins to regard the other for no reason at all, as his enemy" (p.73). Very soon the shadow of communal frenzy casts its evil spell on Rafiquddin's locality. The houses of the Hindus, including Devenderlal's, were looted and burnt down. The atmosphere was charged with hatred. The "horses of rage were whipped into murderous frenzy by hatred and envy, religious groups spread poison everywhere, and the flames of communal frenzy were fanned by the police and the bureaucracy"(p. 75). Most shocking things were happening all around. A doctor was stabbed by a relative of the patient he had gone to examine while another nobleman and his family who had, in fact, given shelter to homeless people were first arrested by the police and then shot dead by the armed guards themselves. To his utter despair and helplessness the madness of the time becomes clear to Rafiquddin by and by when he is forced to turn Devenderlal out of his house or else is threatened with dire consequences. With pressure from other Muslims mounting on Rafiquddin Devenderlal decides to leave his house but Rafiquddin arranges a shelter for him in a small dark room in a neighbour's house. Both the friends wonder what is happening in the name of freedom. And Devenderlal's hideout is worse than the government prison. This brings out the bitter truth how one is virtually 'imprisoned' by one's own people.

The sane and the normal like Rafiquddin and Devenderlal are agonised at the happenings but find themselves utterly helpless to check the frenzy. Devenderlal is provided food and shelter by his friend's friend, one Sheikh Sahib, for some days but then his benefactor only tries to kill him by giving him poisoned food. This leads to utter loss of faith in his benefactor. How could one believe the 'other' during those bad days? The saviour had turned the murderer. Devenderlal ponders over the whole situation rather philosophically, "One had told him that he would force him to stay back, but had turned him out of his house. The other had not only offered him shelter, but had also given him poison". (p. 82). The faith that had taken centuries to be cemented between the Hindus and the Muslims was butchered overnight. The non-Muslims were joining hands on one side and the Muslims on the other which shook the foundations of love, friendship, brotherhood and faith.

Devenderlal sadly realises that "the danger in the world lay not in the strength of evil, but in the weakness of good" (p. 82). And yet the biggest consolation amidst all inhuman killings, looting and burning is that good, however weak, persists in the most desperate times. Sheikh Sahib's daughter, Zaibu, warns Devenderlal about poison in his food and thus saves his life. Devenderlal jumps over the wall and escapes from that house and finally reaches Delhi. In response to his appeal on radio to his family in India he receives a note from Pakistan, understandably from Zaibu, thanking God at his safe escape and asking him to similarly remember his duty towards other human beings. And this provides the most optimistic word in the whole story, the *selfless* human concern for another human being in distress. Goodness, however weak, prevails even in the face of monstrous evil.

Similarly, the close friendship between Arun and Munir, in *Azadi*,[9] loses its faith, natural ease and spontaneity. The communal frenzy and the ensuing change do cast its sinister shadow on their 'instinctual love' and amity. It is right after coming back from Bill Davidson's house where they had been discussing the Partition that they find that the old feeling of easiness is gone. "Even Munir and Arun feel a tension towards each other" (p.124).

II

UNHOLY ACTS OF THE 'HOLY WAR'

The brutal violence during the communal riots left deep scars on the life of the victims. Freedom of India brought with it a bitter harvest of death when millions of lives were lost in the religious frenzy. Some of the stories particularly record the horrors of monstrous violence. While some of the historians are partial enough in their judgments since they either hold the Muslims responsible for the Partition riots or the Hindus, the short-story writers and novelists, in fact, give a fairer picture of the Partition riots. For instance, Khushwant Singh sums up the reality of the situation by laying the blame on both the communities: "The fact is, both sides killed. Both shot and stabbed and speared and clubbed. Both tortured. Both raped."[10] While the historians have ignored the voices of the victims with "astonishing silence,"[11] novelists and storywriters have particularly focused on the pain and suffering of the victims.

No doubt, religious irrationality and distortions leading to "religious intolerance" resulted in hatred between the Hindus and the Sikhs on the one hand and the Muslims on the other. Though riots did take place in the 1920s and 1930s they were different from those during the Partition. Earlier the riots were caused by different issues such as cow slaughter, the playing of music before the mosques, the performance of *arti* or *namaj* or the defilement of religious symbols and places. On the other hand, the Partition violence broke out purely on the political issue of transfer of power. "The violence at this time has a definite political orientation and was closely connected with the question of independence and partition".[12] The riots that took place in 1937, when the Muslim League failed to muster majority even in the Muslim area, too, were different from the riots of 1947. Anders Bjorn Hansen has rightly asserted:

> The violence in 1937 mainly was a case of consensual violence, since the aim was to reinforce the communal territories among the three communities. However, in 1947 the violence changed into non-consensual violence and appropriated genocidal features, because the aim of the violence turned into an act of survival.[13]

Once the riots were triggered, they took a ghastly turn, as people from all the communities were involved. The Partition violence aimed at forced conversion and its effort was to 'dishonour' the other community particularly by molestation of females.[14] The violence was also used to 'ethnically cleanse' minority communities. Meanwhile some selfish political leaders were busy in creating the feeling of animosity and "the Muslims were even talking of civil war and the tone in public speeches was becoming belligerent."[15] Now riots not only reflected existing tensions, but also polarised communities where one looked at the other with hatred and distrust. In addition to communal hatred another reason for attacking, looting or murdering people of the other community was materialistic or economic. As in "The Owner of Rubble" we learn Rakkha had killed his friend Chiragdin for grabbing his newly built house. So also in other instances of arson and murder greed was a motivating force. People were ready to destroy each other with anything—bamboo-sticks, hockey, ice picks, knives, clubs, swords, hammers, bricks and clawing fingers. People of different religion were busy with "spontaneous and irrational slaughter"[16] The short-story writers have recorded the scenes of bloodshed, looting, arson and abduction so minutely that they shock the readers and give them an idea of the dimensions of the tragedy. These stories are written by people of conscience who knew that during the days of the Partition the "monstrous was a part of all communities."[17]

Ironically, all the inhuman acts of violence, bloodshed and destruction were glorified by sections of people as "a holy war" and on this account youngsters particularly were being encouraged to participate in it.

Yashpal's story "A Holy War" vividly describes how a city of beautiful gardens and bustling crowds, Lahore, was "paralyzed by fear and mutual hatred amongst all the communities" (p. 193).[18] The riots brought with them devastation and destruction all around. All the Hindu families were forced to flee even though Gangu-ki-Gali was a Hindu dominated area. The eerie and gloomy atmosphere in the street is very effectively portrayed by Yashpal with the recurrent use of such words as "darkness", "deep silence", "curfew", "darkness terrifying and unbearable", "darkness and silence", "desolation" and "sadness" which was "oppressive" and made night "even more gloomy and suffocating" (p. 193). The author has created an atmosphere of fear and loneliness in the story so solidly that it seems the whole scène is taking place before our eyes. The darkness is so thick that "not a ray of light filtered through the cracks in the doors." And "there was no sign of life in any house... only fear haunted the abandoned and ruined houses..."(p. 193).

The response to this situation is represented by two Muslim characters, Fazzay the dyer and his son Nasru, who had a small shop at the corner of the street where they lived also with their bare minimum possessions. Fazzay is pained to see the deserted street and nostalgically remembers the earlier days: "After all the children, the young men and the young women of the lane had called him Mama for years. And the wives and daughters of the neighbourhood had often come to his shop without bothering to cover their heads or veil their faces, to give him sarees, *chunnies* and turbans to dye" (pp. 194-95). He fondly remembers the time when the children would "sneak up to his shop and steal a bit of starch to fix their torn kites and then run away" (p. 195).

By contrast his son, the youthful Nasru, feels "elated" when he sees the Hindus run away from the lane. "He clenched his teeth in anger" and said, "Let the kafir bastards go to hell! Pakistan doesn't need kafirs"! (p.197). When he sees people looting and burning the houses and shop of the Hindus his mouth also "began to water with greed" and he asks his father if he could also get "a few bales of cloth or a few sacks of sugar and flour?" (p. 198). While Fazzay is mad with rage at this thought of his own son, Nasru still tries to argue with his father, "why, everyone is looting. They say they are collecting the just rewards of a holy war"(p. 198). Nasru is among those who have completely accepted the mad logic of calling it "a holy war" and he is keen to participate in this "holy war" with a religious passion despite his father trying to restrain him. Here Nasru is representative of all those youngsters mad with communal frenzy who failed to understand that "Islam stands for the unity and brotherhood of mankind, not for disrupting the oneness of the human family."[19]

Contrary to Nasru's faith in religious frenzy Fazzay represents a humane response to the mad violence of communal riots and seeing the abandoned house of his neighbours, he sighs, "Yah, Allah! What a catastrophe! After all these people leave, how will I carry on in this desolate place! How will I live in this ghost-haunted place! (p.197). He still cherishes the bond he had with the members of the other community.

In the looting and arson that was carried on for days together unabated in the name of a "holy War" the prime motive was indeed greed, to grab the property of others. And people of both the communities were involved in this pursuit. "A Holy War" depicts the Muslim goons busy in looting and arson. Similarly, the Hindu goons are shown looting the property of the Muslims in "The Owner of Rubble". Hence both the communities were greedy for the property of the others. They had nothing to do with religion. As Larry Collins and Dominique Lapierre write:

> A motive that had nothing to do with religious fervour was more often behind the Moselm attacks on Hindus and Sikhs in Pakistan. It was greed, a simple, often carefully orchestrated effort to grab the lands, shops and wealth of their neighbours.[20]

Inevitably another thought that swept the Muslims was that if Pakistan was theirs so too were the shops and houses in it. And so even the old and innocents, like Moolan Tai were not spared. When all the Hindus had fled only Moolan Tai, an old Hindu woman, had continued to stay on. One night Nasru notices her quickly going out of her house with a small bundle. He thinks she was going to run away with her gold and money, etc. and at once he rushes towards her and stabs her with the desire to possess her wealth. But all that he finds in the bundle is "the stone idol of her God" (p. 200). Sadly, even now Nasru fails to see the senselessness of his acts, instead he "laughed derisively"(p. 200) while his father curses him angrily, "May you burn in Hell for murdering an innocent old woman... You are really a great Ghazi, you have saved your God!" (p. 201).

The voice of sanity, of humanity is still alive, as is depicted in Fazzay, but the sad fact is that it becomes ineffective in such mad times.

The author very subtly portrays the contrast between the two times—of peace and of violence—through two contrary pictures of the father and the son sleeping in their small shop. In earlier times, "Fazzay would sleep on the platform next to the shop and Nasru would lie on mat which he would spread out in the street, leaving some space for people to walk past. Often he sat late into the night singing *Heer* and folk songs" (p. 194). On the contrary during bad times those peaceful days had given place to the days overcast with darkness and fear. There was curfew outside, "Fazzay didn't feel like making food". Fazzay and Nasru lay down side by side on the mat on the floor of the room. "It was pitch dark in the lane outside and it was even darker inside the room. The night was absolutely still and silent. The sky was covered with heavy, rainless clouds. It seemed as if the clouds had lidded the new city so tightly that its brick houses didn't have the chance to cool down.... The old city lay as if it was stunned" (p. 199).

Ghulam Abbas's "Avtar: A Hindu Myth"[21] gives an equally graphic account of looting, torture and murder of the Muslims on this side of the border by the Hindus. The story begins and ends in a surrealistic mode with realistic depictions in the middle describing one community's struggle for survival in a hostile world. The writer describes how the Hindus who were in majority and were hunting for the Muslims attacked Sambhal town in Muradabad district. It was due to communal frenzy that "armed gangs of Hindus attacked Muslim localities, burnt down their houses, butchered countless men, women and children. Those Muslims who survived the massacre fled from the town" (p. 193). The Hindus took possession of the houses, shops and other properties of the Muslims (p. 194). Small children were killed ruthlessly. The mad irrationality of the Hindus is clear from their act when they surrounded one old Muslim man. He was "tied with ropes and his virginal daughters were raped before his eyes and cruelly butchered" (p. 201). Afterwards they sprinkled kerosene around the house and set it on fire.

The story also portrays an instinct for survival and the challenges one has to face for survival. The Muslims who survived the massacre set up a colony far away from the town in a forest. It is the instinct for survival that one is even ready to live under most difficult circumstances. This reminds us of

Devenderlal of "The Refuge" who gets ready to live hidden in a dark room and where his friends also think it best to imprison him so that he may survive. Even when the Muslims of Sambhal town tried to settle down quietly and peacefully in an isolated area some miscreants from the majority community still keep on bothering them due to the hatred against them. The women are not allowed to take water from the well near the temple on the outskirts of the city. Thus they are deprived of even the basic needs for their survival. They face deprivation at every step. When Muslim women try to fetch water from the well at night they are "ambushed" and the Hindus pounce upon them like "hungry wolves" (p. 202) and rape them. Those who resist their breasts are "cut off" (p. 202). The minority community is terrorised and intimidated into keeping quiet or to face the consequences.

As said earlier, the story begins and ends in a surrealistic mode. The communal passion is so intense and the violence and hatred so ghastly that even the earth finds these horrors unbearable. The horrors of religious hatred are so mind-numbing and shaking that the earth gets fed up and goes to the courts of gods and pleads,

> "May Indra Maharaj be praised. Maharaj, there is no religion left anywhere in the world. The darkness of sin has spread over it. In every city, in every town, in every village, innocent people are being slaughtered. Villages have been reduced to ash. Unborn children have been plucked out of the wombs of pregnant women, impaled on spears and brandished in the air. Breasts of women have been cut, noses of men have been chopped off, people have been roasted alive in fire. Human beings have become more ferocious than the beasts. I can no longer watch such horror, Maharaj. Permit me to leave this hell and sink into the nether world" (p. 191).

This is where in fact the story begins. In between there is detailed realistic depiction of suffering humanity as a result of communal assaults. The ending is again surrealistic and suggestive of hope that one day God will take the form of a human being to save the world from evil. People of the Muslim community have a revelation of an *avtar.* The Muslims have a vision of an *avtar*. When a Muslim woman, Sara, cries out as the Hindu goons are throwing her husband into fire, there is "a deafening burst of thunder in the sky" (p. 203). The earth shakes and fire is extinguished. The Hindus are terrified. A handsome boy appears before them on a horse. There is a long burning sword in his hand. There is a strange light on his face. He declares himself *avtar* of Kalki whose coming has been announced in the *Vedas.* He is the last *avtar* of Vishnu. He reproaches the Hindus for their cruelties and teaches them that the "final goal of all religions is the same" (p. 204). Finally he declares that this time he has been born in the house of a Muslim—a poor ironmonger. Thus it is through a vision seen by the Muslims or through "the author's use of surrealistic mode that a hope of good time is revealed where evil is punished for its bad deeds. It is also good that though the writer of the story is a Muslim he draws upon the myth of the *avtar* of Vishnu and believes in Vedas and its teachings for the benefit of mankind.

"The City of Sorrow"[22] by Intizar Husain, particularly records the degradation of human values—social as well as moral. The story develops in the form of a conversation among three men who are not given any names. The story is written in a surrealistic mode where two dead men are talking to a third one who is alive. But as they recall the events prior to their death one gets graphic details of most monstrous crimes against humanity, and particularly against women, how they were forced to be stripped by their own relatives and then publicly raped and butchered. Both the men had raped and killed without any sense of shame. They know that, symbolically, their faces are disfigured because they had let lose the hell on their enemies. But now they are afraid of themselves. They can neither find a place in any society, nor a spot on the earth in which they can bury their own corpses. One of these three men had forced a

Hindu boy to strip his "sister naked" and then he raped her in the presence of her brother (p. 85). The same Hindu boy took revenge later on by forcing a Muslim to strip his wife naked (p. 86). The story depicts how men of both the communities had gone mad with communal frenzy.

No doubt, religious frenzy leads to mad acts of inflicting violence and humiliation on the 'other' but its true impact and meaning is felt when it recoils on one's own self. It was only when the daughter of the First man was stripped and raped, and then she disappeared, that he realised the horror of his act he had done earlier. It was here that he died—a moral death. The story also tells that one realises the sufferings of others only when one suffers oneself. The suffering and trauma of one's 'own' made the First man realise the dimensions of pain and torture he inflicted on others. All this made him realise the moral death he had met with. Since then, as he says, he has been carrying his corpse and looking for a place to bury it.

The author does not mention the religion of the three men in the story. They may belong to any religion, which is suggestive of the fact that the Hindus as well as the Muslims were equally involved in the ghastly acts of raping and killings. They did a great loss to the humanity. That is why faces of the three men, mentioned in the story, are disfigured and their characters are tainted. They committed one crime after another. Though the Third man is not involved directly in these gruesome acts, he is equal accomplice in these acts, as he does nothing to protect those in distress. He is representing millions of those who, during the Partition, had witnessed mutely the heinous crimes against mankind but did nothing to save those who were victims of violence or those suffering in the worst way. Face of the Third man is also disfigured as he had turned his back towards his fellow human beings. He himself admits, "My face was disfigured when I turned my back on those people" (p. 98). His condition is worse than those who are dead. The other two men force him to realise that he is also dead. Indeed, he is morally dead.

The most gruesome and nerve-racking depiction of mass killings during the Partition is perhaps Krishna Chander's "The Peshawar Express"[23]. The moving account of the man-made cruelties and bestial activities emerging from the communal passion leaves one stunned. The Hindus and the Muslims were inflicting the worst kind of violence on each other with "sadistic fury".[24]

The train carrying Hindu refugees from Pakistan (Peshawar) to India is personified. She provides a very moving, mind-boggling and heart-rending account of the train killings, looting, abduction and rape. The train was carrying refugees since "overcome by a sense of grave insecurity in Pakistan, they were trying to escape to India" (p. 207). The refugees were so grieved that even the train "felt so weighed down under their cataclysmic grief that it slowed down" her speed (p. 207). People looked depressed and horror was reflected in their eyes. The evacuees who were escaping to India as refugees were not fortunate enough to continue their journey uninterrupted. The train was time and again made to stop by the rioters who harassed and butchered the passengers. At Taxila railway station a procession of Muslim rioters appeared carrying the corpses of the Hindus. "Every Muslim in the procession was carrying the corpse of a Hindu on his shoulder" (p. 208). The unfortunate Hindus were trying to escape when they were caught and killed mercilessly. The Muslims in the procession put ten or fifteen corpses in each carriage. These two hundred Hindus suffered for no fault of their own. They were sacrificed at the altar of communal insanity. Before the train left the station the rioters picked out two hundred Hindus, a few from each carriage. The guards guarding the refugees helped rioters to fulfil their mad designs. Ironically, the guards pushed a few Hindus out and "entrusted" them to the care of the mob. All the Hindus were made to stand up in line and were killed one by one. Thus the rioters thought or claimed that they were serving the cause of their religion.

Ironically, this heinous crime against mankind takes place

at a place which once "boasted of being the leading university of Asia, where thousands of students flocked from distant places to study civilisation and culture" (p. 209). Yes, this 'holy' land was Taxila where "its museum housed unique images and inimitable jewellery, representing the finest example of ancient art" (p. 209).

But now people of the land had gone so mad with communal passion and hatred that they piled up skulls and corpses to 'decorate' the museum. This was the land of the Buddha, the great champion of humanity who had preached the gospel of non-violence. It seemed as if human beings had stepped into the realm of old, bestial, cruel and wild life.[25] The station had turned "red with the blood of the victims and the scène was so traumatic that even the train was shaken, "...when I pulled out of the station my wheels seemed to be slipping from the rails" (p. 209). The women were the worst sufferers amid bloodshed and killings. At the Rawalpindi station the Muslims appeared with fifteen non-Muslin women and they boarded the train. These women were crying pitifully. Later they were dragged to jungle where the Muslims had their "way" with those women. To the train "it appeared the whole earth was covered with the dark forebodings of Doomsday" (p. 210).

At the Wazirabad station massacre took place again. But the train was looted first and then four hundred passengers were pulled out from the train and they were massacred. It was done out of revenge since the Muslim rioters had seen that four hundred Muslim refugees were missing from the train from Amritsar. Not only this, a procession of naked women was seen at this station. These naked women ranged from "old grannies to young virgins" (p. 211). They were made to sit naked among the refugees in the train. The women had to face humiliation and torture at the hands of the rioters. A little child asked, "Ma, why are you sitting naked?" He wondered if she was returning from her bath. "The old woman forced her tears. Today, the sons of her land had given her a sinister bath" (p. 211). The story depicts how men had degraded to the level of beasts.

Similar acts of communal violence were carried out on the other side of the border. The Hindu and the Sikh rioters were doing the same things—killing, looting, raping and abducting the Muslim refugees. No doubt, the cataclysm had shaken the human conscience. People had become rolling coffins.[26] On this side of the border too, people were mad with similar kind of communal frenzy. They had become so callous and ruthless that even children were not spared from the wrath of rioters, "A jat impaled the body of an infant on his spear and jubilantly flung it in the air" (p. 213).

The happy and prosperous land of Punjab was tarnished and mutilated beyond recognition:

> In those very fields, where barns were brimming with the golden wheat, where the mustard flowers smiled, where young women, fed on the love legends of Heer-Ranjha and Sohni-Mahiwal, bent like tender stalks under the loving gaze of their husbands, the marauders hastily improvised temporary brothels under the peepal and rosewood trees. Here fifty women were made to serve five hundred ravishers. Fifty sheep and five hundred butchers (p. 213).

Both the communities were similarly responsible for bloodshed and arson. Both were responsible for the humiliation of the women. Both had fallen.[27]

III

CHILDREN: THE MUTE SUFFERERS

The feeling of hatred, violence and animosity stupefied the sensibility of the Hindus, the Sikhs and the Muslims so much so that even children were not spared from the wrath of communal forces. Children who did not know what religion was or what two-nation theory meant were killed mercilessly. Many of them fell victim to another kind of violence, in that they became orphans. What is more painful and shocking is that no history of the Partition has anything to say about the sufferings of children. Even after the partition was over the two countries did not fight over children as they did over women.[28] There were numberless children who were left behind and sometimes even abandoned willingly. We have no record of these children. Some parents abandoned their children since under the shadow of death their first thought was to save themselves.[29] Urvashi Butalia has done much in this field by talking to the sufferers personally. She has recorded that history through memory. She has talked to a person called Kulwant who describes, "...the six month old daughter, first of all they did Ardas and threw her into the fire, and they said, 'bibis our *izzat* is in danger, will we save our honour or our children'. And then turn-by-turn they threw their children into fire..."[30] These people preferred their so-called 'honour' to the lives of children. God knows which religion had taught them to sacrifice the lives of innocent children to save their own honour. Like women children too fell victim to intra as well as inter-community violence. Equally painful was the fate of those children who were born to abducted women. During the rehabilitation work while some families were ready to take their women back they refused to accept their children, as they were of mixed breed. They were considered polluted as they belonged to the Muslim fathers or vice versa.

Bhisham Sahni's rather long story "Pali"[31] captures the agony of a small child who fell victim to the Partition violence. His fate shifts like a pendulum. He not only faces an identity crisis but also the ruthlessness of fundamental forces.

Pali was just four years old when he got separated from his parents. His parents—Manohar and Kaushalya—were leaving Pakistan for India as refugees along with their children. Pali got lost in the large crowd when they were boarding the lorry. Manohar and Kaushalya kept crying but no body tried to stop the lorry and help them find the child. People had become so callous that everyone was for himself. "The heart of the refugees had dried up of all sentiments" (p. 121). No one had pity for the lost child. One of the refugee cried, "Get down, you! If you want to search for your child, get down and let us proceed" (pp. 121-22). The parents had to leave without Pali. The mother had to leave without her child. The trauma of losing a child was so great to the mother that she almost went mad. She kept crying all the time, shedding tears for her child. Kaushalya's "plight was like that of a bird whose nest was being destroyed before its very eyes" (p. 121).

Meanwhile, Pali was picked up by a Muslim called Shakur. He brought him to his house. Shakur and his wife, Zenab adopted the child. They were a childless couple. Pali kept crying the whole night. But gradually the love and warmth showered by Zenab consoled him and he accepted his new parents. However a few days after Pali was brought home by Shakur a Maulvi came to Shakur's house and threatened him for sheltering a "Kafir's child" (p. 126). He insisted that the child must be circumcised as required by the Muslim religion. The Maulvi called the child "snake" and that the child was "polluted" (p. 127) since he belonged to a Hindu. The next day the circumcision was performed. "Little Pali was terrified at the sight of the razor and clung to Zenab's legs" (p. 127). From now on Pali was brought up in a Muslim way. And from Pali he became Altaf. The name 'Pali' was buried under the so-called religious rituals, which were rather meaningless even for Shakur and Zenab but were forced on them by the community. Life was still not going to be happy and peaceful for Pali alias Altaf. Suffering still lurked in his life. The wheel of fortune took another turn. After drifting for a long time from one place to another Pali's father comes to know of the whereabouts of Pali. And he comes with police officials to claim Pali from Shakur and Zenab. He is happy to find his child being affectionately brought up by his foster parents but he insists on taking Pali back as his own wife, who had lost Pali and her little daughter was killed by the rioters, had gone virtually insane and was dying. Now when the child had adopted the Muslim ways and had settled happily with his new parents once more his identity was at stake. He was supposed to learn the Hindu ways. The situation brought an upheaval in his life. Once more he would bear the severe blows released by the so-called religious bosses. The drama, which had been enacted in Pakistan, was now to be enacted in India by the Hindu fundamentalists. When the child read *namaz* in India, people watched him with "feeling of disgust (p.140). One Hindu man cried, "He must at once get rid of this nasty habit. We don't want to have a Muslim among us" (p. 140). He further says, "Those Mussallas have planted the poison of fundamentalism in his mind. And at such a tender age!" (p. 141). How ironical! Were they not going to do the same thing? The people of both the religions had played with the emotions of the child. They had thrust upon him the useless rituals. The child had become a puppet in the hands of religious bigots. When in India, the Hindus forced their own religious rituals upon him. He was made to sit on the mat like a sacrificial lamb and his head was shaved. "As long as the ceremony lasted, the boy sat with his head bowed and sobbed" (pp. 141-42). The child could not forget his parents in Pakistan. When his head was shaved, he got up in fright and cried, "Ammi, Ammi, Abbaji !" (p. 142). Poor child did not know who he was and what his identity was.

Religious distortions create unlimited agony for the little child. The maulvi slapped him at a tender age for being the son of a Hindu while in Pakistan. In India, too, in Manohar Lal's house one of the religious men gathered there almost slaps Pali. He "glared" at the boy. When Pali told them his Muslim name the man said, "Repeat that name again and see what happens. I'll pull out your tongue!" (p.141). Thus Pali was terrified. He suffered at the hands of the people of both the religions. Both had enforced their respective rituals on the innocent child to purify him. If this was the way to keep one's God happy the way or style was, no doubt, disgusting as well as awesome. This brings forth the hypocrisy and callousness of the people of both the religions.

There is irony of situation, as Pali became victim of

circumstances. There is no direct villain in the story who kidnapped him. It was all due to circumstances that he got lost and fell in the hands of a childless Muslim couple. Though the Muslim parents showered affection on him the so-called custodians of 'religion' are rough with him and repeatedly create a crises of identity for him. In addition to the emotional pain and confusion the poor child has to suffer in repeatedly getting separated from his parents and adopting new parents.

The suffering of the two mothers is equally touching. Pali's mother is on the verge of dying due to the separation from her child. Zenab is jolted out of motherhood when she has to give up Pali at the request of Manohar Lal for the sake of suffering Kaushalya.

The agony of the two mothers, the real one and the foster mother, is also central to Gurumukh Singh Musafir's story "The Abandoned child."[32] It revolves around an infant girl Mubina who gets separated from her parents during the riots. During the Partition when communal riots broke out, Zeenat and Qasim left their house for fear of attack on them. They abandoned their daughter under a tree because they feared that if the child cried the rioters would find them out and they would be killed. It was the instinct for survival that made them leave behind their daughter. Although Zeenat was not ready for this, yet Qasim forced her to abandon the child. Here the attitude of men versus woman is portrayed so clearly. Even during difficult times women can never be callous like man. That is why when Qasim told her about his plan to leave the child, she just said, "I don't think we should do that" (p. 183). Even when she leaves she is worried about Mubina that she must be hungry since she has not drunk anything.

Like Pali, Mubina, is fortunate to fall in the hands of a childless Muslim couple who adopt her and fondly look after her. They shower their love and affection upon the child. But very soon the real parents come to claim the child. The foster mother is not ready to hand over the child. She has developed a bond with the child and does not want to lose her. Now the two mothers are victims of the same feelings. Both are at a loss. It is difficult to part from the ones you love too much. The foster parents decide not to hand over the child to its parents and hence they lie that the child has died. The real mother faints at this and does not come to her senses for long. Her trauma is indescribable. She is the worst sufferer. But woman can never be so cruel as man can be. A change is noted in the foster mother. She realises the pain of losing one's child. She places the child in Zeenat's lap that gives a new life to her. The woman appears like an angel in her eyes. She feels that the woman who has saved her child has much greater claim on the child than the one who has given birth to it. Finally, a solution is sought and they all start living together. Krishna Sobti's "Where is My Mother?"[33] records the trauma of a little girl who has lost her mother in the riots. She has lost not only her mother but also her father and brother in riots. She has witnessed the carnage and arson caused by communal frenzy. She has seen how "children were thrown into fires" (p. 135). Yunus Khan, a Muslim soldier picks her up from the roadside when she was wounded and unconscious. "Her salwar was soaked with blood" (p. 136). It seemed that the little girl was raped. It was really terrific that communal frenzy had turned man into a beast and had filled his heart with cruelty and such callousness that he did not show any pity for the innocent children. Even little girls fell victim to man's onslaught upon their tender bodies through rape and molestation. The girl could not forget that "her brother's head had been chopped off with a scythe!" (p. 139). This reminds us of Roshan of "Post Box" who, too, had witnessed his mother being butchered. Thus both the children—one a Hindu and another a Muslim—were equally victim of communal violence that had left permanent scars on their mind. They had seen the death and merciless killings of their dear ones. Those ghastly and heart rending incidents had terrified them. The girl, though picked up by the Muslim soldier, had no faith in him because he was a Muslim. Communal riots had created a wedge between the two communities and people were unable to decide whom to believe and whom not. Even small children's minds were contaminated as they too witnessed the worst cruelties against one another. This made them believe blindly that the 'other' was their enemy. That is why the girl showed indifference towards the soldier's offer to help her. She was not ready to go with him as she had witnessed the cruelties inflicted by the Muslims upon her dear ones. She kept repeating, "Where is my mother ... where is my mother?" The girl remained terrified. Her trauma cannot be explained.

N.G. Gore's "A Mouthful of Water, A Mouthful of Blood"[34] is a vivid description of beastly attitude of man, particularly of killing a Muslim child without even an iota of pity. The story depicts how a saviour turns into a killer. Communal frenzy had suspended all the rationality out of a human being making him beastly.

During peacetime Udham Singh was a soldier in the Indian army who met a Muslim child, Anwar, during one of his journeys, in the train. Very soon both of them developed a sort of relation—a bond of love. The child called this Sikh man "chachaji" and played with his long beard calling him a "lion." The Sikh called him "rabbit" out of love. Anwar felt thirsty and his mother had no water with her. Udham Singh offered to bring water for the child from the station. He said to Anwar's mother "Behnji, give me the lota, I'll fill it and bring it back in a moment" (p. 220). He almost missed the train for the sake of the child. He was happy that he could quench the child's thirst. The next few hours were spent with the child. It was a composite picture of good humanity. But during the riots the same man became a killer. Within the short span of two years after this incident the Partition of the nation took place, leading to widespread communal riots. The bonds of love between the communities snapped leaving the common man aghast. Friends became strangers overnight. Udham Singh, too, migrated to Delhi where he started running a shop. The child, Anwar, whom Udham Singh had met in the train was also now in Delhi. When the narrator told about the child, Udham Singh showed no interest or love for the child. He was not the same man who had once played with the child, had brought him water. Communal frenzy had changed the attitude of people replacing love with hatred and animosity. Udham Singh merely replied with bitterness in his tone, "Yes, doubtless, a golden lad, but a snake all the same" (p. 224). All the emotions, it seems, had dried up. Even today people fail to understand that communal politics is essentially the manipulation of social consciousness based on religion for political pourposes.[35] The communal politics had polluted the mind of common man to the extent that within a few years a 'rabbit' became 'snake', and love turned into hatred. What 'they' did in Pakistan was to be repeated in India. Delhi, too, "started to moan and groan! Into the eyes of Hindus and Sikhs had began to descend murder, and into the eyes of Muslims, the dark shadow of fear!" In a few days from the sea of people in Delhi rose just one roar—"revenge! Vengeance! Justice!" (p. 225).

Communal carnage and hatred filled such poison into the minds of people that "even known persons began to look strange. Because from their known faces, familiar expressions had been erased" (p. 226). How could Udham Singh be an exception? He, too, declared, "Tomorrow will come to Delhi, Judgement Day. All snakes will be crushed!" (p. 226). And the Day of Judgment did mark its presence felt. He had caught hold of little Anwar. The little bird was crying helplessly in the "clutches of a falcon!" (p. 228). Before the narrator could stop Udham Singh from killing the little child, "the edge of Udham Singh's Kirpan has met the tender heart!" (p. 228). Ironically, it was the same child whom Udham Singh had once said jokingly, "No one would shoot a Chirruping Bulbul like you...?" (p. 220). And it was the same man who had quenched the thirst of the child. The same man killed the 'bulbul', the innocent child without an iota of pity or any sense of guilt.

The writer has deftly depicted the change in man, "the

human layer on our bodies was dropping off. Instead on them were sprouting wolfish eyes, tiger's claws, tusks of wild boars, and he goat's satyr penis!...trampling all these loved, sacred, sweet things under the heel, drowning their desperate cries in our monstrous laughter, shamelessly displaying our hands lathered in our kin's blood,—we, who had become human beasts— having stripped naked...man had brought upon man the occasion to see, in broad daylight, the desecrating hand violating his mothers' breasts, his wives' thighs, his claws at his innocent children's throats !" (p. 225).

Anwar was not only the one who had been butchered. There were many Anwars who were slaughtered during the Partition amidst communal frenzy. The atrocity, thus committed against the children, surpassed medieval barbarity. Lal Bahadur has rightly quoted the words of an eyewitness in his book:

> Even small boys and girls were killed by mobs. In one place a three-year old child is stated to have been killed and nailed to the door. Fiendish mobs raiding residences are said to have thrown down children from second and third floor balconies in some places.[36]

The most tragic of all these stories is probably S.H. Vatsayan's "Post Box".[37] It is the story of Roshan, a five-year-old boy, who becomes an orphan due to the riots. His father had gone to bring his sister and he never returned while Roshan's mother was mercilessly killed before his eyes. The attackers first tried to abduct her and when she resisted a man "finally managed to push her away from him, had thrown her down on the ground, and then smashed her face in with the blunt end of his axe" (p. 107). When Roshan opened his eyes he had seen that "her eyes, nose, jaws had been reduced to a bloody pulp" (p. 107). Such dreadful happenings made a permanent scar on his psyche that even an adult would be shattered at such harrowing happenings and here Roshan had to bear it all at the tender age of five.

The child had to walk several miles on foot to reach the

refugee camp. There were "dry wounds on his legs and his feet were swollen. He was bare headed... and his eyes, which still had the innocence of childhood seemed to be full of sufferings" (p. 106). The child lives in the camp where "all the others were strangers to him" (p. 108). He still has no one to speak to. He has lost all his dear ones. But he still has a hope that one day his father would come to him. And so he writes a letter for his father and stands near the post box, and it is here that the narrator of the story finds him. He wants the narrator to help him post the letter. But the letter cannot be posted because there is no address on it. The child, of course, does not know where his father is. When the narrator tells him that the letter cannot be posted till he writes his father's address his eyes are filled with tears. He is disappointed but he still hopes that someone will one day "tell him how to send his letter to his father" (p. 109). The hopeless hope that the innocent child is cherishing of meeting at least his father some day makes his tragedy all the more painful and moving.

NOTES

1. Anders Bjorn Hansen, *Partition and Genocide: Manifestation of Violence in Punjab, 1937-47* (New Delhi: India Research Press, 2002), p.13.
2. Ibid.
3. Urvashi Butalia, *The Other Side of Silence: Voices from the Partition of India* (New Delhi: Viking Penguin India, 1998).
4. Mohan Rakesh, " The Owner of Rubble", trans. Alok Bhalla, in *Stories About the Partition of India*, Vol. I, ed. Alok Bhalla (New Delhi: Harper Collins, 1994), p.67. All subsequent references to the story are to this edition and have been incorporated in the text.
5. K.N. Panikar, "Introduction" in *Communalism in India* (ed.) K.N. Panikar (New Delhi: Manohar Publications, 1991), pp.7-8.
6. Ved Rahi, "Death", trans. Alok Bhalla, in *Stories About the Partition of India*. Vol. III, ed. Alok Bhalla (New Delhi: Harper Collins, 1994), p. 229. All subsequent references to

the story are to this edition and have been incorporated in the text.

7. Larry Collins and Dominique Lapierre, *Freedom at Midnight* (1976, rpt; New Delhi: Vikas Publishing House, 1977), p. 284.
8. S.H. Vatsayan, "The Refuge", trans. Alok Bhalla and Rachna Sharma in *Stories About the Partition of India*, Vol. II, ed. Alok Bhalla, (New Delhi: Harper Collins, 1994), p.73. All subsequent references to the story are to this edition and have been incorporated in the text.
9. Chaman Nahal, *Azadi* (1979; rpt. Delhi: Orient Paperbacks, 1988), p. 124.
10. Khushwant Singh, *Train to Pakistan* (New York: Grove Press, 1956), p. 128.
11. Swarna Aiyar, "August Anarchy: The Partition Massacres in Punjab, 1947" in *Freedom, Trauma, Continuities: Northern India and Independence*, ed. D. A. Low and Howard Brasted (New Delhi: Sage Publications, 1998), pp.15-38.
12. Swarna Aiyar, ibid, p.16.
13. Hansen, *Partition and Genocide: Manifestation of Violence in Punjab, 1937-47*, p. 18.
14. Ian Talbot, "Literature and the Human Drama of the 1947 Partition" in Low and Brasted (ed.), op. cit., p. 40.
15. Hansen, *Partition and Genocide: Manifestation* of *Violence in Punjab, 1937-47*, p. 117.
16. Collins and Lapierre, *Freedom at Midnight*, p. 285.
17. Alok Bhalla, "Introduction", in *Stories About the Partition of India,* Vol. I, ed. Alok Bahalla (New Delhi: Harper Collins, 1994), p.xix.
18. Yash Pal, "A Holy War", trans. Alok Bhalla in *Stories about the Partition of India,* Vol. I, ed. Alok Bhalla (New Delhi: Harper Collins, 1994) p.193. All subsequent references to the story are to this edition and have been incorporated in the text.
19. "Gandhi on the Partition of India". Excerpted from *The Way To Communal Harmony* by M.K. Gandhi, ed. U.R. Rao. *The Tribune* (Sunday Reading) June 22, 1997, p. 1.
20. Collins and Lapierre, *Freedom at Midnight*, p. 288.
21. Gulam Abbas, "Avtar: A Hindu Myth", trans. Alok Bhalla and Vishwamitter Adil in *Stories About the Partition of India*, Vol. III, ed. Alok Bhalla (New Delhi: Harper Collins,

(1994), p. 191. All subsequent references to the story are to this edition and have been incorporated in the text.

22. Intizar Husain, "The City of Sorrow", trans. Alok Bhalla and Vishwamitter Adil, in *Stories About the Partitions of India* Vol. II, ed Alok Bhalla (New Delhi: Harper Collins, 1994), p.185. All subsequent references to the story are from this edition and have been incorporated in the text.
23. Krishna Chander, "The Peshawar Express", trans. Jai Rattan, in *Stories About the Partition of India*, Vol. II, ed. Alok Bhalla, (New Delhi: Harper Collins, 1994), p. 207. All subsequent references to the story are from this edition and have been incorporated in the text.
24. Collins and Lapierre, *Freedom at Midnight*, p. 292.
25. Narhar Vishnu Gadgil, *Satta ka Sach* (Hindi) (New Delhi: Parveen Parkashan, 2000), p. 54. My translation.
26. Collins and Lapierre, *Freedom at Midnight*, p. 298.
27. *Living Thoughts of Mahatma Gandhi,* ed. Mulk Raj Anand (New Delhi: NCERT, 1998), p. 41.
28. Butalia, *The Other Side of Silence: Voices from the Partition of India*, p. 187.
29. Ibid., pp. 188-89.
30. Ibid., p. 191.
31. Bhisham Sahni, "Pali", trans. Jai Rattan in *Stories About the Partition of India*, Vol. III, ed. Alok Bhalla (New Delhi: Harper Collins, 1994), p. 119. All subsequent references to the story are from this edition and have been incorporated in the text.
32. Gurmukh Singh, "Abandoned Child", trans. B.M. Sagar and Alok Bhalla in *Stories About the Partition of India*, Vol. III, ed. Alok Bhalla (New Delhi: Harper Collins, 1994), p. 181. All subsequent references are to this edition and have been incorporated in the text.
33. Krishna Sobti, " Where is My Mother?" trans. Alok Bhalla, in *Stories About the Partition of India*, Vol. II, ed., Alok Bhalla (New Delhi: Harper Collins, 1994), p. 135. All subsequent references are to this edition and have been incorporated in the text.
34. N.G. Gore, "A Mouthful of Water, A Mouthful of Blood", trans. Sudhakar Marathe, in *Stories About the Partition of India*, Vol. III,ed. Alok Bhalla, (New Delhi: Harper Collins, 1994), p. 217. All subsequent references are to this edition

and have been incorporated in the text.

35. Panikar, *Communalism in India*, p. 8.
36. Lal Bahadur, *Struggle for Pakistan: Tragedy of the Triumph of Muslim Communalism in India (1906–47)* (New Delhi: Sterling Publishers, 1988), p. 258.
37. S.H. Vatsayan, " Post Box" trans. Alok Bhalla, in *Stories About the Partition of India,* Vol. III, ed. Alok Bhalla (New Delhi: Harper Collins, 1994), p. 105.

3
Individual, Community and Crises of Identity: The Plight of the Refugees

The freedom of the country ironically meant, for large sections of masses, the loss of freedom to live peacefully, safely and happily in their homes. The birth of a new country Pakistan and the redefining of the boundaries of 'free' India meant uprootedness, loss of life and property, rape, abductions, rendering thousands of people penniless, homeless and lonely, becoming orphans, as discussed in the previous chapter. This chapter focuses on one sensitive aspect, in many ways most agonising for the survivors of the Partition violence and that is of people becoming refugees overnight due to one political decision.

The Partition led to one of the largest ever processes of forced migration.[1] It was estimated that by March 1948, six-million Muslims and four and half million Hindus and Sikhs had become refugees bringing about a virtually complete and forcible exchange of population[2] making the movement what O.H.K. Spate asserts, "absolutely unparalleled in the history of the world."[3] Horace Alexander has rightly asserted, "There must be many examples in the bloody history of mankind where the extent of violence has been as great or even greater but it is probably true that there has never been such a huge exchange of population."[4] The exodus of the two communities was not at all peaceful. Once the Boundary Award was declared, the country witnessed the worst kind of communal frenzy. Since the country was partitioned along religious lines which meant India for the non-Muslims and Pakistan for the Muslims, the mass violence that followed seemed inevitable.[5] Some fled for the fear of becoming a minority on either side of the border while others were forced to flee by those who were greedy to grab their land and property, as they believed it now rightfully belonged to them.

What was more tragic and gruesome was that even mass migration did not take place peacefully. Those who were fleeing towards safety and security were attacked by small and well-organised bands of hooligans consisting of the people of other community. Overcome by communal hatred people became so callous that they spared no one whether one was a child, a woman or an old man. Even patients were not spared. It is said that the Muslim patients were thrown out of the T.B. Sanitarium at Kasauli by the Hindu doctors.[6] On the other side, in Pakistan, a few *sadhus* of an ashram were driven out of the place where they had devoted their lives to prayer, meditation and yoga. It was their own land. They had never even dreamed that they would be thrown out of it one day. Their abode was set ablaze afterwards by a mob.

A large number of refugees started their journey on foot. They were crawling like columns of ants across the border. These caravans of refugees were so large that one of them consisted of 800,000 people.[7] This was really mind-numbing in dimension. Their journey was not smooth or easy. The refugees had to undergo innumerable sufferings *en route*. They had awful and traumatic experiences. They kept on crawling towards their unknown destiny with their eyes and throats raw with dust. Their feet were wounded and bruised by stones or the searing asphalt, and the scorching sun overhead added to their misery. The unfortunate evacuees kept on creeping amidst hunger, thirst and bearing the stench of urine, sweat and defecation. Most of the refugees were barefoot and their clothes were falling into pieces. These refugees had nothing to eat except one or two *chapatis* and a few sips of water. But they had to complete their journey, not one or two miles but hundreds of miles. The same was the story of the cattle of these refugees who kept pulling their starved bodies. It was, in fact, a grotesque exodus in which human being and cattle were facing the same pain and trauma. Larry Collins and Dominique Lapierre write about the plight of refugees:

> It was not just a brief trip to another village those Indians and Pakistanis were making. Theirs was the trek of the uprooted, a journey with no return across hundreds of miles, each mile menaced with exhaustion, starvation, cholera, attacks against which there was often no defense. Hindu, Moslem and Sikh, those refugees were the innocent and unarmed, illiterate peasants whose only life had been the fields they worked, most of whom did not know what a Viceroy was, who were indifferent to the Congress Party and the Moselm League, who had never bothered with issues like Partition or boundary lines or even the freedom in whose name they had been plunged into despair.[8]

At each step the miseries were increasing. People had become so degraded morally that they were bargaining with the unhappy evacuees over the few possessions they were going with. The price dropped with each passing mile until the desperate refugees were ready to give away their possessions for even a cup of water. It happened so that at the end they were left with nothing at all. Besides, the refugees from both the sides were attacked by the gangs of their 'rival' community. On both the Indian and Pakistani sides horrible atrocities were committed against those who travelled on foot. The convoy refugees were attacked mercilessly till the roads were "clogged with corpses."[9] Women had been the worst sufferers as they were ambushed and then raped and abducted. At night, when the women were asleep, they were picked up by the hooligans and raped.

Millions of refugees headed towards their new countries by train. Those trains were the best hopes for the uprooted people to avoid the nightmares they were surrounded with. But these unfortunate ones failed to perceive that for the majority of them those trains would become mobile graves. For many of the refugees that voyage to safety never even began. The refugees who migrated by train had to encounter a terrifying ordeal as the refugee trains were also attacked time and again and the passengers were butchered without a grain of pity, and the women were abducted. Khushwant Singh has rightly said about the refugees who were travelling by trains, "...trains were attacked and sent across the borders with bogies jammed with slaughtered passengers. No quarter was given to the sick or the aged or even to infants. Young women were occasionally spared only to be ravished."[10] The railway stations were easy targets as most of the victims were killed on the stations since the refugees had gathered on the railway stations that stink of human excreta and urine. The swarms of flies and mosquitoes spread the infection from the dirt and filth all around. The condition was disgusting. These stations became veritable death traps.[11] The Sikhs attacked the refugee trains on their way to Pakistan methodically. They were looted and those who refused to leave were butchered. Similarly, Frontier Mail and Karachi Mail were attacked in Lahore city, in which non-Muslims were slain. The police and army also harassed refugees. The worst instance of such conduct was that of a police officer at Kamoke, district Gujranwala, where non-Muslim girls were distributed among police officers, their friends and relatives after the massacre of the passengers of a refugee train there.[12] The refugees were not provided with food, of water and medical help in the trains, and many refugees died of starvation and shortage or water.[13] Krishna Chander's "The Peshawar Express"[14] discussed in the previous chapter captures some of the agony of the people trying to escape to safety in trains, as "overcome by a sense of grave insecurity in Pakistan, they were trying to escape to India" (p. 207). They had loved the land and had lived there for centuries. But now they were "anxious to get away from the land where their families had lived for countless generations" (p. 207). The same land "had forsaken them, refusing to shower its bounty on them" (p. 207).

Those who were fortunate enough to survive the onslaughts of their enemies were housed in refugee camps. Even here their condition was terrible. Their misery and wretchedness became no less in the camps either. The refugees were forced to live under miserable condition. There was no provision for fresh water and food. Some inmates were noted defecating and vomiting in same pool of water in which women were washing their cooking pots.[15] Cholera broke out at some of the places that caused death of many refugees. Due to scarcity of basic necessities even in the camps one often found hostility, suspicion, insecurity and violence. There seemed to be no end to the sufferings of those uprooted from their land. They were forced to live in cramped government-run relief camps. They were provided with insufficient rations. They were treated as no better than beggars,[16] as is clear from the stories, "God's Dog" and "The Parrot in the Cage".

As mentioned earlier the historians on the Partition have largely ignored the human aspect of this political event. The historians have largely covered the tragedy in terms of figures and numbers and not at the level of human detail. Nevertheless the numbers indicated by them, or studies conducted by them do give an idea of the scale of suffering while real glimpses of agony and trauma suffered by the refugees on both sides of the border came through literature. This chapter particularly focuses on their irretrievable losses. The chapter discusses in detail the agony of the refugees and how the Partition created unresolved dilemma in their life. The Partition also caused identity crises in the life of refugees. These refugees were uprooted from their homes because they belonged to a particular community. They were forced to flee from their native land leaving their homes and hearth behind. And when they took refuge in the land supposed to be their 'own' and joined the community which too, was supposed to be their 'own' they were not welcome there. They had to live amid the atmosphere of animosity and alienness among the people of their own community. The short stories taken for detail study dealing with these themes are: "The Claim", "Separated from the Flock", "Toba Tek Singh", "The Parrot in the Cage", "God's Dog", "Mother of Dhiren Muzumdar", "An Unwritten Epic", "Getting Even" and "A Grave Turned Inside Out".

I

BEGGARS IN THEIR "OWN" COUNTRY

With rise of communal animosity the individuals were completely identified with their religious communities—both from within, i.e., solidarity was felt among the members of one community, and from without, i.e. as seen by the others. And it was essentially due to their religious identity that individuals had to flee leaving behind their land and home if they were on the wrong side of the newly created border, that is, the non-Muslims had to flee from Pakistan and the Muslims had to flee from India. They were forced to run away from their respective homes on the plea that they should go to their 'own' country, where they rightly belonged. So they fled to their respective countries in the hope of finding a home and living in security amidst people of their own community.

However, as the communal violence subsided those who had survived it and had crossed the border safely did not find any welcome from their own communities. They were received with apathy and with suspicion as possible contenders. To their shock they found they were reduced to beggars in what was supposed to be their 'own' country. Some of the stories quite poignantly capture the deprivation and degradation of these uprooted people.

The greatest calamity that can ever befall a man is the snatching away of his home and hearth. Our psyche acclimatises itself most concordantly within the four walls of a home. We feel safe in our home as the four walls of our home guarantee security to us. We are like plants that grow deep in our own soil. We wilt and wither when uprooted. Our soul is seared and our mind shrivels when we wander desperately in search for shelter.

Mohan Rakesh's "God's Dog"[17] is a poignant account of a refugee who along with other members of his family suffers a lot after he is uprooted. The story depicts the mental pain of this old Sikh refugee. The religious bigots in "communal inferno" killed his brother.[18] He migrated to India with his brother's widow and his son and daughter. All of them are in a destitute state as they are virtually starving. The brother's son is suffering from tuberculosis and the daughter is of marriageable age. It gives pain to the old man to see all these persons in a miserable condition. After reaching India he applies for the land. It takes seven years before he is allotted a useless piece of land that he cannot cultivate to grow food for the family. The old man feels it is making a mockery of his misfortune. For two years he has suffered the indifference of the administration. He had given an application for the change of this land for a better piece of land so that he may earn his livelihood, but in vain. Due to this deprivation, and the apathy of the administration he is forced to drag himself along with his family to Deputy Collector's office where he starts his protest against the indifference and cold attitude of the authority. He is very sad that no one takes any notice of his problems and the agony he has been undergoing.

Uprooted from their homes, in their 'own' country they are nobody's responsibility, it seems. For seven years the old Sikh has suffered, no land for seven years and then a pit in the name of land, which is of no use to him. But no one seems bothered about him and millions other like him rendered homeless. Even basic human necessities of food and shelter are not available to them. Such is the degradation of these humans that they are reduced to mere numbers, not individuals. When anyone asks him about his identity he doesn't give his name but only his number 1226/6. And it seems to the administration that the refugees are not human beings but just numbers. Unable to take the apathy of the administration anymore he decides to shake the administration out of its stupor by a shocking act. He decides to appear before the collector naked so that he at least takes note of him and of his problem. And he cries out, "Ha, ha ... your police will beat all my royalty out of me! Call the police! I'll stand here naked before the police and say, come beat the royalty out of me!" (p.122). The story gives an idea of the desperation of the millions of refugees who had to run from pillar to post like him.

The story is also a bitter satire on the apathy, indifference or sluggishness of Indian administration. The story of personal agony is equally about society at large as it portrays how common man suffers at the hands of government servants. The apathy of the system becomes more painful because now it was supposed to be people's "own" government, not of any foreign rulers.

The protagonist of the story is the victim of the system and those officers who have turned their backs on the afflicted ones. The corrupt clerks and officers are blind with selfishness, cupidity and avarice. One Surjit Singh is helped in the story only when he bribes the clerk. The miserable condition and deprivation force the old man to be shameless. It is the instinct for survival that as the last desperate measure he decides to sit before the office and protest. He decides to appear naked before the Deputy Collector. Maybe the government appeared apathetic due to the large number of the refugees as it became difficult to help them. But part of the truth is that the refugees had to suffer because influential local people or influential displaced person had grabbed a large area of evacuee land, while common people suffered. As Satya M. Rai reports:

> A sizeable section of the revenue staff, zaildars and patwaris itself was engaged in grabbing land, and since the fate of

the refugees continued to be entrusted to those men, the incidence of bribery, corruption and nepotism was increasingly intensified.[19]

The attitude of the officers makes the old man rage with anger. He stretches his legs fully. He attracts the attention of others and cries out loudly:

> The government takes time! In five to ten years the government will decide whether my petition should be accepted or not-Bastards! Even Yamraj keeps count of our days. When the days allotted by him are over, I'll find out that government has accepted my petition (p. 121).

He feels so broken and full of agony that he spreads his turban on the ground and makes his family sit on it. He says in desperation:

> Look, today I have arrived here with my entire family. Now you can take as much time as you want. After starving me for seven years, the bastards allotted me a pit three acres wide, so that I could burry the bones of my ancestors in it! ... I am starving, but the application is still being considered" (p. 121)

It is only after he gives up all sense of shame and takes off his clothes that the administration wakes up from its stupor. The Collector takes up his case immediately–after two years—and he is allotted a piece of land, which may sustain his family.

All the uprooted were fated to suffer. There was no bar of age, class, caste or religion. Even the old and the poor were not spared from the onslaughts of violence, callousness and apathy. Mulk Raj Anand has vividly recorded the trauma of uprootedness of an old refugee woman in "The Parrot in the Cage",[20] who has only a parrot to keep company with. She used to earn her living by working as a domestic help. She is representative of millions of those who are uprooted and wander like a lost soul from pillar to post expecting some help from the government. But they are not fortunate enough to get even both ends meet. They were kicked out of their native places for the only reason that they belonged to a particular religious community that had no right to stay in Pakistan which was carved out for the Muslims. Rukmani escaped the rioters as a Muslim helped her. She says, "I only know if Fato had not given me a burqah to escape with, I should not be there ..." (p. 86). But surviving the bloodshed has only added to her misery. She has nothing to eat, nowhere to live. The community which had given her an identity, and which identity was responsible for her being driven out of her home, however has nothing to offer her here. She is left to fend for herself. All she can look up to is help from the government that is finding it hard to handle the large number of refugees and which is equally incompetent because of corruption and apathy.

Rukmani is a helpless victim of the Partition violence and her fate as a refugee is awesome. She hopes that the Deputy Collector will compensate her for the loss as she has come to know that the government will give what they have lost. Uprooted from her home and without work she is reduced to the state of a beggar. She waits for the Sahib in the scorching sun. Every passing moment is full of agony and sorrow for her. She has nothing to eat. She tells the roadside gram-seller, "I am waiting for the Sahib, so that he can give me some money to buy bread with..." (p. 87). She is hurt. Her mind drifts between hope and despair. She is full of agony, "Oh, why did I leave home to wander like this from door to door! ...Oh, why did you have to turn me out of my room in my old age, God...Oh, why... why didn't I tie rupees I had earned in a knot on my dupatta! ... Hai Rabba! ..." (p. 87). She keeps moaning while waiting for the help and her eyes are filled with tears. And when the Deputy Collector arrives, the refugees rush towards him and, like beggars, they cry, "Hujoor, Mai Bap, hear us! Sarkar! Deputy Sahab! ... We have come on foot all the way from Lahore…you…" (p. 87). The old woman, Rukmani, too, rushes grimly on. But they get nothing. They are left as destitute as they were. A furious whirlwind rises from the opposite direction and "a posse of policemen charged the refugees with lathis and angry shouts which drowned the chorus of voices of which Rukmani's sighs and her parrot's cries had been a part" (p. 88). Poor Rukmani is brushed aside by some desperate arm. She reels and falls down where she had been sitting and waiting for the Sahib. But she does not lose hold of cage in which her parrot is sitting. The parrot keeps repeating as before, "Ruknaniai! Ni Rukmaniai! Ni tun kithe hain! Ni tun ki karni hain!" [Rukmani, where are you? what are you doing?] Ironically, Rukmani cannot reply since she herself does not know where she is. The writer wants to suggest that she is rootless. She has no destination. There is darkness all around her. That is why she replies to the parrot, "Han han, son, han my son...I don't know where I am! I don't know …" (p. 89). She has nowhere to go. She is fated to bear the brunt of sufferings and the irretrievable losses, like the loss of her dignity. She used to earn her living as a domestic help and now she has to beg for food, which she doesn't even get.

Rukmani, like other refugees, is a victim of the callousness of the government officers and their apathy towards refugees. No doubt, the officers may be unable to compensate for the losses because of the problem of large numbers of refugees. But the officers also seem to be insensitive of their sufferings probably since they themselves are not uprooted. This apathy of the administration only adds to their agony. Amidst so much despair and anguish a healing touch comes from a stray individual. The gram-seller on the roadside who had been talking to Rukmani and watching her, picks up Rukmani who had fallen on the ground and helps her sit under a shade and gives some grams to the parrot. It is probably such small gestures of goodness that soothe suffering humanity in the worst of times.

II

IRRETRIEVABLE LOSSES

One of the themes that emerges repeatedly in the short stories is that the Partition brought with it not only physical and material loss but also unbearable emotional losses. Material losses could be compensated to some extent as one could claim the loss of the lost house, land or wealth but emotional loss was irretrievable as it tore apart the victims mentally. The antipathy, chagrin and animosity with which the victims had been treated during the Partition made deep scars on their psyche and it was not easy to erase those scars. Once the refugees were extirpated from their land their life was devastated entirely. A sort of trepidation was created in their minds through bestial cruelties they experienced and witnessed during the riots. They suffered emotionally remembering the good old days when all the communities lived happily. It was through memory and nostalgia that their mind drifted between past and present that still added more pain to their heart and lacerated their wounds. It was the emotional loss that created a vacuum in their life. Added to this were the degradation and humiliation they had to undergo in the refugee camps and also while asking for compensation or 'claim'.

The most touching account of the emotional shock to individuals appears in Saadat Hasan Manto's classical story, "Toba Tek Singh",[21] which is also a subtle satire on the madness of the whole idea of the Partition of India. The story moves around the character of Bishan Singh who is known as Toba Tek Singh as he has large land holdings there. He is a lunatic and is entrusted to the care of an asylum in Pakistan. Once the Partition is declared he, along with other non-Muslim lunatics, is forced to migrate to India as both the governments have decided to transfer the lunatics along with other people. Though Bishan Singh is mad he loves his land very dearly. The thought of leaving his land gives him immense pain. Before he is forced to migrate to India he wants to know whether Toba Tek Singh is in India or in Pakistan. When he comes to know that it is in Pakistan he becomes very sad. He is not ready to go to India.

Here, Bishan Singh is representative of millions of people on both sides of the borders who never wanted to leave their homeland but were forced to forsake their land due to whims of their political leaders. The masses have to pay for the fancy and malevolence of these 'leaders' who fail to feel the trauma of the people. Bishan Singh loves his land so much that he will die but not leave the country that belongs to him. When the evacuation process is going on he refuses to enter the other country. He is left standing and is not coerced to go. He remains in the place where he stands while transfer of other lunatics continues:

> Before the sun rose, a piercing cry arose from Bishan Singh who had been quiet and unmoving all this time. Several officers, and the guards ran towards him; they saw that the man who, for fifteen years, had stood on his legs day and night, now lay on the ground, prostrate. Beyond a wired fence on one side of him was Hindustan and beyond a wired fence on the other side was Pakistan. In the middle, on a stretch of land, which had no name, lay Toba Tek Singh (p. 7).

He dies there stretched on the no man's land.

Not only Bishan Singh but other lunatics like him are also sad at heart when they are told about the transfer. One of them, a Muslim, first climbs onto a tree and when the guards order him to come down he goes still higher up. He is then threatened by the guards but he says, "I want to live neither in Pakistan nor in Hindustan—I will live on this tree" (p. 2). When he comes down, he embraces his Hindu and Sikh friends, cries bitterly and is saddened by the thought of their impending departure to India (p. 2).

The story really gives a poignant account of the emotional

loss caused by the Partition. Even lunatics intensely feel the sense of loss. They have nothing to do with the materialistic pursuits since they are mad. They don't love money, power and pelf but they love human relations. They, too, have feelings and love for land and the bonds they have enjoyed with their fellow human beings. The lunatics of the asylum "cursed all the leaders both Muslim and Hindu, who were responsible for splitting Hindustan in two" (p. 3). So the real 'lunatics' were those leaders who divided the country for their vested interests and created a vacuum in the life of masses. The loss of these lunatics is, no doubt, irretrievable. While the material losses could be compensated to some extent by providing partial compensations by the government, however delayed, but the emotional losses suffered by the masses are irretrievable as they can neither be claimed nor can be paid back by way of compensation. No body can give back one's lost dreams, relations, love for soil and the friends one has left behind. Sadhu Singh is such a sufferer in Mohan Rakesh's "The Claim"[22] who lost much during the Partition holocaust. He lost everything—his land, house, trees and even his wife. He came to India like others as a refugee. Here he starts plying a tonga to earn his livelihood. The other refugees make claims in the rehabilitation office. He faces various problems and difficulties but is not broken in the face of sufferings. He does not claim anything. It does not mean that he has not lost anything or that he is earning a lot. He earns his livelihood with difficulty. He does not want to beg for any claim, as his claim can never be compensated. He is unable to fill up the form for the claim for what he has lost. Material losses are immaterial for him. Whatever he has lost has caused pain and anguish to his psyche. The government cannot compensate for the trauma he has undergone. The Partition has shattered his dreams.

Earlier, Sadhu Singh had a blissful life with his wife, Hiran. They had dreamt of a happy life echoing with the joyful sounds of their children. He had planted a mango tree that started giving fruits. Though he had been living in a rented house, "that nine rupee-a-month house had come to seem like his own" (p. 39). When Hiran would try to stop him from eating unripe mangoes, he would reply, "It's the fruit of my own tree, darling! My teeth wouldn't spoil eating it" (p. 39). But all the joys were overcast with the dark clouds of communal hatred and bloodshed. Things turned against him and he lost everything. "The mangoes had turned from green to yellow and from yellow to red when the riots began. Blood flowed in every street of Pattoki" (p. 39). His wife was abducted and he became homeless.

Now in India he is lost in the past memories. He dreams of the mango tree "eating whose green fruit he had been spoiling his teeth—the years of the future to be spent in the shade of the tree" (p. 40). Here he is missing "the house's own special smell which emanating from a bundle of clothes enveloped everything right up to the walls of the courtyard" (p. 40). The 'Claims Office' cannot return the "evenings, which were spent lying in the courtyard staring at the sky" (p. 40). Sadhu Singh had made so many plans. He had been living with his wife happily teasing her and laughing with her. How can he claim for those memories, that feeling, that thrill and that imagination? His pain is incurable. No claim can compensate for his losses, which are irretrievable. He will live with this agony forever.

Despite suffering in the new environment, Sadhu Singh has adjusted himself to the changed time and new life. He now has a friend in his house, Afsar, his horse. At one point he feels like "having the shopkeeper make him a glass of limejuice and then perhaps lying in the shade for a while" (p. 39). But he doesn't have sufficient money to buy juice. He just wets "his lips with his tongue" and turns the horse's face in the direction of the city. And yet hope still persists in his life. He says to his horse, " If God keeps you well, Afsar, the old days will return again. Eat! Fill your belly! Your claims must be filled" (p. 41). But one can see that the vacuum in his life can never be filled.

Similar feelings are expressed in Narain Bharti's story of the same title, "The Claim."[23] The protagonist of the story, Joharmal, is so broken and sad to leave behind his land and relations that he does not make any claim for material losses. The things he has lost behind cannot be compensated. He is "stupefied" by the formalities required by the Claim Office since they ask tiresome questions. When the typist asks Joharmal, " How much property have you left behind in Pakistan? How many houses, how much other property?" Joharmal is surprised to hear such questions. He says, "I have left the whole Sindh in Pakistan. I am now putting in the claim for the whole of Sindh; it should be given back to me. The proof of the claim is that Joharmal is a Sindhi, his language is Sindhi and his culture is Sindhi," (p. 221). Joharmal is right. No body can perceive his loss, the pain of separation from one's land, soil and fellow human beings with whom one has spent his life. He would like to claim the emotions, which can never be redeemed. He is right as he is speaking in the context of the culture he shared with those left behind; the language he used to share with the natives of Sindh. How can one return to him his ethnic group? Undoubtedly he has lost much and he would like to fill up a claim for Sindh! : "Every part of my body is replete with memories of Sindh. I am a Sindhi and Sindh is mine. I have the right to put in a claim for it" (p. 221). Joharmal's eyes are full of tears for those Muslim friends he had left behind. He says, "I shall never meet my brothers Rajab, Ramzan and Mehboob, the barber. Can I get back their friendship?" (p. 222). Joharmal does not claim any house or land. He says, " My friends, their friendship was dearer to me then my fields" (p. 222). The story, thus records the emotional losses suffered by the refugees, not only seen in the light of an emotional response to loss of personal friends but also equally importantly of the collective identity.

Joharmal finally succeeds in making the typist realize that Joharmal is right and whatever he says is true. The typist, too, remembers his "friends in Sindh—Anwar, Hussain, Ahmad and

Ali, with whom he used to go to the Ramzan garden for a stroll" (p. 222). It is Joharmal's love for the lost friends and land that ignites the emotions of the typist as well and Sindh with its fields, friends and the entire community arises before his eyes. They have really lost much. Their losses are irretrievable. No Claim can be made for that.

Like Mohan Rakesh's "The Claim" this story, too, despite the agony of the uprooted people ends on an optimistic note that even in the face of sufferings hope does not completely perish. That is why the typist thinks, "Korea was also partitioned like this and even today the people are fighting for a united Korea" (p. 222). He is hopeful of the day when their claim will be fulfilled. He says, "When there is true democracy in India and Pakistan, this artificial wall will be demolished and you—all of us, shall certainly get our claim" (p. 222). They are all hopeful that the day will come when their agony will end and their emotional losses, though at present irretrievable, will be redeemed.

An extended portrayal of the agony of leaving home, particularly one's birthplace, is given in Syed Mohammad Ashraf's "Separated from the Flock."[24] The narrator tells his own story of sufferings. He suffers not because of material loss. He is a Superintendent of Police in Pakistan and is well off. Still there are wounds in his psyche that can never be healed nor can his loss be compensated. He was uprooted from India, as he was a Muslim. The Muslims got Pakistan as their country but the narrator is not happy. The uprootedness has resulted in agony for him. He longs for the lost home and friends in India. He holds the land dear where he learnt to speak the first words. The story very vividly brings out the trauma and poignancy after he is uprooted.

The narrator is on his way to a lake for duck hunting along with his driver, Gulam Ali. He shows a deep urge and longing for the lost home. He does not want that Gulam Ali should remind him of his past because it adds to his pains. And yet he almost wants to share with Gulam Ali, "I no longer have any relationship with that part of the earth where my childhood was spent listening to my mother's lullabies, where, as a boy, all the small things I beheld were dear to me—and where, in my youth, I first felt life's upsurge and learnt to test my wings" (p. 2). But he does not tell Gulam Ali even a single word since he feels Gulam Ali will not understand the pain of losing one's birth place. The Partition has brought with it desperation for the narrator, "The hard deep lines of Partition have erased the signs of all other feelings—feelings which belong intimately to that place where a human being first opens his eyes on earth and catches a glimpse of the sky" (pp. 2-3). He takes refuge in the world of memories.It is through the reeling memory that the sadness of the narrator is laid bare before us. Though all his relations have also migrated along with him, still he is sad, as he has left behind the world without which he feels incomplete. It is not only the family one wants. One longs for friends, environment and the memories. That is why nothing can "console" (p. 3) him. He has lost much that is not material and nothing can compensate for the loss of those good days he had left behind. He had also loved a girl in India. He failed to marry her. Both were separated. He had to sacrifice his love because of the partition of the country.

By a rare coincidence, during the hunting trip he comes across his old friend, Nawab. Nawab, too, is uprooted like the narrator. He is a good and wealthy businessman who also suffers in a similar way. His loss, like the narrator's, is not material. He too suffers from the agony of being uprooted. Both the friends embrace each other and tears flow as they remember the childhood spent together in India. On seeing Nawab, the memories rage within the narrator like "uncontrollable wild fire" (p. 11). Both the friends are victims of the same fortune. Both had been in love with young girls there. Both had to sacrifice their blissful love. Recounting their past love stories with an aching heart adds to the poignancy of their experience. They can never forget that land, those lanes, houses, fields, fairs, their friends, school and their childhood.

Both feel trapped by the circumstances and the changed reality. They cannot go back. The narrator says to himself:

> It occurred to me that neither of us had any control over our lives; that we are helplessly trapped by circumstances over which we had no influence; that we were utterly defenceless... if I were to resign my job and go to India, how would my family survive; and, Nawab, if you were to neglect your factory and leave Pakistan, who would compensate you for loss...? Yes, both of us are paralysed, are unable to make a move..." (p. 12).

This helplessness, the inability to go back adds to their agony and they feel broken. Their business and job have become a hindrance between their past and present. That is why it is only in memory that they can go back to their past, 'their childhood'. Both are suffering since both of them feel 'separated from the flock'.

It is through the use of metaphors that the tormented psyche of the narrator and others like him is exposed. The narrator and his friend are hunting ducks and when the ducks are shot at, their "wings are broken"; they beat the water frantically with their broken wings, "desperately trying to get away from the hunters" (p. 14). The 'wings' are here used metaphorically. The wings of the narrator and Nawab are also broken as they are tied to their jobs and business. They, too, try desperately to get away but in vain. The ducks are migratory who have left their land behind like these refugees. But they will soon go back, when the season changes. But some ducks never reach their land, as their wings are broken or they get lost in the way, they get "separated from the flock" (p. 14). The condition of the refugees is no better than the ducks with broken wings. They, too, get lost and are separated from the flock. Both the friends feel like these birds with broken wings. The longing for the lost home tears their heart apart. The memories of the past torture their whole being.

Even worse is the suffering of Gulam Ali's wife, Jameela

and Vaziruddin's wife who are similarly victims of this uprootedness. They, too, belonged to India. During the Partition they had to migrate to Pakistan. Now they want to go back to India to see their homeland. Though they have no relative there, they want to see the land where they had spent their childhood. The longing for that part of the country is so intense that they can do anything to see the lost homes. The husbands of these women consider their longing just a "whim" (p. 4). It is just a 'whim' to those who are not uprooted. They cannot imagine or understand the pain and trauma of uprootedness. They have no value of nostalgia, for the pull towards the past.

Vaziruddin's wife is able to save some money with great difficulty to meet her expenses to visit India and with a lot of effort she is able to obtain a permit also to visit India, to see her homeland, the place where she spent her childhood. But Vaziruddin cannot understand how intense is her longing to go to her village nor does he care for her feelings. At first he tries to argue her out of her strong desire to go to India but when she doesn't agree with him he thrashes her badly and throws her permit into the fire, thus shattering her chance of going back just to see once the place where she lived. He does not want that his wife should go to India because, then, there will be no one to cook his meals. By burning the pass into the fire he has clipped her 'wings' so that she may not 'fly'. Similarity, Gulam Ali, too, wants that his wife should not go to India, as it will cost him some money. He does not want to spend money for her fare etc. The narrator is sad to know all this. He starts hating Gulam Ali and says to himself:

> .... you and your friend will never understand what happens to a man who has been separated from the place where he was born, where he was suckled by his mother, and where he felt his father's affectionate hand ruffle his hair. You won't understand how strongly attached a man is to the place, where he has spent his childhood surrounded by

daily acts of kindness and joy; you can never feel, Gulam Ali, how precious those moments of innocence are, how one nurtures them with one's blood, how they are a part of everything that one has become (pp. 4-5).

And yet ironically even the narrator himself fails a longing, agonized heart by refusing to help his driver's wife Jameela. When Jameela comes to know that the narrator, her husband's boss, is a big police officer she begs before him to get her a permit so that she may go to India "to feel once again the spirit of the place where her mother used to sing her lullabies, to walk once again in the warmth of the village where she had flung her arms out in gladness to welcome her youth" (p. 6). But her wings are also clipped as her husband has already requested the narrator not to accede to her request. Her dreams are shattered. Her condition is like those ducks with 'dreams in their eyes' that get killed and their dreams remain unfulfilled. The image of the ducks dying with 'dreams in eyes' intensifies the anguish of the sufferers. Jameela's longing for the past is buried. She sheds her "last tears for her home and for her dreams" (p. 17). The narrator is very sad because he has not helped her. He just wants to tell her in pain:

"Goodbye, sister. You'll never again see that land where you grew into consciousness—hear its songs, swing from its trees on rainy days, play hide-and-seek in its chicken coops, dye your dupatta there in rainbow colours, collect flower with your childhood friends—never again will you see the place where you gathered tenderness in your hands and pressed it against your heart—Forget that place, sister....Why thrash your wings in vain, a hunter hidden in the shadow of the lake broke them a long time ago—There is nothing left now" (pp. 17-18).

It is true that those selfish political and religious leaders were like hunters who had broken the wings of millions of people. They have created a chasm between people and forced them to live in the land where they have no one their 'own'. Now they have lost everything and are forced to live in the "mirror house" (p. 14) of their memories. These uprooted people have made "terrible sacrifices" (p. 19).

The wounds in their psyche will never heal. They cannot go back to 'their' lost homes. There are so many hurdles in their way—material, jobs, and self-centred callous husbands—that block their way. They can only dream of those fields and friends. The narrator feels agonised to see that the pain has created millions of holes in their heart and soul. This agony comes out very poignantly in the following words, which the narrator wants to say to Nawab:

> We are birds with broken wings and we can never fly back to those fields of desire—we are more helpless and defenceless then those birds because once their wings are broken they are ritually slaughtered—but people like us—our torment never ends, we die slowly, we are tortured at every moment of our lives, we are hunted without mercy and we can only beat our wings in the throes of death, but we cannot die..." (p. 22).

Thus for many uprooted people, like Sadhu Singh, Joharmal, Nawab, Jameela or Vaziruddin's wife or the narrator of "Separated from the Flock," the emotional losses are more painful than the material losses. Although these wounds are not visible, yet they keep on gnawing at their heart all life, refusing to heal.

III

AMBIGUOUS COMMUNITIES: FRAGMENTED IDENTITIES

This part of the chapter deals with the study of ambiguities manifested within the communities—how people of the same community are treated as 'other' and that creates problematic identities of the uprooted. The uprooted struggle with the quest for belonging with no easy solution in sight. There are two stages that show ambiguities clearly. The first stage of identity crisis came when, after the Partition, people were forced to evacuate the land where they had been living for centuries. Suddenly the land as well as the people around became alien. Though the land and homes belonged to them, ironically, nothing was their own now. Those who exhibited affection and attachment to their houses and land and were not ready to leave were threatened first and later slaughtered mercilessly. Earlier, people of different religions lived in Punjab and Bengal but they enjoyed the same culture, celebrated the same festivals and used the same language. The Partition was such a social upheaval that it changed the definition of community and caused fragmentation not only in the lands of Punjab and Bengal but also in the life of its people. Despite belonging to different religions their cultural identities as Bengalis or Punjabis were very strong. The religious distinctions were not so rigid then and they were subsumed under the cultural and linguistic identity. But the situation suddenly changed when the demand for separate Muslim Nation was created. It was during 1930s and 1940s that the differences on religious grounds widened and a chasm between the people of both the religions started appearing. The identities based on Bengali or Punjabi culture and language rapidly came to be fractured along sectarian and religious lines.

Now people started looking upon themselves as Sikhs, Hindus, or Muslims first and Bengalis or Punjabis afterwards. Earlier religious identities used to be secondary but now they became primary. The communities were now redefined and the non-Muslims of East-Bengal and West-Punjab were subjected to the persecution and intolerance and the same was the condition of the Muslims living on the other side. Communalism defined communities very rigidly along religious lines only. And the result of the communal thinking was that each community started looking at each other with suspicion, hatred and vengeance, as discussed in the second chapter.

The second stage of identity crisis appeared when the uprooted people reached India and Pakistan respectively. Instead of welcoming their religious brethren the host communities in both countries treated these new arrivals into their communities essentially as outsiders. In India these uprooted people living in the camps were called "refugees" while those who arrived in Pakistan were called "muhajirs". Their own religious communities refused to accept them as part of their community. They had hoped that it was their legitimate and rightful claim to seek rehabilitation in the land where they were told they belonged. But it seems the definition of communities based on religion seemed no more valid once the fires of the Partition started cooling down. Now the 'other' was no longer the other religious community but people belonging to the same community.

The Hindus who had crossed over to India and the Muslims who had crossed over to Pakistan came in search of new homes in what they were told was going to be their "own" country. Hounded out of their houses as enemies by the other communities they found new shades of animosity or estrangement among the people of their own community as they landed in the refugee camps. Now these uprooted people were subjected to intra-community oppression, suspicion and there was quick loss of sympathy. Earlier when people of one community were tortured by those of the other, then community had shown sympathy and had even taken revenge. That sympathy and fellow feeling turned out to be temporary. The refugees were now seen as a threat to the economy and balance. The neighbouring states, too, were not ready to rehabilitate the refugees, particularly the government of Assam showed open reluctance to the proposal of sheltering Bengali refugees.[25] And when the refugees of West-Bengal tried to settle themselves on the island of Marichjhanpi which lay in Ganga-Brahamputra delta in the Sunderbans region in West-

Bangal, "they were tear-gassed, their huts were razed to ground, and their fisheries were destroyed in several encounters that took place between the police and the refugees. Inevitably, violent clashes followed leading to several deaths and a larger number of casualties."[26] The women were subjected to 'humiliating abuse' by the police. Hence we see that the refugees were not accepted even by their own community. They became people of 'nowhere'. Thus ambiguity in the response of the community to these uprooted individuals led to a terrible identity crisis in the refugees. Where did they belong, who should they turn to for help—to these questions they had no answer. They had become an unwanted community—of refugees or of muhajirs—in their own communities.

Shanti Muzumdar the protagonist of Lalithambika Antharjanam's. "The Mother of Dhiren Muzumdar"[27] is forced to be uprooted twice. It is a poignant story that deals with the identity crisis she has to face after the Partition, and once again after the creation of Bangladesh. Besides, the story also focuses on the sacrifices made by Shanti Muzumdar for her country and her present pathetic condition.

Shanti Muzumdar sacrificed her five children for the freedom of that country which turned its back towards her refusing to recognise her and she was forced to abandon her soil as a "refugee", an "outsider" (p. 199). What an irony! Her sacrifices were not given any importance. Muzumdar family had been a patriotic family. Shanti Muzumdar had taught the lessons of patriotism to her children—to be loyal to the land. She always helped her son, Dhiren Muzumdar in his crusade to liberate India. When she heard about the death of her son in a dynamite explosion during an attack on arsenal, she sang *Vande Mantram*. She was, then, crying, laughing and screaming like a mad woman singing praises of her motherland. India got freedom and the Partition took place. Shanti Muzumdar was very sad and her mind was full of agony at the thought of the Partition. She did not like that Bengal was divided into two parts. It was her deep love for the country that when Bengal was divided in the name of religion and caste she says, "She asked the great emperor Nehru":

> With whose consent did you cut off Bengal's head? With whose permission did you separate us? Here no one is a Hindu, no one is a Muslim. We are all Bengalis. We are one. If the head and the body are separated, then like rahu and ketu they will play a very destructive game. Both the sun and the moon will come under total eclipse. Mark my words! (p. 203).

She was right. The eclipse had taken place that overshadowed everyone. Even then Shanti Muzumdar compromised and decided to remain in East Pakistan. She blessed the people with the freedom of Bengal. Ironically, in East Pakistan her identity remained that of an outsider since she was a Hindu. She had worked hard for the freedom of Bengal, walked along with Gandhiji in Noakhali and opened a sevashram in Chittagong, organised a solidarity meet in Dhaka. Yet the authorities suspected her. Her son, Shubendu, who was a professor in Dhaka, was dismissed. Samrendu was not given the licence to practise as a doctor. And Jogendu died while engaged in relief work. Thus she sacrificed her sons. The people who used to say, "You are our grandmother! May Bengal be liberated with your blessings!" (p. 204) treated her as an outsider and suspected her honesty and integrity. She had to face the trauma of alienness in the land to which she belonged.

Time again took a new turn when East Pakistan became Bangladesh and Bengal got freedom from Pakistan. All the Hindus, though they were Bengalis, were made to flee from there. The Hindus were again uprooted. It was then that Shanti Mutassi was lifted up and carried by her grandchildren, the soldiers of the Mukti Fauj and finally brought to India. She became a victim of double uprootedness. In India she was again an outsider, "...supposedly a refugee! Supposedly a beggar woman! Supposedly an outsider!" (p. 204).

Now in India she remembers her past and her sacrifices that

make her uneasy and add to her agony. She is reminded of her lost identity. Whenever the past torments her she cries out in pain:

> Oh… I am thirsty, my children. My throat is parched … Give me a little water.. cold water… yes ? Recalled all this. After all, I am now just an outsider, who has come here as a refugee begging for your mercy. Dhiren Muzumdar faded from people's memories a long ago. So how can they be now expected to remember his mother? (p. 203).

The story expresses a sense of stunned disbelief at the fact that it could happen at all, that the inhabitants of the land could be so cruelly cut off from the familiar world of their childhood. Truly, the home of Shanti Muzumdar was in a country to which she has no relation now. Her house was there, the village was there, the property did exist but she is homeless. She is a double victim of identity crisis. She was uprooted twice. First, it was when East Pakistan was created, she was detached from India. Her Indian roots were cut off and she became a Pakistani. At that time her own land became alien to her. Secondly, it was in 1971 when East Pakistan became independent and was renamed Bangladesh. Again she was uprooted from Bangladesh, as it was not meant for the Hindus. Earlier East Pakistan came into existence for the people who spoke Bengali irrespective of any religion. And later the issue of language was brushed aside and religion became the dominating factor. Hence, Shanti Muzumdar was double victim of double uprootedness that enhanced her trauma. Her past position and her present condition are so opposed to each other. Her status is reduced to that of a beggar from the status of being a mother of Bangal. She doesn't belong to anywhere.

"A Grave Turned Inside Out"[28] by Ibrahim Jalees is also a story of double uprootedness like "The Mother of Dhiren Muzumdar." The story describes how their Muslim brethren treated the Muslim refugees or 'muhajirs', with the feelings of otherness. The story revolves around Ayesha who migrated from India with her husband to East Pakistan during the Partition violence. But she failed to understand that once uprooted there would be no home for them. In East Pakistan they adapt to the Bengali ways. Even then there was no acceptability.

When Bengalis of East Pakistan started a struggle to get East Pakistan freed all the people of East Pakistan were fighting against Pakistan. But as soon as Bangladesh was created riots based on language started and the Bengali speaking Muslims started troubling the Hindus as well as the Urdu speaking Muslims. The Muslims who were not basically Bengalis particularly had to face the wrath of the rioters. It was then that Ayesha's husband was killed by a Muslim goonda who abducted Nurul's wife. Ayesha's husband tried hard to save Nurul's wife but in vain and he lost his own life amid this struggle. His own daughter was also abducted during this period and Ayesha was thrown at the mercy of Nurul. Ayesha was displaced from Dhaka. She had to flee to Pakistan, as she was a Bihari Muslim who spoke Urdu. She had to abandon the world of Islamic brotherhood promised by their Quaid-I-Azam.

On the contrary Ayesha falls a prey to the deceit and treachery of her fellow Muslim, Nurul, who gives her false hope of support. He also cheats her as he tells her that he has sent her daughter safely to Pakistan whereas it is not true. The notion of community based on one religion proves false here as Ayesha suffers at the hands of a Muslim. Nurul who wants to exploit her brings Ayesha to Karachi. He betrays her faith in him. She "had trusted Nurul like a brother, because they had been neighbours ..." (p. 143). But Nurul wants to use her as a prostitute. In Karachi they take refuge in a poor part of the city near a graveyard. The goons who supervise the slums for Bihari migrants from East Pakistan rape her. They punished Ayesha "for illegally grabbing Government land, made a grab for the land of her body" (p. 151). She was raped and killed. She could belong neither to Dhaka nor to Karachi since she had no identity. She remained an outsider till her death. Death became the final resort for her. The author has also focused on a beastly hankering after female body. Not only her psyche but also her body was mutilated.

The Urdu writer Intizar Husain in the story, "An Unwritten Epic", explores the theme of alienation, lost identity and a search for belongingness with great subtlety.[29] The writer focuses on the problem of mixed identity as well as struggle for belongingness after migration through the character of Pichwa, a young Muslim. He is torn between two worlds none of which is ready to embrace him. Ironically, the men of his own religious community deceive a man who has dreamt of a nation that will belong to him. He is forced to drift from one world to the other and is finally killed mercilessly.

Before the Partition took place, Pichwa had been a hero of Qadirpur in India. Whenever there were fights with the other villagers or attacks from outside he had no match. All were afraid of him. He had, many times, defeated the Hindu wrestlers like Tidda. No body dared challenging him. But once the Partition was declared his identity as a strong and powerful man got lost and he was pained to know that Qadirpur did not fall in Pakistan. Like other Muslim brethren in India he had to migrate to Pakistan and he became a 'muhajir'. Ironically enough, the country that claimed to be the home for the Muslims no longer welcomed the Muslims from India. The Muslims of Pakistan were not like *ansars* who had welcomed the migrants like Prophet Mohammad with open arms.[30] Pichwa of the happy days of the past was no more 'alive'. The man known for prowess and strength was virtually dead. The height and grandeur of his character had been destroyed. In Pakistan Pichwa was reduced to the status of a beggar. He begged and grovelled before the narrator, who himself was a migrant like him, "Miyan, get me some kind of work. I have no damned place even to rest my feet on. Babu, if I can't find a job, at least get a house allotted to me" (p. 69). He had never been worried about daily necessities in Qadirpur, and here he had to beg for food and a roof to cover his head. It is painful to see the plight of this once towering figure. In Pakistan Pichwa went to see Naim Miyan, who had also fled from Qadirpur much before Pichwa, to get some help. Naim Miyam had changed. He did not talk to outcasts now. He scolded Pichwa, "Everyone just marches into Pakistan expecting to get something, as if his father had buried a treasure here. They just don't realize that there is not that much room in Pakistan" (p. 69). But the reality is that there was no room in one's heart for others. People had confined themselves to the narrow selfish worlds. No doubt, it was the same Naim Miyan who had always been tongue-tied in front of Pichwa in India. Pichwa faced double identity crisis. He had been forced to flee from India as he was considered an alien there. On the other hand in Pakistan he was again treated as an "outsider" who was a burden on the land of Pakistan. In Pakistan the orders were issued that "the refugees who have come here can damn well go to India" (p. 69). Pichwa, helplessly, left Pakistan because there was "no longer any room in the hearts of the people." (p. 75). He left defiantly. He felt he had disgraced himself by coming to Pakistan. No body tried to feel his emotions because, "Peopledon't care about human emotions here—the mention of human emotions is still an after thought" (p. 77).

Pichwa, helpless and broken, came to India hoping that the land and its people would own him. But he was wrong and could not understand that "man is no more then a bubble" (p. 75). Qadirpur had become Jatunagar and Pichwa was nothing more than an outsider. He had lost both the grounds. He belonged to 'nowhere'. He got neither Pakistan nor India. He had to take refuge in the lap of death ultimately as the natives of Jatunagar who had been his rivals before the Partition killed him.

Similarly one of the themes *Azadi* deals with is the theme of loss of identity. Men became one with the indistinguishable multitudes fleeing to refugee camps. To the uprooted people the shock of uprootedness is so sudden that it is not possible to adjust oneself from one's personal home to the impersonality of a camp. The trauma which Kanshi Ram, the protagonist of the novel, and his wife, Prabha Rani undergo is indescribable. He suffers the loss most poignantly. Never before in his life had he felt so exposed, so naked, so defenceless. "Out of the dark cave that life was, Prabha Rani had carved a sunny patch for him and then sealed it off. Prabha Rani was still with him but that seal had been smashed. There were too many eyes peering in on them at these camps, too many ears listening. Each one was a curiosity to the other but no one had an identity."[31] The wind that blows non-stop through the tents drives holes through his body. He does not want to go back to a refugee camp. Four months of living in the camp has shrunk his heart. He wants a house, his wife, and his children. So much sorrow for a house, such prostration and such weariness of spirit in his father cuts Arun, the son, to the quick. But once he is under the corrugated roof, with solid walls of brick around him in the hutment of Kingsway camp, he mutters with satisfaction, "Let it rain real hard." The change which 'azadi' brings humiliates man in many ways. There is no dignity left. After coming to India Kanshi Ram stops wearing a turban since a turban is a sign of respect, of dignity. Now he sits bareheaded exposing his humble position to the world.

NOTES

1. Swarna Aiyer, " 'August Anarchy': The Partition Massacres in Punjab, 1947" in *Freedom, Trauma, Continuities: Northern India and Independence*, ed. D.A. Low and Howard Brasted (New Delhi: Sage Publications, 1998), p.15.
2. Sumit Sarkar, *Modern India: 1885–1947* (1983, rpt. Madras: Macmillan India, 1992), p. 434.
3. Quoted in Kirpal Singh, *The Partition of the Punjab* (Patiala: Punjabi University, 1972), p.114.
4. Quoted in ibid.
5. Anders Bjorn Hansen, *Partition and Genocide: Manifestation*

of Violence in Punjab, 1937-1947 (New Delhi: India Research Press, 2000), p.156.

6. Larry Collins and Dominique Lapierre, *Freedom at Midnight* (1976, rpt. New Delhi: Vikas Publishing House, 1977), p. 294.
7. Ibid., p. 319.
8. Ibid., p. 321.
9. Khushwant Singh, *A History of the Sikhs: 1839-1974,* Vol.II (Delhi: Oxford University Press, 1984), p. 282.
10. Ibid.
11. Swarna Aiyar, "'August Anarchy': The Partition Massacres in Punjab, 1947" in *Freedom, Trauma, Continuities: Northern India and Independence*, p. 18.
12. Kirpal Singh, *The Partition of the Punjab*, p. 123.
13. Ibid., p. 136.
14. Krishna Chander, "The Peshawar Express", trans. Jai Rattan in *Stories About the Partition of India*, Vol. III, ed. Alok Bhalla (New Delhi: Harper Collins, 1994), p. 207. All subsequent references to the story are from this edition and have been incorporated in the text.
15. Collins and Lapierre, *Freedom at Midnight*, pp. 330-31.
16. Gyanesh Kudaisya, "Divided Landscapes, Fragmented Identities: East Bengal Refugees and their Rehabilitation in India, 1947-79" in *Freedom, Trauma, Continuities: Northern India and Independence,* ed. D.A. Low and Howard Brasted (New Delhi: Sage Publications, 1998), p. 118.
17. Mohan Rakesh, "God's Dog", trans. Alok Bhalla in *Stories About the Partition of India*, Vol. II, ed. Alok Bhalla (New Delhi: Harper Collins, 1994), p. 119. All subsequent references to the story are from this edition and have been incorporated in the text.
18. Sumit Sarkar, *Modern India: 1885–1947,* p. 435.
19. Satya M. Rai, *Partition of the Punjab* (New Delhi: Asia Publishing House, 1965), p.128
20. Mulk Raj Anand, "The Parrot in the Cage", *Stories About the Partition of India,* Vol. III, ed. Alok Bhalla (New Delhi: Harper Collins, 1994), p. 85. All subsequent references to the story are from this edition and have been incorporated in the text.
21. Saadat Hasan Manto, "Toba Tek Singh", trans. Tahira Naqvi in *Stories About the Partition* of India, Vol. III, ed. Alok Bhalla (New Delhi: Harper Collins, 1994), p. 1. All

Subsequent references to the story are from this edition and have been incorporated in the text.

22. Mohan Rakesh, "The Claim", trans. Richard Williams in *Stories About the Partition of India,* Vol. III, ed. Alok Bhalla (New Delhi: Harper Collins, 1994), p. 35. All Subsequent references to the story are from this edition and have been incorporated in the text.
23. Naraim Bharti, "The Claim", trans. Sree Israney in *Stories About the Partition of India,* Vol.II, ed. Alok Bhalla (New Delhi: Harper Collins, 1994), p. 219. All subsequent references to the story are to this edition and have been incorporated in the text.
24. Syed Mohammad Ashraf, "Separated from the Flock", trans. Vishwamitter Adil and Alok Bhalla in *Stories About the Partition of India,* Vol. I, ed. Alok Bhalla (New Delhi: Harper Collins, 1994) p.1 All subsequent references to the story are to this edition and have been incorporated in the text.
25. Gyanesh Kudaisya, "Divided Landscapes, Fragmented Identities: East Bengal Refugees and their Rehabilitation in India, 1947-79" in *Freedom, Trauma, Continuities: Northern India and Independence,* p. 112.
26. Ibid., p.122. For details see pp. 106-123.
27. Lalithambika Antharjanam, "The Mother of Dhiren Muzumdar", trans. T. Muralidharan in *Stories About the Partition of India,* Vol. II, ed. Alok Bhalla (New Delhi: Harper Collins, 1994), p. 199. All subsequent references to the story are to this edition and have been incorporated in the text.
28. Ibrahim Jalees, "A Grave Turned Inside Out", trans. Vishwamitter Adil and Alok Bhalla in *Stories About the Partition of India.* Vol. II, ed. Alok Bhalla (New Delhi: Harper Collins, 1994), p. 141. All subsequent references to the story are to this edition and have been incorporated in the text.
29. Intizar Husain, "An Unwritten Epic", trans. Leslie A. Fleming and Muhammad Umar Memon in *Stories About the Partition of India,* Vol. III, ed. Alok Bhalla (New Delhi: Harper Collins, 1994), p. 59. All subsequent references to the story are to this edition and have been incorporated in the text.
30. Sarah Ansari, "Partition, Migration and Refugees: Responses to the Arrival of Muhajirs in Sind During 1947-48" in *Freedom, Trauma, Continuities: Northern India and Independence*

(ed.) D.A. Low and Howard Brasted (New Delhi: Sage Publications, 1998), p. 92.

31. Chaman Nahal, *Azadi* (1979: rpt. New Delhi: Orient Paperbacks, 1988), p. 350.

4
Violence Against Women

The term violence has been defined variously. The Oxford dictionary defines violence in its mild form as an outrage, injury or an act contrary to one's feelings or principles, and in its strong sense as unlawful exercise of physical force. Straus (1980) has described a violent act "an act where there is the high potential of causing injury." Geller (1979) defines violence as "an act of striking a person with the intent of causing harm or injury but not actually causing it." Domenach (1981) has described it as "an act of a person which encroaches upon the freedom of another." Kempe (1982) has applied the term 'violence' to "physically striking an individual and causing injury."[1] There are some thinkers who relate violence to Aristotle's concept of 'catharsis' as a release or transformation of emotional pressure or impulse via activity and expression. Catharsis lies in emotions and it becomes essential to release these pent up emotions either through expression or action to feel normal. Some of the repressed emotions are released in such violent actions that they become dangerous.

These definitions of violence are general and not gender specific and they can be applied in the common context of men as well as women. On the contrary violence against women has different forms and purposes. Under patriarchy, a woman's whole existence is seen in relation to man. Man inflicts violence on woman to strike terror in her so that she remains subdued as an object, as a piece of property. Objectifying a living being is the most pervasive kind of violence done to a woman since it amounts to negating her emotions, desires and thinking. Man wants complete control over a woman's body and mind, which means crippling her, choking her, thwarting her. For a man woman's mind has no value, to him only woman's body is important, that too as it is useful to him. Violence is also useful in keeping man healthy, in that he can release his own tension by pouring out these on woman in violent actions. In the context of women, as Women's Aid Federation observes:

> Violence can mean among other things, threats, intimidation, manipulation, isolation, keeping a woman without money, locked in, deprived of food and using her children in various ways to frighten her or enforce compliance. It can also include systematic and belittling comments.[2]

Hence for women violence ranges from the wish to cause physical pain—for instance, by beating her — to humiliating her, putting her in chains, or forcing her to complete obedience in other ways.[3] The force, whether overt or covert, is used to wrest from a woman something that she does not want to give of her own free will and it can take the form of either physical injury or emotional trauma or both inflicted together.

Physical violence is a common and most obvious form of violence against woman. The history of human culture is replete with examples of systematic oppression of woman. In fact, inflicting violence against woman begins often right from her birth and sometimes even before that as the recent figures of census have shown. The practice of female foeticide after sex determination test is common in some parts and is having serious consequences for the social health and balance. Oppression of woman through female infanticide was in vogue in the past when in some parts of India the infant girls were killed mercilessly at their birth. The Kallars of Tamil Nadu and the Rajputs of northern India, both seen as ruling classes in certain small pockets, had the custom of female infanticide.

Infant daughters were killed either by stepping on the throat or by giving a dose of lethal poison, with a little sugar, causing instant death.[4] In both the cases women's choice did not have any importance.

A frequent form of physical violence is wife beating which is not peculiar to any society but is common to patriarchy all over. A husband who is supposed to be a protector and lover of his wife often beats her. It becomes a shattering experience for a woman when she is battered by a man whom she trusts the most. This fact is not confined to India alone. One of the most shocking facts emerging out of 1977 World Health Organisation study was that globally one out of every three women experiences domestic violence at some point in her life.[5] Through pornography, prostitution, sexual harassment, rape, woman battering, suttee and witch-burning man has controlled woman's sexuality for male pleasure. It is shocking how ruthlessness towards woman has been blatantly advocated by some persons:

> Pay no attention to her murmurs, her cries, her pains; nature has made her for our use and for bearing everything: children, sorrows, blows and pains inflicted by man. Do not accuse yourself for hardness. In all the codes of so-called civilized nations, man has written the laws that ranged woman's destiny under this bloody epigraph: Vae Victis! Woe to the weak! [6]

Man evolves fear in the mind of woman by his superior muscular power and by extreme emotional indifference and callousness that make woman so vulnerable. According to a recent review in the *Journal of the American Medical Association.* "Women in the United States are more likely to be assaulted and injured, raped or killed by a current or ex-male partner than all other assailants combined."[7] The same could be said of women elsewhere in the world including India.

One of the most common forms of violence which is simultaneously physical and mental is rape. Rape is considered as a patriarchal weapon used by a man on woman as a threat. Rape is simply one of the tools of oppression.[8] Rape imposes humiliation on the victim. There is ample evidence that rape in India is a phenomenon which goes beyond the variable of sexuality in many ways, e.g., the way in which it is used by landlords to quell tribal uprising.[9] In addition to random rapes, the police also use rape as a very effective weapon in the suppression of leftist movements and tribal uprisings. In these cases the police, local upper-caste landlords and the governments are all embroiled in a complicated system by which they all support each other and benefit from the suppression.[10]

Even the role of judiciary towards there problems is not encouraging sometimes. For instance, rape has been viewed as an attack on women's chastity and not an offence against human rights and dignity.[11] The victim has to bear the trauma of another kind as well. A woman who is raped is looked down upon by the society. She is hated as if she herself is responsible for losing her so-called 'chastity'. Moreover, she is treated as an outcast. Her status in the household is that of an untouchable. Members of the family do not talk to her. Society looks at her in a manner as if she has committed a sin. The biggest irony is that the victim of rape is held responsible for the violence inflicted on her and she is stigmatized. Rape is probably the only crime in which the victim is treated like a crimnal.[12] For these reasons the victim has to suffer silently without sharing her trauma with others. The feeling of shame may prevent the woman from seeking help even from friends, neighbours and relatives.[13] This type of violence is a more subtle form of violence where the wounds remain invisible and are more difficult to heal. It is a more precarious kind of violence also as it ruins not merely the body but the whole being.

Physical and psychological acts of violence are not individual acts of aberrations. They are sanctioned socially to keep woman under control and the violence is inflicted not only for the benefit of individual men but also for the larger structure of patriarchy. Woman is also subjected to socio-psychological violence. In a patriarchal culture, what we get is a masculinist definition of ideals and images of woman. The concept of virginity or chastity or 'izzat' is so deep rooted in our society that it creates problems in the life of woman. Even since the time of Manu woman's chastity mattered much, even after the death of the husband.[14] Even today a woman cannot spend even one night away from her home without the permission of her husband or in the company of a relative. If she does so, she has to pass through an ordeal to prove her chastity.[15] The maker of these regulations is no other than man himself.

The social codes are enforced on woman in the name of morality without trying to understand that morality should be concerned with good and evil[16] of both men and women. Both husbands and wives ought to be faithful to one another.[17] Durkheim has rightly stated in this regard that we do not disapprove of an action because it is a crime, but "it is a crime because we disapprove of it."[18] It means that there is nothing good or bad intrinsically but is made so by society and that morality depends upon social opinion.

Religion and social code make the concept of virginity mandatory for woman. Even Gandhi, who is credited with bringing women into public life to join the national movement and who believed that woman was suppressed under custom and law for which man was responsible[19] nevertheless felt that his 'ideal woman' was the mythical Sita,[20] the self-sacrificing, monogamous wife of the *Ramayana*, who guarded her chastity, and remained loyal to Rama in spite of many provocation.[21]

In most national histories, the countries have idealised the private virtues of woman and public roles of men. Mythology, too, reinforces these perceptions. Sita and Savitri are two characters held up as ideals of Indian womanhood. However, Sita had to prove her fidelity and chastity by undergoing a trial by fire since she had been in Ravana's custody for a while. She is to most Hindu women the epitome of the proper wife. She represents the ideal towards which all should strive.

On the contrary, such ideals or codes are not mandatory for man. He is free to do what he wants and can satisfy his whim for sex whenever he likes, while it is ruthlessly condemned as adultery in case a woman indulges in it even though accidentally. The concept of 'izzat' is so deep-rooted that on the slightest hint of any deviation on her part which may not even involve sex, man turns violent and hostile towards his wife and starts persecuting her. Hardy in *Tess of the D'Urbervilles* and Nanthaniel Hawthorne in *The Scarlet Letter* have shown how women are persecuted and abandoned, whereas men are spared any punishment for the 'sin' which is committed by both. The concept of 'honour' thus can devastate the life of a woman.

Due to this concept of 'izzat' women suffered inter-community as well as intra-community violence during the Partition riots. The Partition period brought with it violence, humiliation and permanent scars in the lives of women. Men of both the community—the Hindus and the Muslims—were worried about their women not because they loved them but because they feared violence of their chastity which would mean shame and humiliation to the whole community. The 'honour' of women at this juncture stood for the 'honour' of the community. Women became symbols of 'community honour', as Urvashi Butalia observes.

> If colonialism provided Indian men the rationale for constructing and reconstructing the identity of the Hindu woman as a 'bhadramahila', the good, middle class Hindu woman as a supporter of her men, independence, and its dark 'other', Partition provided the rationale for making woman into symbols of the nation's honour.[22]

It was due to this changing concept of honour that the men of one community took it as an opportunity to punish and humiliate the 'other' community by inflicting the worst kind of violence upon their women. As a result women became victims of rape, abduction and killing through inter-community violence. On the other hand it was believed that if chastity of women got defiled or polluted, it would be a permanent reminder of a community's insult and dishonour. So women emerged as valuable overnight and the men of the respective communities tried their best to protect and save the honour of their women. Men even killed their women so that they should not fall in their enemies' hands. These women became victim of 'honour killings.' Worse still, even some members of the same community were on the look out for raping and abducting the women of their own 'caste' and community. They were sold into prostitution by their own men. Urvashi Butalia writes:

> ...so many women had been picked up by men of the same village. So many *older* women had been abducted – women in their fifties and sixties. According to social workers, this wasn't uncommon: because abductors often know the circumstances of women they were picking up, they would take away older women, widows, or those whose husbands had been killed, for their property. They would then ask to became their 'sons'—a short cut to quick acquisition of property.[23]

Once the chastity of women was violated by the members of the 'other' community the women were treated as 'untouchables' or social-outcasts. Their own community started looking at them with hatred and indifference. Most of the victims were shunned and ostracized by their own kith and kin, which added to the trauma in the life of these victimized women.

The short stories taken up for in-depth study are replete with the theme of inter-community as well as intra-community violence against women. The Partition of India rendered women vulnerable. They were the real victims during that period as their fate was to suffer the loss of their children, parents, husbands and even their own 'honour'. And it is another tragic irony that the history of the Partition made no mention of women.[24] The historians have not dealt with the pain and trauma faced by thousands of women left alone[25] to suffer. In fact the history of Partition was also a history of deep violation—physical and mental—for women.[26] They were bought and sold like cattle. It is only through the short stories based on partition that the whole tragedy of women is laid open before us. In these stories physical violence ranges from bitter and harsh comments to beatings; from abduction to rape; from restoration to the rejection and further loneliness.

By focusing on numerous women—both Hindu and Muslim—the stories give us an idea of the pervasive violence suffered by women during the communal frenzy of the Partition.

I

INTER-COMMUNITY VIOLENCE

In patriarchy women suffer violence even in peace time but during times of communal riots their suffering is much worse as ghastly crimes are committed against their body and mind. In times of religious hatred women are over and over again singled out specially for humiliating treatment by men of rival community. Women become targets of molestation, abduction, rape, mutilation, forced conversion, marriage and death.[27] The violence inflicted upon them during the Partition displayed communal animosity at its peak. Earlier the rioters defiled mosques or temples to express their hatred for the 'other' community and religion. During the Partition riots their attention shifted towards women "partly to punish their men folk and partly because they are a vulnerable section of society."[28] So by violating the honour of women the whole community was defiled. One recurring factor in these attacks was the emphasis on sexuality and reproduction in the female body which thus presented an opportunity to "conquer the enemy territory."[29] Since women were seen as a symbol of community production, the rival community took it as an opportunity to sow the seeds of their community in the wombs of the women who belonged to the 'other' community. The *modus operandi* included gang rapes, stripping and parading naked women through towns and cities. Besides, their breasts and genitals were marked or tattooed with slogans like 'Pakistan Zindabad' or 'Hindustan Zindabad'. Not only this sometimes their breasts were amputated and some times the wombs were cut opened with knives and foetuses were killed or crushed mercilessly. Even Jawahar Lal Nehru publicly observed at Indian Woman's Conference in December 1947, "The last few months have seen terrible happenings in northern India and women have perhaps been the chief sufferers."[30] Undoubtedly, the incidents of violence against women swept the communities clean of all decency, morality and sense of human values.

The worst kind of violence on women was inflicted through abduction. The abducted women were either kidnapped by the religious fanatics of the other communities or as 'part of a programme of planned retaliation or human lust and insanity but abduction was given the name of 'religious vendetta.' It is estimated that about fifty thousand women were abducted in both the Punjabs.[31] These abducted women became victims of government indifference. Some government officials, too, had kept abducted women. The women were abducted from their homes, refugee trains, refugee caravans and also from refugee camps. These ill-fated women were sold off in bazaar and were treated like commodities. About afflicted souls Anis Kidwai writes movingly in her *Azadi ki Chaon Mein*:

> In all of this sometimes a girl would be killed or she would be wounded. The 'good stuff' would be shared among the police and army, the 'second rate stuff' would go to everyone else. And then these girls would go from one hand

to another and then another and after several would turn up in hotels to grace their décor or they would be handed over to police officers in some places to please them.[32]

The short stories that deal with the agony, trauma and 'shame' of these victims are "Cold Meat", "Open It", "Peshawar Express", "The City of Sorrow" "Kulsum", "Exile", "Lajwanti", "I Shall Live", "Pali" and "The Abandoned Child".

"The men start warring, the women weep" is a popular saying in many cultures.[33,] As men started rioting women became the worst victims. The visible violence through rape was the most pervasive kind of violence which shattered women altogether. There was no limit to men's savagery. In their lust and insanity they were not able to differentiate between dead and alive. "Cold Meat"[34] by Saadat Hasan Manto is a story of such a beastly man, Ishwar Singh—the irony in his name is striking—who forces himself on a dead woman. He kills six men just to satiate his desire for the blood of those who belong to the rival community. This Sikh man spares the life of a beautiful Muslim woman only because he wants to rape her, to taste the "delicacy" (p. 96). He carries her on his shoulder to a canal bank. When he starts raping her he is surprised after a while that girl is making no sound or movement of any kind at all. He is horrified to find that he was mating with a dead woman. The Muslim girl had died while being carried on his shoulder to be raped. But his blind lust had failed to see the difference between a living woman and a dead one. For him she was just a female body to be used. He is shocked to find, "She...was dead...a lifeless corpse...a cold, lifeless corpse..." (p. 96).

After this gruesome act in fact the human in him probably gets pricked and he turns impotent with the shock of realization of what he had done. His wife is frustrated,. angry and suspicious when he fails to gratify her but it is then he makes a confession of his beastly act, his savage infliction on the dead girl.

Sakina[35] the protagonist in "Open It" again by Manto is a similar victim of man's lust. Though she is physically alive, mentally, emotionally she is dead. During the Partition riots her mother was killed. Sakina was with her father. When her father tried to pick her *dupatta*, she wept. Her poor father who bothered about her *dupatta*—a symbol of honour and shame—did not know that the next moment his daughter would be lost. She was picked up by some one to satiate his lust. Sakina it seems was raped time and again and that made her a mental wreck. She was afraid of everyone. When the social workers noticed her standing on the road, Sakina started running in fear. The earlier ghastly experience had left her virtually dead, if not literally. The experience of repeated rape had left her dazed and numb with fear. This fear was further accelerated as she was again raped by the eight social workers who were requested by her father to rescue her. They had betrayed the father as well as the daughter. The effect of the violence was so devastating on the girl that now whenever she heard a male voice, she quietly, as a battered animal, lowered her pyjama and opened her legs. She knows what a beast in man wants from a woman.

The irony and horror of human tragedy comes to the surface when Sakina is later restored to her father who takes her to a doctor. The doctor examines her and says, "Open the windows." The girl stirs a little and "moved her hand painfully towards the cords holding up her salwar. Slowly she pulled her salwar down" (p. 72). The doctor and her father watch her in horror. Undoubtedly, the terror created by the male violence has turned her into a living corpse.

Similar is the fate of Kulsum[36] who too suffers because of inter-community violence inflicted on her. She is saved from riot-hit area and brought to home by an old man, belonging to the other community. The old man saves her neither because he is a good man, nor because he has any pity for the girl. He has some self-interest to fulfil. He intends to use her as a prostitute. The old Hindu man wants to sell her in men's market where he can make money out of her. Kulsum is presented to a schoolmaster as a "gift" which he can "neither eat nor drink" (p. 91). The schoolmaster is ready to "devour" her. She does not want to surrender before him. She wants to save her honour. But the schoolmaster's eyes "burnt with lust" and he smiles "lasciviously" and lunges at the girl. He grabs her and pulls her towards the bed. There is a kind of rage in his eyes, as he wants to rape her. Without uttering a word he continues to "pull her towards the bed" (p. 93). Kulsum is horrified and helpless. She is terror-stricken at his advances. She feels she can save her honour if he marries her first. So Kulsum pleads with the schoolmaster that he should marry her first. But when he turns a deaf ear to her pleadings, she pounces upon him like a "lioness." The schoolmaster is horrified and goes out of the room. He complains to the old man against her behaviour. The old man is enraged at her resistance and rapes Kulsum himself first. This time she does not make any protest. Ironically the saviour has turned into a destroyer. She is looted by her saviour. Now when the schoolmaster approaches her she surrenders without any resistance since she has been turned virtually into a 'corpse' by the man who had rescued her. The impact of the violence is so horrifying and shattering on Kulsum that she too is turned into a living corpse.

Women, irrespective of their religion and caste, suffered male violence inflicted upon them during the Partition, while men of all the communities were involved in persecuting women and that confirms the truth that during the course of rioting, all communities were equally involved.[37] Jamila Hashmi's "Exile"[38] is a story of deep human significance. The writer delineates the true dimensions of the events accompanying the Partition by showing their physical and psychological impact on human life. The story brings out not only the irreparable physical loss, but also the emotional loss—the loss of personality under the stress of this traumatic event. The story is a portrayal of the little world of the narrator enjoying the bonds of love of her parents and brother, and her childlike, placid, easy and happy life before the Partition and then her totally changed life after the storm of the Partition. The story hints at the poignant reality that it is easier to cut a country geographically, but it is hard to snap the bonds of love and life. "Exile" movingly describes the impact of forcible dislocation through abduction, rape and marriage.

The trauma and anguish of the narrator is depicted on three levels. The poignant and sad tale of her sufferings starts from the day she is abducted by a Sikh, Gurpal, who brings her to his home. She may not be as unfortunate as Kulsum or Sakina or the woman of "Cold Meat" who are turned into virtual corpses due to the onslaught on their body, and they are rendered homeless. The narrator in "Exile" at least finds a home, but under most painful circumstances. It is most agonizing for her that the murderer of her parents becomes her husband. The most painful day comes in her life when having slaughtered her parents Gurpal abducts her and drags her to his house. She is "pushed" in like an animal and Gurpal proclaims, "Look Ma, I have brought you Bahu. She is tall and good-looking. Of all the girl who fell into our hands tonight, she was the prettiest" (p. 40). She is too tired to lift even a finger and her feet are bruised and wounded since she had to walk barefoot for miles. Physical exhaustion and mental trauma make her fall at Ma's feet in a heap. Even the cattle are surprised at her helplessness and miserable state as if she belongs to their category. "The cows and buffaloes, who were chained in the courtyard, stopped eating their fodder and turned to look at me in surprise," says the narrator (p. 40). Badi Ma "scrutinizes" her from head to feet as if she is not a human being. She is not happy that a Bahu has come and her response is of indifference. She is rather satisfied as the maid servants have stopped working in the house and the narrator will be a good substitute for a maid servant as is clear from the statement of Gurpal who asserts, "At least, look at her. You won't have to put up with the insolence of maidservants any more. She will be your slave. Order her to grind corn, fetch water. As far as I am concerned, you can ask her to do anything you wish. I have brought you a Bahu!" (p. 40).

The narrator is made a 'Bahu' without any ceremony. No one greets her at the door with music, no songs are sung with beating drums and there is no dancing to celebrate her arrival. Neither is her hair anointed with oil nor is she decorated with jewels and fine clothes, nor is *mehndi* put on her hands. Her dreams of becoming a bride in real sense, bading good-bye to her brother, sitting in a palanquin are shattered. She is made a Bahu by her abductor without applying *sindoor* in the parting of her hair. Ironically, she has become a bride! Her sorrow only increases when even Badi Ma, a woman herself, does not bother to talk to her. She turns her back towards her in indifference and leaves. She suffers for nine long years. She has children from Gurpal but she has never accepted her as a husband. How can she forgive a man who has spoiled her life and broken her dreams?

It is one act of the abduction and ensuing atrocities on her that she feels alienated. She feels all alone even in the company of her family. It is the separation from her 'own' people that tortures her psyche the most. She is constantly anguished over the separation. "The very fact of separation stands like a wall between people who once loved each-other. Once separated they are fated never to see each-other's faces again.... They can never return to their past again" (p. 41). The narrator lives in a state of exile.

It is through the use of myth that her trauma and predicament are made clear. Like Sita she is abducted and separated from her dear ones. She also feels that she is living in Ravana's home. There is a good use of words, images, and metaphor that portray her life effectively. Her two children are retuning from fair holding the images of Ravana reminding her that she has been living among wicked people like Ravana. The words like "darkness", "meander", "mist surrounding them", "empty sky", a "single star" trembling like the "flame of earthen lamp" which make her feel sad convey her traumatic and aching condition so clearly. She says, "In the wilderness of my house, I am like that lonely tree which neither blossoms nor bears fruit" (p. 42). No body tries to soothe her afflicted soul, "After all, one can never know how much a wound hurts, until one is injured oneself" (p. 42). Her loneliness intensifies her trauma and she feels like a "boat without oars". Since her abduction, as she says, "all the lights of my life were extinguished forever. Since then, no ray of light has gleamed in the wilderness that surrounds me" (p. 43).

Remembering about her past, her family and her home makes her feel lonelier. She remembers the days when she would feel safe in the company of her brother. She thinks, "those old bonds, strengthened by sorrow, have not snapped. In fact they have become deeper and stronger. How can I ever forget my past?" (p. 44). Her position is like "a tree and earth" whose bonds are so intact that it is difficult to separate them. Their roots are very deep. She feels that the page on which her life story has been written is so smudged with "black" ink, that it is difficult to find a single straight line one it. She feels lonely without her brother and for her "loneliness is hard to endure. Life is difficult" (p. 45).

She wavers between hope and despair. She hopes that one day her brother will come to rescue her but then she also realizes that her brother must have a wife and children. He must be busy and happy with them. She realizes that "the road to the other land is desolate and passes through a burial ground. There is no one there who waits for me. Whoever paid attention to Sita's lament?" (p. 45). She is right. Woman's fate is to suffer and bear the burden of atrocities done by her own people as well as 'others'. It is the memory of the past that shatters her inner self into shreds. When her brother does not come to help her, she feels sad and thinks, "Oh why do I stand waiting at the door? For whom? How much longer will I have to carry this dead corpse of my hope? Why do my eyes fill with tears when I find that the lane outside is desolate?" (p. 52). She has to yield before her fate.

Gradually, however, she accepts her desolation and submits to her fate. She decides not to lament over her past and also decides to look after her children. She does this not because her brother has deceived her faith, but because she has a greater dilemma as time passes. She is a 'mother' now. Who will accept her with the children of a man belonging to another community? Besides she can never dare to discard her children. She is, thus, forced to accept the home of Ravana. It is nothing but her instinct for survival and love of children that she goes on living. She says, "Like everyone in this caravan of life, I have to keep on walking." Yet she is unable to forget her past and feels sad and says, "I don't know when my journey will ever end" (p. 53).

Rajinder Singh Bedi's short story "Lajwanti"[39] also tells the story of an abducted woman. The story is regarded as a classic in Urdu. The plot revolves around Sunderlal and his wife Lajwanti. Lajwanti was abducted and raped by some Muslims. One incident of abduction devastated her life to the core. Sunderlal had left all hopes of finding Lajwanti. He had made his loss a part of the general loss. He had drowned his personal sorrow by dedicating his own self to the social service. He daily led processions and remonstrated with those who refused to take back their abducted women. He wanted people to accept back into the fold of family when abducted women were restored to them. However when his own wife Lajwanti is restored to him he finds it hard to accept her as easily and naturally as he has been advising others to do. Lajwanti's Muslim style of dress disgusts him when he sees her at the police station. Nevertheless he brings her home. Sunderlal fails to read the signs of pain and humiliation in her face. He cannot imagine how she must have lived with her abductors and how helpless she must have been there. On the contrary he "...was shocked. Lajo looked healthier than before, her complexion looked clearer, her eyes brighter and she had put on weight...she looked different from what he had imagined.... He was startled to see that she had been well treated in Pakistan.

He was puzzled. 'If she had been comfortable and happy there why did she agree to return'?" (pp. 63-64). Sunderlal is unable to feel the real trauma of Lajwanti. He cannot feel that one never feels comfortable and happy when one is away from one's home and hearth and one is forced to surrender to her abductors. How can he feel trauma of uprootedness when he himself is not uprooted? That is why for him the thought of confronting his wife, who had been abducted and raped, was 'strangely disturbing.' In accepting her he has just done his "duty." Lajwanti suffers from the loss of identity as Sunderlal refuses to let her unburden her nightmarish experiences. She has been rehabilitated but not accepted. He treats her, instead, with an over-exaggerated respect calling her 'Devi'. He no longer calls her 'Lajo.' Abduction has played havoc with her identity. 'Lajo' of the past has lost herself somewhere. She wants to be treated like a human being, not like a goddess. She wants to tell her husband, with tears in her eyes, all that she had suffered so that she may feel clean once again. But he always shirks away from hearing her story. On the other hand Lajwanti feels apprehensive about her new life of 'love' and kindness'. Sunderlal just says, "Let us forget the past" (p. 65). He does not understand that forgetting one's past is not that much easy. It is only he who can help his wife to forget the past. But he is not ready to help her unburden her sorrows which remain "locked up" in her breast.

Helplessly, Lajwanti gazes at her own body and realizes that she can never become Lajo of the past. She realizes that since the Partition, it has been no longer her own body but the body of a goddess. She remains a stranger in her own house, among her own people. Her husband has made her feel that she is fragile like a glass and she can be shattered at any time at the slightest touch. She gives up the hope of becoming Lajo as he has neither "eyes to see her tears nor the ears to hear her sobs"(p. 66). The experience of abduction is one of pain and humiliation for Lajwanti. She is as much a victim in her own home as she was at the time of her abduction.

Another damage caused by abduction is the loss of communication. Everything is there. Lajwanti lives with her husband, talks to him. He, too, talks to her but not as a wife, only as a 'devi'. The real contact is missing. Something has driven them apart. Abduction has proved to be sinister and she cannot reach her husband who goes on singing:

Do not touch Lajwanti
For she will curl up
and die…!

Ironically, Lajwanti cannot die at the touch of her husband but she surely will die if her husband maintains a distance from her. She will die not at the touch but because she is forced to live a life of loneliness and alienation.

Similar trauma of abduction is suffered by Lenny's Hindu *ayah* in *Ice candy Man*[40] who is abducted by a Muslim who rapes and marries her forcibly. She cannot accept her captor and says, "I will not live with him…I cannot forget what has happened" (p. 261-62) How can the *ayah* forget and forgive a person who first abducted her and sold her to a brothel where he counted money when she was forced to dance. Poor *ayah* had become the source of entertainment in the male world, where "the girls are the diamonds! The men pay them to dance and sing…and to do things with their bodies. It's the world's oldest profession" (p. 240). The abductor marries her only when he comes to know that Lenny's mother has arranged to have her sent to Amritsar otherwise he "counted money while drunks, peddlers, sahibs, and cut-throats used her like a sewer" (p. 250). It hardly matters to the *ayah* whether her family will accept her or not but she will not remain with the captor.

Urvashi Butalia, too, gives a similar account of a Muslim girl, Zenab[41] who was abducted and sold to a Sikh man called Buta Singh. The girl did not accept him as her husband who has bought her as a 'chattel.' She rejected him and was restored to her relatives. Zenab, too, suffered from a serious trauma of abduction and rape that tormented her soul and shattered her life to pieces. Women were not only abducted but also raped at public places and in the presence of large gatherings. Sometimes relatives of the girls were forced to stand around while they were continuously raped.[42] And rape was sometimes followed by other atrocities as chopping of the breasts, and even death.

There is an astounding account of a parade of naked women in "Peshawar Express". [43] At one of the stations where the refugee train stops a crowd appears with the sound of English band to the accompaniment of cheering and clapping. It is really a ghastly scène that shudders one's conscience and is an evidence of man's lost human values. "In a minute, the crowd had surged over the railway platform, dancing and singing, villagers forming the vanguard, followed by a concourse of naked women ranging from old grannies to young virgins" (p. 211). These women were from the Hindu and Sikh communities. It was Wazirabad station where the Hindus and the Muslims had "celebrated Baisakhi together" for centuries. But now these unfortunate souls were celebrating the most "gruesome Baisakhi" in which the hair of the women was untied, their bodies were marked with wounds, yet they walked erect "as if the death had already cast its dark shadow on their naked bodies" (p. 211). The rival community had taken a sinister revenge upon them by humiliating the communities via women.

A brother is forced to strip his sister naked in "The City of Sorrow"[44] who, when threatened, "slowly, with great effort shaking hands, he reached for his sister's saree. The girl screamed and covered her face with her hands" (p. 86). Next time the same boy took revenge upon the man by forcing him to strip his wife naked. Ironically, the 'revenge' was taken. But it was a woman every time that had to pay for the insanity and communal frenzy of her man. A vivid account of how women were debased is given in "Lajwanti" where "the Uzbek buyer stood before rows of naked women and prodded them with fingers...The women, he rejected stood before him sobbing helplessly, clutching their garments and hiding their faces in shame."[45] All these loathsome incidents remind one of *Azadi* which too depicts a similar parade of naked women at Narowal, "It was the wholesome gathering," Arun had ever seen, "They were all stark naked. Their heads were completely shaven, so were their armpits. So were their pubic regions. Shorn off their body hair and clothes, they looked like the baby girls or like the bald embryos one sees presented in methylated spirt."[46] The descriptions of these atrocities and humiliating acts in literary texts are corroborated by the historical accounts, such as the one presented by Damyanti Sehgal:

> I was told that there was a nawab in Gujarat who would sit on his throne and the abducted girls would be paraded before him and he would choose the pretty ones. The ones who were young, he used to feel them, the older ones he would give away. The girls could not do anything, to protest, nothing. He would say give such and such in category no. 2 and the best ones, keep then in the Zenana.[47]

Train to Pakistan is also replete with blood curdling scenes including humiliation of women. Two incidents from the novel continue haunting the readers for days together. A newly wedded girl Sundri travels with her husband in the train which is stopped on the way. "She who had not really had a good look at Mansa Ram was shown her husband completely naked. They held him by the arms and legs and one man cut off his penis and gave it to her. The mob made love to her. She did not have to take off any of her bangles. They were all smashed as she lay on the road, being taken by one man and another and another.[48]

While violence through rape, abduction or beatings is visible and understandable, women who were victims of this violence were further subjected to a still more intolerable kind of violence that is equally strong and traumatic. The women who became pregnant as a result of rape had to suffer as mothers. Many abducted women when recovered were forced to abandon their children otherwise they were not accepted by their parents, as "the child born of mixed union was a constant reminder of the violation of the women, of the fact that she had sex with a man of the other religion."[49] So women were given a choice either to keep their children with them and stay in ashrams all their life or to give their children up for ever and stay with parents. During riots many innocent children were butchered by the rioters of other community or were killed by their own parents so that they should not deter their movement during their exodus. Urvashi Butalia gives a poignant and touching account where a Sikh man first did *ardas* and threw his six-month-old daughter into the fire and then said, 'bibis, our izzat is in danger, will we save our honour or own children.'[50] Numberless children were also abducted and female children were sold into prostitution later on. Numberless children got lost during riots. Whatever happened to the children, the invisible scars were also made on women's psyche because they had to bear the brunt of losing their children.

It is in "Pali"[51] by Bhisham Sahni that Kaushalya is unable to bear the trauma of losing her child, Pali who gets lost during their exodus to India. As a mother her condition is painful and miserable. Another baby at her breast was killed by rioters in the train. What else could be more distressing for a woman whose two children were lost? In India she kept on mourning all the time "as if she was on the verge of insanity" (p. 130). Nobody else could face and realize the trauma and anguish of a mother. "At the mention of children her condition would worsen; she would start trembling and sometimes she wailed in such a heart rending manner that even Manohar Lal [Her Husband] got jittery" (p. 130).

Similarly, Zenab the foster-mother of Pali suffers who looks after him as her own son and showers her maternal love upon him. Unfortunately for her when Pali is restored to his real parents, Zenab is very sad and depressed since she has brought up the child as her own. A bond of love was created between Pali and Zenab, which snapped leaving her numb. But there is a positive sign in the story that human values still sustain during bad times. First, Zenab protests against handing over the child but later on she resigns to her fate saying, "Take away the child. I do not want an unfortunate woman's curse fall upon me. How could I have known that you had lost both your children?" (p. 137). She suffers silently and the departure of the child inflicts invisible pain to her own being. Raj in "I Shall Live"[52] suffers similarly since she loses her children during the Partition as they are killed mercilessly. She looks after an abandoned child and showers her motherly love upon the child, Dilip. She develops a bond of love with Dilip. But his real parents turn up and Dilip is restored to them. Raj is left behind wailing for the child. Similarly, "The Abandoned Child"[53] is a story of a mother who has to abandon her infant girl whom she places under a tree to avoid the rioters. Her husband forces her to abandon the child so that the rioters may not find them in case the child cries out. But the mother remains a sufferer for a long period till the girl is restored to her after many years. Thus the Partition brought with it another kind of suffering for women whose children were lost or when they were forced to abandon their children.

II

INTRA-COMMUNITY VIOLENCE

During Partition or communal riots as discussed earlier gender differences get obliterated and women were also completely identified with their community. That is why violence is inflicted upon women to punish the rival community. In a way the violence perpetrated by the males of the other community is still not so damaging because it is seen as violence done by enemy and this type of violence takes place now and then only during class conflicts or social upheavals like the Partition. But the scars are much deeper and the pain much more terrifying when the violence is inflicted by one's own community. The suffering caused by inter-community violence may still heal in due course of time but the scars left by the violence inflicted by one's own community are hard to heal as there is no one to soothe their tortured souls. They are forced to remain in constant agony and trauma caused by the violence and the callous attitude of their own family members.

The stories discussed in this section are, "Lajwanti", "Exile", "Separated from the Flock", "Open It", "How many Pakistans?", "Where did She Belong?", "A Grave Turned Inside Out", "I am Game" and "A Visitor from Pakistan".

A woman who is subjected to beatings and bestial ill treatment in her own home finds portrayal in "Lajwanti."[54] Sunderlal, husband of Lajwanti used to often beat her before her abduction during the Partition. It was in a marriage party that she fell in love with Sunderlal, a city boy, and forgot what she herself used to sing, "I shall never marry a city boy/he wears boots and my back is slender..." (p. 56). The fact that husbands were expected "to beat" their wives was a part of their folk songs. After marriage Sunderlal had frequently "thrashed her because he didn't like the way she sat or looked, or the way she served food!" (p. 56). With the passage of time this village girl who was "slender" and "naïve" learned to work, to lift all kinds of heavy weights and even tolerate the beatings he would give her. He became increasingly cruel forgetting that "the patience of any human beings breaks" (p. 56). But Lajwanti never complained and instead she would laugh happily after even the severest beating if she saw a faint smile on Sunderlal's face. The condition of Lajwanti reveals how after marriage the woman becomes the property of the husband.[55] Even though society does not actually say that a man has the right to beat his wife, no one denies that he has the right to tame the woman he marries, or make her to bow to his will.

Lajwanti however undergoes a worse kind of trauma when she is recovered and restored after her abduction by a Muslim. She is unable to forget the trauma she faced when she was in

Pakistan. But another chapter of more intense pain and depression starts after the restoration as her husband, Sunderlal, starts treating her with a sort of suspicion and extra care to which she had never been habitual in the past. He addresses her as 'Devi' and with this address is changed the real self of Lajo.

Sunderlal feels that she had been happy with her abductor and fails to read the "signs of pain and humiliation in her face" (p. 64). He is unable to face his wife who had been abducted but he accepts her just to show the world that he has thrown open the doors of his heart and house. He has just "fulfilled his pledge" because he is the spokesman for the local committee for the rehabilitation of women and leads procession of fellow workers urging people to give a place in their "heart" and houses to the abducted women. This hypocritical attitude of Sunderlal adds more pain to Lajwanti's psyche.

Ironically, with her restoration to her husband Lajwanti loses her old self and identity. She faces identity crises in her life. Neither does she receive the Sunderlal of the past. She is also no more the earlier Lajo now. Her greatest longing is to cease lamenting for the past, to be accepted as a victim of historical circumstances, to be treated as a human being of flesh and blood. On the contrary Sunderlal starts treating her as a goddess that shatters her human self. She wishes be touched, to be embraced as a woman who is physically alive and longs for the generosity of love.[56]

The communication gap that has been created by the behaviour of Sunderlal devoids Lajwanti of expressing her suffering so that she can feel purged and "cleaned again." Had she been allowed to outpour her emotions and sufferings she had undergone, she would have been relieved from the mental pain, a burden which is difficult to carry for long. She is forced to keep silent since her husband shrinks away "from hearing her story" (p. 65). One must, at least, try to see the other side of silence that is more painful and may be more horrifying. Lajwanti's sorrows and emotions remain "locked up in her breast" (p. 65). Now she has realized that she will never get back her old self while she is apprehensive of the new life of a 'Devi'. She now longs for her old life of chastisement and beatings so that she can feel that her relationship with her husband is the same as before. She is now a "stranger" in her *own* house. Her husband has thrust upon her the life of an object that is "fragile" (p. 66) and will shatter at the slightest touch. She has returned home but has lost everything. Her husband has neither the heart to feel her agony nor the ears to hear her sobs. The Partition and its aftermath have played with her person. Her loss can never be compensated. She is left alone for ever and her life reveals the reality about women that women's lives are structured entirely around crises and struggles.[57]

The element of honour or 'izzat' is so dominant in "Lajwanti" that it not only inflicts violence on Lajwanti, the protagonist but also brings in its encompass many ill fated women like Lajwanti. Lajwanti's husband, Sunderlal is a member of a rehabilitation committee, which has a programme to rehabilitate the abducted women. The slogan of the committee is, "Honour them. Give them a place in your hearts" (p. 55). How tragic and sad! The honour for woman is to be *begged* and still it is not given to them. It seems nobody is ready to honour these ill-fated women willingly. In fact the idea of accepting back the abducted women is strongly opposed by the priests of Narain Baba's temple and by others like them who are orthodox and so-called 'good' people of society. Here Narain Baba is a representative of all those who support woman's subordination and emphasise the importance of 'honour' and 'chastity' in women. Undoubtedly, there are numberless Narain Babas in this world who block the way of women's peace, happiness and freedom by quoting social codes and examples from the past legends, and in fact blame women for any thing going wrong in society.

In "Lajwanti" too Narain Baba recites that section of *the Ramayana* in which a washerman, having thrown his wife out of his house, has said that he is not Raja Ram Chandra, who can take Sita back, even after she has lived with Ravana for years. Stung by the rebuke Ram Chandra orders Sita, who has been virtuous and faithful, out of his palace; even though she is pregnant at that time. And people like Narain Baba call it "Ram Rajya!" (p. 59) It is Ram Rajya for them because even the words of washerman are liked and respected in it. Does a Ram Rajya here mean shutting eyes to the violence against woman? What about those men who violate the chastity of women and who inflict the worst kind of violence upon them? What punishment is in store for them? Nothing, of course! They go scot-free. This type of Ram Rajya cannot be an ideal one rather it is spiteful. What is the difference, then, between a washerman's mentality and the mentality of Rama who is adored as God? Both are, of course, crippled mentally. Neither was Sita to blame for her abduction nor the women who fell victim to men's insanity during the Partition. They were innocent. It was Ravana and men like him who are to be blamed for the devastation done to women on the one hand and Rama and men like him who refused to honourably accept their wives, on the after hand.

The abducted women face humiliation even at the hands of their own men who refuse to recognise them when they are restored. Some even go to the extent of saying:

> Why didn't they die? Why didn't they take poison to preserve their virtue and houour? Why didn't they jump into a well? Cowards, clinging to life! Thousands of women in the past killed themselves to save their chastity!.... (p. 58).

So many women were sacrificed at the altar of self-defined social codes, which substituted 'death' for life for the abducted women. Ironically those women are held responsible for their plight and for tarnishing the 'community honour' rather than being admired for their "awesome strength", for the courage they have shown by facing hideous attacks made on them. Sadly they have chosen to carry on living in a world in which even their husbands refuse to "acknowledge them" (p. 58). Though Sunderlal has accepted his wife despite all opposition from Narain Baba and the likes, it is obvious that Lajwanti too falls a victim to the concept of honour laid down by the patriarchal set-up. When she is being brought from the police station by Sunderlal one of the men gathered there shouts, "We don't want these sluts... they were defiled by Muslims" (p. 64). It seems that Sunderlal also, like others, feels guilty to accept her in his home as she is polluted. She can never occupy a place in Sunderlal's heart. The so-called concept of 'izzat' has razed her life and rendered her alienated and broken for ever.

The narrator of "Exile"[58] also suffers from endless pain. Like Lajwanti she is also abducted and her tale of suffering is as poignant as that of Lajwanti. Lajwanti is a Hindu woman while the narrator of "Exile" is a Muslim abducted by a Sikh. This is enough to prove woman's predicament as her fate is the same everywhere irrespective of religion. Though Lajwanti is accepted by her husband after her abduction, she is devoid of that identity which she enjoyed before abduction and she feels alienated. The narrator of "Exile" feels pained because she is rejected by her 'own' brother and her own community. Her sorrows and pain remain buried deep in her heart. Though soldiers do come to her village to rescue her but she feels broken to see that her brother is not accompanying the soldiers. How can she go with strangers? She is tormented, shattered and depressed at the thought. Her condition is like that of Sita in exile who was abducted, rescued and finally rejected. Her predicament can well be felt if we keep in mind Sita's exile. The tragedy of the narrator is more intense as she has to accept her abductor's house as her home finally.

Memory of the past—those good old days in her home—keeps on haunting her and makes her feel sad and lonely. Gurpal, a Sikh, who killed her parents has abducted her and made her his wife. She has children from him. But she is not happy with him. She feels all alone since she cannot accept her abductor. For her "loneliness is hard to endure. Life is difficult" (p. 45). She is alone and lonely as her 'own' people are not with her. She had put faith in her brother but he does not come to rescue her. She says, "I know that a boat without oars sinks; that a boat can sink near the shore; that a simple wave can smash it. Unfortunately Bhai is not with me" (p. 43). She equates herself with a boat that drifts in water rudderless if it has no one to ply it. The realization of this fact intensifies her suffering. She shrinks within. Though Gurpal and children are with her, she is lonely and living in an "extraordinary emptiness and loneliness."[59] She becomes sad and says, "...in the wilderness of my house, I am like that lonely tree which neither blossoms nor bears fruit" (p. 42). She feels injured and there is no one who can share her sorrows. She is right in observing that one can never know "how much a wound hurts, until one is injured oneself" (p. 42). Her daughter, Munni, asks repeatedly about the whereabouts of her *mama.* She wants that like other children's *mamas* he should also visit her with gifts and sweets. Constant reminder and pestering by her daughter make her speechless and hurt her feelings and emotions. She realizes that this is a world where people are self-centered. Poignantly, the narrator thinks:

> After some time people find other things which give them support. Bhaiya's children must be as old as Munni. I am sure that whenever they ask about their *mama*, their parents don't have to either change the subject or direct the attention of the children" (p. 51).

There can be nothing more traumatic and miserable for her than the fact that the circumstances have forced her to live with her parents' murderer and the violator of her honour. Gurpal had killed her parents and dragged her to his house. His presence reminds her of the injuries done to her whole self. It is here that she sees herself as modern day Sita who has to suffer always in times of crises—the ancient and the repeated humiliation of woman by their *own* men.

Like Lajwanti the narrator of "Exile", too, feels a victim to the man-made concept of 'honour' or 'izzat'. She is a Muslim girl who had been loved by her brother; once she is abducted nobody cares for her. No body asks about her whereabouts as she is now a 'spoiled' one. This concept of chastity plays havoc with all the women whether one is a Hindu or a Muslim. It is perhaps because of the social codes that one feels humiliated and dishonoured to meet a 'spoiled' relative. The element of 'honour' is dominant here that deters her brother from facing her. She says, "When the army came to rescue me like a princess in a fairy-tale, I hid myself. How could I have gone with strangers? Why hadn't Bhaiya and Bhabhi come with them? I was angry with them. I have not forgiven them till this day" (p. 51). Her children are also a deterrent in the way of her reunion with her brother. Similarly, Hindu women were victims of similar tragedies during the Partition. Urvashi Butalia writes, "Where there were girls who were carrying children from Musalmaan men, their families were very reluctant to take them back."[60] The narrator sadly tells her daughter, "your mama never came in search of you, Munni. He never came to take me away. Who has the time to look for anybody?" (p. 51).

The element of 'honour' is so dominant in patriarchal society that the parents of the girls are always worried about their daughters not only during peacetime but also during social upheavals when danger is double—from outside as well as inside one's own community. The narrator's mother was also worried about her daughter during the Partition: "It is not our lives alone which are in danger. Our honour too is threatened. We have grown up girls...." (p. 48). Her anxiety to save the honour of the family had a cause because it was a time when "those who had once been ready to die for their mothers and sisters, now began to play cruel games with the honour of women" (p. 48).

How ironical it appears that society whose epic celebrates the defeat of evil every year has succumbed to evil. The story opens on the Dussehra day and is deliberately located in a sanctified context. But the modern Rama and Luxmana are greasy and tinsel crowned actors.[61] This enables the narrator to counter-pose the public remembrance of the acts of Rama, with those of her Sikh husband who now urges her to forget past, as well as, with those of her brother in Pakistan who refused to come to her rescue. The failure, thus, is not only of the Hindus and the Sikhs to remember that evil can only be defeated by one who has a firm grasp over righteousness, but also of her Muslim brothers who susspect her 'purity' and reject her.[62] Though a Muslim, the narrator draws upon the mythic tradition of the Hindus and so points to the fact that these myths are a common heritage of both the communities. Woman belonging to both the communities are equally subjected to persecution in one way or the other. She is subjected to humiliation in all the ages. It is clear that even in the past, cruelty and violence were often perpetrated on women in the name of preserving the social order through the ritual purity of the community.[63]

A similar account of woman's plight is found in *The River Churning*[64] where Sutara, around whom the whole piece revolves, is a sufferer of patriarchal hypocrisy regarding purity and honour of woman. The novel originally written in Bengali is one of the rare examples of Partition novel in Bengali written by a woman. The main focus of the novel is the possible rape of a Hindu girl in East Bengal and her subsequent marginalisation by her own community in post-Partition "secular", India. Jyotirmoyee, the novelist, presents the trauma of the adolescent girl, Sutara, who is a victim of socio-psychological norms as well as class-caste conflict.

It is during the Partition riots that Sutara's parents are butchered and her married sister disappears. The young and adolescent Sutara loses consciousness during her assault and molestation. She is the only surviving member of her family. She is looked after by a Muslim family. Though she struggles to "piece together" the nature of the outrage, the trials of Sutara do not end with the assault on her body or mind. Even more unbearable suffering is experienced by her in the form of indifference from her own family members. Her brothers do come to know about her survival and that she is living in Calcutta. Their response is lukewarm and rather indifferent. The cause behind this attitude of her brothers is quite simple. The brothers are "more concerned about their good name, the honour of the family" (p. 23) than they are about the fate of Sutara. She becomes the victim of social "morality" which emphasizes purity of woman. Urvashi Butalia is right when she observes, "'purity' of the woman was of much more importance within India, to Hindus and Sikhs—perhaps because the Hindu religion places greater emphasis on purity."[65] Sutara becomes the victim of social codes and is abandoned by her family. She is now ostracized and treated like an untouchable. One of the members of her family says:

> ...she has spent so many days in a Muslim household, six long months. What is left of her caste, you tell me! It was good of you to bring her over, that is alright. But keep her away from household work as you would a low caste *hadi* or *Bagdi*. Look at what she is doing, polluting everything. Who knows what she has done, the kind of food she has eaten there! (p. 36).

Sutara's only fault is that she was forced to stay with another community. Though the novelist does not hint that Sutara has been raped even then her family treats her as an outcast only because she stayed with the Muslim who rather saved her and gave her shelter. But she has to pay the price for staying away from her family. It is wrong, of course, in the eyes of man in patriarchy. "Sita was exiled for the same offence" (p. 43). Did king Janak come to the aid of Sita, his daughter? "Even parents refuse to take back such girls" (p. 43). Like Sutara numberless women fell victim to this attitude of their families during the Partition. For several of those who did allow themselves to be 'rescued' or who were forcibly 'recovered', there was another trauma to face. Their families, who had earlier filed reports and urged the government to recover their women, were now no longer willing to take them back.[66] Perhaps the women were aware of this over emphasis on 'chastity' or 'virtue' and the mental attitude of their men hence some of them refused to go back to their families. One of the abducted women says, "Why should I return, why are you particular to take me to India? What is left in me now of religion or chastity?" and another said, "I have lost my husband and have now gone for another. You want me to go to India where I have got nobody and, of course, you do not expect me to change husband every day."[67]

Ipso facto, we are living in a very paradoxical state. Daughters and wives are guarded very carefully in time of upheaval but once they fall into the hands of enemy the women undergo not only the trauma of abduction or rape but even the doors of their own houses are closed for them leaving them totally devoid of any solace or comfort. One of the characters in *The River Churning* confirms the fact, "This is an old story. The powerful fight among themselves, the weak and the insignificant have to suffer. Women have always been a commodity, even in our society. We at least keep the girl from going astray but the exploited girls in the other communities are forced to take to streets" (p. 26). Sutara suffers also because she is now treated as an "outsider" (p. 35). Amulya Babu's sister says in the novel, "Yes, of course, we Hindus have some code of daily rituals. It does not allow such a girl to be accepted back into the family" (p. 42). Sutara's presence can "pollute" (p. 44) the entire family since she is defiled. As a solution Sutara is sent to a boarding house and that is the way to keep her at a distance. Hence, she is devoid of love and care that would have given her solace and would have unburdened her of the trauma she had faced. But she is thrown into a life of loneliness. The families of such women had made their adjustment to their absence, "Why should they now have to readjust, make new space, and take in a person who had become 'polluted'? [68]

This attitude towards woman regarding her chastity is a deep rooted and well-established practice in our society. Perhaps the parents of the narrator of "Exile", or of Sutara or Lajwanti would have disowned them had they been alive at that time. This has been the plight of women since the time of Ambe of the *Mahabharata* and Sita of the *Ramayana*. Society has remained the same since the time of these epics. There is no denying the fact that history repeats itself. Even Gandhi and Nehru were aware of these facts who had to issue repeated appeals to people assuring them that abducted women still remained 'pure'.[69] They, time and again, urged people to give due place to the abducted women.

Not only this, many women and girls were killed or forced to commit suicide to save the "honour" of family or community which would have been lost had they fallen into the hands of the other community. Even girl infants were killed in cold blood. There is an account of such honour killings in various short stories and novels. As depicted in "An Unwritten Epic" when the riots broke out, all the Muslim women of the Quadirpur settlement were collected inside the haveli, and "each women had been clearly told what her duty required her to do in an eventuality, a few nooses had also been set up for good measure."[70] Whether a Muslim, a Hindu or a Sikh, woman is forced to die or even killed mercilessly in order to save her 'honour'. Similar is the predicament of the Sikh women in *Tamas* who jumps into a well one by one to save their honour lest they should fall in the hands of the Muslims.[71] In *The River Churning*, too, Sutara's mother jumps into the pond to save her honour (p. 8).

Urvashi Butalia has also given an account of such honour killings in her book, *The Other Side of Silence*. She has herself recorded these accounts after meeting the persons who have witnessed the Partition upheaval. In one of the accounts she writes about one Mangal Singh and his brother who killed the women and children of their family. They killed seventeen persons in all. Mangal Singh himself tells Butalia, "After leaving home we had to cross the surrounding boundary of water.... And we were many family members, several women and children who would not have been able to cross the water, to survive the flight So we killed—they became martyrs—seventeen of our family members, seventeen lives...."[72]

If Lajwanti is a victim of physical violence in the Hindu community, in the other community Gulam Ali's wife, in "Separated from the Flock",[73] is a similar victim of violence. It was after the Partition that she had to part from her parents in India. Now in Pakistan her greatest desire is to see her own land and relatives in India. But her husband negates this desire of her not because there is some difficulty in it. He works with a senior police officer who can get a permit very easily, but he does not want to spend money on his wife. He himself says to his officer, "I am not concerned about the permit, Sahib. It's not the only problem a man faces in his life, Sahib! It's merely a *whim*—this visit to India. To satisfy that whim, I'll have to waste four to five hundred rupees" (p. 4). Like the most wives the wife here too is a victim of double standards. Gulam Ali himself visits his parents "thrice a year" (p. 6) at Karachi that is at the same distance from Lahore as Hardoi is in India. He satisfies his urge to meet his parents but his wife's desire to meet her parents are merely brushed aside and termed as a "whim".

Another woman, Vaziruddin's wife is also subjected to the same kind of violence and male power. She sells her earrings to get the permit so that she may meet her parents in India. But Vaziruddin steals her permit at night and burns it (p. 4). When his wife accuses him the next day he picks up his stick and goes after her shouting, "Haramzadi, will your mother cook for me while you are away for three or four months" (p. 4). The wishes of a woman are trampled upon most callously as man cannot bear the slightest inconvenience to himself.

Gulam Ali's wife is helpless. She sheds her "last tears for her home and for her dreams" (p. 17). She comes to know that the man has clipped her wings and she should not beat her "wings about in vain." She is merely a puppet in the hands of her husband, his private property, a sexual object. And it is not a new phenomenon. Throughout history women have been viewed as sexual objects. As Karl Marx had said, "Marriage... is... a form of exclusive private property."[74] Let alone the physical violence both the women in the story are also victims of psychological violence. By devoiding them of meeting their 'own' people their husbands inflict pain to their psyche, which they have to bear helplessly.

"Open It"[75] is a horrifying story that suggests that the inhumanity of the Partition had so obliterated the moral realm that there was nothing left to retrieve and nothing to hope for. People had so demeaned themselves that they could only act as beasts.[76] Sirrajudin, a Muslim man leaves India following the Partition riots. He goes to Pakistan but on the way his wife is killed and his young and beautiful daughter, Sakina, is abducted and raped. Sirrajudin is shattered. He takes shelter in a refugee camp where he entrusts eight social workers of his own community with the job of finding out the girl and to bring her to him. They assure him, but they themselves pick up the girl and all of them rape her and throw her away as if she is a useless thing. Her own men inflict violence on her in the form of rape. Later she is brought to the doctor in the camp. A very tragic and poignant thing happens there. When the doctor says, "Open the window", the girl stirs a little and "she moved her hand! Painfully towards the cord holding the salwar" and slowly "pulled her salwar down" (p. 72). The doctor and her father watch her in horror. Yet her father is happy that she is "alive".

Sakina, thus, suffers at the hands of her own men. Poor girl is punished for no fault of her own. The physical assault on her body shreds her life into pieces at such a tender age.

Bano's fate is different from other women's as she is a sufferer of the double-edged sword. In "How Many Pakistans?"[77] Bano's wishes are trampled upon. She is not allowed to marry the narrator, Mangal, for the simple reason that he is a Hindu. The Partition raises insurmountable walls between the lovers. Her community does not allow her to have a relationship with a Hindu since it can cause communal riots, as if the riots broke out in the past only because some Mangal loved Bano. Tradition has always been against woman whether she is a Hindu or a Muslim. The males still have the prerogative to act according to their wishes. During the Partition men abducted the women of other religions or communities. How ironical it is! A man can abduct a woman of the other religion and can marry her forcibly. She becomes his wife but he would not allow his own daughters to choose a spouse belonging to the other religion. Mangal is forced to flee from the village under the pretext that his presence may cause riots in the village, as if riots in 1947 broke out only because of Mangal's relationship with Bano. Bano is married to a Muslim man, Muneer against her wishes. She has to lose her child who is mercilessly butchered during riots. After some time Muneer forces her to go with him to Bombay and when she refuses he trembles with anger and screams, "Do what you like. Sleep with anyone you want to. Find someone to give you a child" (p. 187). Muneer is a drunkard and a shirker who cannot earn livelihood for his family. He sells his blood in Bombay. Man can go to any extent to fulfil his desires. He can sell his wife, as if she is a cattle, in the men's market where her body is demanded most. Bano, too, becomes the victim of male violence and her husband's ruthlessness. Poor Bano is forcibly shoved into prostitution. By chance Mangal visits a brothel one day where he is welcomed by a prostitute who asks, "Is there anyone else?" (p. 187). Mangal is stunned to find out that the prostitute is no other than Bano herself. She truly becomes a victim of male-violence, traditions and hollow social strictures, which are only made for women. It is man's duty to work to protect and to provide for daily needs of his wife and children. Ironically, Bano is sold in the market to provide for the needs of her husband.

Munni is a sufferer right from her birth in Suraiya Quasim's story "Where Did She Belong?"[78] It is right after her birth that she is abandoned by her parents and is left halfway between a mosque and a temple. It is difficult to decide to which religion she belongs. A woman owner of a brothel picks her up and brings her home. She is saved not out of compassion or love for the innocent girl but because the woman plans to earn money out of Munni when she will grow up. With the passage of time Munni grows up and she is pushed into the loathsome business of prostitution. She is the "chief source of income" (p.110) for her 'saviour'. It is the fate of woman in general that nobody helps her without getting something in return. Anyone can buy Munni for the night:

> And possessing her was not difficult—anyone could possess her she lived to be possessed—of course, at a price. Her body was for sale" (p. 109).

Though Munni does not like to do all this but she is forced into the obnoxious act of selling her body. When she refuses to sell her body the old woman gives her a good thrashing and abuses her. Here Munni becomes a victim at the hands of a woman of her own community. The woman whom Munni calls 'Ma'(mother) grows angry and says:

> You eat during the day what you earn at night and you've got to have something to eat if you want to stay alive" (p. 111).

The old woman speaks as if women of the whole world are eating by selling 'themselves'. But the tragedy with Munni is that she "satisfies" as many customers as she can. Her chastity has become a plaything of male society, "The elite of the society had already robbed her of the only precious thing she had ever possessed" (p. 112).

Rajkamal and Zafar Khan are two regular customers of Munni Bai.Rajkamal pretends to love her and promises that he shall "abide by her through thick and thin" (p. 115). On the other hand Zafar Khan claims the same. What is more astonishing as well as detesting is that both the men are married. Are they not doing injustice to their wives by not giving them due love and care? Rajkamal is attached to his wife not because he loves her but only because she belongs to very rich parents and "without whose benefictions he would be out on the streets begging. He has to divide his passion between Munni Bai and his wife" (p. 113). On the contrary Zafar Khan is a poor man. The money he is spending at Munni Bai must be spent at his home on his wife. Both the men pretend to love Munni Bai. But it is her beauty and their lust that draws them to her.

Riots take place and Pakistan is created. Since the owner of the brothel is supposed to be a Hindu, all of them are forced to quit Pakistan for India. Munni Bai is sure that her lovers will come to save her. But they do not turn up which exposes the hypocrisy of men in general. This attitude of both the men gives invisible scars to her mind. Helplessly, she leaves Pakistan for India without any of her 'lovers' with her.

In India they start a new brothel where they 'sell' their bodies. The fate of woman remains the same everywhere. She gets nothing but violence. During the Partition women lost everything and received nothing except violence, humiliation and wounded psyche. That is why Munni Bai asks innocently, "Ma, the Muslims asked for Pakistan and they got it. The Hindus wanted to see the backs of the Muslims and they got Hindustan and are happy. We asked for nothing. Why, then, have we had to suffer much?" (p. 116) These women asked for nothing but got deception, injured souls, hypocrisy and anguish of the worst kind, which they will have to live with for ever.

Even more poignant and gruesome is the story of Ayesha in "A Grave Turned Inside Out"[79] as she is the worst sufferer of intra-community violence. She is not only raped by the men of her 'own' community but she also dies a sad and shameful death. She is a Muslim whose husband, Abdul Waheed gets killed by another Muslim goonda, Hussan Ullah when Waheed tries to stop him from raping his wife's friend Ameena. Ameena is also a victim of intra-community violence in a sense that she, too, falls prey to a member of her own community. Hassan had earlier a wish to possess her as he loves her but she refuses to have any relationship with him. He grows revengeful towards her. He strips her naked, drags her out and throws her in the jeep. Waheed fails to save Ameena, instead he dies while saving her. His 13-year old daughter Razia is abducted. Thus Waheed's wife Ayesha loses both—her husband as well as her daughter at the hands of Muslims.

But this is not the end of Ayesha's suffering and trauma. Ameena's husband, Nurúl now takes the responsibility of 'helping' Ayesha. He feels guilty for Ayesha's troubles since her husband has died in saving Nurul's wife. Ayesha trusts Nurul like a "brother" (p. 143) because they have been neighbours. Ironically, Nurul has a selfish end to fulfil. In the garb of a helping man there is a wolf hidden in Nurul. He wishes to exploit her. He takes her to Karachi. He lies to her that he has safely sent her daughter to Pakistan. Poor Ayesha gets ready to go with him in the hope of seeing her daughter. At one point she tries to commit suicide but Nurul stops her from doing so in the name of her daughter. But once she boards the plane with him to go to Karachi, his behaviour completely changes. He becomes rude and abusive, "Shut up, you bitch, down on earth you used to beg for death and now that you have a chance of embracing death, you lost your nerve…!" (p. 143).

Ayesha finally arrives in Karachi, after a long detour through Kathmandu, accompanied by 'her new husband'[80] whose real plans are to use her as a prostitute. Immediately afterwards, she is raped by the goons who supervise the slums for Bihari migrants from East Pakistan. Here, Ayesha is again a victim of physical violence inflicted by the Muslim brethren who make "a grasp for the land of her body" (p. 151). Ayesha keeps crying for help but no men or women of the settlement help her and when one man tries to come forward for her help, his wife begs him not to help her saying, "Ayesha is already a widow—why do you want us also to became widows…?" (151)

Poor Ayesha dies then and their and her hut becomes her graveyard. Ayesha is killed and buried in the land where she hoped to find her daughter and a home.

Like Ayesha is the fate of Afroj's mother in "I am Game"[81] whose emotions are exploited by the person whom she treats like a brother. But Ayesha and Afroj's mother are victims of the same male lust for money—of the men who want to earn money through women's body. They suffer intra-community violence since both the women are helped by men of their community only to be exploited. Ironically, both are exploited by the persons whom they trust. They came forward to help these women not because they are compassionate or good people but because they have 'big' plans in their dirty minds to use these innocent women as prostitutes.

Afroj's mother has lost her husband in an accident. Now she is thrown at the mercy of others. Besides, the creation of East Pakistan adds to her misery. Afroj's mother has to spend a night in a refugee camp with her daughter in "starvation". They become aliens in their own country. They spend the night in the camp where women are not "above trading their bodies to come by some money" (p. 144).

Majid, her cousin, appears a 'godsend' to help her but "there is no knowing a man" (p. 148). She fails to realize that this male-dominated society is never ready to help the fellow human beings particularly women, without getting anything in return. Afroj's mother is worried because Afroj is growing fast. She is worried because for a woman it is not easy to find out a suitable match for her daughter, since she is traditionally taught dependency on man. Afroj's mother is "tired of the hectic life" (p. 147). Her loneliness is "so intense that she cannot even hear her own voice." She feels entombed in the sprawling rubble of her own existence.

She feels that Majid can help her. He has some "big plans" and "ideas" for Afroj, the young and beautiful girl. But, ironically, he will help her not by finding a suitable match for her but by finding a rich customer for her. Any rich person is ready to "shell out any amount of money" (p. 148) for her only for a night. What else can be more painful, traumatic and awesome to the mother of a daughter on whom "a price" is being "tagged on her youth." Poor mother! She feels "darkness creeping upon her" (p. 149). Majid by offering his plans, is surely "blazing forth red hot lava" (p. 148) before her. But a mother can never bear such humiliation and shame. She says:

> I ... I... never expected this from you of all persons.... You have been like a snake in the grass. I don't want your help. I don't want your money. You evil minded man, get out of my sight! (p. 149).

Unfortunately, woman's fate is to bend and break. How long can she remain alone and without help? Afroj is stopped from going to school. Who will pay her fee? How can she live without food? A mother can remain hungry but she can never see her child famished and dying of starvation. It pains her and she dies inch by inch seeing her child hungry. She has to strike a compromise. She sets out to see Majid wherever he is. When she meets him she tells him in a painful voicc:

> If it concerned me alone, I would have certainty committed suicide without a moment's thought. But I have also to take my daughter into account.... The other day you opened the door of hell for me. I am ready to enter it. Go and fix up with anyone you can find for fifty or a hundred or any amount you can pin him down for" (p. 150).

The mother gets ready to sell herself for the sake of the child and she is forced to enter into this vicious and immoral profession by no other than her own co-religionist—her own relative. She feels broken and desperately tells him," I don't want a customer for Afroj ...I want one for myself. I'm game!" (p. 150).

Saraswati, the protagonist of "A Visitor from Pakistan"[82] faces a dilemma created solely by the Partition. She is separated from her husband, Baldev, following the Partition riots and Baldev is reported to be killed. Saraswati and her parents are rescued by Sunderdas who marries Saraswati and she has, two children from him. Though she has struck a compromise in her life yet she is presently happy with Sunderdas and her children.

The wheel of life takes a new turn when Baldev appears before her bringing a sort of storm in the life of Saraswati. She is surprised to see him alive and she is in fix as to what to do. It is somewhat natural that she cannot ignore the presence of a person who once was her husband. After all she is a human being made of flesh and blood and she, too, has emotions and feelings. She is unable to decide whom to choose—Baldev or Sunderdas. She finds herself in a very awkward situation. When her mother sees her standing before Baldev she pounces upon her, "Why are you sitting here? Have you no shame? Go in at once?" (p. 182). Saraswati feels "hurt and humiliated." What is her fault? Is she not a human being? Is it a sin to stand before a man who had once been her husband? Woman's life is really replete with predicaments. She is held responsible for the sufferings in the house. Saraswati's mother tells her that "death is the only solution left!" (p. 182). It is her tragedy that she had to accept a person who had once been an arch rival of her husband, Baldev and who always felt jealous of Baldev.

Saraswati cries out bitterly and does not know what to do. She is a victim of circumstances which have marked her life with pain. Though Baldev returns to Pakistan without her but the dilemma in the life of Saraswati remains unsolved. Her scars remain unhealed and her agony is intensified after she knows that her husband is alive.

Hence the women of Muslim, Hindu and Sikh communities fell prey to both inter-community and intra-community violence during the Partition. The short stories and novels are directed against the dual control exercised by patriarchy. The riot victim women are hit twice by patriarchy: firstly by the male members of the 'other' community who establish their own identity by exercising their conquest over these women's bodies, secondly by her 'own' community which invokes compulsions of ritual purity to exclude them from the ritually pure domains of hearth and marriage, and drinking water, not to talk of the violence inflicted by lustful callous men of their own communities.

NOTES

1. All four sociologists have been quoted by Ram Ahuja in *Social Problems in India* (1994; rpt, New Delhi: Rawat Publications, 2001), pp. 243-44.
2. Quoted by Bela Rani Sharma, *Women: Marriage, Family and Divorce* (Jaipur: Mangaldeep Publications, 1997), p. 91.
3. Erich Fromn, *The Anatomy of Human Destructiveness* (1973; rpt, Harmondsworth: Penguin, 1977), p. 62.
4. S. Krishnaswamy, "Female Infanticide in Contemporary India: A Case Study of Kallars in Tamil Nadu", in Rehana Ghadially (ed.), *Women in Indian Society* (New Delhi: Sage Publications, 1988), p.188.
5. Raman Mohan, "Healing the Blisters of Domestic Violence", *The Tribune*, March 3, 2002, p.20.
6. Honore de Balzac quoted by Rosemarie Tong, *Feminist Thought: A Comprehensive Introduction* (Boulder: West view Press, 1989), p.206.
7. Bela Rani Sharma, *Women: Marriage, Family and Divorce*, p. 54.
8. Sohaila Abdulali, "Rape in India: An Empirical Picture" in Rehana Ghadially, *Women in Indian Society*, p. 201.
9. Ibid., p. 196.
10. Ibid., p. 201.
11. Sonia Bathla, *Women, Democracy and the Media* (New Delhi: Sage Publications, 1998), p. 58.
12. Bela Rani Sharma, *Women: Marriage, Family and Divorce*, p. 117.
13. Ibid., p. 101.
14. Ramnika Jalali, *Indian Women in Smritis* (Jammu: Vinod Publishers, 1994), p. 3.
15. Recently there were frequent editorials (I forgot to note the dates) and news in some newspapers mentioning how a woman had to undergo several ordeals to prove her chastity, by holding a hot metal rod, only for the simple reason that she had visited Vaishno Devi shrine with her female friends and also spent a night there. On returning from the shrine she was chastised time and again since she had left the house without the consent of her husband.
16. Vidya Bhusan and D.R. Sachdeva, *An Introduction to Sociology* (Allahbad: Kitab Mehal, 1994), p. 680.

17. Ibid., p. 681.
18. Ibid., p. 687.
19. M.K. Gandhi, *India of My Dreams*, compiled by R.K. Prabhu (Ahmedabad: Navjivan Publishing House, 1962), p. 224.
20. P. Thomas, *Indian Women Through Ages* (London: Asia Publishing House, 1964), p.183. He writes, "Sita, whose greatness lies in the annihilation her individuality, in a paragon of feminine perfection, from the time of Brahamanic ideal of wifehood was established, and has been held as an example to be followed by Hindu women, down the centuries to the present day."
21. K. Jayawardena, *Feminism and Nationalism in the Third World* (London: Zed Books, 1986), p. 96.
22. Urvashi Butalia, *The Other Side of Silence* (New Delhi: Viking, 1998), p. 145.
23. Ibid., p. 102.
24. Ibid., p. 95.
25. Ibid., p. 85.
26. Ibid., p. 100.
27. D.A. Low and Howard Brasted, ed. *Freedom, Trauma, Continuities: Northern India and Independence* (New Delhi: Sage Publications, 1998), p. 57.
28. Satya M. Rai, "Partition and Women: The case of Punjab" in *The Partition in Retrospect* ed. Amrik Singh (New Delhi: Anamika Publishers, 2000) p. 191.
29. Anders Bjorn Hansen, *Partition and Genocide: Manifestation of Violence in Punjab, 1937-1947* (New Delhi: India Research Press, 2002), p. 162.
30. Quoted in Low and Brasted, *Freedom, Trauma, Continuities: Northern India and Independence*, p. 57.
31. Kirpal Singh, *The Partition of Punjab* (Patiala University, 1972), p. 154.
32. Quoted in Butalia, *The Other Side of Silence*, p. 112.
33. Shakuntala Narasimhan, "Saying a firm no to war", *The Tribune*, October 28, 2001, p. 20.
34. Saadat Hasan Manto, "Cold Meat", trans. and ed. Alok Bhalla in *Stories About the Partition of India*, Vol. I (New Delhi: Harper Collins, 1994). All subsequent references to the story are to this edition and have been incorporate in the text.
35. Saadat Hasan Manto, "Open It", trans. and ed. Alok Bhalla in *Stories About the Partition of India,* Vol. II. (New Delhi:

Harper Collins, 1994). All subsequent references to the story are to this edition and have been incorporated in the text.

36. Kartar Singh Duggal, "Kulsum", trans. Vishwamitter Adil and Alok Bhalla in *Stories About the Partition of India*, Vol. II, ed. Alok Bhalla (New Delhi: Harper Collins, 1994). All subsequent references to the story are to this edition and have been incorporated in the text.
37. Hansen, *Partition and Genocide: Manifestation of Violence in Punjab, 1937-1947*, p. 94.
38. Jamila Hashmi, "Exile", trans. and ed. Alok Bhalla in *Stories About the Partition of India*, Vol. I. (New Delhi: Harper Collins, 1994), All subsequent references to the story are to this edition and have been incorporated in the text.
39. Rajinder Singh Bedi, "Lajwanti", trans. and ed. Alok Bhalla in *Stories About the Partition of India*, Vol. I. (New Delhi: Harper Collins, 1994). All subsequent references to the story are to this edition and have been incorporated in the text.
40. Bapsi Sidhwa, *Ice Candy Man* (New Delhi: Penguin Books, 1989). All subsequent references to the novel are to this edition and have been incorporated in the text.
41. Butalia, *The Other Side of Silence*, p. 96, for detail see pp. 96-99.
42. Hansen, *Partition and Genocide: Manifestation of Violence in Punjab, 1937-1947*, pp. 161-62.
43. Krishna Chander, "Peshawar Express", trans. Jai Rattan in *Stories About the Partition of India*, Vol. III, ed. Alok Bhalla (New Delhi: Harper Collins, 1994) p. 211.
44. Intizar Husain, "The City of Sorrow", trans. Alok Bhalla and Vishwamitter Adil in *Stories About the Partition of India*, Vol. II, ed. Alok Bhalla (New Delhi: Harper Collin, 1994), p. 86.
45. Rajinder Singh Bedi, "Lajwanti" in *Stories About the Partition of India*, Vol. I, p.63.
46. Chaman Nahal, *Azadi* (1979; rpt. New Delhi: Orient Paperbacks, 1998), pp. 296.
47. Quoted in Butalia, *The Other Side of Silence*, p.118.
48. Khushwant Singh, *Train to Pakistan* (New Delhi: The Book International, 1989), p.177.
49. Butalia, *The Other Side of Silence*, p. 121.
50. Ibid., p. 191.
51. Bhisham Sahni, "Pali", trans. Jai Rattan in *Stories About the*

Partition of India, Vol. III, ed. Alok Bhalla (New Delhi: Harper Collins, 1994). All subsequent references to the story are from this edition and have been incorporated in the text.

52. Vishnu Prabhakar, "I Shall Live", trans. and ed. Alok Bhalla in *Stories About the Partition of India* Vol. II (New Delhi: Harper Collins, 1994), pp. 207-218.
53. Gurmukh Singh, "The Abandoned Child", trans. B.M. Sagar and Alok Bhalla in *Stories About the Partition of India,* Vol. III. ed. Alok Bhalla (New Delhi: Harper Collins, 1994), pp. 181-190.
54. Rajinder Singh Bedi, "Lajwanti" in *Stories About the Partition of India*, Vol. I, p. 63.
55. Flevia, "Violence in the Family: Wife Beating" in Rehana Ghadially, ed. *Woman in Indian Society* (New Delhi: Sage Publications, 1988), p. 154.
56. Alok Bhalla, "Introduction" in *Stories About the Partition of India*. Vol. I. (New Delhi: Harper Collins, 1994), pp. XXV-VI.
57. Jyotirmayee Devi, "Beginnings", trans. Rimli Bhattacharya in *The River Churning* (New Delhi: Kali for Women, 1995), p. VIII.
58. Jamila Hashmi, "Exile", trans. and ed. Alok Bhalla in *Stories About the Partition of India,* Vol. I.
59. Butalia, *The Other Side of Silence*, p. 122.
60. Ibid.
61. Bhalla, "Introduction" in *Stories About the Partition of India*. Vol.I., p. XXIV.
62. Ibid.
63. Jyotirmoyee Devi, *The River Churning* , p. XXVI.
64. Jyotirmoyee Devi, *The River Churning,* trans. Enakshi Chatterjee (New Delhi: Kali for Women, 1995), All subsequent references to the novel are to this edition and have been incorporated in the text.
65. Butalia, *The Other Side of Silence*, p. 121.
66. Ibid., p. 120.
67. Kirpal Singh, *The Partition of Punjab*, p. 117.
68. Butalia, *The Other Side of Silence*, p. 123.
69. Ibid., p. 121.
70. Intizar Husain, "An Unwritten Epic",trans. Lesie A. Fleming and Mommad Umar Memon in *Stories About the Partition of India.* Vol. III, ed. Alok Bhalla (New Delhi: Harper Collins, 1994), p. 61.

71. Bhisham Sahni, *Tamas*, trans. Jai Rattan (New Delhi: Penguin Books, 1988), p. 199.
72. Butalia, *The Other Side of Silence*, p. 147.
73. Syed Mohammad Ashraf, "Separated from the Flock" trans. Vishwamitter Adil and Alok Bhalla in *Stories About the Partition of India*, Vol. I, ed. Alok Bhalla (New Delhi: Harper Collins: 1994). All subsequent references to the story are from this edition and have been incorporated in the text.
74. Quoted in Juliet Mitchell, *Women's Estate* (New York: Vintage Books, 1973), p. 110.
75. Saadat Hassan Manto, "Open It", trans.and ed. Alok Bhalla in *Stories About the Partition of India*, Vol. II (New Delhi: Harper Collins, 1994). All subsequent references to the story are to this edition and have been incorporated in the text.
76. Alok Bhalla, "Introduction" in *Stories About the Partition of India*. p. XXI.
77. Kamleshwar, "How Many Pakistans?" trans. Vishwamitter Adil and Alok Bhalla in *Stories About the Partition of India* Vol. II, ed. Alok Bhalla (New Delhi: Harper Collins, 1994). All subsequent references to the story are to this edition and have been incorporated in the text.
78. Suraiya Quasim, "Where did she Belong?" Trans. Vishwamitter Adil and Alok Bhalla in *Stories About the Partition of India*, Vol. II, ed. Alok Bhalla (New Delhi: Harper Collins, 1994). All subsequent references to the story are to this edition and have been incorporated in the text.
79. Ibrahim Jalees, "A Grave Turned Inside Out", trans. Vishwamitter Adil and Alok Bhalla in *Stories About the Partition of India*. Vol. II, ed. Alok Bhalla (New Delhi: Harper Collins, 1994). All subsequent references to the story are to this edition and have been incorporated in the text.
80. Alok Bhalla, "Introduction" in "*Stories About the Partition of India*. p. XIII.
81. Sultan Jamil Nasim, "I am Game", trans. Jai rattan in *Stories About the Partition of India*. Vol. III, ed. Alok Bhalla (New Delhi: Harper Collins, 1994). All subsequent references to the story are to this edition and have been incorporated in the text.
82. Ram Lal, "A Visitor from Pakistan", trans. And ed. Alok Bhalla in *Stories About the Partition of India*. Vol. I (New Delhi: Harper Collins, 1994). All subsequent references to the story are to this edition and have been incorporated in the tex.

5
Beyond the Communal Divide: Survival of Human Values

The Partition of India, as discussed in the previous chapters, was really a turbulent and traumatic period in the history of the sub-continent when the worst passions were aroused in the name of religion. Freedom, the long cherished dream of Indian masses, turned into a bloody nightmare. What followed the Partition was so violent that, "It rudely shocked the conscience of the civilized people all the world over, and made them shudder with anguish and dismay at man's wolfish cruelty to man in the name of religion."[1] It was a period when all—young and old, children and women, the Hindus and the Muslims—fell prey to communal insanity. The crimes against mankind were so ghastly that it seemed that the world that lay before us:

> Hath really neither joy, nor love, nor light,
> Nor certitude, nor peace, nor help for pain.[2]

People lost faith in one another giving place to hatred and malevolence. A split in the amicable relationships appeared. People were forced to flee from their houses. They had to take refuge on the other side where their co-religionists lived. It appeared as if goodness had been eclipsed altogether and there was rule of evil and wickedness. The unbearable existential trauma is emotionally reflected through various short stories at length in the previous chapters.

Though human values were hit hard on the anvil of communal fury yet there is no denying the fact that goodness still survived giving place to hope and optimism. Even after so much bloodshed, arson, rapes, abductions and lootings good emerged like the mythical bird phoenix from its ashes and showed a ray of hope. We can't hope for an ideal world of Shakespearean comedies and we cannot escape from the worldly realities. We have to face them with courage. The earth, despite many evils and sorrows, seems a good and suitable place to live even to a pessimist poet like Robert Frost who says:

> Earth is the right place for love
> I do not know where it is likely to go better.[3]

Even after large scale bloodshed and a sense of insecurity the Muslims and the Hindus gave a show of amity and brotherhood. Mohammad Mujeeb, the vice-chancellor of Delhi's Jamia Millia Islamia, had a strange experience in Bihar soon after the orgy of violence had taken a heavy toll of human lives. He visited the grave of a Sufi saint, on the bank of river Ganges, after peace was restored. He found that the Muslims living in the shrine had left. Soon a group of the Hindu women turned up and performed the same rituals that their ancestors had observed earlier. It appeared as if nothing had happened that affected their sentiments of respect for the tomb of a Muslim saint.[4] On the other hand Phillips Talbot was struck by the expression of Hindu-Muslim cordiality during the Independence celebrations:

> ... at the climax of Independence celebrations this week, Hindus and Muslims mixed together freely. Many Hindus visited mosques on the 18th and distributed sweets to Muslims who were observing their ld festival.... Similarly, in Delhi and Bombay I saw Hindus and Muslims playing hand in hand.[5]

Even today there are many on both sides of the border who do think that the Partition had been a blunder. The people who agitated for the Partition with violence and who did not feel hesitate to massacre their fellow human beings are today the most troubled. The leader of 'Mohajirs' says that Partition was the biggest mistake in history. Even the man who worked to achieve Pakistan, Mohammad Ali Jinnah, saw in his last moments that the Partition of India was a tragedy.[6]

Though the short stories vividly reveal one of the darkest eras in the history of the sub-continent there are also many which reveal the best in man. Despite the terrible consequences of the Partition they confirm that human values can never die. Though the short stories taken for study are full of trauma and pain suffered by the victims of the Partition yet their final impression is not one of nihilism or pessimism. The stories do not lead to despair. Rather they affirm our faith in life. They convey a message that death is not the end of life. Individuals may die but life endures, it continues. There were many whose dear ones died but life, for them, continued. Despite sorrows and the worst kind of traumas the victims craved for life. They wanted to forget every sorrow and pain. They had a longing for winning the war against heavy odds. The life-force in human beings causes them to carry on. Life carves out its course among the graves also. On the one hand there were piles of dead bodies everywhere, on the other mothers were giving birth to babies. The process of life and death was going on side by side.

In this worst of human tragedies there were also instances of extreme human goodness, of individuals who cared for humanity, for human values, irrespective of the fact whether those they helped were Hindus or Muslims.

I

SAVIOURS EMERGE PHOENIX-LIKE

The Partition period witnessed the worst kind of loss of human values. As soon as the Partition was declared people belonging to both the religions started killing one another. But this was also the period that displayed the courage of humanity. There were many who "risked their own lives to save others."[7] On the one hand people were busy dragging out their 'enemies' from their houses, on the other there were also those who despite the protests and threats from their own men saved 'others' from the danger. The Muslims protected the Hindu and the Sikh refugees and vice-versa often risking their own lives. Not only this, they also opened the doors of their hearts and homes to those who were uprooted from their homes.[8] They not only gave shelter to the threatened individuals but also protected them from the outside danger. One of the most famous affirmations of the heroic in human nature is Khushwant Singh's portrayal of Jugga's self-sacrificing thwarting of attack on the refugee train in the classic novel, *Train to Pakistan*. He sacrifices his own life to save the life of those refugees who were heading towards Pakistan in a Train. It is Jugga who foils the nefarious plan of some miscreants to kill those Muslim refugees.[9] On the other hand, the Muslim woman, Rajo, in *Tamas* is an example of true humanity. She gives shelter to the Sikh couple Harnam Singh and Banto while the male members of her family are out looting and killing people of other communities. She fully realizes the problems that would arise in the family by her act of sheltering the couple, but still she does not hesitate in hiding the couple. She is aware of her husband's and son's temper and their fanaticism towards Hindu or Sikh community, but being a truly God-fearing woman and basically a kind-hearted person she helps Sikh couple saying, "You have knocked at my door. You came here with hopes of safety. Come back. What ever happens I shall face the consequences!"[10] She not only gives them shelter in her house at her own risk, but later even goes out to leave them till a certain safe distance and gives the rifle back to Harnam Singh. She is sympathetic to the suffering of other people irrespective of their religion or community. Besides, there are various short stories that depict the goodness of mankind that sustain the world. Some of these stories are: "Parmeshwar Singh", "The Refuge", "The White Horse", "Pali", "The Abandoned

Child", "Mozel", "A Leaf in the Storm", and "How Many Pakistans?".

"Parmeshwar Singh"[11] is a fine story written by Ahmad Nadeem Qasmi. The story depicts how an old Sikh saves a Muslim child from being killed by a Sikh mob. The child, Akhtar, is surrounded by the Sikh mob and they are ready to kill him. When all the Sikhs laugh cruelly in an inhuman way, Parmeshwar Singh is sad at heart to see the frightened child. He argues with the other Sikhs, "Don't laugh, yaroon. This child was created by the same Waheguruji as the one who created you and your children" (p. 159). To the people like Parmeshwar Singh "all human beings are one race", as echoes the *Rig Veda.*[12] To him true religion is the service of mankind and not killing of innocents in the name of religion. He knows that no religion teaches hatred against one's fellow human beings. Here Parmeshwar Singh is an embodiment of goodness. When one of the Sikhs in the mob threatens to kill Akhtar showing him kirpan his eyes fill with tears, as he is frightened. The child looks at Parmeshwar Singh as if "he was looking at his mother" (p. 160). Akhtar tells the rioters that his mother "found him in hay in a small barn" (p. 160). At this Parmeshwar Singh sobs like a child and wails, "All children are alike, yaroon. My Kartara also used to say the same thing. He too had been found by his mother in hay in a small barn" (p. 160).

Parmeshwar Singh has also lost his son, Kartara, during the Partition riots. Maybe he had been killed by some Muslim or had been picked up by someone. Even then he loves a Muslim child dearly. He stops other Sikhs from taking revenge. He is an epitome of humanity who has a faith in what Shakespeare says:

> ... the rarer action is
> In virtue than in vengeance...[13]

It is due to the resistance of Parmeshwar Singh that the Sikh rioters have to give in. Eventually, they decide that he may look after Akhtar as his own son. But he should grow his hair and should give him a Sikh name. Communal hatred has turned people so narrow-minded that they fail to realize the real aim and meaning of religion. How strange! We can convert one from Muslim to a Sikh or Hindu or vice-versa through meaningless rituals and the moment one is converted we start looking at him as if he belongs to us. Ironically, we don't care to turn one into a human being by inculcating in him virtues of love and tolerance.

Parmeshwar Singh also faces protests from his wife and daughter who do not want to accommodate Akhtar in their house. He is a lone fighter against his co-religionists. He showers his love upon the child and treats him like a son. He does not want to convert Akhtar into a Sikh. Rather, he assures him that when the ripe time comes, he will send him to his parents. He sobs like a child and says, "Forgive me, Akhtar. I swear by your God that I am your friend. If you go away from here by yourself, someone will kill you.... I'll take you to Pakistan myself and leave you there" (p. 165). He does not want to enforce Sikhism on the child. When a neighbour resists he says, "How can you be so cruel, yaroon? You want to make Akhtar, Kartara, but supposing someone were to make Kartara, Akhtar? You'll call him evil, won't you?" (p. 166). Parmeshwar Singh is a saintly man who does not want to torture an innocent child in the name of religion. When other members of his community persist on converting the child he grows angry and roars, "No, this boy will remain a Muslim. I swear by Darbar Sahib. I'll take him to Amritsar and get his hair cut in the English style. What do you take me for? I am a Khalsa. The heart of a lion beats in my breast, not the heart of a chicken" (p. 166). Undoubtedly, he is a true Khalsa who is ready to fight against evil. But unfortunately he has to accept defeat before the *granthi,* the religious leader, and he agrees to grow Akhtar's hair as a Sikh grows. Even after that he allows Akhtar to recite the *Koran* whenever he likes to do so. One day when he cannot sleep, Parmeshwar Singh goes to him to know the reason. Akhtar says, "I keep remembering my mother. My mother says that if one can't sleep, one should recite 'Que huwallah-ho-ahad' thrice. That will help one to sleep. I was about to sleep when Amar Kaur's [Parmeshwar Singh's Daughter] shriek frightened me." (p. 130) Parmeshwar Singh says, "Recite it again and go to sleep... Recite it everyday. Loudly. Never forget to do so..." (p. 170). He often enjoys listening to Akhtar reciting *the Koran*. He believes that every religion of the world teaches us how to become more human. He does not hate the Muslims for what they have done, neither does he longs for any vengeance. He has the virtues of strength and greatness in his character. He is great by forgiving his enemy since "forgiveness is the attribute of the strong."[14] It is his better self that incites him to mercy. It is far nobler to show mercy than to take vengeance.

The day, at last, comes when Parmeshwar Singh plans to send Akhtar to his parents. He accompanies him to the border from where Akhtar tries to cross it. But the two soldiers stop him and snatch his turban. His comb falls down. He cries for the lost comb. Meanwhile the soldiers find out Parmeshwar Singh and one of them shoots at his thigh. When the soldiers approach him he says, "Why did you shoot me? I had forgotten to cut Akhtar's long hair. I come to give him back his religion, yaroon" (p. 178). He has come there so that he may cut Akhtar's hair so that others should not mistake him for a Sikh. When Parmeshwar Singh is talking to the Pak-soldiers, in the distance he sees Akhtar "running towards them, his loose and dishevelled hair streaming in the wind" (p. 178). The running of Akhtar towards Parmeshwar Singh Symbolises victory of good over evil.

True religion binds man to God and man to man. The religion that teaches antagonism to other religion is not a religion at all. Those who emerged to help others during troublesome period were true followers of their respective religions. "The White Horse"[15] is a story by Ramesh Chandra Sen about a groom and coachman who is a Muslim. He loses his horse. The Hindu boys save the horse. They take care of the horse and play with it. Jamuna Prasad, a mischievous boy always rides on the back of the horse. When peace reigns for some time, the groom appears in search of his horse. The boys hand over the horse to the groom despite knowing that the old man is a Muslim. Suddenly the riots resume and the old Muslim is frightened as presently he is in a Hindu-majority area. When the killings begin the old Muslim looks around and "tries to find reassurance from the boys" (p. 132). Even the horse has a "piteous look too; perhaps he realizes the danger to his master" (p. 132). The boy, Nontey assures him, "you have nothing to fear", though he knows that the old man is a Muslim. But meanwhile a number of rioters advance from the crowd towards the old man with the intention of harming him. It is worth appreciating that amid hatred, selfishness, cruelty against mankind and thirst for one another's blood the good still prevails. Good cannot be eliminated so easily. All the boys—Jamuna, Habul, Nontey and others—"make a cordon round the old man" (p. 132). An elderly Hindu, Hirshikesh Babu also argues with the rioters, "This man is innocent. Don't beat him up" (p. 132). The rioters call the old Muslim a "devil". They want to take revenge upon him only because somewhere else the Muslim may have tortured the Hindus. One of the boys cries out, "No one can touch the groom", and the boys are ready to fight with their co-religionists to save this Muslim. The rioters throw brickbats at the boys. Still they are determined to help the old man. Meanwhile the army turns up and the rioters run away. Jamuna Prasad drags the old man to a safer place. He saves him. Ironically, it is the same Jamuna Prasad whose shouts are the loudest whenever there is an attack on a temple. The same boy forgets everything else now and does a great service to mankind by saving the life of the old man and also by saving the human values which are at stake. This noble act of the boys reveals the truth that no one is wicked basically. Such incidents affirm our faith in human goodness and sanity even in the worst of times.

Similarly, Ayesha and her father Qasim Sahib are good Muslims in "A Leaf in the Storm"[16] who try their best to save some Hindus women from the cruel claws of Muslim rioters. During the Partition when the Muslim communalists start killing and raping in Pakistan, Ayesha wants to help her friend, Jyoti, and other Hindu women to escape Pakistan. She requests her father to help them, and she plans to send them by her father's bullock cart which goes on its usual trips near the border. All are made to hide themselves under the bundles of hay. Unfortunately, the rioters find them out and drag them away one by one. The reality remains that at least Ayesha and her father show us the nobler side of humanity. Despite protests and threats from their own people individuals like Ayesha and Qasim Sahib still dared to help those in distress. The goodness in mankind refuses to be extinguished, though it may be under a cloud for a while.

Mozel is a Jewish girl in "Mozel".[17] Saadat Hasan Manto brings out the divine qualities in Mozel, a Jewish girl. She is a girl with a humane nature who sacrifices her own life to save the life of a Sikh girl. When Mozel comes to know from Tirlochen, her friend, that his beloved Kirpal Kaur is confined in her house which is situated in a Muslim-majority area, Mozel offers herself to bring Kirpal Kaur out of danger. She also makes fun of Tirlochen and calls him a "coward" (p. 165). Though she too loves Tirlochen, she hates him at the same time for his overindulgence in religious rituals like growing a beard, hair and putting on a turban. She laughs at him for all these things since these have no meaning for her. Once Tirlochen shaves his head just to make her happy, as he wants to get Mozel's love. When Tirlochen insists on wearing a turban, she stops him from doing so as they plan to go to the Muslim area to rescue Kirpal Kaur. Mozel snubs him, "Oh, your love be damned! I ask you, are all Sikhs stupid like you? It's a question of her life and you insist on wearing your turban" (p. 166). Mozel enters the Muslim locality along with Tirlochan. She tells the people that Tirlochen is a doctor and a Jewish like her. No one harms them, as Mozel is a Jewish. At Kirpal Kaur's house she gives her own skirt to Kirpal Kaur so that rioters will take her for a Jewish. Now Mozel is naked. She tells her plan to Tirlochen, "I'll open the door .... You run after me, I'll go up the stairs…you follow me…these men at the door will forget everything and come after us…. your, what's her name, will use the diversion to get away and no one will bother her in that dress" (p. 171).

Mozel starts climbing the stairs blindly. The rioters, who seconds ago were attempting to break down the door, turn and follow Mozel and Tirlochan. Unfortunately Mozel's foot slips and she comes "stumbling down the stairs, her body hitting every stone stair and the steel banister as she fell, landing finally on the cement floor" (p. 171).

Her nose starts bleeding and the blood trickles from her mouth and ears. Even in this condition she wants to know from Tirlochen, through gestures, if Kirpal Kaur has escaped. When Tirlochen tells her about Kirpal Kaur's safe escape she is pleased. Mozel dies for others' happiness. Her sacrifice is great. In fact she is a true lover. She believes in what Gandhiji has said, "Love never claims. It ever gives. Love ever suffers… never resents, never revenges itself"[18] Mozel symbolises goodness and she is merciful. Though her own community faces no danger, it has no fear of any riot or killings still she dies for the sake of others.

Similarly, Lenny's mother and God-mother are humane characters in *Ice Candy Man*[19] who save the lives of many Hindu and Sikh families by helping them reach across the border safely. Lenny's mother tells Lenny, "We were only smuggling the rationed petrol to help our Hindu and Sikh friends to run away…. And also for the convoys to send kidnapped women, like your ayah, to their families across the border" (p. 242). Not only this they also get the *ayah*, who has been abducted, freed from her captor and God-mother consoles her saying:

> That was fated, daughter. It can't be undone. But it can be forgiven…. Worse things are forgiven. Life goes on and the business of living buries the debris of our pasts. Hurt, happiness…all fade impartially…to make way for fresh joy and new sorrow. That's the way of life (p. 262).

God-mother's words apply a balm on any afflicted soul, and the healing becomes easier. They are like a gospel that soothes one's tortured self and give a new hope of life. These helping women are from Parsee community and like Mozel they have no threat to their lives but they live for others. In others' safety and happiness they find their own contentment and pleasure. Such exemplary show of human values erases the dark smudges left by evil.

Once the Partition was declared on the basis of religion majority of the people were busy throwing 'others' out from their homeland. Yet there were many who were sad at heart to bid farewell to their neighbours. They did not want to snap the bonds of love and friendship they had enjoyed together for centuries. This was a positive sign and implied that human values were still intact even amid the clouds of hatred and suspicion against one another. S.H. Vatsayan's "The Refuge"[20] depicts such emotions of two friends—one a Hindu and the other a Muslim—who are about to part from each other. The story is set in Lahore that is burning with communal passion. Though all other Hindus of the *mohalla* have escaped to India, Devenderlal continues to stay there as his Muslim friend Rafiquddin insists on him staying there. Rafiquddin assures his safety as he sincerely feels that it is his duty to protect his Hindu friend and neighbour. Whatever is happening around is shameful in the eyes of Rafiquddin. He is a man who places love and friendship for friends and neighbours above any religion. He is, thus, a true Muslim with the virtues of love and understanding. He persuades Devenderlal not to leave Lahore saying, "No, we'll lose face! How can you leave your own home and become a refugee in your own city? We'll not let you go—we will force you to stay. It is the duty of the majority to protect the minority, and to make sure that they don't abandon their homes and run away" (p. 73). Here Rafiquddin is one with Mahatma Gandhi who believed that "the only protection on which a minority could count on was that given by neighbours to neighbours".[21]

Unfortunately the day comes when the Muslim communalists threaten Rafiquddin for sheltering a Hindu. He is forced to turn Devenderlal out of his house. Nevertheless, he arranges a shelter for Devenderlal in a neighbour's house where he is sheltered in a very dark room. Rafiquddin's friend, Sheikh Sahib, provides Devenderlal with food and shelter. But one day this benefactor tries to kill his guest by giving poisoned food. However, Devenderlal is lucky as 'good' makes its appearance in the form of Shiekh Sahib's daughter Zaibu. She warns Devenderlal about the poison in food and thus saves his life. Devenderlal jumps over the wall and escapes from that house and finally reaches Delhi. In response to his appeal on radio to his family in India he receives a note from Pakistan, understandably from Zaibu, his soviour saying:

> I cannot but praise God a thousand fold for having helped you to escape. I hope that you are once again united with the people to whom you appealed over radio. I want to ask your forgiveness for what my father did or tried to do. It was I who foiled his plans. You don't owe me a favour—my only request is that, if you come across someone in your country who is in a similar situation, don't forget this incident. I make this request, not because that person may be a Muslim, but because you are a human being! Khuda hafiz! (pp. 82-83).

And this noble act of Zaibu provides the most optimistic word in the whole story, the *selfless* human concern for those who are suffering. Her action speaks louder than worlds. Zaibu reminds us of Miranda, Shakespeare's loveliest and sweetest creation, 'Eve of an enchanted paradise'. The simplicity and tenderness of her character are at once laid open when she seems to echo words of Miranda:

> Oh, I have suffered
> With those that I saw suffer.[22]

Zaibu is, no doubt, a true follower of the principle of universal brotherhood and of *Ahimsa* since she acts upon what Gandhiji had taught, "True *Ahimsa* should mean a complete freedom from ill-will and anger and hate and should have an over flowing love for all."[23] Zaibu is really an embodiment of 'good' whose noble features convey that goodness, however weak, prevails even in the face of monstrous evil.

Rafiquddin's friendship with Devenderlal can be compared to that of Chaudhry Barkat Ali and Kanshi Ram in *Azadi.*[24] Barkat Ali is almost broken and choked to the emotion when he bids good-bye to his friend and his friend's family. He fails to control himself and utters in a rather prophetic tone, "We are one people and religion cannot separate us from each other" (p. 276). He forces his friend to leave at once as there is danger all around. Though he is a Muslim by faith, he has not ceased to love his Hindu friend and neighbour. He is very sad to know about the atrocities being perpetrated on the Hindus by his Muslim community. He rather considers them devils and not Muslims. He believes that a religious man is always amenable to reason. He agrees with Gandhiji who believed that "Islam does not teach enmity to any man.... No religion teaches man to kill fellow man....[25] The ultimate objective of religion is to kill evil or the brute in us. Barkat Ali says almost in utter desperation, "All my arguments of peace have failed with my brother Muslims; they have ceased to be Muslims and have become Shaitans" (p.138). Fortunately in every society there are men like Barkat Ali who understand that religion doesn't consist in rituals and ceremonies or in detesting people from other religions but in loving and respecting all humanity.

Barkat Ali is, thus, a true Muslim who has absorbed the true essence of religion. Though he witnesses the brutal dance of communalism, hatred and animosity, he does not lose his poise. He is a good Muslim not because he observes some of the Muslim rituals but because he acts upon the ethical values of Islam. He believes in the unity of all religions. To him God is one whether one prays to Him in a temple or a mosque. To him "the Hindu next door was as much his brother, more his brother than an unknown Muslim living elsewhere" (p. 103). He reminds one of Juggat Singh in *Train to Pakistan*[26] who also symbolises goodness and humanity as he risks his own life to save the people of other community.

II

CLEARING OF THE FOG: RESTORATION OF GOODWILL AND FRIENDSHIP

Communal frenzy poisoned people's mind so much that they started looking at each other with hatred and ill will. Evil possessed the people of both the religions and the faith in one another that had cemented their bonds of love for centuries was shaken. Even those kind souls who could never think of doing harm to their neighbours were misguided and swayed by the virulent slogans and speeches against each other. Once the masses were blinded in the name of religion they forgot to differentiate between good and evil. A sort of fog of hatred cast its spell on the mind of those who were good otherwise. Stories like "Neighbours", "Roots" and "The Death of Sheikh Burhanuddin" reveal how 'good' was eclipsed temporarily and finally the fog of misunderstanding and hatred was lifted and it was triumph of 'good' over 'evil'.

Shaikh Ayyaz brings out the best in man in "Neighbour"[27]. The story reveals vividly how the mind of a Muslim barber, Khannu from Sindh, is perturbed and stirred by the slogans raised by his co-religionists and he, too, starts looking at his Hindu neighbours with hatred and suspicion. The suspicion in his mind is aggravated when he reads about the disturbances in Bengal and Bihar in the newspapers. He comes to know about the ".... dreadful tales of murder and brutality. People seemed to have lost their humanity. Woman were being mutilated and raped, children were being dispatched to the valley of death, brothers were playing holi with the blood of their brothers. The same was happening at Lahore, Bombay and at other places near the border" (p. 187). Khannu has also seen some horrifying photographs in the newspapers. He often thinks about the cruelties committed by the Hindus of Bihar on the Muslims and their woman. All bring about a sudden change in his mentality. A thin veil of hatred against the Hindus is cast on his good and kind heart. He starts thinking, "Are we going to avenge the killings of Bihari Muslims? Should I, for example, cut the throat of this Seth with my razor?" (p. 188).

Khannu's mind thus wavers between 'good' and 'evil'. He is caught in the web of momentary hatred and ill-will against the Hindus. He quietly wonders, "What will I do if disturbances break out in Sindh tomorrow?...Will I cut the throat of this Seth with my razor? Sethji's son goes to a local college and also comes here for a hair cut" (p. 189). But meanwhile he remembers the day when he has celebrated with them. The atmosphere was filled with love and "there was no difference between the Hindus and the Muslims" (p. 189). The memory of the past relations with the Hindus removes slowly that veil of hatred and misunderstanding from his mind and heart. He remembers the good old days and says to himself:

> The water of the Sindhu river did not know the difference between the two sects. It was not as if the water would let the Hindu drown and the Muslim swim across. Besides, the same sun shone on the heads of both the communities. Both the communities took a dip in the same water to cool when it got too hot. It wasn't as if the sun gave shade to the Muslim and burnt the Hindu. If nature did not differentiate between the Hindus and the Muslims, who was he to differentiate between the two? Was he the creator of the universe? And when the Lord Himself didn't treat people differently, how could he do so? He wondered how, after having lived with the Hindus and their children for so long, he could possibly kill them? (p. 189).

Gradually these good and noble ideas nullify the

wickedness that tries to overpower his mind. He cannot harm his Hindu friends as "the lives of the Hindus and the Muslims were so intimately woven together that they were a part of the same cloth", thinks Khannu (p. 190).

One day a Hindu woman, Pesu Ram's mother comes to him enquiring, "I have heard that there is a lot of hatred being spread. Muslims are going to start a riot. If this happen, I will come and live with you" (p. 190). Khannu says teasingly, "I belong to the Muslim League and I wear a Jinnah cap. You should be afraid of me" (p. 190). But the woman has placed faith in Khannu and she believes that 'good' persons like Khannu can never harm anyone. She says, "Do not talk like that, Bhaiya. You will always remain Khannu Bhai for me. How can you kill us? You often say that neighbours are like our own father, mother, brothers and sisters. You always send us Phiru on Id and share our sweet bread during Sheetla.... But even if I die at your hands, I will be happy and satisfied" (pp.190-91). Here comes the moment when all the fog in his mind is lifted giving place to purity and innocence in his heart. He wonders, "Can I kill this woman? She is asking for refuge. Can I kill her? No. Never. It cannot be.If the Hindus in Bihar have killed the Muslims, Pesu Ram's mother has nothing to do with it. She has always been our neighbour.... No. No Never. We cannot have any rioting in the country of the Sufis" (p. 191). It is worth appreciating that people like Khannu were still there who did not allow their mind to be contaminated so easily. Even during the darker days good still emerged out of the smoke and ashes of evil and pessimism and desperation gave way to optimism and love.

The Partition violence and hatred created a gulf between those who had lived together happily sharing one another's joys as well as sorrows. "Roots"[28] by Ismat Chughtai reveals how two families used to live together before the Partition. Despite their religious difference they lived amicably celebrating one another's festivals. Roop Chand, a Hindu doctor, is a close friend of the narrator's Muslim family. For every decision the

Muslim family consulted Roop Chand. In fact both the families had been closely related to each other for "three generations" (p. 11). There are many episodes in the story that give evidence how much two families loved one other.

However, as soon as the Partition is declared a chasm appears between two families dividing them physically as well as emotionally. The new situation pollutes both the families. Their visits to each other's houses virtually come to an end. "The distance between the two houses seems to crawl with venomous snakes" (p. 14). Earlier when there had been fights among the children of both the families, their elders would give them a thrashing for that. But now time has changed and things have taken an ugly turn. The elders support their children and praise them for their courage. It seems as if a fog has cast its obnoxious spell on the minds of the elders as will as the youngsters.

The day comes when the narrator's family decides to leave for Pakistan. But the narrator's mother is not ready for that. She cannot leave behind her house and land where she has spent her life; where she has given birth to her children and brought them up. She stays behind alone. She feels heart broken. Roop Chand does not try to persuade them not to leave, though he too is sad at heart. Slowly the fog that has smothered the 'goodness' in Roop Chand starts clearing away. He paces up and down his verandah and curses and shouts at everyone in his house.

> He was particularly angry at the empty house across the road which seemed to mock at him. It was as if he had, with his own hands, demolished it brick by brick. He wanted to brush something out of his mind. Wanted to peck it out with all his strength. But he was irritated by his inability to get rid of it. He couldn't uproot it from his soul because it had gripped him like the roots of an ancient tree" (p. 18).

Slowly a change appears in Roop Chand. He is free from all ill-will and malevolence against his neighbours. A similar change appears in the women of his house also. Roop Chand's daughter-in-law "entered the narrator's house, through the back door, like a thief, with two plates full of food in her hands" (p. 18). She and the narrator's mother sit across each other without saying anything. The daughter-in-law brings food to the mother of the narrator showing faith in true religion. Dr. Radhakrishnan had defined Hindu religion in three words, "do the right,"[29] and this is perhaps equally applicable to all the faiths and religions. Roop Chand also displays true humanity in him by bringing back the narrator's family before they cross the border. He showers a lot of joy on the mother by bringing her family back. "A smile began to play on her lips. She was overwhelmed with happiness. All her sorrows…swirled into the surrounding darkness and vanished" (p. 19). As Roop Chand demands his fees for bringing her children back the old woman's face glows with a smile and "slowly two teardrops rolled down her face and fell an Roop Chand's wrinkled hands" (p. 20). Hence, Roop Chand fanally symbolizes a man with true human values. Evil fails to contaminate his mind for long.

"The Death of Seikh Burhanuddin"[30] by Khwaja Ahmed Abbas is a story of a Muslim whose mind was full of antipathy and hostility against all the Sikhs, right from his childhood. His name is Sheikh Burhanuddin and he is also the narrator of the story. He tells how he hated Sikhs and disliked even to look at them or to talk to them. But the day also comes when he realizes that he had been nurturing wrong notions about the Sikhs. It is the day of his defeat, or rather the death of his old self, which hated Sikhs. It is only when his heart is enlightened by the encounter with the truth that all the dirt and fog of wrong notions is washed off his mind and it is enriched with a new light of love and adoration for those whom he hated.

The narrator was only six years old when he first saw a Sikh. He disliked the Sikh at the first sight for having long beard and hair like women. As he got older, "this dislike developed into hatred for the entire race" (p. 223). The fault does not lie with the narrator. It is all due to our elders that our mind is contaminated against other races and castes right from our childhood. The narrator, too, says, "It was a custom amongst the old woman of our household to heap all afflictions on our enemies" (p. 223).

When the narrator goes to University for higher education even there education failed to remove the feeling of contempt off his mind. Here he had got a Muslim boy called Ghulam Rasul as a room-mate. Ghulam Rasul also hates Sikhs and has many anecdotes about the Sikhs' stupidity. He also finds them "stupid" and "incredibly filthy" (p. 226). He consideres the Sikhs to be "cowards" and holds Muslims in high esteem for their bravery. Having completed his education the narrator comes to Delhi and starts living there as a head clerk. He has a Sikh as a neighbour who has fled from Pakistan during riots. Even here the narrator hates his neighbour and snubs him whenever he gets a chance.

During the Partition Sheikh Burhanuddin had sent his family to Pakistan and he had stayed in Delhi because he wanted to draw money from his provident fund. Though he felt proud of Islam when he saw "Sikhs who had fled from Rawalpindi" (p. 227), he was also afraid that they might avenge themselves upon him. All his fear and apprehensions about the Sikh neighbour, however, proved false as the old Sikh came to him when the riots broke out in Delhi. The Sikh reassured him, "Sheikhji, do not worry! As long as I am alive no one will raise a hand against you" (p. 229). Even now the narrator was not free from doubt against the Sikh and he said to himself, "How much fraud is hidden behind this man's beard! He is obviously pleased that the Muslims are being massacred, but expresses sympathy to win my confidence, or is he trying to taunt me? (pp. 229-30). But it was not so. When non-Muslim rioters attack the narrator's house, it is the same Sikh who gives shelter to the narrator. He hides him in his house. The rioters start looting his house. The Sikh stops the rioters and gathers some belongings saying, "We have prior claims over our neighbour's property. We must get our share of the loot" (p. 231). He calls his children and all of them gather whatever they can lay their hands on. The narrator thinks that the Sikh was really looting him. But the Sikh hands over all the belongings they had collected to the narrator saying, "Here you are, take your things" (p. 232). The narrator is dumb-founded. The Sikh had not only given him shelter but has also protected his goods as much as he can. He has done a great service to the man who hated him. Meanwhile the rioters come to know that the Sikh had given shelter to the narrator. They come back. But the Sikh locks the narrator inside a room and argues with the rioters. The rioters shoot at the Sikh and go away. Before his death, the Sikh tells the narrator that he has paid the debt as a Muslim called Ghulam Rasul in Rawalpindi also saved him. The Sikh was really great—an angel who sacrificed his life to save his neighbour. The veil of hatred or the myth that the Sikhs were bad and contemptuous was removed with the supreme sacrifice of the Sikh. Overwhelmed by the goodness of the Sikh Sheikh Burhanuddin, the narrator now identifies him with his grandfather. He says that the Sikh "reminded me of my grandfather with his twelve-inch beard. How closely the two resembled each other!" (p. 233).

This transformation in the attitude of the narrator was the result of the love and concern and of the supreme sacrifice of the Sikh who in turn was protected and helped by a Muslim in Pakistan. Thus the chain of good deeds keeps one's faith in humanity and human values alive even in the worst of times. It ennobles the hearts and minds of men like Sheikh Burhanuddin and builds bridges of faith and goodwill.

III

REDEEMING WOMEN FROM TRAUMA

We have discussed in the previous chapter how women had been the worst sufferers during the Partition. They were time and again attacked physically as well as emotionally, being the most vulnerable class. They had to face the trauma of molestation, rape, abduction and killings. Their husbands and children were butchered before their very eyes and the women were spared only to be raped. Their lives became desolate. Their 'own' people refused to own them as they were 'polluted'. Despite pervasive violence against women there were still some men who risked their lives to rescue women who were in danger of being violated or killed. Anis Kidwai, who was a social worker in the refugee camps in Delhi at that time tells in her novel *Azadi ki Chaon Mein* about a Hindu Jat rescuing a Muslim girl in the face of hostility from his villagers.[31] There were also families which gladly welcomed the rescued women.[32] Many husbands readily agreed to own their abducted wives without any ill will or contempt against them. These were the men who symbolized 'good' 'social values' and who held relationships dear and did not succumb to the false notions of honour or chastity.

Though Sunderlal the husband of Lajwanti[33] has some dilemmas and difficulty in accepting his wife as naturally as one would wish yet he does a great service by publicly creating an atmosphere for the acceptance of restored women. He is the main spokesman of the local committee for the rehabilitation of women. He leads morning processions of fellow workers urging people to treat women with love and care. He wants that due respect and affection must be showered upon those who had been abducted. He pleads, "Honour them. Give them a place in your hearts" (p. 55). He does not like that they should be treated as defiled and polluted. Sunderlal is, thus, doing a great service for the suffering women. Since he himself was a sufferer as his wife had also been abducted. The so-called morally self-right and priest-beguiled critics get silenced at his great service. Sunderlal's concern and gentle regard for these women, is not "hypocritical".[34] Though his behaviour towards Lajwanti undergoes some change, he treats her with exaggerated care and regards her as *devi* after her rehabilitation, yet his acceptance of his wife creates a climate for others to come forward for similar acts of acceptance of restored women. He at least gives his wife a place in his home—a shelter where she has no fear of onslaught on her body and psyche from outside, nor does she have to remain at the mercy of relief camps.

Not only this, Sunderlal also argues with the priest of the temple, Narayan Baba who opposes the rehabilitation of abducted women saying they are impure and defiled. He argues:

> Yes, Baba.... There are many things in this which are beyond my comprehension. Yet, I believe that in Ram Rajya, men cannot commit a crime against his own self. To inflict pain on oneself is as unjust as it is to hurt someone else...Even today, Lord Ram has thrown Sita out of his home because she was forced to live with Ravana.... Did Sita commit any sin? Wasn't she, like our mothers and sisters today, a victim of violence and deceit...Is it a question of Sita's truthfulness, or is it a question of Ravana's wickedness? (p. 60).

Sunderlal breaks down and weeps. He is right. The women were not to blame for their sorrows. It was the demon in men that had led them to suffering. He is a good man who shows a good way to others to follow the right path. "A Visitor from Pakistan"[35] is a story of a man called Baldev who got separated from his wife during the Partition riots. Some Muslims saved him. He did not know whether his wife, Saraswati, was alive or not. After ten years when he comes to know about the whereabouts of his wife he comes to India to stay with her. Despite knowing the fact that she has been staying with another man and also has children from him, he is ready to own Saraswati. He begs before her to come with him. Saraswati faces a dilemma as she is between the devil and the deep sea. Sunderdas, her present husband, has given her shelter and Baldev is her real husband. Baldev has been suffering for the last ten years lonely and silently. He has not married again. He is a faithful husband. When all the people oppose Saraswati's going with him he says:

> Saraswati is my legal wife and she can never forget that I love her. Instead of giving her back to me, for she is rightfully mine, you want me to go and knock at the doors of the court for justice. I am sure the courts will be just. But the process will take long. I don't know how many years will pass by. I shall, instead, knock at the door of another court, ...in that court I shall be dealt with justly (p. 186).

He goes near Saraswati and asks, "Saraswati, give me an answer. I don't want to ask anyone. I want an answer from you and only you" (p. 186). Saraswati breaks down for she has been in fix and does not know what to do. Meanwhile a man appears on the door and asks, "Is there a visitor from Pakistan in this house?" After reading the paper in his hand Baldev just says," Yes, he is here but he will return to Pakistan today"(p.186). Baldev resigns before circumstances and gives up his claim so that no disturbance is caused to others. He is really a good man who is ready to give due place to Saraswati in his life and yet he does not force her to go with him. Baldev is among those who instinctively seem to be able to act correctly, according to the norms of a humane social order.

Vishnu Prabhakar's "I Shall Live"[36] reveals the best in man. Raj is a woman who lost her child and other relations when she was fleeing from Lahore. She picked up a small child and looked after the child. In India she is helped by a good man, Pran. He gives shelter to her and takes care of her. When Raj had lost everything she found consolation in the child, Dilip whom she found "as a gift" (p. 211) when she was coming from Lahore. Unfortunately, the real mother of Dilip turns up one day and claims the child. Raj is sad at heart. When she refuses to hand over the child to the real mother, Pran persuades her calmly saying, "Raj! There is something even more precious then being a mother, and that is protecting the motherhood of someone else" (p. 212). Pran is a noble soul who is fair, caring and considerate in his behaviour. He can imagine the agony of the real parents of the child, hence he tells Raj, "I am not asking you to do anything. He's their child. You can do a good deed by returning it to them. By performing your duty, you'll find the kind of peace that you will never find by doing anything else." (p. 212). Prans's words have so much effect on Raj's mind that she hands over the child to the real mother. Raj is broken and sad. No life is left in her. On the other hand, Pran is also broken and wants to see Raj happy. He symbolizes humanity in true sense. "He wanted to see Raj lose herself in the innocent play of a child again. He often went to an orphanage in the hope of adopting a child, but never succeeded in taking one home" (p. 213). But Pran is an optimist who hopes that "the moment the circumstances changed, she too would change" (p. 213).

Time takes a strange turn when Raj's husband appears before Pran and tells him that he feels ashamed, as he could not save her. He wants to take Raj along with him. Pran asks him if he has any doubt about her, as she had been staying with a stranger. The man replies, "Doubt? Why should I add to burden of my sins by doubting her?" (p. 215). Pran feels elated when he comes to know that one of Raj's children is also alive and is with her husband. Pran appreciates the man, "Before people can make mistakes, but it is against their nature to deceive someone" (p. 216). Raj's husband also shows goodness of heart, as he does not care for the social constructs like 'honour' and 'purity' but values humanity to the core. He knows that Raj had been living with Pran but he does not suspect her purity. It is enough for him that he has found his wife. He takes Raj gladly with him. On the other hand, Pran is adorable as he makes great sacrifices for the happiness of others. He protects the motherhood of a woman by restoring her child to her. Though he has lived with Raj, he never tried to exploit her physically. In the end he restores her to her husband. It is almost incredible even to dream about such great and noble souls on earth during such violent and monstrous upheavals. Pran had lost all the members of his 'own' family. His wife and her parents were swept away by a river. His children had died one by one on the way from Lahore to India. He has lost everything and yet he finds solace and pleasure in the happiness of others. He, in fact, embodies the essence of '*dharma*', as real '*dharma*' lies in the right conduct which includes love, truth, non-violence, concern for others and equanimity of mind.[37]

IV

QUEST FOR SURVIVAL

For the countless families rendered homeless and uprooted during the Partition and treated as 'others' in their new places of refuge, it seemed as if their life had come to a stand still and the rest of the life would be spent mourning for the lost past—their land, home, hearth and dear ones. But it was *not* to be so. These uprooted people faced the changed circumstances with courage and equanimity. They picked up the broken shreds of their life to weave them again into a whole. It was not for the first time in human history that people had suffered. For centuries the sordid and the sublime, the mean and the exalted, the ugly and the beautiful had been existing side by side. Such is the strength of the vital life force that even in the worst circumstances one does not lose the urge to live. One cannot spend one's whole life in mourning and lamenting for what is not there now. As Huxley observed that Homer had told the whole Truth in his *Odyssey*. Homer knew that the most cruelly bereaved must eat and that hunger is stronger than sorrow and that its satisfaction takes precedence even over tears. He knew that "when the belly is full (and only when the belly is full) man can afford to grieve and that sorrow after supper is almost a luxury. And finally he knew that, even as hunger takes precedence of grief, so fatigue, super venting, cuts short its career and drowns it in a sleep all the sweeter for bringing forgetfulness of bereavement. In a word, Homer refused to treat the theme tragically. He preferred to tell the Whole Truth". [38] While the short stories tell a lot about evil they also tell us about the good which too is an integral part of the human beings. The writers of the short stories do not paint life with morbid and pessimistic strokes alone. They reveal characters with a strong urge for survival despite sufferings and calamities. They want to struggle tooth and nail to survive in the face of death. They wish to strive, to seek, and not to yield to sorrow or helplessness for ever. "Weeds", "Exile", "Claim" and "Getting Even" particularly focus on humanity's struggle for survival.

As mentioned in the previous chapter the narrator of "Exile"[39] was abducted by a Sikh and was married forcibly. She also has children from him. She longs for her lost home and relations. Her mind wavers amid hope and despair. She hopes her brother will come one day and take her to his house. But he never comes. It is time that proves to be the greatest healer. Despite the fact that she can never love Gurpal, her abductor, she resigns to the circumstances. She cannot stop living. She knows that "the caravan of life moves on forever. Even if one has no fixed destination, one must keep walking, over straight and winding paths, across confusing, and bewildering ways. Keep walking. Always. Even if one's feet are bruised and one's heart is empty" (p. 42). How can, then she stop her journey? Sorrows and sufferings are but part of one's life and the realization comes that "the wheel of life revolves between happiness and suffering" (p. 44). She remembers what her brother had told her, "Bibi, water has its own force. It always finds its own path" (p. 46). Her brother was right because like water life-force also forces us to find our own paths. She reminds herself, "It's a sin to give up hope" (p. 47). The instinct for survival is clearly manifested through her love for her daughter, Munni. She realises that apart from being a sister she is also a mother of Munni. How can she go to her brother leaving behind Munni. The village, Sangraon, now seems her own. She says in a very optimistic tone, " My life had taken roots in Sangraon, and the roots had spread wide and deep. Who wants life to wither and die? After all, every girl has to bid farewell to her parent's house and go to her husband's place. Every bride had to leave her children home after marriage. So what if my brothers had not been present at my wedding?" (p. 50). With the resolve that "Like everyone else in this caravan of life, I have to keep on walking" (p. 52). And she reconciles with her present situation and devotes her self to the nurturing of her children. Hence she does not lose mental balance and is not given to despair.

Similarly, "Weeds"[40] is a story of an abducted woman who does not want to go to the house of her 'own'. She wants to stay where she is. The narrator, an officer for the rehabilitation of the abducted woman approaches her to rescue her. She is in a very sad state. She is seriously ill and her health is deteriorating. She has accepted her abductor's house as her own because she wants to live. She just wants that her young sister-in-law who was abducted by some Muslims should be brought back to her. She begs for this favour from the officer. She says, " Give her my regards. I am her eldest sister-in-law. I raised her and looked after her as my own daughter. If she comes to live with me, I will find someone for her. My health, my position, here, too, will improve. At last, I will be able to call someone my own" (p. 208).

Symbolically, too, "Weeds" convey the message of optimism that one should always strive for survival even in the face of death. 'Weeds' are symbolically used hare to represent those struggling always to survive. The narrator also recalls the words of a Jat who had told his son, "If you look carefully, nothing much has happened! The population of the world has always wandered from one place to another and then found a place to rest. Everything will soon find its proper place and then life will settle down once more" (p. 204). The words of the Jat appear like a useful sermon which advises us to look at tragedy and waste in a larger perspective and derive strength from the fact that soon life will take roots and start afresh. He tells his son who is rather broken and desperate at seeing all the miseries and troubles caused by the Partition:

> ...Look at those weeds. When the sowing and planting season begins, the farmer ploughs the field and pulls them up by their roots. He gathers them together with all the wild plants and throws them away. But after a few days the weeds sprout again. A month later, it seems as if the field had never been ploughed (pp. 204-05).

The worlds are so reassuring that the human spirit could never be extinguished, no matter how grim the tragedy may be.

Sadhu Singh, the protagonist of "The Claim"[41] has lost everything, his land, his house and even his wife who was abducted during the Partition violence. He has come to India where he has started plying a tonga. His customers are often those uprooted people who go to the claim office to fill up claims for their loss. But Sadhu Singh has never tried to put a claim for his lost property. He knows that his loss cannot be claimed. No body can give back his wife, the mango trees and that smell which he used to feel at his native place. There can be no claim for emotions and feelings. He is still rather hopeful of a bright future ahead. That is why he says to his horse, Afsar, "If God keeps you well, Afsar, the old days will return again. Eat! Fill your belly! Your claims must be filled. May your life be blessed!" (p. 41).

There were also those who had lost everything and did not know where to go. Even then they wanted to live. S.H. Vatsayan records an incident in "Getting Even"[42] that takes place in a train. The story focuses on the identity crisis of the two Sikhs, a father and a son. The Sikhs have fled from Pakistan for the fear of massacre during the Partition. They do not know where to take refuge. They have lost their home and land and with the loss of their land their identity has also been lost. They become aliens in their own country and flee as refugees. They find refuge in a train, which is on its way to Aligarh. Here the train is a symbol of abridged spaces and the death of old structural certainties. When one of the passengers asks the elder Sikh to which place he belongs, the Sikh replies, "Where ever I happen to be, there is my home! One corner of a railway compartment" (p.121). It is nothing else but the spirit of adjustment that even after becoming rootless the two Sikhs keep on travelling in the train to and fro without having any grudge against anyone, and thus find a purpose, a meaning in life by escorting lonely women to safety between Delhi and Aligarh.

Even after having suffered extensively the Sikh man keeps his faith in human values still alive. He assures a Muslim woman in the compartment of her safe journey. He protects and escorts her up to her destination. There is a note of optimism in the story. If bad people are there good persons, too, exist among us. Human feelings eventually emerge victorious. When a Hindu passenger tries to give details of the riots and torture of the Hindu women by the Muslims, the elder Sikh forces him to keep silent and not to aggravate tension by such ghastly narrations. He tells him, "A woman's dishonour is woman's dishonour—it is not a Hindu's shame or a Muslim's shame, in her the mother of all mankind has been dishonored" (p. 124). Though the Sikh has been made to flee by the Muslims, he does not wish to take revenge because he thinks, "there can be no adequate vengeance for all that took place there! I can only get even after a fashion so that whatever happened to me should never happen to another" (p. 124). He is a sufferer, has no identity of his own but he is a good man representing the positive in humanity. Both the Sikhs are without any shelter except one that they have received temporarily in the train. Yet they are trying to alleviate the suffering of the others.

This great spirit of adjustment and survival depicted in these short stories can be compared to something similar in *Azadi*.[43] Despite troubles and tribulations Kanshi Ram, the protagonist of the novel, does not develop a defeatist attitude. It is the instinct for survival and the life force that assert through him and he is ready to face new challenges that life brings before him. "Hitherto he had only died—in various ways. It involved no act of the will on his part; the death came suddenly and swiftly and offered no alternatives. The act of creation on the other hand demanded a slow nursing, a careful watch" (p. 274). During this struggle there is much in him that had died and yet there is something still alive in him too. Not accepting defeat in the face of death is the real victory of life. His personal loss has not demoralized him. His own suffering has made him more sensitive to the sufferings of others. He protects Sunanda and her family like a father. He shows love and concern towards Isher Kaur. He lost his own daughter Madhu, but he becomes a father to all those unfortunate ones who look up to him for love and concern.

Like Khannu of "Neighbours", Roopchand of "Roots"and Sheik Burhanuddin of "The Death of Sheikh Burhanuddin", Kanshi Ram finally completely gets rid of any feeling of hatred and finds himself in a position where he can love his enemies as fellow brethren. Here love represents the life force that forces one to live. While crossing Ravi, Arun leaves behind three great rivers forever. But he does not feel sad and sorry for he is carrying along with him a far sweeter and more exuberant, moveable river and that river is the river of love. As long as this river of love continues flowing in human hearts—Man will endure.

Not only the events and the characters, the style and structure of the stories are also used to convey an optimistic massage. Some of the recurrent images in the stories are 'train', 'bridge' and 'river'. 'Train' symbolizes continuity as well as a device that minimizes the gap between places and people. 'Bridge' also joins two divided lands and hints at the truth that there is hope of joining the divided hearts. 'Bridge' also minimizes the gaps and distances and brings the separated ones close to one another. The 'river' is also a fine symbol of continuity that implies that life goes on continuously despite heavy odds. At the close of *Azadi* Sunanda's sewing machine also symbolizes continuity of life. "The machine went whirring on, its wheel turning and its needle moving up and down, murmuring and sewing through cloth. The door of both the rooms shook with its vibration" (p. 371).

Though the writers of the short stories have depicted evil and wickedness incarnate in their stories, they are not closing their eyes to essential human goodness in simple hearts. The writers pin up their hope on the elemental goodness in human nature. No doubt, goodness and evil co-exit in the world almost everywhere. The short-story writers deal with the destructive force of evil but they present the events in such a way as not to shake our faith in human goodness or shatter our belief in the ethical order of the world. Evil rather cautions us to desist from evil. Goodness may be rare in the world, yet its very existence is a redeeming feature. We are reminded of Macduff's comment in *Macbeth*: "Angels are bright still, though the brightest fell." The stories on the Partition despite their harrowing narratives of monstrous acts of violence, fortify our faith in the essential human goodness. If there are people like Nasru eager to loot others' property and giving it the name of 'holy war' there are also like Fazzay who disapprove looting and killings and consider them a 'sin'. On the other hand if there are wicked characters like Nurul who help women only because they want to use them as prostitutes, there are angels like Pran who not only save and give shelter to women but also honour their chastity and purity. There are cruel vampires like Udham Singh who spear children just to quench their thirst for blood, but there are also god-like people like Zenab and Shakur who not only save children but also bring them up like their own children. If there are diabolical Muslims exulting in sadism, there lives in the very streets of Narowal (in *Azadi*) a Muslim who weeps over the loss of the unfortunate Hindu women and prays to Allah to protect their honour. His angelic tears seem to purge the sins of his race. If there are non-Muslim who are hacking the Muslims in the name of religions there are also Sikhs like the one in "The Death of Sheikh Burhanuddin" who sacrifices his life to save the Muslim neighbour from the wrath of rioters. All this affirms that despite the outburst of insanity neither has humanity completely died nor have the springs of human kindness totally dried up.

NOTES

1. K.K Sharma, "The 1947 Upheaval and India English Novel," in *Exploration in Modern Indo-English Fiction,* ed. R.K. Dhawan (New Delhi: Bahri Publications, 1982), p. 30.
2. Mathew Arnold, "Dower Beach", ll. 33-34, in *Victorian Prose and Poetry*, ed. Lionel Trilling and Harold Bloom (New York: Oxford University Press, 1973), p. 594.
3. Robert Frost, "Birches", ll. 52-53, in *American Poetry and Prose*, ed. Norman Foerster and Robert Falk (1934, rpt.Boston: Houghton Mifflin Company, 1960), p. 914.
4. Mushirul Hasan, "Memories of a Fragmented Nation" in *The Partition in Retrospect* ed. Amrik Singh (New Delhi: Anamika Publishers, 2000), p. 346.
5. Philips Talbot, "Thus Independence came to India", *Hindu*, 4th and 24th August 1997.
6. K.F. Rustamji, "Two Nation Theory Fails: The Triumh of Secularion", *The Tribune,* Dec. 2, 2000. p. 12.
7. Ian Talbot, "Literature and the Human Drama of the 1947 Partition" in *Freedom, Trauma, Continuities: Northern India and Independence,* ed. D.A. Low and Howard Brasted (New Delhi: Sage Publications, 1998), p. 43.
8. Ian Talbot, "Partition in Retrospect" in *The Partition in Retrospect*, ed. Amrik Singh (New Delhi: Anamika Publishers, 2000), p. 322.
9. Khushwant Singh, *Train to Pakistan* (New Delhi: Time Book International, 1981), p. 181.
10. Bhisham Sahni, *Tamas.* Trans. Jai Rattan (1974; rept. New Delhi: Penguin, 1988), p.177.
11. Ahmad Nadeem Qasmi, "Parmeshwar Singh", trans. Vishwamitter Adil and Alok Bhalla in *Stories About the Partition of India* Vol. I, ed. Alok Bhalla (New Delhi: Harper Collins, 1994), p.159. All subsequent references to the story are to this edition and have been incorporated in the text.
12. Quoted in "Communal Harmony", editorial in *Campetition Success Review,* August 2002, p. 16.

13. William Shakespeare, *The Tempest,* Act I, Sc.II, Lines 5-6.
14. *Living Thought of Mahatma Gandhi,* ed. Mulk Raj Anand (New Delhi: NCERT, 1988), p. 56.
15. Ramesh Chandra Sen, "The White Horse", trans. Mihir Bhattacharya, in *Stories About the Partition of India,* Vol. II, ed. Alok Bhalla (New Delhi: Harper Collins, 1994), p. 127. All subsequent references to the story are to this edition and have been incorporated in the text.
16. Lalithambika Antharjanam, "A Leaf in the Storm", trans. Naraya Chandran, in *Stories About the Partition of India,* Vol. I, ed. Alok Bhalla (New Delhi: Harper Collins, 1994), p. 137. All subsequent references to the story are to this edition and have been incorporated in the text.
17. Saadat Hasan Manto, "Mozel", trans. Tahira Naqvi in *Stories About the Partition of India* Vol. Ed. Alok Bhalla (New Delhi: Harper CQllins, 1994, p.153. All subsequent references to the story are to this edition and have been incorporated in the text.
18. *Living Thoughts of Mahatma Gandhi*, ed. Mulk Raj Anand (New Delhi: NCERT, 1988), p. 48.
19. Bapsi Sidhwa, *Ice Candy Man* (New Delhi: Penguin Books, 1988). All subsequent references to the story are to this edition and have been incorporated in the text.
20. S.H. Vatsayan 'Ajneya', "The Refuge", trans. Rachna Sharma, in *Stories About the Partition of India,* Vol.II, ed. Alok Bhalla (New Delhi: Harper Collins, 1994), p. 73. All subsequent references to the story are to this edition and have been incorporated in the text.
21. In. B.R. Nanda, "Foreword", Bhasyan Kasturi, *Walking Alone* (New Delhi: Vision Books, 1999), p. 8.
22. Shakespeare, *The Tempest,* Act I, Sc. II; Lines 5-6.
23. *Living Thoughts of Mahatma Gandhi*, ed. Mulk Raj Anand (New Delhi: NCERT, 1988), p. 23.
24. Chaman Nahal, *Azadi* (1979; rpt. New Delhi: Orient Paperbacks, 1988). All subsequent references to the novel are from this edition and have been incorporated in the text.
25. "Gandhi on the Partition of India". Excerpted from The Way to Communal Harmony by M.K. Gandhi, ed. U.R. Rao. The Tribune (Sunday Reading) June 22, 1997, p. 1.
26. Khuswant Singh, *Train to Pakistan* (New Delhi: Time Book International, 1981).

27. Shaikh Ayyaz, "Neighbours", trans. Saroj Vashistha in *Stories About the Partition of India,* ed. Alok Bhalla (New Delhi: Harper Collins, 1994), p. 187. All subsequent references to the story are to this edition and have been incorporated in the text.
28. Ismet Chughtai, "Roots", trans. Vishwamitter Adil and Alok Bhalla in *Stories About the Partition of India,* ed. Alok Bhalla (New Delhi: Harper Collins, 1994), p. 9. All subsequent references to the story are to this edition and have been incorporated in the text.
29. N.L. Gupta, *Nehru on Communalism,* ed. (New Delhi: Sampradayikta Virodhi Committee, 1965), p. 66.
30. Khwaja Ahmad Abbas, "The Death of Sheikh Burhanuddin", trans. Khuswant Singh, in *Stories About the Partition of India* Vol. II, ed. Alok Bhalla (New Delhi: Harper Collins, 1994), p. 223. All subsequent references to the story are to this edition and have been incorporated in the text.
31. Andrew J. Major, "'The Chief Sufferers': Abduction of Women During The Partition of The Punjab" in *Freedom, Trauma Continuities: Northern India Independence,* ed. D.A. Low and Howard Brasted (New Dehli: Sage Publications, 1998), p. 60.
32. Ibid., p. 65.
33. Rajinder Singh Bedi, "Lajwanti", trans. Alok Bhalla, in *Stories About the Partition of India,* Vol. I, ed. Alok Bhalla (New Delhi: Harper Collins, 1994), p. 55. All subsequent references to the story are to this edition and have been incorporated in the text.
34. Alok Bhalla, "Introduction" in *Stories About the Partition of India*, ed. Alok Bhalla, (New Delhi: Harper Collins, 1994), p. XXV.
35. Ramlal, "A Visitor from Pakistan", trans. Alok Bhalla, in *Stories About the Partition of India,* Vol. I, ed. Alok Bhalla (New Delhi: Harper Collins, 1994), p. 179. All subsequent references to the story are to this edition and have been incorporated in the text.
36. Vishnu Prabhakar, "I Shall Live", trans. Alok Bhalla, in *Stories About the Partition of India,* Vol. II. ed. Alok Bhalla (New Delhi: Harper Collins, 1994), p. 207. All subsequent references to the story are to this edition and have been incorporated in the text.

37. N.L. Gupta, *Nehru on Communalism*, p. 66.
38. Aldous Huxley, *Music at Midnight* (Chandigarh: Vishal Publications, 1974), pp. 7-8.
39. Jamila Hashmi, "Exile", trans. Alok Bhalla, in *Stories About the Partition of India,* Vol. I, ed. Alok Bhalla (New Delhi: Harper Collins, 1994), p. 39. All subsequent references to the story are to this edition and have been incorporated in the text.
40. Kulwant Singh Virk, "Weeds", trans. Alok Bhalla and Gurupadesh Singh in *Stories About the Partition of India,* Vol. I, ed. Alok Bhalla (New Delhi: Harper Collins, 1994), p. 203. All subsequent references to the story are to this edition and have been incorporated in the text.
41. Mohan Rakesh, "The Claim", trans. Richard Williams, in *Stories About the Partition of India,* Vol. III, ed. Alok Bhalla (New Delhi: Harper Collins, 1994), p. 35. All subsequent references to the story are to this edition and have been incorporated in the text.
42. S.H. Vastsayan 'Ajneya', "Getting Even", trans. Alok Rai, in "*Stories About the Partition of India*", Vol. I, ed. Alok Bhalla (New Delhi: Harper Collins, 1994), p.119. All subsequent references to the story are to this edition and have been incorporated in the text.
43. Chaman Nahal, *Azadi* (1979; rpt. New Delhi: Orient Paperbacks, 1988). All subsequent references to the story are to this edition and have been incorporated in the text.

6

Fifty Years After: The Partition in *What the Body Remembers*, *Blood Brothers* and *Kitne Pakistan*

"Stories are not told for the telling, stories are told for the teaching."

The stories of the Partition no longer seem so remote. People from the same country, the same town, the same village, can still be divided by the politics of their religious differences, and, once divided, could do terrible things to each other.[1] The bitter and dark memories of the Partition once more became redolent when ruthless violence was let loose in 1984 when the then Prime Minister, Indira Gandhi was assassinated by none other than her own security guards who happened to be Sikhs and the riots broke out which were equated with the Partition by none other than Congress President Sonia Gandhi.[2] For days afterwards Sikhs all over India were attacked in an orgy of violence and revenge. Many homes were destroyed and the mayhem took nearly 4,000 lives[3]. At that time Rajiv Gandhi had reacted to the riots with a laconic, "When a big tree falls, the earth is bound to shake". [4] Yes, the earth did shake so badly that it created so many 'partitions' in the heart and mind of those who had been living amicably for the centuries. Innocent Sikhs were butchered mercilessly after by being doused in kerosene and than set alight.[5] They died horrible and gruesome deaths. The ghastly killings remained the painful memory of those who had come to Delhi as refugees in 1947 as they remembered that they had been through a similar terror before.

'We didn't think it could happen to us in our own country', they would say, 'this is like Partition again.'[6]

The truth, then, is that the Partition was not over in 1947. It is not a thing of the past. The mistrust between communities, the communal divide and the irrational killings—all these features of the Partition are still hovering around and a small violent happening anywhere and at anytime can let loose similar frenzy. If the Sikhs became targets of communal fury in ghoulish riots in 1984, countless Muslims were slaughtered in 1989 in Bhagalpur in Bihar once the communal riots broke out. Another wave of communal riots swept through the country in the wake of demolition of the Babri Mosque on December 6, 1992. The demolition of the Mosque and its bloody aftermath are termed as the third tragedy in the Indian historical series.[7] The Muslims looked at the demolition as an onslaught on their religion and the incident led to the most religious fury as some communalists retaliated through a series a bomb blasts in Mumbai in 1993 where hundreds of innocent people, irrespective of any religion, died a sad death. All the more, it resulted in a chain reaction from both sides and thousands of Muslims were targeted in Surat and Ahmedabad. Obviously, the line between the two communities has been drawn so deeply along religious lines that a minor incident can lead to ghastly communal riots. Undoubtedly, the current happenings have their roots in history, in the Partition of the country.[8] In each of these instances, the Partition stories and memories have been used selectively by the aggressors.[9]

The irrationality of the religious divide can be easily understood as even after more than fifty years of independence the religious communal divide and its use by politicians for personal gains seems to be still the same. Alas, even today the specter of communalism veiled behind religion still haunts us. The memory of the Hindu pilgrims being burnt alive in the railway coaches in Godhra in Gujarat in 2002, and the horror of the retaliating strikes in Gujarat leading to the killings of

Muslims several times more in number is a recent one. These riots were less communal and more 'political'.[10] It is, indeed, a tragic irony that the home of Mahatma Gandhi who opposed the Partition on religious lines should see such communal carnage.[11] The role of the state machinery has often been questioned in the case of these riots as also in the case of anti-Sikh riots in 1984. The role of various political leaders during such riots has also been questioned.

All this seems to underline the fact that the 'Partition' cannot easily be effaced or set aside as a thing of the past. Even after more than fifty years of independence the Partition is not a closed chapter of history. If we look at the gory tales of arson and murder of 1984, Ayodhya, Godhra and many more, they enable us to recognize how "ever-present Partition" [12] is in our lives and it can no longer be easily put away inside the covers of history books.

No wonder even after more than half a century, the Partition still becomes the subject of exploration for several creative writers. There are many novelists and authors who still realise that the Partition was more than just a political divide, or a division of properties, of assets and liabilities. It was also, to use a phrase that survivors use repeatedly, a 'division of heart'.[13] Several creative writers still remember the untold suffering, tragedy, trauma, pain and violence wrought in the life of communities who otherwise lived together in some kind of social contract. The recurring incidents of riots and communal clashes drag creative sensibilities back to the ghastly incidents of 1947 when people had really gone mad. The Partition has surfaced as a major theme in such recent novels as Shauna Singh Baldwin's *What the Body Remembers* (1999), M.J. Akbar's *Blood Brothers* (2006), and Kamleshwar's *Kitne Pakistan* (Hindi, 2000), translated into English as *Partitions* (2006) by Ameena Kazi Ansari. One of the reasons why the Partition is time and again remembered is also that creative minds wish to revisit it to learn about the past and derive some lessons from that for the present as Roop asserts in *What the Body Remembers*,

"Stories are not told for the telling, stories are told for the teaching."[14]

The novels about the Partition once again express the inexpressible, thus giving voice to silence, to pent up emotions and agony. On the one hand, these recent novels depict the collective as well as individual anguish of those who were being drifted away from their 'homes', at the same time these focus on the religious cynicism and human savagery generated as a result of the 'splitting' of the sub-continent. Communal hatred became so blatant on either side of the border that irrational and fanatical Hindus, Muslims and Sikhs immediately asserted their respective religious identities and loyalties. Mutual animosity, hatred, fear-psychosis and distrust had resulted in psychological restlessness as "friendship became secondary to faith".[15] The novels particularly highlight how the politics of communalism devastated the normal life of those who had nothing to do with the politics of power.

I

Shauna Singh Baldwin's *What the Body Remembers,*[16] written by a half-Sikh woman, is somewhat different from the other two novels as its main emphasis is on the people belonging to the Sikh community who have been marginalised in the Partition literature in general. Set in the Partition background the novel focuses on the tragedy of a Sikh family. The novel makes it clear how the meaning of community gets changed and the Sikhs who have been living in Lahore for centuries become outsiders following the Partition violence. Riots force them to quit Lahore which will now belong to the Muslims. The novel poignantly records the bloodshed, madness and violence of the Partition. Gender issues are also important in the novel.

What the Body Remembers clearly and movingly depicts how the Partition is revisited by a second wife. The author becomes a mouthpiece of all those who were directly or otherwise affected by the tragedy of the Partition. It is the author's attempt to inform the readers about the marginalisation of the Sikhs during the Partition. The novel underlines communal tension in the wake of the Partition. The setting is a small village in Punjab, India, aptly called Pari Darwaza. The hearts of the people belonging to different religious communities are poisoned by the selfish politicians and religious bigots who masquerade to fight for the betterment of their respective communities. In an atmosphere of acrimony and hostility all around the readers witness, from Pari Darwaza, "the beginning of the tense and tumultuous decade that culminates in the violent and still controversial Partition."[17]

This powerful saga of a Sikh family set against the independence movement revolves around three main characters—Sardarji, his first wife Satya and the second wife, Roop. Rawalpindi born, U.K. educated, with a degree in engineering Sardarji is a man caught in the midst of transition on more than one front. He builds canals that criss-cross Punjab and makes energetic blueprints for modern canal-irrigated India. Sardarji's first wife Satya is childless. The story truly begins when Sardarji, a-42-year-old man, takes a 16-something innocent village belle Roop as his second wife. However, behind this family tale of two wives for survival and control of the family the dominant theme of the novel is that of communal tension during the final phase of Indian national Movement followed by the Partition and more gruesome communal violence.

The novel opens in the year 1937 and by then the Muslim leaders had started demanding a separate country—Pakistan—for the Muslims. It was leaders like Jinnah, of course, instruments in the hands of the British who wanted to perpetuate their rule over India by dividing its people on religious lines. Jinnah "continues to press his demand for Muslims representation to be guaranteed when India became self-Governing ..." (p. 286). It gave birth to tension and fear among the people of different communities as they started treating the minority neighbours as 'outsiders' and started seeing each other with suspicion and hatred despite having lived together for centuries. Even before the Partition the bitterness is noticeable in the relationship of the two childhood friends, Roop and Huma. When in 1944 in Shimla Roop meets her childhood friend Huma, who is now Rai Alam Khan's third wife, the conversation between Roop and Huma reveals how communal feelings have poisoned the minds of even good friends:

'Huma,' says Roop. 'Where do you think Pakistan will be?'

'My abu says,' Huma is reciting now, 'wherever there is one Muslim village, there is Pakistan.'

It is not a Muslim village.'

'It is a Muslim village except for tum-log.

Tum-log. You people. A shudder passes through Roop; with one word,

'And where are hum-log—we people—to go?'

'You can go to Hindustan,' says Huma, as if it is all resolved. 'But you can't stay in Pakistan. We don't like Hindus here.' She looks at Roop's shocked expression and gives a high pitched giggle. (p. 350).

Thus the polarities are clearly drawn and an atmosphere of tension prevails among friends and neighbours. The escalating tension reflects the religious and political dynamics that will lead to the cleaving of India.

One Radcliffe line plays havoc with the sentiments of the people as it divided the land and people overnight. It comes as a shock to Roop and Sardarji because for them it is incredible and mind boggling that Lahore would go to Pakistan. Her shock is natural as Lahore had Hindus and Sikhs in majority.[18] To them Radcliffe line sybolises more than a boundary line. "Sir Cyril Radcliffe's boundary line has cut Punjab in two as a child might tear a newspaper.... And the Radcliffe line has done more than break railway connections between cities, or tear headworks from canals—it has severed ties, severed all pretensions to culture, informed everyone of the savagery of which neighbours are capable" (pp. 432-33). Through the tension of Roop the novelist emphasises that the Sikh community was the worst sufferer as the Sikhs were made to flee from the place where they were in majority. Sardarji, representative of every Sikh, feels that people like him are pushed into this Partition. It was due to irrationality, haste and insanity of political leaders that the Sikhs had to suffer. Worse, Radcliffe knew nothing about India and had no fixed rules to go by when he drew the boundaries. Besides, he was given very little time to finish his work.[19] He pleased the leaders but shattered the lives of many.

Roop's family is forced to leave Lahore. It pains her heart to cut off her ties with the native earth. Her journey is fearful and poignant as she is surrounded by fear everywhere. Danger prowls at every step. Circumstances force her to witness many horrifying scenes ranging from molestation of women to rapes and killings on her way to Delhi. She encounters the caravans of terror-stricken refugees who begin to crawl along inadequate roads like her. Their trauma is reflected in her eyes. This was an awful time when all the fountains of love, amity and other such human feelings had dried up giving place to ill-will and hatred. When Roop's eyes fall on her childhood Muslim friend, Huma, being abducted by some Sikh soldiers, she does not raise a cry to save her even once. She thinks "compassion is weakness, disloyalty to the Sikhs". During terrible moments everyone is for oneself. She thinks, "Beware of pity. Pity charmed Sita, pity for an old beggar lured her out of her circle so Ravan could steal her away from Ram" (p. 403). It is from inside the car that she observes with panic many tragic scenes—the tired, old and sick refugees dragging away their own bodies with trepidation all around. She watches "vultures feeding on bodies from a Hindu or a Sikh village!...Bodies, purple-black and bloated, show in patches where the satiated vultures cannot eat anymore. Clawed feet tear and rip, featherless heads delve into flesh, strong beaks peck away eyes" (p. 429). Roop is shattered to see all the mayhem brought in the lives of those who were contented to live a life of their own. They had no complaint against anyone. Why, then, were they pushed into this mad dance of inhumanity? Roop's heart is aggrieved to think:

> Is this India we fought for god-chosen or godforsaken? She is like a woman raped so many times she has lost all count of the trespasses across her body. Who will rescue and pyre the bodies of my quom? What use now to be Hindu, Sikh, Muslim or Christian, what use of quom, the biradari, the caste, the compartments that order our lives? What do they do for us now in time of chaos when person meets person and the question between us is only this: Can you feel as I feel? Do you agree to let me live if I let you live? And will you keep that promise even when no one watches, under cover of sand-storms, when the veil is snatched away, will you be kind? (p. 429).

Roop's state of mind is a clear manifestation of what happened to millions of innocent people across the border in the wake of the Partition. She herself is frightened to see the naked dance of irrational forces wreaking havoc on innocent people in the name of religion as if they had been the real defenders of the community they belong to. She hears the war cries of *Allah ho Akbar!* "It is a small section of sepoys whose bodies forgot all Koranic admonitions as they drank the contents of a bhang still in the last Sikh village they raided....In a few short miles on the Grand Trunk Road their bodies have already learned that any man who kills, maims, hurts or rapes one of another religion finds his second and his third become easier, and easier" (pp. 421-22).

A Sikh novelist though Baldwin is, she does not exonerate the members of her own community from charges of violence. They are shown equally guilty of chaos wrought in the life of others. Nowhere has she betrayed any emotional bias for the Sikhs or against the Muslims. When men turn savages, they behave alike irrespective of their religion. Hence all the major communities share the blame. Baldwin succeeds in maintaining a balanced approach towards different communities throughout the novel.

What the Body Remembers also highlights the plight of refugees who become homeless for no fault of their own. Through the eyes of Roop we observe the miserable condition of the refugees who have lost their land and houses. Carol Batchelor, Chief of UNHCR, the Refugee Agency, defines a refugee as someone who had crossed an international border due to a well-founded fear of prosecution.[20] Ironically, during the Partition the refugees didn't even know clearly where the 'international' border was. They left their homes just to save their life by looking out for the safest haven but faced death at every step during their journey to the land that, too, was alien to them. This is the backdrop against which the Partition riots break and the mass exodus of millions of uprooted and embittered people across the borders drawn arbitrarily by one Sir Cyril Radcliffe begins:

> In all the centuries since it was first incarnated in cobbled stone to carry the armies of Alexander the Great and Sher Shah, then Mughal, then Sikh armies, the two lanes of the Grand Trunk road have never felt the press of so many sorrowing men and women as this day. On bullocks carts and rickety ekkas, pushing three-wheeled rehris, wheeling rusted bicycles, Sikhs and Hindu move east across Punjab, while Muslims from India pour north and west into the province carrying their old, their sick, moving not in hope of freedom and independence, but from the fear their bodies remember from other ages.
>
> And since they know not where the border will be, know not where to stop (pp. 394-95).

The novel is a clear manifestation of the dimensions of forced migration and subsequent suffering and wretchedness. Everywhere there are problems of food, sanitation and shelter. In Delhi Roop tries to comfort others like her. She is shocked to see the heartrending condition of the refugees. They were no better than beggars in the countries they choose as a haven for spending the rest of their life. The similes and metaphors the novelist uses to reveal the trauma of refugees are particularly striking. It is a time when "women and children are being sorted between the two countries like apricots brought in from the orchard. The sorting baskets are the old ones: religion, class, caste, quom" (p. 466). Admittedly, the condition of those who were uprooted was worse than animals.

II

M.J. Akbar's *Blood Brothers*[21] is partly autobiographical in its setting and sequence of events. The past, in the form of the Partition, is revisited by the author to understand the present. The Partition led not only to the inexpressible sufferings but it also divided the Hindus and the Muslims on communal lines in a way that even today both look at each other as 'enemies' and 'others'. Being a Muslim in India may have led to some uneasy moments to the author personally. The question of identity might have surfaced time and again. The theme of communalism is dominant in the novel showing how the meaning of community changes time to time giving place to loss of faith and generating hatred among those who otherwise live amicably during peaceful moments. However, the novel concludes on a very positive note that basically both the Hindus and the Muslims are brothers. And the need for this reminder comes up because violent communal divisions keep on taking place even after more than fifty years of the Partition. It is a skillfully crafted family saga down three generations who witnessed the Partition with choking emotions. Partly autobiographical, the novel is a fine blend of fact and fiction, history and creative imagination. The novel does underline the bitter reality that people can still be divided in the name of religion by none other than selfish leaders who masquerade to be the champions of their respective communities. The novel highlights how the two communities living together amicably before the Partition start treating each other enemies as soon as the division of country is declared on the basis of religion. Religion becomes the basic factor of community identity and its misuse brings about catastrophe in the life of innocent masses.

The novel is set in the pre-partition times of communal harmony in a small jute mill town some thirty miles north of Calcutta along the Hoogly River—Telinipara where the Hindus and the Muslims live amicably. Telinipara is a safe haven for migrant Bihari workers— both Hindus and Muslims; for Bengalis, poor as well as those who are slightly better off. The Sahibs live in the safe 'foreign' world of Victoria Jute Mill in the town.

It is in this surrounding that Prayaag, a Hindu child, whose parents died due to famine around 1870 is saved by none else than a Muslim called Wali Mohammad, the owner of a tea shop. This angel, Wali Mohammad, becomes a symbol of piety and humanity who "retained a stony sympathy for the wrecks of famine" (p. 5). Like Wali Mohammad his wife, Diljan Bibi—a true mother— is a woman full of love and kindness for the child. The childless couple not only saves the child and pulls him out of the jaws of death but decides to adopt Prayaag as their son. Diljan believes that "Prayaag was Allah's answer to her prayers for a son" (p.7). Prayaag is brought up by the Muslim couple and then one day, years later, he is converted into Islam and christened as Rahmat before he gets married to a Muslim girl, Jamila. The conversion is not forced upon him. Maulvi Taslimuddin asks him if he is there out of his free will or if there is a pressure on Prayaag (p. 23). The Maulvi emphasizes:

> I have to insist on these questions because in the Holy Quran, and by the precepts of the Holy Prophet Muhammad, peace be upon him, it is illegal to forcibly

> convert anyone to true faith. You are welcome into the redeeming radiance of Allah only if you come by free will. It is said clearly in the Holy Quran—and remember that every word in the Quran is sent by Allah, it is Allah's book—in verse 256 of the second chapter: *La Ikraha fi ad—deen*. Let there be no compulsion in religion… (p. 23).

The novel, it seems, is also an attempt on the part of M.J. Akbar to make his readers aware of the true nature of Islam. Prayaag's conversion to Islam is quite in contrast to the general reporting of forced conversions to Islam during the Partition.

Rahmatullah or Rahmat as he is called knits Telinipara into a harmonious community where Hindus and Muslims live together sharing each other's culture, joys, happiness, sufferings and sorrows. Friendship, love, trust and faith run deep in this community. However, cracks appear in the harmonious relationships giving way to mistrust and hatred among communities as soon as religion is used as an instrument to divide people by the British. They wanted to create 'partitions' in the hearts of Indians for each other. It is always greedy politicians, rulers with vested interests and the religious fanatics in every community that create the trouble. In *Blood Brothers* one such religious bigot representing the fanatic forces is Nazir Mian, Imam of Rishra, a neighbouring town of Telinipara, who insists on sacrificing a cow on Bakr'Id in 1896. The flame of bigotry also reaches Telinipara when Hazi Zakaria, a businessman, attempts to help the Muslims to sacrifice a cow on Bakr' Id in the quest of Muslim's "struggle for self-respect" (p. 54). A good man like Talat Mian knows that God never claims the life of an innocent animal. He knows that the Muslims want to sacrifice a cow "Not because they want to worship Allah, but because they want to create trouble" (p. 56). There is no religion that demands the life of innocent animals. On the other hand Mangu Qasai, who has opened a butcher's shop near the mosque, plans to sell beef to the white sahibs. It will serve double purpose—sacrifice of a cow on Bakr'Id and a supply of beef to the sahibs.

Rahmat feels burdened by the trust that the illiterate, uncertain community has placed in him. He is worried as "there had never been any trouble between Hindus and Muslims here; there would inevitably be a first time" (p. 57). Rahmat, however, is able to avert the trouble with the help of Burha Deewana, a fakir, a dervish who sets the women of Telinipara against cow slaughter. It is Zubeida and Saira, Rahmat's mother-in-law, who sit squatting before the shop of Mangu Qasai. They insist that Mangu Qasai "would have to swear upon the Holy book that he would not sacrifice a cow on Bakr' Id" (p. 69). They emerge victorious as by the sunset Mangu Qasai pledges, "hand on Quran, to sacrifice a goat the next morning". (p. 69). Saira takes home his cow and returns it only after the festival is over. The victory doubles the elation of a festive eve and peace is regained in Telinipara. All celebrate Id with pleasure. Had the trouble not been averted, it would have caused hatred and bloodshed.

Unfortunately, the selfish leaders who are bent upon dividing 'brothers' and causing ignoble "partitions" among them do not sit in peace. They leave no stone unturned to create trenches of mistrust among them. Trouble once more revisits Telinipara when the kind godsend Dervish dies and it seems as if peace, too, has died with him. With the arrival of Maulana Jauhar Kanpuri to Telinipara communal tension flares up once more. He wants to divide the Muslims in the name of launching reforms in the life of Telinipara's imperfect Muslims by purifying them. Maulana Jauhar brings a tremor in the life of Muslims by insisting, "If Rahmatullah wants to prove that he is a genuine sheikh of Muslims, he should sacrifice a cow on Bakr'Id. The blessings of Allah are five times as great in the case of a cow as compared to a goat" (p. 136). Rahmat is in a fix. He is well aware that cow slaughter will not only lead to trouble and riots but also cause a great blow to the unity and amity that he has established in Telinipara among the Hindus and the Muslims. Somehow Rahmat forces Maulana to blurt that "the sheep, the goat and the camel" are considered lawful for sacrifice. He also tells Rahmat that of all the camel is the most "meritorious for a believer" (p. 138). Maulana is clever enough as he knows that it is not easy to manage a camel in Telinipara. However, a good man like Rahmat can. He will never let his brothers be divided. For a few days he remains silent but on the eve of Id he is relieved to find as Syed Ashfaque Alam who has secretly been entrusted with the duty by Rahmat turns up with a camel. Rahmat heaves a sigh of relief as no cow will be slaughtered the next morning. Ashfaque tells everyone that arranging a camel was not a joke. "More over, they had to keep it secret for who knew what demand Maulana Jauhar would come up with were he given time" (p. 140).

Thus Rahmat and Ashfaque save their small Telinipara from violence, ill-will and bloodshed. Rahmat symbolises what the Quran advocates "*adl, ih.an, rah... mah and h...ikmah*" i.e. justice, benevolence, compassion and wisdom. None of these concepts by itself would promote violence.[22] However, those were the days when communalism raised its ugly head repeatedly as the selfish leaders would not sit in peace. Rahmat, too, falls a victim to the politics of communalism. How long can he save his Telinipara when the selfish leaders of both the communities insist on division of hearts? Rahmat realises that "the Id festival of 1945 was the last time they laughed together (p. 207)." By then like other cities and towns of India Telinipara too becomes the centre of the ominous activities of the RSS and Jamiat-e-Islami. Both order "their brothers to oil the rust of their swords" (p. 207). Both Congress and the Muslim League decide to choose the path of communal divide. Jinnah shows his fury and declares on 29 July 1946, "The time has now come for the Muslim nation to resort to 'Direct Action Day' to achieve Pakistan" (p. 208). Telinipara falls victim to this virus of communalism, as soon as the pamphlet published by the Muslim League reaches the town with an ambiguous massage:

> The Bombay resolution of the All-India Muslim League has been broadcast. The call to revolt comes to us from a nation of heroes.... The day for an open fight which is the greatest desire of the Muslim nation, has arrived. Come, those who rise to heaven.... The shining gates of Heaven have been opened for you. Let us enter in thousands. Let us all cry out victory to Pakistan.... Be ready and take your swords...We shall show our glory with swords in hands and will have a special victory (p. 209).

A good man like Ashfaque who does not endorse Jinnah's idea of Pakistan is killed by the Hindu fanatics on the Holi festival for the simple reason that he is a Muslim. Festivals symbolise togetherness, love and amity. But those who hold irrational views about religion create trouble on festivals such as Holi and Id to create 'divisions' between communities. It is a matter of regret that such religious festivals as Dussehra, Ram Navami, Janam Ashthami, various Puja days of local gods and goddesses, Muharram, Ids, Shaab-e-Barat, and birthdays of Sikh gurus... etc. are being communalised[23] even today.

Communalism emerges victorious on 16th August 1946—the 'Direct-Action Day" when it shows its most hideous face. The author gives a horrendous detail of the communal frenzy of that time:

> Mobs began operating from a little after dawn; curfew was not imposed till nine at night. Policemen were invisible, even traffic policemen. By the nineteenth, the only civil force in the city, the army, was wearing masks to mute the stench of dead bodies piled on carts and shoved into drains. The government offered five rupees per corpse. Nearly 16,000 were killed, and if the Muslims were the "victors" of the opening bouts of frenzy then proportions had evened out by the second and the third day (pp. 209-10).

No doubt, communalism reaped a rich crop of corpses. Innocent people suffered for the madness of those who played with religion for their selfish motives as there is no denying the fact that communalism is a specific form of political use of religion.[24] Rahmat feels shattered when he comes to know that India will be partitioned to create a divided Pakistan, half of it in the west and the other half in Bengal. In a state of dismay and shock he worries with simple logic, "Pakistan has been found for the Punjabi Muslim in the west and the Bengali Muslim in the east. No Pakistan has been offered to Bihari Muslims" (p. 211). He will move to nowhere. He loves his land and people. Once freedom is granted to India on 15th August, 1947, Telinipara, too, hears the periodic clamour of communal tension that spared neither the Hindus nor the Muslims.

M. J. Akbar shows fanatics on both sides who were equally responsible for dividing people and who brought catastrophe in the life of those who were enjoying their normal life. At the assassination of Gandhi, the greedy politician Ram Chatterjee drinks rum and gloats, "Gandhi is dead!" with an exaggerated swivel, he asks, "Who will save these Muslim bastards now?" (p. 217). At the same time he is not happy as Gandhi's death has led to calm. "No one wants to kill Muslim bastards any more." He asks himself repeatedly, "Why had not a Muslim killed Gandhi? Life would have been so uncomplicated" (p. 217).

It is Ram Chatterjee representing communal forces on the Hindu side, who brings trouble in the life of Rahmat after the Partition. Chatterjee lives in Chandernagore. His methods are uncomplicated. He loots grain from wagons at the railway station and sells the food in the black market. In Rahmat's eyes it is a great sin. He confronts Syed Shah Bukhari, the Police officer and gets Ram Chatterjee arrested once he is caught red handed looting the wagons. He is sent to British jail. Now after the Partition it is Chatterjee's turn to avenge himself upon Rahmat. Pullock Sanyal, manager of Satyajit Benerjee's estates instigates Chatterjee to wreak revenge upon Rahmat. He claims that Rahmat is a Pakistani. So, "your duty is to rid our holy land of Pakistanis!" (p. 219). Soon Surjya Modak hears a talk in his restaurant that Ram Chatterjee is planning to kill Rahmat in revenge for sending him to jail. People like Ram Chatterjee have used 'Pakistan' as an excuse for perpetuating further 'partitions' to fulfil their selfish motives. Admittedly the partisan politics have often permitted and sometimes encouraged the intrusion of religion into politics.[25] Rahmat, a representative of the first generation has seen many ups and downs. Even the second generation represented by his son, Akbar, is not spared and it too falls victim to the communal politics. Akbar's friend Benoy Chaudhary comes over to Akbar and tells him that "he must leave Telinipara with his family at once." Rahmat is shocked, "Go where?" he asks as if there is "no place on earth apart from the home he had built two and a half decades ago" (p. 223). Rahmat, who has taught both the Hindus and the Muslims the gospel of love and peace, becomes an 'outsider' overnight. He is seen as a 'Pakistani'. The Partition wreaks havoc on him. Enmity takes the place of Friendship.

Communal feelings have vitiated the mind of people so much so that even a good man like Rahmat is forced to leave his country for Dhaka. The trauma of leaving his hearth and home is noticeable, "I don't want to leave Telinipara," he whimpers. "Let me be... please let me be... I am an old man ... let me be" (p. 225) Rahmat's family is taken to Calcutta in his jeep by Simon, a British officer. They are chased by Ram Chatterjee's gundas in jeep loads. At last it is only due to a virtuous character like Simon that they reach Calcutta where they spend the night in a hotel that serves as a refugee camp. Akbar's son dies there and his wife becomes hysterical due to this shock. Akbar turns cold. Ram Chatterjee fails to kill Rahmat's family. He returns to Telinipara, loots Rahmat's house and kills his friend, Abdul Ghani known as Bauna Sardar. Religion was thus also used as an excuse to grab others' property. People of religion hated the 'others' not out of love for their own religion but to loot their assets. It was nothing but their hypocrisy in the name of their religion. Akbar is so deeply attached to Telinipara that he brings back his family from Dhaka as soon as peace returns to the area. Once again Rahmat, his Hindu friend, Bhagwan Singh and others are together. "Bhagwan Singh would not let go his friend Rahmat's hand." Good days return but Rahmat "seemed in awe of his destiny: he had been reborn twice" (p. 235). When one day the author asks his father, Akbar, as to why he had returned from Pakistan in 1948, he tells a long story in a few words, "There were too many Muslims in Pakistan", as he answers (p. 235).

It is through the author representing the third generation born a few years after the Indian independence that we come to know that even long after the Partition riots do take place and the Muslims in India are seen as 'others'. And every time it is the selfish leaders who keep fomenting religious sentiments to bring about more "partitions".

The Partition remains a permanent reminder of pain and agony to the author as it has occupied a permanent place in the hearts of his family and other Muslim brethren who suffered its onslaughts. Even long after the Partition the bitterness is visible among friends. The irrational communal frenzy and the Partition have caused loss of faith, friendship has given place to bitterness, suspicion and hostility against one another. Even the third generation starts talking of the Partition. Involved in the Partition talks are all friends—Shyam, Mustafa, Jaipal, Kamala and the author himself. Shyam reprimands Muslims and says, "Muslims must make up their mind, they go to Pakistan when they like, they live in India when they want. We Hindus cannot do that" (p. 261). Jaipal, too, is angry at Mustafa's staying back while his father has left for Pakistan. He responds, "Ha! You stayed back because you want the property that your father left behind! You go and see him whenever you want. What difference does it make to you? Only Hindus suffered in the Partition of their motherland" (p. 261). But it is the good and noble boy Kamala who cools them down. He is always for peace among friends. He interferes, "What is there to argue about? Indian Muslims marry among us, so they are one of us" (p. 261). Kamala, the author's friend is always anxious to find balm in the most obscure cupboard, for he hates confrontation of any kind. Confrontation over the Partition among the boys of third generation implies that the virus of hatred creeps from generation to generation causing havoc to the harmonious fabric of India and making way for more 'partitions'.

Communalism in the wake of the Partition has given way to further 'partitions' and suspicion so much so that Akbar, author's father, is sent to jail, during war with Pakistan in 1965, only because his in-laws live in Pakistan. Nobody can deny the reality that Akbar, like his father, Rahmat, stands for Hindu-Muslim unity and is loyal to his country. It is his love and devotion for the nation that he exhibited during Indian war with China by donating his ring for the national defence fund. Again the selfish politician, Ram Chatterjee plays havoc with Akbar's faith by forging a letter and making the authorities believe that he is a traitor and supplies information across the border. Akbar feels humiliated as the tag of a 'traitor' is attached to the one whose family symbolises love and unity among the Hindus and the Muslims. This single action changes his life. His own "brothers" shatter his faith. Many Muslims suffer even today as their integrity to the nation is seen with suspicion because borders are created between them—borders which are the embodiments of violence bred by politicians.[26] The creators of 'divisions' are the ones who use religion for their partisan politics and selfish purposes. These are the people like RSS man Kanhaiyalal Sahu and Zahid Quereshi from Jamaet-e-Islam who play in the hands of selfish politicians like Ram Chatterjee and greedy businessmen like Girdharilal Gupta who use people for selfish ends and make them fight for their own benefit. They stealthily supply arms and ammunitions for bloodshed and divide people as they also find the policy of "divide and rule" of the British useful. Girdharilal Gupta, the new owner of Victoria Mill, pays money to politicians to create trouble through labour unions just to deviate workers' mind from their demands. The author asserts that such politicians are experts in creating 'divisions' among innocent people. Hence even after independence and the Partition the process of dividing people through riots and hatred has not come to an end. Wali, the rickshaw-wallah, is killed long after independence during a procession on a festival. Wali "was a simple man, a poor man, an innocent trying to make a miserable living so that he might eat a few vegetables along with his rice every day. His murder was neither revenge nor accident; it was the lust of venom" (p. 339) Likewise, Mohan Teli and Jalil Mastan become victims of hatred and get killed. All this causes a rift between the Hindus and the Muslims and they start distancing themselves from each other. Most start leaving Telinipara and go to Bihar. Others take shelter with their relatives. However, the author's father does not let the few Hindus in his neighbourhood leave, and they stay back.

Time and again irrationality is manifested in the miscreants like Ram Chatterjee and the communalists like him who paste posters presenting Prophet's caricatures on the walls of the mosque. The procession on Muharram is attacked with crude bombs supplied by the men of Chatterjee eclipsing peace in Telinipara. This leads to bloodshed and finally the death of Kamala, the author's friend, a custodian of Hindu-Muslim unity. Thus we see that the selfish politicians, religious bigots and irrational people continue to create more "partitions" among people who wish to live in peace.

III

Kamleshwar's *Kitne Pakistan*[27] laments the various divisions made on the basis of religion. While examining the Partition on the Indian sub-continent he very artistically uses Pakistan as a 'metaphor' to explain how various similar 'divisions' are created all across the world along lines of religions or ethnicities. Such divisions of humanity along communal grounds are in fact happening all over the world leading to immense suffering, violence and uprooting of innocent people.

At the same time he also touches upon the very sensitive gender issue explaining how women had been the worst sufferers during those terrible days. Doing this, however, he never appears pessimistic as the novel ends on an optimistic note hoping for a peaceful beginning. *Kitne Pakistan* deals mainly with the Partition of India and its aftermath. The main reference of the novel is the turmoil created by communal forces altogether during India's partition in 1947. The theme of communalism dominates the novel. However, the novel presents a limitless canvas against which the extraordinary trial in the history of mankind runs its course. Present in a court that transcends space and time are those emperors, rulers and dictators of the past who brought havoc to the mankind. Along with political leaders there are present in the court of adeeb, littérateur, religious zealots and scheming gods of mythology. All stand accused of creating countless fractured nations, leaving a never ending trail of hatred and distrust.

The novel can be analysed and studied at various levels. It is not based on a single theme or incident. It has various themes running through its backdrop. The most significant and extraordinary feature of the novel is that it has no hero or villain.[28] The protagonist is a nameless adeeb or littérateur. The novelist does not want to limit his protagonist to specific confines by giving him name and place. He is made to transcend time and space in the course of the narrative. He is a contemporary Everyman, a man of a many parts and personae. He is introduced as a writer who has lived through India's partition, experiencing the trauma of hearts and mind being divided as the contours of Pakistan are drawn up by the British. Since he stands for Everyone, the adeeb plays multiple roles. In interrogative discourse, the adeeb questions everyone. He is a journalist who questions the establishment. He is also playing the role of an unrequited lover whose mistress lives across a volatile border. He is a historian who questions pantheons of divinity as well as civilisational myths and history, and finally he is an activist who rails against massacres, in imperialism and nuclear proliferation. In each of these roles, the adeeb comes across as a person with an extremely sensitive conscience which makes him take a position of critical moderation. He articulates common man's concerns which have gone largely unheard in history's relentless march of time. It is through surrealistic technique that Time calls all those to his court who had brought havoc to the civilisation in the past centuries.

Kamleshwar, unlike historians and other novelists, does not hold any particular person responsible for the Partition and ensuing mayhem. He insists that even Mohammad Ali Jinnah was "deliberately made a trump-card by the Englishmen" (p. 282). He failed to comprehend the nefarious designs of the British and fell an easy prey to their communal policy. The author, it seems, is not happy with Mountbatten who could not rationally justify the two-nation theory based entirely on religion. By putting the onus of decision on Jinnah, Mountbatten would never be able to acquit himself.[29] It was the tragedy of Jinnah that he was unable to retract statement he made in public. Mountbatten himself tells his wife Edwina:

> Having openly demanded the partition of India, he cannot take back his words, no matter how much he regrets them now. If he does, he will lose all credibility and no politician can bear to do so. This is the strength as well the weakness of movements that are born from stirred passions. A statement, once issued cannot be retracted even if, in hindsight, it is discovered to be incorrect or inappropriate. Whenever this happens, brute forces, opposed to change, rear their ugly heads (p. 42).

Jinnah, though, wanted time to think over the issue of Pakistan, he was not allowed to do so by Mountbatten. Jinnah was helpless and too aware that in the game of political chess, "he was a mere pawn in the hands of the British. He was being paid back in his same coin—Pakistan!" (p. 45). Jinnah to whom Pakistan "was an impossible and ill-considered dream..."

(p. 279) fell easy prey to the communal politics of the British government that projected him as the leader of the Muslims in India. It was the nefarious plans of the imperial government, otherwise "God-fearing, pious Muslims in India would never have accepted this pork-eating atheist as their leader" (p. 282). Over and over again, Mountbatten has held Jinnah responsible for insisting on Partition. By putting the onus of the decision on Jinnah, "Mountbatten has acquitted himself" (p. 285). It is a reality, then, as the adeeb is told by one in the court, "Jinnah did not make history... he was created by the powers of imperialism" (p. 96). It was that imperialist power that turned Jinnah into a staunch communalist who would not agree for anything less than a separate country for the Muslims. Similarly, Mountbatten had thrusted Cyril Radcliffe to write the destiny of millions of people of this land. He was neither a sociologist nor a geographer then, how could he mark the boundary line? As Kabir resents, "This barrister, in whose hands you've thrust the butcher's knife, cannot even distinguish between wheat and barley! And this butcher is going to divide Punjab?" (p. 319). Along with the marks on the map, mass passions were aroused in the pre/post partition era leading to a holocausts, mass rapes, abductions, cold-blooded murders, and communal frenzy drew the lines of two nations:

> So, India witnessed the agony and ecstasy over the massacre and festivities engendered by its partition.... No one knew where exactly Cyril Radcliffe's line had ripped the land in two. But for those who mourned or celebrated, this line was clearly visible. The area littered by the corpses of Hindus and Sikhs was Pakistan; the region strewn with the corpses of Muslims was India. The corpses alone determined where the borders lay (p. 324).

The common man had to pay the price of freedom as he was the worst victim of communal violence. Religious arrogance and bitterness spread by colonial politics had split the national identity into two—India and Pakistan—but a human being is not a geographical territory who can be cut up and parceled off anywhere.[30] The "trauma of hearts and minds being divided as the contours of Pakistan are drawn up by the British"[31] is a main characteristic of Kamleshwar's *Kitne Pakistan.* The life of common people was devastated in the wake of communal violence so much so that they were not happy with the Partition. The common man is represented in the novel by Tannu, Major Hasan—an army officer who returns from the World War II after the Armistice has been declared. He comes to his village Gangauli and is pained to learn about the plan of India's partition. He loves his village and people so much that the idea of Pakistan does not appeal to him at all. He remembers the days in the battlefield and tells others, "I have witnessed the macabre dance of death in the battlefield. When death came close, I remembered Allah and was reminded not of Mecca or Karbala, but of Gangauli.... If Allah is everywhere, what is the difference between Gangauli and Mecca, the indigo warehouse and Kaaba, the waters of Zamzam and that of our pond?" (p. 49). Tannu tries to reason with the Hakim Sahib, a staunch Muslim, who calls Tannu blasphemous for having so moderate views about religion, "Anything built on the foundations of hatred and fear can never flourish" (p. 49). Tannu represents all those rational Muslims, Sikhs and Hindus who were against the idea of Pakistan and the Partition. People who were forced to migrate to the 'other' country were equally dejected. Communal tension and violence made the shift from the known to the unknown apprehensive as it was a journey from sanity to madness. Search for a new roof and the economic insecurity made everyone so uncertain and distressed on both sides of the border that they wept days and nights. Tannu ironically states about Jinnah that,

> If he so desires, he can exhume his wife Rati's remains from her grave here and carry them to Pakistan, because he has no bond with the soil. But kulsum can neither take away her ancestor's graves nor that of her dead son 'muntaj' to

Pakistan. If all the graves of Hindustan are carried away, the country's very soul will be ravaged. Muslims will certainly get a fragmented state to themselves, but they will leave behind their hearths and homes. ... I am a Muslim and I love this village because, I am this village ... (pp. 48-49).

Salma, Zainab, Buta Singh Vidya and Surjit Kaur are other representatives of common people like Tannu who were against the Partition and whose lives were ruined by the Partition violence. They lived in the new country with fragmented identities. Communal frenzy absolutely ruined their peaceful lives. Through these characters the novelist hints at the madness of creating 'partitions' and how 'partitions' bring pangs of separation in the lives of people. Admittedly, it is religious obscurantism, narrow-mindedness and bigotry in the name of going back to fundamentals that tends to divide people whom life and history have brought together.[32]

Kamleshwar, like M.J. Akbar, underlines how the political use of religion caused rift and hatred among the Hindus and the Muslims in India. The selfish politicians and religious leaders maneuver religion for political use and divide people along religious lines creating hatred among them. About one such religious leader, Kulsum, a Muslim woman, reports, "Arrey, that man who has arrived from Aligarh, the one who wears a black sherwani and ... brandishes a cigarette... he referred to the number of times in the Koransharif that Allah exhorted the mians to vote for the Muslim league" (p. 46). Likewise, the Hindu bigots exploit their brethren. One Hindu pandit with the tilak mark on his forehead tells how the god Krishna has declared, "O, Arjun, I am the Supreme Power. There is none but I. Today, beloved Bharat of the Gita sends forth a clarion call to each Hindu, exhorting him to rise and banish these vile Muslims from the sacred banks of the Ganga and Jamuna" (p. 46). This is how the illiterate people are deceived in the name of religion and God and made to hate each other. An Afghan common man turned into a mujahid, weeping, appears in the adeeb's court and complains, "We were not blood-thirsty mercenaries to begin with. Like all children, we were born innocent, but self- interest and the lust for power transformed us into beasts.... How I wish we had been trained to work in the fields and factories" (p. 179). Similarly,' Nikhil Chakravarthy tells adeeb why Hindu Pandits are demanding a Hindu homeland or the version of Pakistan, "Pakistan carries on giving birth to more Pakistans.... It is an infectious disease. As long as religion, race, caste and imperialist ambitions continue to hold mankind in thrall, as long as lust for power and supremacy thrives, this planet will continue to witness the birth and evolution of many such monstrous Pakistans" (pp. 181-82).

Badruddin Umar is right that communalism as a specific form of political use of religion appears in India with the rise of national movement in the fourth quarter of the nineteenth century.[33] In this context Salma reminds adeeb in his court how Lokmanya Tilak, "sought to identify the quest for independence with the Ganpathi Utsav celebrations and turned the former into a purely Hindu movement" (p. 94).Thus he divided the hearts. 'Pakistan', thus, stands for a metaphor for division of hearts leading to mistrust when there is lust for power by using religion for political ends. Even today the practice is being repeated. Kamleshwar uses Pakistan as a metaphor for communal divide leading to bloodshed in the name of religion.

The time of independence in 1947 was a time of strange paradoxes. The opening lines in *The Tale of Two Cities* poignantly sum up the state of affairs that prevailed in the wake of India's independence:

> It was the best of times, it was the worst of times, it was the age of wisdom, it was the age of foolishness, it was the epoch of belief, it was the epoch of incredulity, it was the season of light, it was the season of Darkness, it was the spring of hope, it was the winter of despair, we had

everything before us, we had nothing before us, we were all going direct the other way....[34]

Sadly, the independence brought with it massacres, rapes, abduction, hatred and suspicion, and in the name of religion there was large scale bloodshed which no religion on the earth preaches.[35] *Kitne Pakistan* is the voice of a man who happened to live through, and keenly felt those troubled times.

Besides religious insanity, every kind of irrational discrimination comes under Kamleshwar's scrutiny and interrogation. Casteism, too, gives birth to 'divisions' among fellow human beings. It is Salma who claims that casteism has destroyed religion by segregating it within mutually exclusive compartments. Through Salma, Kamleshwar questions the caste system among the Hindus. She tells the adeeb, "Your caste system has become your true religion. ... By asserting that individuals are born from different parts of Brahma's body, they have established a faith built on the difference between one human being and another. In today's terminology, one could well say that your Brahmins have created a Pakistan for themselves" (p. 93). Similar 'Pakistans' are created among the Muslims as well, as an old man of history says, "Even in Hindustan, Islam becomes the victim of a kind of outdated Islamic Brahminvad, controlled by the vested interest of priests. ... In Hindustan, the priests moulded Islam into the Hindu system of caste" (p. 136). It was perhaps under its impact that Aurangzeb who followed and perpetuated this system in the name of Islam became a Muslim Brahmin." Who "gave precedence to religion over humanitarian concerns" (p. 136).

Kamleshwar in *Kitne Pakistan* also holds some historians responsible for spreading communal ideology through their writings that pave the way for more divisions among people. He, very candidly, lambastes those historians who create many 'Pakistans' or 'partitions' of hatred through subjective and partial accounts of history. The adeeb questions, cross examines and passes strictures against those historians who brought havoc with the future generations by writing speculative histories and paved way for more 'partitions' among those who had been living together enjoying the mutual love and goodwill, for the centuries.

The adeeb fumes with anger against those historians who have evolved their own histories relating to Babri Mosque. Until 1857 there was no question of a Ram temple at Ayodhya but the wrong information about Babar was presented before people to divide Indians on religious lines:

> The two crucial pages of *Babarnama* which prove that the king had gone to Avadh and not to Ayodhya, mysteriously disappeared. Having played this dirty trick, the British and, particularly, H.R. Neville, the Faizabad gazetteer, went a step further. The latter placed on record the falsehood that Babar had stayed in Ayodhya for a week and ordered the demolition of the Ram Mandir (p. 61).

This one incident of tempering with 'history' has cost thousands of lives of innocent Hindus and Muslims so far. Besides, it has led to permanent feuds, distrust and hatred and 'partitions' among them. The historians give religious tinge to every battle and those irrational arguments change the parameters of social, religious and historical realities and lead to animosity among people. And as the adeeb observes, "The vanquished deliberatively erase truth and memory. They record in word and deed a history warped to suit their own perspective" (p. 141).

The adeeb rebukes the historian Shibli Nomani for his biased version of history in which he defended the cruel ruler, Aurangzeb. The adeeb is right in asserting, "History written in blood and recorded under coercion can never be other than suspect. Such accounts are written by professional historians who are paid to do so" (p. 195). The attacks on Hindu states are wrongly recorded as attacks on 'kafirs' by the biased historians which leads to more 'partitions' even today and people look at each other with hatred and enmity. The adeeb lashes out at Hazrat Shibli Nomani for his bigoted version and vision of history. He says:

> For faith and religion rarely keep up with the realities of life and invariably lag centuries behind. It is the discrepancy between religion and reality that lays the foundation for the many "Pakistans" that have no grounds at all for taking root (p. 196).

Thus, the adeeb, through arguments with those summoned in his court, asserts that such biased and opinionated history must be brushed aside and eschewed if we want to have love, peace and harmony across the world.

From a particular event Kamleshwar moves on to a world-wide phenomenon. Hence Pakistan emerges as a 'metaphor' for more politically motivated divisions and hatred in the name of religion. One ghastly event of the Partition bred many 'partitions' in the time that followed. Since 1947, many Pakistans are being carved out not only in India but in different parts of the world. Politicians, religious diehards and even the common men failed to learn lessons from the past mayhem and continue to give in to anti-social elements in the name of religion. Accordingly, *Kitne Pakistan* is not about India alone. It has a wider perspective—a macro study of people all over the globe who have undergone injustice, oppression and dislocation of various kinds. It is about those who have suffered the partition of one or the other kind. The adeeb as an everyman expresses his anger as many 'Pakistans' are being created all over the world let alone India.

The adeeb gives a very painful account how the process of creating more 'Pakistans' is escalated through terrorism and religious fanaticism. He explains how ULFA, LTTE and those in Punjab brought massacres one after another in the wake of terrorism (pp. 50-51). Behind all these terrorists the sustaining power is always selfish politicians who divide people by creating differences. The narrator expresses his anger against Simranjit Singh Mann and Abdullah Bukhari, the Shahi Imam of Jama

Masjid who so often instigate their brethren from their respective communities. Abdullah Bukhari announced, "If the Babri Masjid is demolished, rivers of blood will flow. This is the Shahi Imam's decree" (p. 51). Similar is his annoyance against the leaders of Vishwa Hindu Parishad and the Bajrang Dal who keep on crying hoarse, " the Ramjanmbhoomi Mandir will be built, in fact, we shall not rest till we liberate Krishna Janambhoomi and the Kashi Vishwanath mandir" (p. 51). All are bent upon creating their own Pakistans. All the accused are summoned in the court of the adeeb along with the victims who are crying in the court pleading for justice. The adeeb's peon is right when he says, "It took birth in the harvest of 1947. It urges both Hindus and Muslims to be zealots" (p. 57). Even today innocent people suffer death throes due to the prevailing communalism. The adeeb witnesses how "the corpses screamed and shouted and moaned. It was unclear as to who was killing whom, because blood thirsty citizens of the world's many 'Pakistans' were shooting their own people" (p. 80).

The adeeb regrets many 'Pakistans' being carved out all over the world. In the court of the adeeb Comrade Imam Nazish, too, laments the creations of many 'Pakistans'. He admits that it is wrong to "determine national creations on the basis of religion." Today, he explains:

> Efforts are on to create Pakistans of hatred in every nation in the world. That's what happened in Bosnia, Cyprus, the fragmented Soviet Union and the new Russian Federation. And it is happening in Afghanistan today. Using hatred as a prop, everyone is involved in creating new Pakistans against the interest of their own people" (p. 83).

It is true. Time has changed and hatred determines man's identity and caste today. It is hatred that enriches the soil of ill-will and strengthens the resolve of revenge.

Besides, Kamleshwar adds some fictional episodes to highlight the irrationality of the division. This is done to indicate that 'Pakistans' are also wrought in human relationships in the form of distances and rifts among people. Such a 'Pakistan' was created between two brothers after the Partition of India. It was in 1965 Indo-Pak war when two brothers were facing each other. Major Yaqub Khan, the elder one, fought for Pakistan and Caption Yunus Khan for India. The war had lent another dimension to the painful tragedy of partition when two siblings were ranged against each other—a 'Pakistan' was created between brothers and both were paying the price of the Partition of the land. Sadly, Yaqub Khan could not save himself and was killed by no other but his own brother (p. 327).

IV

The Partition stories often tell us that women are vulnerable for being women and for their sexuality. They are also victims of the gender dimensions of ethnic nationalism. Women had been the worst targets of sexual violence during the Partition. The 'other' community was punished and avenged by assaulting their women. The common crime that took place during the Partition violence was rape and sexual abuse culminating in psychological consequences that included wounded psyche, guilt and shame. During those troubled days of communal frenzy women were sexually assaulted to dishonour the opponent community and nation. Women were raped and impregnated with the seed of the other religion, and in this way, not only were they rendered impure individually, but through them, the entire community could be polluted for they would give birth to 'impure' children. Women suffered for no fault of their own. Even then the history of national movement does not give due place to these suffering lots. For decades their voices had been rendered unheard and, of course, the emotional linkages outweighed the political historiography. However, as we revisit the Partition, a human view of the event is an imperative. In fact, as Urvashi Butalia has put it, "the only memorial to this colossal rampage is its literature."[36] With the renewed focus on the partition literature there emerged a new school of thought which spoke of the women's point of view which earlier was not taken note of. This, in fact, is the only medium to transmit the anguished experiences.[37]

What the Body Remembers and Kitne Pakistan can well be studied from gender perspective also. Both the novels illustrate how women had been the worst victims of the Partition violence and communal hostility, and simultaneously also highlight their suffering and victimization in patriarchy. Shauna Singh Baldwin's *What the Body Remembers*[38] is a fine account of violence against women inflicted in the name of tradition in patriarchy. Roop, the main character of the novel, suffers due to patriarchal values, besides the Partition violence. Hence, she becomes a victim of intra as well as inter-community violence.

Woman is victimised right from her childhood. Roop has cherished some dreams about her marriage that are shattered. She, as a young girl, dreamed that "She won't marry a village lambardar like Papaji—she is as beautiful as (her) Mama and can marry a man higher than a headman. May be a military man, a trading, and money lending sahukar, a land owing jagirdar.... May be a raja" (p. 68). She would often dream that "she will have a palanquin made in London and perhaps her husband -to- be will come for her in a wedding procession with an English bagpipe and drum band, instead of an Indian shehnai and dhol-drum band. She'll tell Papaji to ask her husband to bring trumpets—she likes trumpets—they'll play 'Nikka Mota Bajra' just for her" (p. 95). This motherless daughter knows that marriage is the only passport out of Pari Darwaza where she lives. So when she learns that she is to be married to a wealthy Sikh landlord, she is expectedly elated and overjoyed. She thinks that she would be a beloved wife of her husband and agrees readily to leave her present life to the unknown as the second wife as since her childhood she has been taught by tradition to say "hanji and yes-ji" and never "nahinji and no-ji". She is taught to speak "softly" and to "never feel angry, never, never" (p. 85). The tradition has trained her not to rebel against the decisions taken by the male members of the family. Even in her childhood after the death of her mother, her father Bachan Singh wishes that her aunt, Revati Bhua must teach her "the great importance of her chunni, her modesty, the danger of unknown men, and the importance of obedience 'for her own good'(pp. 83-84). The custom does teach woman obedience to her husband and elders. Woman is groomed up for her marriage as Revati Bhua demands of Roop, "you want to make a good marriage; you must be more graceful, more pleasing to your elders" (p. 85). Besides, Roop is taught to "speak softly, always softly!" and "never feel angry. You might be hurt, but never ever feel angry" (p. 85).

Violence is wreaked on Roop's heart and mind when her father decides to get her married to a man much older than her because he is a rich man and may be a great help to Roop's father. We see that in view of their economic and social-political significance the choice of relationships is determined by the elders.[39] Roop is not even given a choice. So she is married away. It reminds us of Hir of the Punjabi legend who falls prey to the tradition held dear by the elders. Custom or tradition did not allow women to take decisions in matter relating to their marriage. "Against her wishes Hir is forcibly put in the palanquin and taken to her in-laws.[40] Ironically, in Roop's case there are no dreams, no trumpets and no palanquin.

Sardarji's "little brown koel", innocent and childlike Roop fails to realise that Satya, Sardarji's first wife, will end up belittling her and will look for ways to get rid of her. And it is clear that Satya will make her feel small, insignificant—intimidated by her supremacy and authority over her. Satya "will have to show Roop an example. Examples create fear, fear keeps control" (p. 170). Thus both the women are pitted against each other by none other than patriarchy. Satya, who manages Sardarji's flour mill, controls all the workers and keeps all the accounts and has full control over his property, treats Roop as inferior—a low-class-born girl. She plans one day that she will throw Roop out of Sardarji life as soon as Roop bears children for Satya. Her rival is not only 25 years younger, but of considerably lower social rank, and her husband's obvious infatuation with Roop rankles her considerably. Roop goes through the pain and agony of giving birth to her children; watch the children till their naming ceremony and then handing them over to childless Satya as "gifts". She bears the birth pangs of her children only to give them away against her wishes. Sardarji, her husband, forces her to go for "sacrifice, the happiness of giving" (p. 175). Nobody has the heart to feel what she desires. Neither has anybody ears to listen to what she wishes to say:

> But I like babies. I want my own. I know how to look after them.... I love their soft cheeks, their tiny feet. I love the way they look at their mothers (p. 175).

Roop is easily cowed down by patriarchy as she knows that "If she refuses, she can be sent home a failure, a burden to Papaji. Tongues will flap in the village. Papaji's izzat will be dragged in the mud. ..." (p. 176). Through the use of Sita's myth the novelist conveys to the readers that woman is made to pass through a test— an ordeal. "This is a fire test, the kind of test Ram asked Sita to take when he become unsure that Sita was worthy to be his queen" (p. 176). Roop faces an ordeal and she has to prove her faithfulness and obedience to Sardarji by giving away her children to Satya. Even after centuries nothing has changed for women as the mindset of males has not undergone a considerable change.

Unfortunately, the marriage turns out to be a nightmare for the young and innocent Roop. One day when suspicion overpowers her that Satya might poison her, she goes back to her father's house, leaving behind here children. However, she does not get warm welcome as women in patriarchy are considered 'no responsibilities' of parents as soon as they are married off. Their happiness is no consideration for the parents. Roop needs support and comfort which, however, she does not get. On the contrary, her father reprimands her severely for leaving her husband's house. Says Bachan Singh, her father:

> 'Beti'.... 'You should go back to him. You have been here since after Diwali, but you are staying too long; we all will be disgraced. Go back, before the eyes of the world are turned upon us, before men in the village council begin raising questions about you.... You have come back without your children, and everyone in Pari Darwaja will say you are here without Sardarji's permission (p. 269).

Thus daughters are not welcome if they come back to stay with their parents for ever. They are seen "as outsiders" once they are married off. This practice is perpetuated in the name of custom, and unmindful of the agony to the women. They are left at the mercy of in-laws.

Anyhow, she joins Sardarji on one condition that she will not give any one of the children to Satya. The struggle between the two women for the control of children and for the husband reaches a poignant end when, eventually, Roop demands the ouster of the elder one from the household and Satya is sent away to Rawalpindi where she is all alone, looks after Sardarji's haveli and finally dies a sad death.

Satya, on the other hand, is equally the victim of violence through patriarchy. It is clear that "Satya was Sardarji's tool, the instrument by which he tortured Roop, then stood back complaining how women fought like cats, never giving him any peace. But so too was Roop the instrument by which he tortured Satya" (p. 331). He fails to bring around conciliation between his two wives. He lets them fight. Had he tried to negotiate their conflicts he would have saved the separation of the two wives. In fact, Satya is a victim of violence to her whole being. Sardarji cheats Satya as he decides to bring Roop as his second wife. Satya is pained that Sardarji chose to get married quietly and it is "a secret betrayal, a marriage with no music, no relative, no dowry" (p. 320). Satya is not even once asked about the marriage because men are also conditioned by patriarchal code which teaches them that women's words are of no consequence. Wisdom lies with men.[41] This betrayal rankles in the heart of Satya till she breathes her last. She remains loyal to her husband. However, he deceives her loyalty. When Roop forces Sardarji to oust Satya, it is a big shock to her. Even the son that was given to her is claimed back. Now she is left all alone to fend for herself and "alone, she ate when hungry, slept when tired, bathed when she felt it necessary to feel clean limbs. Alone, she spoke aloud to herself, spoke her mind as a woman much older..." (p. 29). Sardarji discards her as a useless thing only because she fails to bear a child. How can one abandon his wife for the simple reason? Why are there choices with men only? If the fault lies with man, the woman is not allowed to go for another marriage. Isn't it hypocrisy on the part of men? Sardarji represents the double standards in the patriarchal set up. He very simply and coarsely says, "Satya, I have decided. When I take up my posting at Lahore, you will remain here. You will be looked after, you will want for nothing. But you cannot come to Lahore. You fight too much—I never get any peace" (pp. 298-99). Perhaps Sardarji does not try to understand that it is not food and clothes that a woman needs. She can even live without basic needs of life if she is with her husband; if the person she loves, loves her. Satya's ego is severely wounded when she feels that even her servants had started talking. She hears "poor men laugh at her in the bazaar beyond the gate" (p. 300). She has become a laughing stock for those who dared not stand before her. Tears come in her eyes as the absence of Sardarji 'began to fester like a wound that would not heal. Sardarji's indifference shudders her to the core. She is persecuted for the simple reason that she has failed to produce an heir. For this reason she is reduced to the level of an object—throw it if useless. Sometimes she asks herself in desperation, "Could he not have kept her with him, like these useless things" (p. 300).

Satya feels so bad that she expresses an identity crisis. She experiences as if she belongs to nowhere:

> I am not wife, my husband has abandoned me. I am not widow, for he still lives. I am not mother, for the son he gave me is taken away, I am not sister, for I have no brother. With no father, I am but daughter of my Bebeji. And so I am no one (pp. 314-15).

It is the tragedy of Satya that she suffers for no fault of her own. She hopes, "Surely there will come a time... when just being can bring izzat in return... when a woman will not be owned, when love will be enough payment for marriage, children or no children. ... (p. 316). Satya is the embodiment of thousands of women who suffer at the hands of their husbands who persecute wives in the name of tradition. Hence, agony of both the women due to patriarchy is captured against the backdrop of the partition suggesting irrationality of both.

Above all *What the Body Remembers* categorically explains how women had been the worst victims of the Partition with violence perpetrated on them through honour killings, abduction and rape. The novel gives a heartrending account of women's suffering caused by uprootedness. Roop, Huma, Kusum, Revati Bhua and Jorimon are all the sufferers of the ferocity caused by the Partition. All these women are victims of Communal violence in one or the other way.

The wounded psyche of all the uprooted and victimised women is manifested through Roop. She observes every poignant scene with bewilderment and fear. The traumatic condition of every woman is reflected through the anguish Roop undergoes. Roop leaves Lahore with her children because her 'earth', home and people are partitioned. Roop has no choice but to leave Lahore for Delhi for the simple reason "where the men go, their women and children must also go" (p. 394). She has no identity without her husband. Roop's story is not just a tale of what might have happened to her in Lahore; it is the story of thousands of Hindu, Muslim and Sikh women who fell victims to the orgy of violence to their mind and body. Roop's story is the story of the division of lives as seen and experienced by her. Lahore and its people become strangers for her overnight. The religious senselessness has rendered people so insensitive that even Mani Mai, a Muslim maid servant "watched them leave too cheerfully" (p. 396). Revati Bhua surrenders herself before the Muslim hooligans and agrees to undergo conversion in order to save her family. Sardarji entrusts Roop and children to the care of his car driver as he himself will join her later at Delhi. Her journey towards India is full of dangers as she witnesses countless gory sights of death and destruction on her way to India.

During such episodes she witnesses her childhood friend Huma being abducted by none other than her own Sikh brethren. For a moment she also fears onslaught on her body from the Muslim soldiers who surround Roop and Jorimon. Though Jorimon is a Muslim, she is assaulted by none other than the Muslim soldiers. She is about to be raped when Roop fights back courageously and saves her. Roop thinks "If men treat a woman they know to be of their quom in this cruel way, can any woman be safe?" (p. 425). Roop is right. Woman has no religion of her own. She is made to satisfy the lust of male members of any community. Roop saves her life by lying that she is a Muslim showing the attackers the name engraved on her wrist in Persian script and tells them that her brother is a soldier like them. She is mystified to hear of "women abducted, mutilated, always by *them* –never by *us.* Men etch their anger upon woman-skin, swallow their pride dissolved in women's blood" (pp. 433-34). Having reached Delhi she views the same tragic scenes of bloodshed, abduction and rape. She hears the same stories of women's trauma. For her the country has changed, people have changed but their attitude to women remains unchanged. In Delhi too women belonging to the rival community were treated with the same cruelty as "rape is one man's message to another: 'I took your pawn. You move'" (p. 450). The rape and sexual molestation of women during communal violence played an important part in reinforcing the communal terror.[42]

Roop's soul is wounded to see "so much shame, so little izzat for girls and women" (p. 438). She can bear it no more. Her blood seems to boil in her veins. She is angry and feels sickened by the endless tales of women being raped and killed. Her anger turns into a bitter protest. In a melodramatic scene overlaid with sentimentalism, Roop, like a mad woman starts tearing her clothes on the platform where she has been endlessly waiting for her husband who has yet not turned up from Pakistan and she does not know whether he is alive or not. Her trauma is so inexplicable and intolerable that "she wants to walk through the hushing crowd wearing nothing .... She wants to scream:

> See me, I am human, though I am only a woman. See me, I did what women are for. See me not as a vessel, a plaything, a fantasy, a maidservant, an ornament, but as Vaheguru made me (p. 439).

Admittedly, *What the Body Remembers* is a poignant story of every suffering woman. The ordeal of women in general and of Roop in particular is manifested through Roop's portrayal.

What the Body Remembers is not only a tale of suffering in the wake of Partition. It delineates so deftly the condition of women in traditional cultural context. It is a social history capturing the customs, traditions and mores of rural Punjab at a particular time. The novel depicts how woman is seen in relation to community honour and it is her responsibility to save her community's honour even at the cost of her own life. Baldwin's portrayal of the Partition is made even more poignant in the sacrifice of Kusum, Roop's dutiful sister-in-law who is killed in the name of community honour. Before leaving Pakistan for India, her father-in-law holds a kirpan over her submissive neck and mercilessly she is sacrificed to save the honour of the quom so that men of other religions are not able to soil her honour and in turn soil the community's honour through her. Kusum represents thousands of her tribe who fell victim to violence perpetrated on them in the name of 'honour'.

On April 15,1947 *The Statesman,* an English daily newspaper, had carried the story of 90 women of the little village of Thoa Khalsa, Rawalpindi district...who drowned themselves by jumping into the well during the recent disturbances.... They revived the Rajput tradition of self-immolation when their menfolk were no longer able to defend.[43] Similarly, the Sikh women, in the past too, committed suicide to save their virtue after the death of their husbands. After the tragic death of Maharaja Ranjit Singh eleven women burned themselves with his dead body.[44] During the Partition many men killed female relatives to save 'their honour'[45] and to maintain the purity of the religion.[46] Kusum is sacrificed on the altar of so called 'honour'. Kusum is humiliated even after her death. The Muslim hooligans mutilate her dead body. They rip off her womb as if saying, "This is a war against your quom, for all time. Leave. We take the womb so there can be no Sikhs from it, we take the womb, leave you its shell" (p. 450).

During the Partition there were thousands like Kusum who were sacrificed to save the honour of their family and community. They are, even today, treated as martyrs who threw themselves into the well and their 'Shahidi Diwas, or Martyrs' day is celebrated to commemorate their martyrdom on March 13 every year, when the following words are repeated as a tribute to them

sura to pehchaniye
jo lade din ke het
purza purza kat mare
kabhi no chode khet
Know him as the brave one
who fights against the enemy
let his body be cut into a hundred pieces
but never will he give up his faith[47]

Thus, Baldwin has very clearly delineated the condition of the Sikh women who became the target of molestation, rape, abduction and murder or died in the name of honour killings in the wake of the Partition. Violence to women through tradition or religion and the dimensions it had during the Partition is one of dominant themes in the novel.

Kamleshwar, like Baldwin, gives an account of violence against women and their subsequent suffering in the wake of the Partition in *Kitne Pakistan.* Nonetheless, doing so he does not concentrate his attention merely on the women of Indian sub-continent, he uses 'Pakistan' as a metaphor for further divisions and violence against women in the name of those irrational 'divisions'. He moves a step ahead and brings the women across the world under the ambit of his study, transcending all borders and boundaries.

In the context of the Partition in 1947 Salma is one such sufferer who is separated for ever from her lover, the adeeb, as she has to flee to Pakistan, the geographical territory. The Partition has ruined many Salmas like her, "Whether a woman belonged to this side of the border or the other, she was never whole. The Partition has diminished her even further."[48] Not only Salma's but even her child's life has been fractured because the Partition split apart one nation, one identity and one culture. Side by side the novel is a truthful and poignant study of two lovers belonging to two different communities. They stand for India and Pakistan forced to stand apart. However, even though the lovers could marry they keep meeting discussing the trauma of separation. They represent millions of people who wish to meet and share the trauma even after more than fifty years of the Partition. Salma and the adeeb are involved in extra marital love as well defying all the confines symbolising anger against the boundaries created by the politicians. Their love transcends all man-made boundaries. Through these lovers the author projects a vision of transcending hatred and divisions.

Similar is the plight of Zainab who is about to be ravished when she is saved by a Sikh called Buta Singh. He not only saves her honour but also gives her shelter and marries her giving legitimacy to their relationship. They have a daughter called Tanvir. But the day comes when Zainab is restored to her parents in Pakistan. Buta Singh manages to reach Pakistan, pleads for his wife, converts himself to Islam but they would not give in. Zainab is forced to keep quiet all the time and both her voice and choice are strangled. Woman has no choice in the matter of even her own life. Buta Singh commits suicide by throwing himself before the train along with his daughter. The lovers are separated for ever for the simple reason that Buta Singh belongs to 'other' religion and country. Zainab suffers the trauma of unfulfilled love as 'Pakistan' is created between her and her lover with whom she enjoyed blissful conjugal life. On the other hand, Surjit Kaur's excessive love for Multan signifies the love of every uprooted one for her or his home. She represents the tragedy of many suffering women during the Partition. It was during those troubled days when she had fled from Multan with her son whom she gives a dose of opium so that he does not cry along the way. She is raped and left almost mad with the violence inflicted on her body and mind. Her son never opened eyes again. Her perennial meanderings have been continuous since 1948. Carrying her comatose son shrouded in a sheet on her shoulders through the years 1965, 1971 and 1999, she has been anxious if her Multan is safe. The adeeb tells about her agony, "Whenever war breaks out between India and Pakistan, she always comes to me asking about her Multan, hoping that it hasn't been bombed" (p. 318).

Vidya undergoes a similar tragedy of separation from her land, relatives and the people she loves. Two boys of her own community abduct her and use her "to satisfy their Hindu lust" (p. 333). They rape her repeatedly. Thus a 'Pakistan' of hatred is created in her mind for her hometown as it has begun to terrify her. She loses her parents in the wake of riots. It is the tragedy of woman that her body is always traded.

Kamleshwar laments that man has learnt nothing from the past tragedy and the use of religion is time and again manipulated for political ends. Consequently, more 'partitions' keep recurring wreaking violence on women. Such a 'partition' takes place in 1971 when Bangla Desh is created. Bengali women fall prey to the lust of soldiers who belong to none other than their own Muslim community. Woman of the Bengali bastis in Karachi are molested and raped. One of the soldiers breaks into the house where a Bengali woman has been staying with her husband. "He tied her hands behind her back.... the officer now tore her clothes, so that not a shred of a cloth remained on her body...he thrust himself deep into her naked flesh a couple of times, then with a jerk, pushed her away" (p. 344). After that the woman is raped by many soldiers. They leave behind a battered, naked woman who repeatedly asks herself, "Who, after all, was the real enemy?" (p. 345). Admittedly, those blood-soaked days inflicted gaping wounds on woman's psyche.

Kamleshwar also highlights violence against women all over the world during such sectarian divisions. They provide an opportunity to the men to reveal the beastly side of their selves without any check. The adeeb tells that even in Yugoslavia Christians have brutally tyrannised Muslims and driven them away. "Muslims women are abducted and subjected to such humiliation and torture that even the Pakistan army's maltreatment of Bangladeshi women during Bangladesh's war of independence pales into insignificance .... The bestiality endured by Muslim women in Sarajevo has no precedent" (p. 174). Women suffered because Serbs and Croats have compelled their Muslim compatriots to create their own 'Pakistans'. And women suffered for male's insanity and irrationality. Kim Huk Sun of Korea was such a sufferer of male violence. At the age of 17, she was abducted by Japanese soldiers from Beijing. She tells the adeeb in his court, "They raped me fifty times a day without respite" (p. 79). She also laments, "Forty thousand women were forcibly conscripted here and every single day, each one of us was forced to sexually satisfy more than a dozen Japanese soldiers" (p. 79). This is a universal phenomenon about violent victimization of women. The psychology or mindset of the male members of society is the same everywhere as they ravage female bodies. Women have to pay heavy prices for the irrationality of male members of their communities. The psyche of woman is wounded so much so that their mental ailment and trauma are left uncured for ever. Their scars are left fresh and bleeding for ever. More Salmas and Zainabs are separated from their lovers, thus changing geo-political partitions into matrimonial partitions, emotional partitions, more Vidyas and Surjit Kaurs are raped making them victims of delirium as many 'Pakistans' are erected over their bodies even today whenever communal violence is let loose in any part of the world.

V

While all the aforementioned novels do give detailed and graphic accounts of brutalities committed against humanity during the Partition they do not have a dark and depressing effect on the whole. Interspersed among the accounts of pervasive monstrosities and human suffering are stories of human goodness, of individuals who even during those dark times did not hesitate in helping or protecting others. Risking their own lives many gave shelter to threatened friends and neighbours or escorted lonely men and women to safety. Many women and children were provided with love, care and shelter by persons of 'other' religion. Such stories of human concern and care save us from despair or pessimism. They also convey this note of optimism that positive, humane actions can still be done at the individual level even when the society is in the grip of insanity, and that the life force in humans is so strong that even after having suffered unbearable losses human beings still embark on the quest for survival and for mutual love and sharing. The novelists emphasise that to overcome such a heart-rending tragedy people need the shoulders of friends to rest on. All the while, "creative powers and pens have persisted in their efforts to make the world a better place" (p. 81). The blind Kabir, for instance, in *Kitne Pakistan,* is the archetype of unity and hope. His repeated visits to Pakistan and India imply a bridge between the two fragmented nations. He begs outside temples, churches and Mosques in both the countries symbolising unity and brotherhood as all give him alms without caring for his religion. Kabir is a blind beggar in the novel. Ironically, the real blind are those who cannot see the love and humanity in the mankind, who go on dividing people in the mad pursuit of religious bigotry and voracity. Kamleshwar does not assume a negative and cynical approach in the novel. He is hopeful of peaceful existence and a world sans 'partitions'. To eliminate hatred and control the urge to divide and destroy he prescribes a panacea. He exhorts that we should not disown our cultural roots as,

> No culture allows the creation of "Pakistan". Culture is not restrictive by nature. It is liberal, comprehensive. It celebrates not decay but continuity of life. Cultural assimilation is imperative, because it respects the value of life (pp. 175-76).

Ultimately, it is the blind Kabir whom the adeeb does see going towards Pokhran and Chagai to plant banyan trees because like "Shiva the roots of the banyan can absorb all poison" (p. 367). His dignified aim is to see the humanity happy. He is the true embodiment of religion, and the words of Dalai Lama expressed in *Freedom in Exile* fit the character of Kabir. Dalai Lama believes that all religions aim at making people better human beings and that despite philosophical differences, some of them fundamental, they all aim at keeping humanity to find happiness.[49] Ironically, it is the blind beggar who is made to show the way to a subcontinent's troubled populace and the novel significantly ends on an *optimistic* note.

Likewise, M. J. Akbar, too, tries to assert in *Blood Brothers* the harmonious co-existence of the Hindus and the Muslims in India which was there before the imperial policy of dividing the people and which needs to be remembered now. The novelist does introduce good characters like Rahmatullah,

Burah Deewana, Simon Hogg, T.P. Singh and the author's friend Kamala who stand for human goodness and always work for peace and brotherhood between the Hindus and the Muslims. At the end of the novel it is the death of Kamala at the hand of miscreants that forces evil to surrender and repent. Zahid Quereshi, a Muslim troublemaker appears at the funeral pyre of Kamala and places "a cache of weapons at Kamala's feet" (p. 346).[50] From the ashes of Kamala's funeral pyre the good resurrects like the mythical phoenix. And life begins anew for all.

Thus the novel is a reminder to the warring groups to follow the path of harmony and mutual goodwill as both the Hindus and the Muslims, as the author affirms, are blood brothers.

Like other two novels *What the Body Remembers* does not give the final impression of negation either. It is not a tale of despair despite violence and suffering. Rather it affirms our faith in life. Despite trials and tribulations Roop does not develop a pessimistic attitude towards life. Life force asserts itself through Roop and she is prepared to face the challenges before her. She waits for Sardarji for eight days without losing hope. It is on the platform that she comes across a refugee like herself from Rawalpindi. This small boy Zorawar tells Roop that his father has been killed and his mother is living in the refugee camp. He sells newspapers and tells Roop that he "can look after her" (his mother). It is the boy who stirs hope in Roop who thinks:

> My people, Punjabi Sikhs, will survive; this Zorawar's spirit is in them. They will not beg, they will not die, they will work and build their lives again. I will survive, even if Sardarji is gone—I made two sons.[51]

Even after the death of Satya, Roop draws inspiration from her. It seems to her as if Satya is showing her the way. At last Sardarji reunites with Roop. She says consoling him, "We must all keep our strength, keep our tears for bigger losses.... **This is only a beginning**" (p. 442). Roop shows courage in the face of suffering and hardships. The novel is also strewn with good and virtuous characters who prevent the readers from adopting a gloomy and cynical stance. Roop saves Jorimon from the soldiers who are about to rape her. Revati Bhua surrenders herself before the Muslims hooligans and agrees to undergo conversion in order to save her family. Burhan-e-din, a Muslim, risks his own life to help Sardarji and Atma Ram escape safely from Lahore. Abu Abrahim tries to argue with his Muslim brethren to save the life of his friend Bachan Singh and his family. Roop gives her ornaments to her father so that he may venture a new beginning. Roop does not accept defeat and not accepting defeat in the face of death is the real triumph of life. Her own sufferings have made her more responsive and sensitive to the sufferings of others. In *What the Body Remembers* the body remembers good and evil, joys and sorrows and pain and pleasure as one is incomplete without the other.

Thus all three novels highlight the irrationality of communal frenzy that divides people and creates artificial boundaries of countries. They affirm that it is madness in naming 'others' as enemies though all are humans alike. The major concern of the novelists is to assert human values which survived, and which should survive, at the times of such communal violence. They assert that humanism and peaceful existence should blossom not only in the Indian sub-continent but across the world. The following piece from Ibne Insha's "Our Country" is worth referring as it forces us to the irrationality of the Partition:

"Who lives in Iran?"
"The Iranians live in Iran."
"Who lives in England?"
"The English live in England."
"Who lives in France?"
The French live in France."
'What country is this?'
'This is Pakistan.'
"The Pakistanis live here, don't they?"

"No, the Pakistanis don't live here. The Sindhis live here. The Punjabis live here. The Bengalis live here. This community lives here. That community lives here."
"But the Punjabis also live in Hindustan. The Sindhis also live in Hindustan. Why was another country created?"
"Sorry, it was a mistake. We shall never repeat it again."[52]

Like this poem the three novels and several short stories discussed earlier do emphasise the irrationality of the Partition, of dividing people who were one, living together despite their linguistic cultural or religious diversities for centuries. And at the same time it is a universal appeal of the authors, like of this poet, to shun all the 'divisions' despite religious differences. The people must learn from the past blunders and try to bridge the gaps created by those who tend to divide the masses for their selfish motives. It is time they lived like blood brothers, and learnt lessons from the past mistakes.

NOTES

1. Urvashi Butalia, *The Other Side of Silence* (New Delhi: Viking, 1998), p. 4.
2. Manraj Grewal, "The Wounds", *Indian Express,* Chandigarh: Nov.16, 1998. p. 13.
3. Ibid.
4. Ibid.
5. Quoted in Butalia, *The Other Side of Silence*, p. 4.
6. Ibid.
7. Madhu Limaye, "Ayodhya Time Bomb" in *Changing face of India: Essays in Honour of Balraj Puri,* ed.Ved Bhasin and Om Parkash Saraf (Delhi: Konark Publication Ltd., 1994,) p. 62.
8. Ibid, p. 65.
9. Butalia, *The Other Side of Silence*, p. 7.
10. Tanveer Jafri, "Sampradayik Vichardhara Pratibandhit Ho" (Hindi), *Divya Himachal,* Dharamshala, 31st August, 2006, p. 8. My translation.
11. S. Nihal Singh "Communal Killing in Gujarat", *The Tribune*, Chandigarh, March, 5.2002, p. 8.
12. Butalia, *The Other Side of Silence*, p. 5.

13. Ibid.
14. Shauna Singh Baldwin, *What the Body Remembers* (New Delhi: Harper Collins, 1999), p. 336.
15. Parveen Mirdha, "Partition Fiction: Between Madness and Humanism" in *Perspectives on the Partition Fiction of the Indian Sub-continent*, ed. Tejinder Kaur, Kulbhusan Kushal and N.K. Neb (Jalandhar: Nirman Publications, 2007), pp. 105-6.
16. Baldwin, *What the Body Remembers.* All subsequent references to the novel are to this edition and have been incorporated in the text.
17. Deepika Gurdev, "Partition revisited by a second wife", an analysis of "What the Body Remembers", *The Sunday Tribune,* Chandigarh, January 4, 2001, p. II.
18. "Line of division : Real and imagined", excerpts from Kuldip Nayar, "Scoop, Inside Stories from Partition", The Tribune, Chandigarh, September, 24, 2006, p. 1.
19. Ibid.
20. Humra Quraishi, "No concern for the displaced people", *The Tribune*, Chandigarh, September 24, 2006, p. 13.
21. M. J. Akbar, *Blood Brothers* (New Delhi: Roli Brothers, 2006). All subsequent references to the novel are to this edition and have been incorporated in the text.
22. Asghar Ali Engineer, "Islam and Non-Violence" in *Changing Face of India: Essays in Honour of Balraj Puri,* ed. Ved Bhasin and Om Parkash Saraf (Delhi: Konark Publication Ltd., 1994,) pp. 132-33.
23. Bipan Chandra, *Communalism in Modern India* (1984; rpt., New Delhi: Vikas Publishing House, 1996), p. 327.
24. Badrudin Umar, "Communalism: a Specific Form of Political Use of Religion" in *Communalism in Contemporary India* (Calcutta: Burdwan University, 1994), p. 61.
25. Bipan Chandra, "Communalism Today—The Way Out" in *Communalism in India* (1984; rpt., New Delhi: Vikas Publishing House, 1996), p. 311.
26. "When Bhisam Sahni broke down at Wagah", a news item, *The Sunday Tribune,* Chandigarh, July13, 2003, P. 6. It was only in November 1999—52 years after the Partition of the country—that Bhisam Sahni stepped on the soil of Wagah from where he aired his views on the physical dissection of the land that caused irreversible damage not just to the people of India and Pakistan but also to the very spirit of

humanity. He had visited Wagah in connection with the shooting of a documentary on his life.

27. Kamleshwar, *Kitne Pakistan* (Hindi), trans. as *Partitions* by Ameena Kazi Ansari (New Delhi: Penguin Books, 2006). All subsequent references to the novel are to this edition and have been incorporated in the text.
28. Kamleshwar, "Author's Note" in *Partitions*, trans. Ameena Kazi Ansari (New Delhi: Penguin Books, 2006). p. vii.
29. Mirdha, "Partition Fiction: Between Madness and Humanism" in *Perspectives on the Partition Fiction of the Indian Sub-continent*, p. 102.
30. Ibid, p. 101.
31. Ameena Kazi Ansari, "Translator's Note" in Kamleshwar, op. cit., p. ix.
32. Bipan Chandra, "Communalism and Communal Violence in Modern India" in *Communalism in Contemporary India* (Calcutta: Burdwan University, 1994), p. 35.
33. Badrudin Umar, "Communalism: a Specific Form of Political Use of Religion" in *Communalism in Contemporary India*, p. 61.
34. Charles Dickens, *The Tale of Two Cities* (1993; rpt., Hertfordshire: Wordsworth Classics, 1994), p. 3.
35. S.K. Kulkarni, "Relevance of Secularism" in *Challenges* (Mumbai: Jaico Publishing House, 2001) p. 65.
36. Gurpreet Kaur, "Two Facets of Partition: The Feminine and The Gender" inquoted in *Perspectives on the Partition Fiction of the Indian Sub-continent*, ed. Tejinder Kaur, Kulbhusan Kushal and N.K. Neb (Jalandhar: Nirman Publications, 2007), p. 76.
37. Ibid.
38. Baldwin, op. cit. All subsequent references to the novel are to this edition and have been incorporated in the text.
39. Pankaj K. Singh, *Representing Woman: Tradition, Legend and Panjabi Drama* (Shimla: IIAS, 2000), p. 49.
40. *Hir Waris*, ed.Jit Singh Sital (Delhi: Navyug Publishers, 1963), p. 213.
41. Pankaj K. Singh, *Representing Woman: Tradition,Legend and Panjabi Drama*, p. 49.
42. Anders Bjorn Hansen, *Partition and Genocide: Manifestation of Violence in Punjab 1937-1947* (New Delhi: India Research Press, 2002) p. 194.

43. Butalia, *The Other Side of Silence*, pp. 148-49.
44. B.K. Ghatak, *A Macrostudy of Women in India—Over the Ages and Qut of Scripture* (New Delhi: Dhillon Group of Publications, date not mentioned) p. 40.
45. Hansen, *Partition and Genocide: Manifestation of Violence in Punjab 1937-1947*, p. 180.
46. Butalia, *The Other Side of Silence*, p. 270.
47. Ibid, pp. 273-74.
48. Kamleswar, *Partitions*, p.130. All subsequent references to the novel are to this edition and have been incorporated in the text.
49. M.G. Chitkara, *Indo-Pak Amity: A New Concept,* (New Delhi: Ashish Publishing House, 1994), p. 59.
50. Akbar, *Blood Brothers,* p. 346.
51. Baldwin, *What the Body Remembers*, p. 441.
52. Ibne Insha, "Our Country", trans. and ed. Alok Bhalla in *Stories About the Partition of India,* Vol. II (New Delhi: Harper Collins, 1994), p. 105.

Bibliography

PRIMARY SOURCES

Abbas, Gulam. "Avtar: A Hindu Myth" (Urdu). Trans. Alok Bhalla and Vishwamitter Adil, in *Stories About the Partition of India*, Vol. III, ed. Alok Bhalla. New Delhi: Harper Collins, 1994.

Abbas, Khwaja Ahmad. "The Death of Sheikh Burhanuddin" (Urdu). Trans. Khuswant Singh, in *Stories About the Partition of India,* Vol. II, ed. Alok Bhalla. New Delhi: Harper Collins, 1994.

Akbar, M.J. *Blood Brothers*. New Delhi: Roli Brothers,2006.

'Ajneya', S.H. Vastsayan. "Getting Even" (Hindi). Trans. Alok Rai, in "*Stories About the Partition of India*", Vol. I, ed. Alok Bhalla. New Delhi: Harper Collins, 1994.

'Ajneya', S.H. Vastsayan. "Post Box" (Hindi). Trans. Alok Bhalla, in "*Stories About the Partition of India*" Vol. III, ed. Alok Bhalla (New Delhi: Harper Collins, 1994.

'Ajneya', S.H Vatsayan. "The Refuge" (Hindi). Trans. Rachna Sharma, in *Stories About the Partition of India,* Vol. II, ed. Alok Bhalla. New Delhi: Harper Collins, 1994.

Anand, Mulk Raj. "The Parrot in the Cage" in *Stories About the Partition of India,* Vol. III, ed. Alok Bhalla. New Delhi: Harper Collins, 1994.

Antharjanam, Lalithambika. "The Mother of Dhiren Muzumdar" (Malayam). Trans. T. Muralidharan in *Stories About the Partition of India*, Vol.II, ed. Alok Bhalla. New Delhi: Harper Collins, 1994.

Antharjanam, Lalithambik. "A Leaf in the Storm" (Malayalam). Trans. Naraya Chandran, in *Stories About the Partition of India* Vol. I, ed. Alok Bhalla. New Delhi: Harper Collins, 1994.

Ashraf, Syed Mohammad. "Separated from the Flock" (Urdu). Trans. Vishwamitter Adil and Alok Bhalla, in *Stories About the Partition of India*, Vol. I, ed. Alok Bhalla. New Delhi: Harper Collins, 1994.

Ayyaz, Shaikh. "Neighbours" (Sindhi). Trans. Saroj Vashistha in *Stories About the Partition of India,* ed. Alok Bhalla. New Delhi: Harper Collins, 1994.

Baldwin, Shauna Singh. *What the Body Remembers.* New Delhi: Harper Collins, 1999.

Bedi, Rajinder Singh. "Lajwanti" (Urdu). Trans. and ed. Alok Bhalla, in *Stories About the Partition of India*. Vol. I, New Delhi: Harper Collins, 1994.

Bharti, Narain. "The Claim" (Sindhi). Trans. Sree Israney, in *Stories About the Partition of India*, Vol.II, ed. Alok Bhalla. New Delhi: Harper Collins, 1994.

Chander, Krishna. "The Peshawar Express" (Urdu). Trans. Jai Rattan, in *Stories About the Partition of India*, Vol. III, ed. Alok Bhalla, New Delhi: Harper Collins, 1994.

Chughtai, Ismet. "Roots" (Urdu). Trans. Vishwamitter Adil and Alok Bhalla, in *Stories About the Partition of India,* ed. Alok Bhalla, New Delhi: Harper Collins, 1994.

Devi, Jyotirmoyee. *The River Churning*, Trans. Enakshi Chatterjee. 1995; rpt. New Delhi: Kali for Women, 1998.

Duggal, Kartar Singh. "Kulsum" (Punjabi). Trans. Vishwamitter Adil and Alok Bhalla, in *Stories About the Partition of India*. Vol. II, ed. Alok Bhalla. New Delhi: Harper Collins, 1994.

Gore, N.G. "A Mouthful of Water, A Mouthful of Blood" (Marathi). Trans. Sudhakar Marathe, in *Stories About the Partition of India*, Vol. III, ed. Alok Bhalla, New Delhi : Harper Collins, 1994.

Hashmi, Jamila, "Exile" (Urdu). Trans. Alok Bhalla, in *Stories About the Partition of India,* Vol. I, ed. Alok Bhalla. New Delhi: Harper Collins, 1994.

Husain, Intizar. "The City of Sorrow" (Urdu). Trans. Alok Bhalla and Vishwamitter Adil, in *Stories About the Partitions of India*, Vol. II, ed Alok Bhalla. New Delhi: Harper Collins, 1994.

Husain, Intizar. "An Unwritten Epic" (Urdu). Trans. Leslie A. Fleming and Muhammad Umar Memon, in *Stories About the Partition of India*, Vol. III, ed. Alok Bhalla. New Delhi: Harper Collins, 1994.

Jalees, Ibrahim. "A Grave Turned Inside Out" (Urdu). Trans. Vishwamitter Adil and Alok Bhalla, in *Stories About the Partition of India*. Vol. II, ed. Alok Bhalla, New Delhi: Harper Collins, 1994.

Kamleshwar. "How Many Pakistans?" (Hindi). Trans. Vishwamitter Adil and Alok Bhalla, in *Stories About the Partition of India*. Vol. II, ed. Alok Bhalla, New Delhi: Harper Collins, 1994.

Kamleshwar. "Kitne Pakistan" (Hindi). Rajpal and Sons, 2000. Trans. Ameena Kazi Ansari as *Partition*. New Delhi: Penguin Books, 2006.

Manto, Saadat Hasan. "Mozel" (Urdu). Trans. Tahira Naqvi, in *Stories About the Partition of India,* Vol. II, ed. Alok Bhalla. New Delhi: Harper Collins, 1994.

Manto, Saadat Hasan. "Cold Meat" (Urdu). Trans. Alok Bhalla, in *Stories About the Partition of India,* Vol. I, ed. Alok Bhalla. New Delhi: Harper Collins, 1994.

Quasim, Suraiya. "Where did she Belong?" (Urdu). Trans. Vishwamitter Adil and Alok Bhalla, in *Stories About the Partition of India*, Vol. II, ed. Alok Bhalla, New Delhi: Harper Collins, 1994.

Manto, Saadat Hasan. "Open It" (Urdu). Trans. Alok Bhalla, in *Stories About the Partition of India* Vol. II, ed. Alok Bhalla, New Delhi: Harper Collins, 1994.

Manto, Saadat Hasan. "Toba Tek Singh" (Urdu). Trans. Tahira Naqvi, in *Stories About the Partition of India,* Vol. III, ed. Alok Bhalla. New Delhi: Harper Collins, 1994.

Nasim, Sultan Jamil. "I am Game" (Urdu). Trans. Jai Rattan, in *Stories About the Partition of India,* Vol. III, ed. Alok Bhalla. New Delhi: Harper Collins, 1994.

Nahal, Chaman. *Azadi*. 1979; rpt. New Delhi: Orient Paperbacks, 1998.

Prabhakar, Vishnu. "I Shall Live" (Hindi). Trans. Alok Bhalla, in *Stories About the Partition of India,* Vol. II. ed. Alok Bhalla. New Delhi: Harper Collins, 1994.

Qasmi, Ahmad Nadeem. "Parmeshwar Singh" (Urdu). Trans. Vishwamitter Adil and Alok Bhalla, in *Stories About in Partition of India,* Vol. I, ed. Alok Bhalla. New Delhi: Harper Collins, 1994.

Rakesh, Mohan. "The Owner of Rubble" (Hindi). Trans. Alok Bhalla, in *Stories About the Partition of India*, Vol. I, ed. Alok Bhalla, New Delhi: Harper Collins, 1994.

Rakesh, Mohan. "The Claim" (Hindi). Trans. Richard Williams, in *Stories About the Partition of India*, Vol. III, ed. Alok Bhalla. New Delhi: Harper Collins, 1994.

Rahi, Ved. "Death" (Dogri). Trans. Alok Bhalla, in *Stories About the Partition of India*. Vol. III, ed. Alok Bhalla. New Delhi: Harper Collins, 1994.

Rakesh, Mohan. "God's Dog" (Hindi). Trans. Alok Bhalla, in *Stories About the Partition of India*, Vol. II, ed. Alok Bhalla. New Delhi: Harper Collins, 1994.

Ramlal. "A Visitor from Pakistan" (Urdu). Trans. Alok Bhalla, in *Stories About the Partition of India*, Vol. I, ed. Alok Bhalla, New Delhi: Harper Collins, 1994.

Sahni, Bhisham. "Pali" (Hindi). Trans. Jai Rattan, in *Stories About the Partition of India*, Vol. III, ed. Alok Bhalla. New Delhi: Harper Collins, 1994.

Sahni Bhisham. *Tamas*. Trans. Jai Rattan. 1974; rpt. New Delhi: Penguin Books, 1988.

Sen, Ramesh Chandra. "The White Horse" (Bengali). Trans. Mihir Bhattacharya, in *Stories About the Partition of India*, Vol.II, ed. Alok Bhalla. New Delhi: Harper Collins, 1994.

Sidhwa, Bapsi. *Ice Candy Man*. New Delhi: Penguin Books,1989.

Singh, Gurmukh. "Abandoned Child" (Punjabi). Trans. B.M. Sagar and Alok Bhalla, in *Stories About the Partition of India*, Vol. III, ed. Alok Bhalla, (New Delhi: Harper Collins, 1994.

Singh, Khushwant. *Train to Pakistan*. New Delhi: The Book International, 1989.

Sobti, Krishna. "Where is My Mother?" (Hindi). Trans. Alok Bhalla, in *Stories About the Partition of India*, Vol. II, ed., Alok Bhalla. New Delhi: Harper Collins, 1994.

Virk, Kulwant Singh. "Weeds" (Punjabi). Trans. Alok Bhalla and Gurupadesh Singh, in *Stories About the Partition of India*, Vol. I, ed. Alok Bhalla. New Delhi: Harper Collins, 1994.

Yash Pal. "A Holy War" (Hindi). Trans. Alok Bhalla, in *Stories About the Partition of India*, Vol. I, ed. Alok Bhalla, New Delhi: Harper Collins, 1994.

SECONDARY SOURCES

Books

Ahuja, Ram. *Social Problems in India*, 1997; rpt. New Delhi: Rawat Publications, 2001.

Anand, Mulk Raj, ed. *Living Thoughts of Mahatma Gandhi*. New Delhi: NCERT, 1988.

Atwood Margaret "Colonisation and Responsibility" in *Free Women: Ethics and Aesthetics in Twentieth Century Women's Fiction*. ed. Kate Fallbrook, London: Harvester Wheat sheaf, 1990.

Baig, Tara Ali, ed. *Women of India*. Delhi: The Publication Division, 1958.

Bathla, Sonia. *Women, Democracy and the Media: Cultural and Political Representations in the Indian Press*. New Delhi: Sage Publications, 1998.

Beauvoir, Simone de. *The Second Sex*. Trans. and ed. H.M. Parshley. 1953; rpt. Harmondsworth: Penguin, 1983.

Bhattacharjea, Ajit. *Countdown to Partition*. New Delhi: Harper Collins, 1997.

Bhasin, Ved and Om Parkash Saraf. *Changing Face of India: Essays in Honour of Balraj Puri*. Delhi: Konark Publication Ltd.,1994.

Bhusan, Vidya and D.R. Sachdeva. *An Introduction to Sociology*. Allahbad : Kitab Mahal, 1994.

Butalia, Urvashi. *Other Side of Silence*: *Voices from the Partition of India*. New Delhi: Viking Penguin, 1998.

Chandra, Bipan. *Communalism in Modern India*. 1984; rpt. New Delhi: Vikas Publishing House, 1996.

Chandra, Bipan and others. *India's Struggle for Independence (1857-1947)*, New Delhi: Penguin Books, 1989.

Chandra, Bipan. *Modern India:* A Textbook of History for XII. 1990; rpt. New Delhi: NCERT Publication, 1998.

Chandra, Satish. *Medieval India*. 1978; rpt. New Delhi: NCERT. Publication, 1988.

Chitkara, M.G. *Indo-Pak Amity: A New Concept*. New Delhi: Ashish Publishing House, 1994.

Collins, Larry and Dominique Lapierre. *Freedom at Midnight*. 1976; rpt. New Delhi: Vikas Publishing House, 1977.

Das, Manmath. *Partition and Independence of India: Inside Story of the Mountbatten Days*. New Delhi: Vision Books, 1982.

Dev, Arjun, ed. *Jawahar Lal Nehru: Samgharsh Ke Din: Chune Hue Vaktavya* (Hindi). Trans. Devesh Chandra. New Delhi; National Book Trust, India, 1996.

Devender, Kiran. *Changing Status of Women in India*. New Delhi: Vikas Publishing House, 1962.

Dickens, Charles. *The Tale of Two Cities*. 1993; rpt., Hertfordshire: Wordsworth Classics, 1994.

Dubey, S.C. *Indian Society.* 1990; rpt. New Delhi: National Book Trust, 1994.

Dubey, S.M. and Dinesh Sharma. *Sociology: An Introduction*. Trans. Susheela Dhobal. New Delhi: NCERT, 1990.

Engineer, Asghar Ali and Moin Shakir, ed. *Communalism in India*. New Delhi: Ajanta Publication, 1985.

Foerster, Norman and Robert Falk. ed. *American Poetry and Prose*. 1934; rpt. Boston: Houghton Mifflin Company, 1960.

Fraser, Wayne. *The Dominion of Women: The Personal and the Political in Canadian Women's Literature.* London: Greenwood Press, 1991.

French, Marilyn. *Beyond Power: On Women, Men and Morals,* 1985; rpt. London: Jonathan Cape, Abacus, 1986.

Fromn, Erich. *The Anatomy of Human Destructiveness*. 1973; rpt. Harmondsworth: Penguin, 1977.

Gadgil, Narhar Vishnu. *Satta Ka Sach* (Hindi). New Delhi: Parveen Parkashan, 2000.

Gandhi, M.K. *India of My Dreams*. Compiled by R.K. Prabhu. Ahmedabad: Navjivan Publishing House, 1962.

Ghadially, Rehana, ed. *Women in Indian Society*. New Delhi: Sage Publications, 1988.

Ghai, Premvati. *The Partition of the Punjab 1849-1947.* New Delhi: Munshiram Manoharlal, 1986.

Ghatak, B.K. *A Microstudy of Women in India: Over the Ages, in and out of Scriptures*. New Delhi: Dhillon Group of Publications, Date not mentioned.

Ghosal, H.R. *An Outline History of the Indian People*. Trans into Hindi by Dheera Verma as *Bharat ka Sankshipt Itihas*. New Delhi: Publications Division, 1962.

Grover, B.L. and S. Grover. *A New Look at Modern Indian History* (1707 - Present day) 1983; rpt. New Delhi: S. Chand and Co., 2000.

Gupta, N.L. ed. *Nehru on Communalism*. New Delhi: Sampradayikta Virodhi Committee, 1965.

Gupta, Padmini Sen. *The Story of Women in India*. New Indian Book Company, 1974.

Hansen, Anders Bjorn. *Partition and Genocide: Manifestation of Violence in Punjab* 1937-1947. New Delhi: India Research Press, 2002.

Haralambos, M. and R.M. Heald. *Sociology : Themes and Perspectives*. New Delhi: Oxford University Press, 1980.

Hussain, Sabiha. *The Changing Half: A Study of Indian Muslim Women*. New Delhi: Classical Publishing Company, 1998.

Jain, Pukhraj and B.L. Faria. *Bhartiya Shashan Evam Rajniti* (Hindi). Agra: Sahitya Bhawan Publication, 1999.

Jalali, Ramnika. *Indian Women in the Smritis*. Jammu: Vinod Publishers, 1994.

Jayawerdena, K. *Feminism and Nationalism in the Third World*. London: Zed Books, 1986.

Jha, Devichandra. *Mahatma Gandhi, Congress Aur Bharat Ka Vibhajan* (Hindi). New Delhi: Abhiruchi Parkashan, 1998.

Kappuswamy, B. *An Introduction to Social Psychology*. Bombay: Asia Publishing House, 1980.

Kasturi, Bhasyan. *Walking Alone: Gandhi and India's Partition*. New Delhi: Vision Books, 1999.

Kaur, Tejinder, Kulbhusan Kushal and N. K. Neb, ed. *Perspectives on the Partition Fiction of the Indian Sub-continent.* Jalandhar: Nirman Publications, 2007.

Kidwai, Sheikh M.H., *Women*. Delhi: Seema Publications, 1976.

Kopp, Clarie. B. *Becoming Female: Perspectives and Development*. New York: Plenum Press, 1979.

The Koran, Trans. J.M. Rodwell. Herts: Everyman's Library, 1909.

Kothari, Milap. *Ab Bharat Ko Uthna Hoga* (Hindi). 1993; rpt. Jaipur: Rajasthan Patrika. 2000.

Kudchedkar, Shirin and S. AL-Issa. *Violence Against Women: Women Against Violence.* Delhi: Pencraft International, 1998.

Kulkarni, S.K., *Challenges.* Mumbai: Jaico Publishing House, 2001.

Lal, Ramji, ed. *Communal Problem in India: A Symposium*. Karnal: Dyal Singh College, 1988.

Low, D.A. and Howard Brasted, ed. *Freedom, Trauma, Continuities: Northern India and Independence*. New Delhi: Sage Publications, 1998.

Madan, G.R. *Theoretical Sociology*. Delhi: Atma Ram and Sons, 1983.

Mahajan, V.D. *Ancient India*. 1960; rpt. New Delhi. S. Chand and Co., 2000.

———. *India Since 1526*. 1978; rpt. New Delhi. S. Chand and Co., 1980.

Majumdar, R.C. ed. *The British Paramountcy and Indian Renaissance,* Part X, Mumbai: Bhartiya Vidya Bhawan, 1982.

Manusmriti, III, 56: *Manav Dharama Shashtra*. Trans. and ed. Graves Chamnen Houghton, Vol. III. New Delhi: Cosmo Publication, 1982.

McLeod, W.H. *The Evolution of The Sikh Community*. Delhi: Oxford University Press, 1975.

Menon, Indu. *Status of Muslim Women in India: A Case Study of Kerala*. Delhi: Uppal Publishing House, 1981.

Millet, Kate, *Sexual Politics*. 1969; rpt. London: Rupert Hart Davis, 1971.

Moi, Toril. "Feminist Literary Criticism" in *Modern Literary Theory*. ed. Ann Jefferson and David Rubey. 1982; rpt; London: B.T. Batsford, 1986.

Naqvi, Mustaq. *Partition: The Real Story*. Delhi: Renaissance,1985.

Neshla. *Atrocities against Women*. New Delhi: Harman Publishing House, 1997.

Pandey, Akhileshwar, *Savtantra Bharat Me Hindu-Muslim Samasya Ke Ayam* (Hindi). Delhi: Raj Publishing House, 1998.

Panikar, K.N. ed. *Communalism in India: History, Politics and Culture*. New Delhi: Manohar Publications, 1991.

Rai, Satya. *Partition of the Punjab*. New Delhi: Asia Publishing House, 1965.

Roy, Shibani. *Status of Muslim Women in India*: B.R. Publishing Corp. 1979.

Sadasivam, S.N. *Party and Democracy in India*. New Delhi: Tata Mc. Graw Hill Publishing Co., 1947.

Sarkar, Sumit. *Modern India 1885-1947*. Madras: Macmillan India Ltd., 1983.

Sarswat, Anand Prakash, ed. *Communalism and Indian Society*. Meerut: Sarup and Sons, 1989.

Sharma, Bela Rani. *Women: Marriage, Family and Divorcé*. Jaipur: Mangal Deep Publications, 1997.

Sharma, Ram Sharan. *Ancient India*. 1947; rpt. New Delhi: NCERT. 1986.

Showalter, Elaine, ed. *The New Feminist Criticism*. London, Virago, 1986.

Sharma, K.K. *Partition in Indian English Novels*.

Sherwani, Latif Ahamd. *Partition of India and Mount batten*. Karachi: Council for Pakistan Studies, 1986.

Singh, Amrik. ed. *The Partition in Retrospect*. New Delhi: Anamika Publishers and Distributors, 2000.

Singh, K. *Principles of Sociology*. Lucknow: Prakashan Kendra, 1980.

Singh, Khuswant. *The History of the Sikhs, 1839-1974.* Vol. 2 Delhi: Oxford University Press, 1984.

Singh, Kirpal. *The Partition of the Punjab.* Patiala: Punjabi University, 1972.

Singh, Pankaj K. *Representing Women: Tradition, Legend and Panjabi Drama.* Shimla: IIAS, 2000.

Sital, Jit Singh, ed. *Hir Waris.* Delhi: Navyug Publishers, 1963.

Spear, Percival. *History of India,* Vol. II. New Delhi: Penguin Books, 1990.

Stoller, Robert. J. *Sex the Gender.* New York: Science House, 1968.

Thomas, P. *Indian Women Through the Ages.* London: Asia Publishing House, 1964.

Tong, Rosemarie. *Feminist Thought: A Comprehensive Introduction.* Boulder: Westview Press, 1989.

Trilling, Lionel and Harold Bloom. ed. New York: Oxford University Press, 1973.

Tyagi, Desh Bandhu. *Bhartiya Rajniti: Hindu-Muslim Sambandh* (Hindi). Jaipur: Jain and Jain, 1998.

Communalism in Contemporary India. Calcutta: Burdwan University, 1994.

Articles

Ahmad, Karuna. "Studies of Working Women in India: Trends and Issues". *Economic and Political Weekly*, Vol. XIV, No, 33, 1979.

Aiyar, Mani Shankar. "Who wanted Pakistan: The Muslims or Muslim Leaguers?" *Sunday,* 14-20 March 1993, p. 18.

Baig, Tara Ali. "Who says the Sati System is Dead". *Femina*, 23 December 1983—7 January 1994. p. 58.

Bhardwaj, K.K. "Indian National Movement: Communal Politics." *Competition Success Review.* Vol. XXV. No.5. November, 1998, p. 51.

Chaddah, R.P. "The Trauma and Turbulence of Partition: A Convincing Portrayal of Novelists." *The Tribune,* 5 December 1997, p. 2.

Chaudhary, D.R. "Unending Female Persecution: Haryana Society in Throes of Change." *The Tribune*, 20 September 2000, p. 10.

Chopra, Ashok. "Moving Testaments to Pain of Partition." *The*

Tribune, 18 June, 1998, p. 4.

Dang, Vimla. "Feudal Mindset Still Dogs Women's Struggle: A Fair Deal, Equitable System Urgently Needed." *The Tribune*, 19 June, 1998, p. 1.

Dutt, Nirupama. "Where has a Girl Child gone?" *The Tribune*, 24 June, 2001. p. 21.

Gandhi, Nandita. "Women: Introduction Feminist Perspectives in Academia." *Economic and Political Weekly*, Vol. XIV No. 4, 1984.

Giri, Mohini. "Women are not just commodities: Get rid of Duplicity, be more egalitarian." *The Tribune*, 19 June, 1998. p. 4

Grewal, Manraj. "The Wounds of 84". *The Indian Express*, 16 November, 1998. p. 13.

Gurdev, Deepika. "Partition revisited by a second wife." *The Sunday Tribune*, 4 January, 2001. p. II.

Hameed, Syeda Saiyidain. "Throwing Veil over Reason". *The Tribune*, 7 October, 2001. p. 20.

Jafri, Tanveer. "Sampradayik Vichardhara Pratibandhit Ho" (Hindi), *Divya Himachal,* 31st August, 2006. p. 8.

Jefferson, R. Leshvan. "Pathar Se Mar Kar Saja-e-Maut Aurat Ko" (Hindi). *Divya Himachal*, 29 August, 2002.p. 8.

Joshi, Sharmila. "They Succumb to Violence due to Economic Dependence: Yet Woman in India Survive, Grow and Achieve so Much." *The Tribune,* 19 June, 1998. p. 2.

Kak, M.L. "Adam for Field, Eve for Hearth no longer Relevant: We have to Change the Patriarchal System." *The Tribune,* 19 June 1998, p. 3.

Kang, Diljit Kaur. "Sati Barbarous Survival." *The Tribune,* 4 October 1987, p. 3.

Madhok, Sujata. "A Vast Majority Lives in Abject Poverty: Gender Bias, Infanticide Bane of Indian Women." *The Tribune*. 19 June 1998, p. 2.

Mohan, Raman. "Healing Blisters of Domestic Violence." *The Tribune*, 3 March 2002, p. 20

Mukherjee, Meenakshi. "Reality and Realism: Indian Women as Protagonists in Four Nineteenth Century Novels." *Economic and Political Weekly*, Vol. XIX, No. 2, 1984.

Murthi, Luxmi. "Indian Women is Advertisements: Moving Ahead; but not Quite There." *The Tribune*, 17 July 2001. p. 21.

Nagar, Sheela. "What Ails the Veiled Women of Haryana: Gender

Discrimination and Rigid Customs." *The Tribune*, 8 October 2000. p.12.

Narasimhan, Shakuntala. "Saying a Firm no to War." *The Tribune*, 28 October 2000. p.10.

Quraishhi, Humra. "No concern for the displaced people." *The Tribune*, 24 September, 2006. p.13.

Ravindranath, P.K. "Jinnah's Role in Partition of India: A Reappraisal." *The Tribune*, 16 December 2001. p. 8.

Singh Hari Jai. "Pangs of Wounded Nation: Looking Beyond the Gujarat Divide." *The Tribune*, 8 March, 2002. p. 10.

Singh Khuswant. "What Makes a Man Great?" *The Tribune* (Windows), 9 June 2001. p. 3.

Singh, S. Nihal. "Communal Killing in Gujarat." *The Tribune*, 5 March,2002. p. 8.

Tanwar, Reicha. "Combating a Mindset that is a Fortress." *The Tribune*, 15 July 2001. p. 21.

Wadhera, Amarnath and Randeep Wadhera. "Is Religion Relevant Today?" *The Tribune* (Sunday Reading), 10 December 2000. p. 1.

"Gandhi on the Partition of India." An excerpt from M.K. Gandhi, *The Way to Communal Harmony*. Compiled and ed. by U.R. Rao. *The Tribune*, 22 June 1997. p.1.

"Line of division: Real and imagined", execerpts from Kuldeep Nayar, "Scoop Inside Stories from Partition", *The Tribune*, 24 September, 2006. p. 1.

"Psychology of Communalism." Editorial. *The Hindu*, 24 March 1993. p. 3.

"Women Lose out to Mithuns." A report under the Column, "Trends and Pointers." *The Tribune*, 7 December 2000. p. 9.

Index